Amertine

R.T. Smeltzer

ISBN: 978-1-6964-6458-1

First Edition

Cover Design by Claire Winter

To Amber

Lots of love

Tanya
Snett

CHAPTER 1

She didn't know why she was here. Maiya shielded her eyes from the sun as she exited the engineering building. The mountains were beautiful today, the green of the trees more vibrant in the afternoon light. Over three hundred days of sunshine, surprisingly mild winters - if you didn't mind the snow, and environmentalists abound, the location was a gleaming advertisement for the good life. Even the campus was positively glowing with students ready to turn their dreams into reality.

Maiya stood among them, yet she feared she would never be one of them. She had never intended to go to graduate school, but faculty and family pressures pushed her down the road that landed her here. It was a mistake. Before it even began, she dreaded the decision, yet she couldn't deny her supporters the pleasure of seeing all their efforts come to fruition. If she didn't follow through, she would be forced to face their degrading opinions. Even worse, she would have to acknowledge her own opinion of herself. It was with this daily thought that she arrived here at year two, surrounded by brilliant and friendly people who thought they shared a common interest. Three o'clock already, but not nearly late enough. Only one more class to go. Or skip.

Maiya began the long walk back to her car as she dialed her parents' number. Since she had come here, this had become an almost daily ritual — attend class, skip another, and call home as feelings of guilt washed over her.

"Hello?" Her mother answered the phone, sounding slightly winded. One positive note about Maiya's routine was that she had come to align it well with the end of her mother's afternoon jog. It seemed monotony ran in the family.

"Hi."

"Waiting for the bus?"

"No... I drove today. I'm just, I don't know. I want to quit again." Maiya flinched every time she heard herself say that word. She'd never quit anything in her life, no matter how much she hated it or wanted to give up, and had always accepted the consequences of putting up with something she didn't want to do.

Her mother's reply was the same as usual. "If you're unhappy, you shouldn't do it for other people."

"I know."

And thus it went day in and day out. A twenty-minute drive later, and she arrived home to find her two-bedroom apartment as she left it – two cats, begging to be fed and otherwise uninterested in comforting their owner. Maiya continued her daily ritual – feed the cats, make a meal of her own, and settle into bed with a book. Rinse and repeat.

Maiya woke the next day with the book still in hand and smiled to herself when she realized this day was free of classes. Whether it was the escape from her disinterest or routine altogether, she didn't care. She found comfort in knowing that, except for a group meeting for her Software Engineering class, the day was her own. She drove to her meeting with a smile on her face and looked for her teammates when she arrived at the coffee shop.

"Hey," Mike beckoned her over to a corner table, laptop and coffee cup dutifully at the ready. Maiya couldn't help but think he looked like he was setting up camp.

"Hey! Where's Steve?"

"He's...somewhere around here," Mike waved his hand dismissively toward the opposite end of the shop, "Anyway, let me catch you up. We were talking, and we think we can make some of this concurrent."

The group had been working on a "video mosaic generator" for generating a photo mosaic of a selected image from frames in a selected video. The content of the project held no real significance, but the class had been studying a specific type of development process that the group was expected to adhere to when creating their software. As Maiya had completed a very similar project in the past, she immediately knew which part of the program Mike was referring to, and truthfully, dreaded any unnecessary work. Not wanting to hold the group back out of her personal disinterest, she forced herself to refrain from sharing those thoughts.

"Oh, okay. Sounds good, as long as it doesn't require a lot of time."

"Nah, it shouldn't. We're already ahead as it is, so we figured 'why not?' You don't mind do you?"

"Oh... no. I'm assuming you're talking about the processing of the video frames, right? I could make those changes this weekend, probably."

"That'd be awesome! You're sure you don't mind?"

Maiya shook her head and gave him a reassuring smile. And yet, she wondered to herself, why do I always volunteer to do extra work? For a moment Maiya was distracted; she was almost certain someone had been watching her. A man in a suit and tie briefly caught her attention before Steve's voice drew her back to the task at hand.

"Oh, hi Maiya," Steve took a seat between the two and quickly reviewed what he had accomplished throughout the week. Maiya did so accordingly and Mike concluded their meeting by reiterating how ahead of schedule they really were. They said their good-byes and assigned work for the following week. All in all, it was a rather quick meeting and served its purpose as painlessly as possible. And through all of this, Maiya thought, *I can't quit now and leave them in the dust.*

Her drive home consisted of much the same thoughts, but as she approached her apartment complex, those thoughts faded, and a new day seemed to await her. This might finally be the day she takes that trip to Rocky Mountain National Park, or perhaps just a hike along a mountain trail. Maiya began to toss about the possibilities in her mind, planning, as she always did, every preparation that would need to be completed before she could be on her way. As it was still well before noon, there was little doubt in her mind that this day would be anything less than exceptional; at the very least, it would be a much-needed break from an otherwise monotonous life.

Maiya was so engulfed in her thoughts that the typically twenty-minute drive felt closer to five. One final turn, and she was parking next to the fitness center on the complex grounds, ready to pack a lunch and head into the mountains. As she stepped from her car, those hopeful thoughts quickly faded. The cheerful chirping of birds and sounds of the town that would normally meet her ears were mysteriously absent, the sort of bleak silence that sends shivers across the skin. The sun was welcoming, but the urge to be inside suddenly washed over Maiya as the silence prevailed. The contrast was so extreme that Maiya feared a panic attack was coming on, though what could have triggered it remained elusive to her.

Crossing the threshold into the apartment, Maiya felt as though she had pierced the perimeter of a bubble, a slight resistance tugging at her clothes. The cats were nowhere in sight, yet another alarming sign that something wasn't quite right. Maiya locked the door and walked cautiously through the apartment, checking each room in turn for any indication that someone else had been here. Finding the cats on the bed and no signs of disturbance, she let out a calming sigh, mentally kicking herself for allowing herself to become so paranoid over the unusual silence. Reassured, she reached down to give each cat a scratch behind the ears and went back to the living room.

"Hello, Maiya."

Maiya halted in her tracks, her breath catching in her throat as her heart felt ready to burst from her chest. Before her stood a trim man who appeared a few years older and several inches taller than herself, his short dark hair and goatee neatly groomed. He was clad in a fine, black suit that brought to mind images of government officials and the unexplained disappearance of individuals. He was very much a sharp-dressed man, his suit free of lint or wrinkles, and himself almost unnaturally perfect in his elegance. The man seemed decidedly composed, looking as comfortable and casual as a person lounging in his own home.

When her eyes met his, Maiya found it was difficult to look anywhere else, as the deep azure of each iris seemed present solely to capture one's attention. Had the circumstances been different, she would have found herself rude for the stare she delivered.

"Who are you? What do you want?" Maiya demanded. Though she tried her best to remain composed, her voice trembled when she spoke. "You're the man from the coffee shop…"

The man smiled, making a gesture of introduction. "My name is Mahdon. I came here as an ambassador for my people. I have come here for you."

Maiya blinked and quickly scanned the room for any weapon to fend off the intruder. She half dove for the only item within range - a textbook on natural language processing. She held the book out in front of herself like a person preparing to squash a bug. "Who put you up to this and how did you get in here?"

"I must apologize. Have I frightened you? That was not my intention. I am not entirely familiar with human customs. I have spent a good deal of time studying, but I am afraid this is my first interaction."

Maiya gave him a vacant stare, considering the possibility that she had fallen asleep and was trapped in a rather vivid dream. The man didn't look crazy, but what he was saying most assuredly was. And did crazy people ever really look crazy? Some must, of course, but it certainly wasn't a necessary criterion. Who did she know that would go to the trouble to pull such a prank? Her mind came up blank and Maiya realized she didn't really know many people at all; none of them knew where she lived.

"Why do you know my name?" said Maiya.

"After we found you, we watched you. Please excuse my curtness, but we should be leaving. I will be more than happy to answer any questions you have after we depart."

"You're a stalker then."

Mahdon crossed to the balcony, going out of sight for a moment only to return with a woman who could have been Maiya's twin. Every detail about her was identical to Maiya, the dark brown eyes and way she held herself, down to the tiniest misplaced hair. The introduction of this new woman sent another wave of uneasiness over Maiya as she tried to piece together what was happening. In a matter of minutes, Maiya had gone from thinking someone had broken into her home to being utterly confused and now faced with the idea that she was being replaced.

"Are you going to kill me?"

A bemused look settled on Mahdon's face. "Of course not. Why would we do that? Do you always assume the worst?"

"Then why is… she… here? Who is she, and why does she look like me?" said Maiya, indicating the other woman.

"We cannot very well have you believed dead; you may be gone a long time." Mahdon nodded toward the woman. "Lahna will care for your animals and give the illusion of your presence until your return."

Maiya shook her head. "I never agreed to go anywhere. You haven't even told me where you want to take me. You haven't even told me why! What reason do I have to trust you? Nothing you've said so far makes sense and yet you expect me to just hop in your car with you and drive away while someone else takes over my life? How stupid do you think I am?"

Mahdon frowned slightly, gave her a puzzled look, and then turned to Lahna in question. "Car? I am unfamiliar with that term."

"It's one of the primary modes of transportation on this planet. The vehicle she arrived in is a car," Lahna said.

"Ah, yes. I remember now. Seems inefficient." Turning once more to Maiya, Mahdon smiled. "I did not mean to imply that you are stupid, and if I have done so, I again extend my apologies. Clearly I have much to learn."

Maiya took a step back, once again aiding in Mahdon's confusion. Had he not been polite and understanding? He briefly considered apologizing once more, but soon thought better of it. The ambassador ran a hand through his hair, pacing for a moment. Bringing his hands to his hips and turning his head to one side, he let out a short sigh. To Maiya's eyes, he seemed to be pondering a thought, his mood bordering on frustration. Her lack of cooperation clearly perplexed him.

"Walk with me." Mahdon gestured for Maiya to follow, not especially surprised when she held her ground. "If we wanted to harm you, would we not have done it already?"

Mahdon placed a hand at the crook of her arm and gave her a slight tug. Glancing back at the other "her," Maiya relented and allowed Mahdon to lead her away. Mahdon took her to the balcony where a small craft hovered just above the ledge.

Mahdon sent Maiya a wide grin. "Perhaps seeing how I arrived will soothe your fears."

Maiya stood staring in awe, fully aware that her mouth was hanging open and she likely looked like she'd just seen a ghost. "How…?"

Mahdon laughed. "Believe me now?"

Maiya walked down the length of the balcony, trying to get a better angle of the craft. She reached out a hand to touch it, half expecting it to be an illusion. "Why hasn't anyone noticed this? Where is everyone?"

Mahdon pointed to a small figure that seemed to be frozen in the sky. "See that flying creature? It has no idea it is no longer moving as it was. Neither do they. They never even saw us arrive, and when we leave, they will never know we were ever here."

"You stopped time!"

"Slowed it," said Mahdon.

"Why aren't we affected?"

"We left time untouched in your home."

"But it was silent when I got back; wasn't time slowed then? I wasn't in my apartment yet."

"Another little trick of ours," said Mahdon.

Maiya laughed in disbelief. "I don't even know what to say. This has to be a dream. Albeit a very realistic dream."

"If this is only a dream, then what is stopping you from leaving?"

Maiya shook her head; she knew she should have an answer to that question, but she didn't. Her life really wasn't that bad, was it? She had a place to live, pets to keep her company, and hope for a future - yet it all paled in comparison to an unknown adventure. After several minutes of mulling it over, she still wasn't satisfied with a decision one way or the other.

"I need a day to think about it," Maiya said at last.

Mahdon seemed disappointed once again but did his best to conceal it. "Of course. It will be a big change for you. This would be easier if you remembered who you are."

Maiya wasn't sure what he meant by that, but it wasn't quite clear to her what was going on, so she let it slide. Maiya stepped back inside and sat on the couch expecting her "guests" to leave, but soon found that they were all too comfortable waiting around for her to decide. Mahdon, in particular, seemed fascinated by every little thing in her apartment from the cats to the empty candy dish. Maiya found his curiosity especially odd when compared to that of Lahna, who was content to sit idly by Maiya in silence.

"I'm going to go for a drive. I'd ask you to leave, but I have a feeling you can just let yourself back in whenever you want anyway."

"This should be most interesting. Where are we going?" Mahdon asked.

Maiya sighed. "I'm going alone. I can't be expected to make a decision without time to think, and I can't think with a stranger following me around and waiting for an answer."

Maiya grabbed her keys and left without giving him a chance to respond. It took a moment, but she soon realized that all the expected sounds had returned to the outdoors and the craft Mahdon showed her was no longer visible along the side of the apartment. Mere seconds had passed, and suddenly everything felt normal again. She considered going to the police before quickly determining that it might just make her look crazy. However bizarre and unnerving the intrusion was, she couldn't explain the vehicle or doppelganger.

Maiya let the windows down and drove on into the foothills. She allowed her mind to wander as the roads began to twist and turn and tall canyon walls rose on either side of the road. She always felt more at ease and free when she drove these roads, but something was missing. She only felt in control of her life on days such as this, when she didn't have to think or try to convince herself that what she was doing would make her happy in the long run. She was always happiest when she had no idea where she was going.

The canyon walls gave way to a valley surrounded by snow peaked mountains, and Maiya recognized the city below as Estes Park. It was stunning, and yet she had no one with whom to share it. Maiya pulled off to the side of the road and stepped outside to admire each peak in turn, but no answers came to her. She stood and watched for hours, until the sun began its descent behind the mountains, and she shivered from the now even more apparent drop in temperature. With one final glance, she got in her car and headed back home.

When Maiya arrived back at the apartment complex, the sun had finished its trek to the horizon, and the birds had settled in for the night. She half expected Mahdon and Lahna to have departed, but instead found them just as she'd left them - Lahna sitting contently on the couch, and Mahdon fascinated by everything he could get his hands on.

Mahdon was visibly delighted when he saw her. "You returned! I had begun to worry you would not. Have you made your decision?"

Maiya nodded. She thought she'd made up her mind, anyway. She could think of no reason why she should stay. It had always been a fantasy of hers simply to quit the career path she was on and do something else, anything else. Yet she couldn't just drop everything and leave, could she? Now that the moment finally presented itself before her, as surreal as it was, it all felt too real.

Her feelings bounced between excited and terrified in a matter of seconds, and she realized she had two choices: stay and wonder, potentially missing the biggest opportunity of her life, or make that leap and take the biggest risk of her life.

If this isn't a dream, then at least I won't wake up to feeling trapped in my own life, she thought. After all, it wasn't just the monotony that had gotten to her - it ran deeper than that. It was an inexplicable void in her life that she felt every day, one so vast that nothing could ever seem to fill it. Despite the fear, she felt she had to do this. A slow smile crept across Maiya's face. "Yes. I'll go."

Mahdon beamed. "Excellent! We will depart at once."

Maiya shook her head. "First we need to clear a few things up. Where are we going? You weren't exactly clear on that. Or why. And shouldn't I pack or something?"

"To Amertine. We need your help…" Mahdon paused, considering his words, "…guiding my people. That is as specific as I can be without spending a great deal of time elaborating, and I will gladly do so on the journey over. As for anything else you need, arrangements have already been made. You will require nothing except yourself."

"Amertine? I'm not familiar with that name."

"I would not expect you to be. We have not had a reason to make any contact up until now."

Something about the way Mahdon dodged Maiya's questions and supplied only the simplest answers only served to feed her curiosity. The man's insistence that they needed her, the very concept that she had been sought out, was thrilling. Even given the location's name, Maiya had no idea where they were going or if this was all some complex facade, but that all seemed less important in her mind. The presence of the strange, hovering craft and bird frozen in time were enough to make the risk seem worthwhile.

Maiya smiled. "Okay. I'll go. Let's do this."

CHAPTER 2

Maiya's hands shook with nervous energy as the side door closed and the vehicle began to rise. She was not only going against her better judgment, but any logic that surrounded dealing with strangers and the unknown. And worse, she surmised, if something should happen to her, her family would never be the wiser.

Directly before boarding, the other woman, Lahna, had presented Maiya with the trivia she had obtained about her life. She knew who Maiya's family was, her routine from one day to the next, and a disturbing amount about her past. Details, she was told, which were collected in only a week's time. Imagine what she could learn in a month. Maiya feared that Lahna would be even better at playing herself than she was.

Maiya tilted her head toward Mahdon, who was looking rather pleased with himself, a smirk on his face that she read as "mission accomplished." Beyond that, he seemed neither more nor less threatening than he had when there was access to an escape route. Catching her stare, he pointed a finger toward her window.

"I think you may find this enjoyable. This is the best part."

"I know. I've flown before."

"Not as high as we are flying; of this, I am certain."

Mahdon held a hand over the console and Maiya felt a sudden jolt as the craft began to accelerate upward much more rapidly. To Maiya's eyes, he hadn't appeared to have done anything to cause the craft to move, and the more she thought about it, she was unsure how he had even been able to steer. The vehicle didn't appear to have any means of doing so, but Mahdon seemed confident in his control over their movement.

Maiya gaped at what she saw. Mere seconds passed before she found herself staring down at clouds and then whole continents, the earth's curvature coming into view as it met with space. They soon passed satellites and the international space station, tracing a path toward a ship like none she had ever seen before. It was immense and largely cylindrical with what appeared to be rows of solar panels running the length of it.

As the smaller transport docked within the ship, Mahdon released the door and stood to exit. Maiya hadn't spoken since they had broken the atmosphere and still sat awkwardly, apparently speechless. Mahdon tapped her lightly on the shoulder.

"Are you well? You appear…" Mahdon pondered her expression for a moment, "…hungry?"

Maiya turned to him with a look that puzzled him further, then shook her head slowly. "No, I'm fine… just wow. I thought we were going to another country; I never thought I'd be in space. It's remarkable. But why would anyone choose me to come here? I don't have any training for space. Hell, I'm not even that smart."

"I think the time has come to have that conversation you wanted."

Mahdon sat in a large, cushy chair across from Maiya, in a room he had designated as her quarters for the remainder of the journey. A king-sized bed, moderately sized closet, and door to a separate bathroom area filled the rest of the room. Maiya found that the closet not only contained clothes, but they seemed tailored specifically for her. Further examination of the room found nothing else of interest.

As sparse as the accommodations seemed, Maiya observed that the room had a far warmer feel to it than the rest of the ship. The corridors were all bare and the ship seemed devoid of life. In fact, she hadn't seen a single person as Mahdon led her to where they now sat. He had left her for a solid half an hour when they first arrived, only to return in less formal attire, bringing with him a bottle of water which he offered to her as he took a seat. Maiya took a sip and waited for him to speak.

"I trust the room is acceptable?"

Maiya nodded.

Mahdon smiled. "Good. It is my desire that you be as comfortable as possible during your time with us."

"I had no idea this technology even existed. Who provides your funding? None of this can be cheap. Does the U.S. government know you have this kind of tech?"

"They are not aware."

"Where is Amertine located, exactly?"

"Our solar system shares a galaxy with yours and is approximately 180 parsecs away."

Maiya suddenly felt light-headed when it finally dawned on her what he had been saying all along. She had thought the way he talked was peculiar but had failed to pay attention to the obvious signs. She was so focused on the outlandish situation that she had ignored what was actually being said. She immediately felt like an idiot.

"You aren't human, are you?"

"No."

She took a deep breath and let it out slowly. "Okay. I think I understand now. I really need to learn to pay better attention. So… you speak English."

"Yes."

"I always assumed that aliens would speak something else."

"We do. My native language is Pandornu. When we found your planet, we studied the five most commonly spoken languages. English was one of them. Once we pinpointed your location, it was between that or Spanish; English seemed the most likely."

"And you learned all of them?"

"Yes. It took a few of your hours, but…"

Maiya blinked. "Hours? Wow. I wish I could do that."

"We are fast learners."

"That's an understatement. Based upon that woman who looks like me and the fact that you aren't from here, I'm guessing you don't normally look this way either."

"No. This seemed most appropriate for your arrival on our planet."

"With all your knowledge and capabilities, what do you need me for?"

"You are incredibly special to us. Roughly 3,500 Earth years ago we were offered a choice – live with our mortality or be given a way to prevent death. I was young at the time compared to many others, and like many in my generation, I was intrigued by the prospect. Why die when we could live forever? So, naturally, most of us chose to accept the extension of our lives. Not everyone did, however, and much of the generation before us has passed with time. But for those of us who chose life, we have known no death or disease. Mortal bodies and illness had become a thing of the past."

Mahdon paused to lean forward on the table. "Recently sickness has become prevalent across the main continent of Amertine. We have no idea why or how to stop it and our people are dying. So much time has passed without procreation; there has been no reason for it. We are not even certain it is a possibility anymore. Yet now we face the threat of extinction."

"If you have the capability to take on other forms, isn't it possible to reproduce that way?"

"It may be, yes. However, we overcame such physical urges many hundreds of years ago. The mere concept of the reproductive act is repugnant to us. Please forgive me, as I do not wish to offend you."

"None taken. What about the ancestors of those who chose to keep their shorter lifespan?"

He looked saddened by the question. "Their population accounts for less than one-percent of our total number."

"Even after thousands of years?" Maiya was suddenly well-aware of the absurdity of the situation. "Wait a second. You're saying you were alive back then? That you're over 3,500 years old?"

"Yes. 3,604 years, actually."

"Wow. I'm sorry, but this is a little much to take in. I can accept the technology, but how is it possible for you to be that medically advanced? You're talking about basically being immortal."

"It was a gift. We would never have figured it out on our own. But that can wait; you can learn about it when we arrive. For now, we need to discuss your role in all of this."

"I'm not sure I can be very helpful at preventing a race from extinction, but I'm flattered you think I might be able to."

"You clearly are not aware of your full potential. You may not remember it now, but you were reborn for this purpose, and I have waited my entire life for your return."

Maiya started at his statement. "Whoa. Reborn? As in reincarnation? I don't mean to demean your way of life and, realistically, given what I've seen I shouldn't be talking, but still… that isn't possible. And if it is, then why be so afraid of death and extinction?"

"Most of us never get to experience another life, but you are different," Mahdon smiled slightly as he chuckled to himself. "It seems strange that I should explain the ways of the universe and life to one of the creators herself, but it is as you planned."

Maiya blinked several times, thinking she must have misheard him. "One of the what, now?"

"One of the creators. It is unfortunate that you do not remember more; I do not believe I can do you justice in any description I paint of you. But never mind that, it is as it is, and I am honored to be the one with this opportunity. Even in that form, you are and will always be the re-embodiment of Jovienna, the goddess of life."

Maiya blushed, wondering if she should deny the title placed upon her. To be called a savior was one thing, to be called a goddess, another. Modesty seemed the best policy, yet denial would, she decided, be no more effective than saying nothing at all. Desperate or not, Mahdon seemed sure of her identity, having left his own planet to locate her on another. Whether or not she agreed with this evaluation of her identity, she had already unknowingly accepted the position when she opted to join Mahdon in the shuttle craft. It seemed pointless to say anything now. After what seemed an extensive moment of silence, Maiya submitted to the notion of at least humoring Mahdon. If she tried to help and failed, could they really fault her for trying?

"Assuming you're right and I am this goddess, what exactly do I need to do to help?"

"We do not know."

Maiya's heart sank. "You don't know? Then how do you know that I'm the one you're looking for? How can I help if I don't know what I'm supposed to do? I'm not sure if you're aware, but I don't exactly have healing powers. I'm only human."

Mahdon didn't seem fazed by her reaction, rather, he smiled. "I understand that you are worried that you will disappoint, but the prophecy regarding your return was clear. We did not contact you lightly. When we arrive, I am certain you will know what to do."

14

She didn't find his words reassuring, but from the bottom of her heart she hoped he was right. The thought of disappointing another person, or a whole race of people in this case, wasn't an idea she relished. She counted herself fortunate that he didn't recognize the look of terror in her eyes. At the very least, his lack of understanding human facial expressions would allow her to sustain the illusion that she wasn't expecting to fail.

"I suspect this must be a lot for you to learn at one time." Mahdon once again smiled at her as he rose from his seat. "Are you hungry? A meal can be prepared for you at once. While you wait, I would be honored to introduce you to the others."

"So there ARE others?" Maiya moved to meet Mahdon at the door. "I was beginning to think we were alone on this massive ship. I didn't see anyone else when we arrived. Come to think of it, I didn't even hear anyone else."

Mahdon chuckled as he swiped a hand over a panel by the door. "Of course there are others. You may soon be surprised."

The door opened swiftly, and he motioned for Maiya to exit first. Stepping into the corridor, the same stunningly white walls expanded before her in three directions. Mahdon turned to the left and Maiya followed.

"Why are all the walls so blank? I don't have any design sense, but even for me they're a bit bland."

"You may change them if you like."

Maiya gave him a sideways look. "How?"

"What would you like to see?"

Maiya shrugged. "I don't know. I like pictures of the mountains and forests, but I'm not sure that's appropriate for a spaceship."

As Maiya spoke, the corridor shifted in color to a pleasant teal and a wide array of photographs from nature appeared evenly spaced along the walls. Beautiful mahogany and dark-cherry wood frames, each bearing a unique and intricate design, accented the images perfectly. The hallway had shifted so much in appearance that it resembled that of a house.

Maiya's face brightened, once again impressed. "Very nice! How did you do that?"

"I did not. You did. Much of the decor can be modified by your thoughts. Ah…" Mahdon stopped before a door at the end of one of the hallways. "We have arrived at the dining hall."

Mahdon once again ran his hand past a sensor and the door slid open. The room beyond the threshold of the doorway was unlike anything Maiya ever expected to see on a ship. Hundreds of interlocking parts created the hardwood inlay of the dining hall, and crystal chandeliers hung down over the half a dozen circular tables in the room. Each table had a white table cloth with a burgundy overlay, and five place settings of fine silverware.

What appeared to be windows along the perimeter of the room showed forests, fields, mountains, and desert scenes. So realistic were the images that the slightest breeze in the fields and the leaves of the trees could be detected. Yet they did not appear to be videos either; it was as if a person could step right into one of the backdrops with no bothersome glass to act as a barrier. Only one panel of the wall revealed the truth of their surroundings. Even so, if not for her own logic reminding her that they were no longer on the ground, Maiya could have just as easily been fooled by the images.

"Do you like it?" A new voice startled Maiya, causing her to jump reflexively. She turned her head sharply to the right to spot a man with olive complexion and thick, black hair standing only a few feet away. He was dressed in long, white and red embroidered robes, and stood roughly as tall as her. His clothing reminded her of something a man might wear to a wedding in India, but the outfit seemed to suit him well. She figured she must have been too distracted by the elaborate decor to notice the man enter the room.

"I designed it myself." The man continued, waving a hand about the room. "I find your choice in planet most fascinating. The decorations alone vary greatly. They are quite vibrant in every culture I studied."

"Yes, it's all very nice. Your design, I mean. I really like the walls; I haven't seen anything like that before. You can't even tell the trees aren't real."

The man smiled and then gave a slight bow. "Please excuse my rudeness. I am Naliz. As the Ambassador may have informed you, I am a member of the High Council."

"I'm Maiya." Maiya extended a hand and Naliz took it in both of his.

"I know very well who you are. It is the finest pleasure to make your acquaintance." Naliz kissed her hand lightly before releasing it. "As much as I would love to continue this conversation, I gather you are not here to talk. I took the liberty to have the chef prepare a meal for you. I will have him bring it out for you at once."

"Why don't you join us?" Maiya asked. "Mahdon has told me some stuff, but I wouldn't mind having someone else to talk to."

"Thank you for the invitation, but I have other business I must attend to." Naliz gave Mahdon a slight smile, "It was kind of you to allow me along, Mahdon. Now if you'll excuse me, I will speak with you later this evening."

He promptly turned and exited the room. Not a minute later, the one Maiya presumed to be the chef entered and presented her with a platter of food fit for a king. The presentation was beyond impressive, so much so that she nearly felt guilty for wanting to indulge in the food that was set before her. The brightest and most aromatic fruit she'd ever laid her eyes upon was nothing less than heavenly to her taste buds. The steak was prepared perfectly to her liking and she savored every bite of it like she'd never tried anything so succulent in her life.

Throughout the meal, Mahdon sat silently with elbows on the table and hands clasped. Maiya had been so engrossed in her own food that she'd hardly taken notice of the fact that Mahdon hadn't eaten a single thing. When she realized this, a tiny bit of panic about being poisoned welled up in her chest. She quickly dismissed these fears as absurd when she thought back on Mahdon's earlier comment. *If they wanted me dead, they would have done it already.*

Maiya set down her fork, leaned back in her chair, and let out a satisfied sigh. "That was fantastic! It was seriously the best meal I've ever had in my life. Aren't you hungry? You didn't eat anything."

"I am glad you enjoyed it. I have not required food in a very, very long time. I cannot imagine starting now."

"But don't you miss it? I'd love it if I didn't have to eat, but I think I'd miss the taste of food. You should at least try something new every once in a while. Just my opinion."

"Perhaps another time. Are you ready to meet the others? I can give you a tour of the ship as well…"

"I'd like that. Are the other members of the High Council on board? Are you a member?"

"No, they are not. I am an advisor to the council, but nothing more."

"Are they the leaders of your country?"

"In a sense, yes. They are more than that – religious, spiritual, and political leaders. We have what you might consider countries, but their reach is more widespread than that. Every individual on Amertine looks to them for guidance. Regretfully they do not take much interest in science or exploration..." Mahdon seemed lost in thought for a moment, and then shook his head and stood. "Shall we go?"

Mahdon offered his hand and Maiya rose to accept it. The route they took now moved toward the outer hull of the ship and Maiya could see streaks of light and color as they walked past full walls of windows.

"Have you visited other inhabited planets?" Maiya said.

"Yes. Two. Many years ago."

"What were they like?"

"Wonderful!" The passion in his voice was palpable. "The first was a planet with far more basic lifeforms, but they were new and unlike anything we have on Amertine. We studied thousands of species while there; they were all new to us, but I never suspected it would get better.

Then there was Krae. We did our best to remain invisible as we did on your planet but still managed to get close. The gift certainly proves its worth in such situations. The inhabitants of Krae were far more advanced than any we had encountered before - except on Amertine, of course. I imagine they would be only slightly more advanced than your kind are at this time."

"I'm jealous... but with a ship like this, I assumed you'd be traveling all over the place."

"I had hoped for that. This ship was designed for research and exploration. However, when the disease spread, locating you became our new priority. This is the first time we have left our solar system with the vessel."

"That's unfortunate."

"Indeed. Perhaps after the people have been cured we will make use of the ship as intended. When that time comes, I would very much like it if you would join me."

"Isn't it a bit early to make that offer? I hardly know anything about you."

Mahdon smiled. "I suppose so. When you have lived as long as I have, you learn to say what you think before you even think it. Please do not feel obligated to say 'yes' if you would rather not. In the future I will try not to be so forward."

Their path once again turned inward and then forward toward two windowed sliding doors. Even from here Maiya could tell they had reached the bridge, though it appeared to be abandoned as the rest of the ship seemed to be. As they got closer, three individuals formed before them on the opposite side of the doors, seemingly out of thin air.

Maiya stopped in front of the door and looked up at Mahdon. "Am I seeing things, or did they just show up out of nowhere?"

"I imagine it must seem that way to you. They have been there all along, though not in human form. Perhaps the greatest thing the gift has given us is this - true freedom, the freedom to take on any likeness or none at all."

"Any at all? What about your identity? Wouldn't it be easy for someone to pretend to be someone who they're not? And how do you know someone is there if you can't see them?"

"Why would we impersonate another?" Mahdon seemed legitimately shocked that Maiya would ask such a question.

Maiya blushed. "Dishonesty tends to run rampant amongst people, I'm afraid."

"That is sad to hear. We have had our share as well, I am certain. That being said, I do believe it is difficult to impersonate another, though I have never tried. We can sense each other regardless of the form we choose to take. Everyone's energy is different."

The door swept open and Maiya was greeted by three overly excited individuals - two men and a woman. Though much of the ship's processes were automated, Maiya learned, there was a moderately sized crew in the event that manual override or repairs were necessary. She was informed that should that crew be needed, they would likely already be dead.

Maiya yawned. She wasn't sure how long she'd been up at this point, but all at once she felt exhausted. She hoped they wouldn't take offense if she asked to return to her quarters. To her surprise, the woman, who had introduced herself as Daera, smiled sweetly when she saw Maiya yawn.

"Are you tired or bored? It's been so long since I've seen someone do that. It's like looking into the past." Maiya had never before heard someone sound so thrilled to witness something so minor.

"I'm sorry... I'm tired. It's been a very long and interesting day."

"I can show you the way back to your room if you are ready," Mahdon said. Maiya thought he looked a bit disappointed, though she wasn't sure why.

She bid the three crew members farewell and followed Mahdon back down the corridor in the direction they had come. For a moment Mahdon said nothing, then stopped after they rounded the first corner.

"May I ask something of you?"

Maiya turned to look at him, wondering what more he could possibly ask of her. She was already feeling a bit overwhelmed. "What is it?"

"I fear I may not be the best advisor for you. Unlike Lahna and several of the others, I did not study your life or culture as closely as I should have. My focus has been much more related to history and prophecy. I was hoping that you might allow me to become acquainted with you in person."

"Oh!" Maiya wasn't expecting such a simple request. It seemed odd to her that he should ask; most men she'd gone on dates with didn't even ask for permission before they tried to kiss her. It seemed chivalry wasn't dead after all. Maiya smiled, "Yes, of course. I'd like that."

Mahdon looked relieved as they began walking once more. "Thank you. Do you require much rest? I am eager to learn as soon as you are ready."

Maiya shrugged. "I don't know what time it is, but I guess that doesn't really matter much anymore. Eight hours maybe? Aren't you tired?"

"I am not. I do not require rest. I have not since Alurine first presented the gift. If I were to remain in this form for too long I would, but I have no intention of doing so past what is necessary."

"I see… is it uncomfortable?"

"In a sense, yes. Once you have tasted freedom, it is hard to stay confined for so long…"

"Please don't feel you have to stay this way for me."

"Truth be told, that is not the only reason we have chosen to appear to you as such." Mahdon's tone was markedly more somber than earlier.

"Oh? Then why else?"

"In every case that we have seen, the disease only afflicts those who have not taken on a more permanent form. We are not certain why, but we seem to be immune to the effects otherwise. Yet if one tries to shift after they have already been infected… it is too late."

"So you'll stay this way until you find a cure?"

"If we must, yes. I do believe we are safe from the disease while on this ship, however, so those aboard have taken the opportunity to shift freely." Mahdon stopped before Maiya's quarters and swept his hand over the sensor. "We have returned."

They stepped into the room and Mahdon handed her a device roughly the size of a quarter. It looked similar to a walkie-talkie, though it lacked an antenna. He pointed to a small button on the side.

"Should you need anything, you may contact me by pressing this button. You can speak into it and I will be able to respond. You are also welcome to move freely about the ship if you desire, so there is no need to feel confined to this room." Mahdon smiled. "I would hate for you to feel you are a prisoner. Is there anything further I can assist you with before I leave?"

"No. This is perfect. Thank you."

"I wish you a restful sleep."

He promptly turned and exited the room. Maiya set down the communicator on the table and began rummaging through the closet for sleepwear. What she found ranged from silk to fleece, and all articles felt pleasing to the touch. If the bedding was half as nice as the sleepwear, she thought, this would be the most restful sleep she'd have in her life.

Maiya settled on a purple silken negligee and climbed into bed only to discover that her expectations had been more than exceeded. As with everything else Mahdon had allowed her to experience, the bed was fantastic. Even in such a tight space, they had spared no expense to please her. As Maiya drifted off to sleep, she thought, *I could get used to this.*

After bidding Maiya farewell, Mahdon shifted out of his human form and headed to a lower deck that consisted primarily of small biology labs which had never been used. He made his way to the back of the ship where several larger rooms had been designed for holding conferences. Upon his arrival, Mahdon found Naliz sitting at a long table and indulging in a rather large plate of strawberries. He shifted back and took a seat across from Naliz.

21

"You should try these. They're quite good." Naliz finished a strawberry and smiled. "All these years and I can still appreciate the taste of something new."

Mahdon frowned. Naliz wasn't one for small talk. Mahdon knew from past experience that whatever reason Naliz had for calling him here, it had nothing to do with enjoying the gifts life had to offer.

"What was it you wanted to discuss?"

"I think you already know." Naliz's expression darkened as he leaned forward across the table. "Brandon isn't going to be very happy with you."

Mahdon sighed. "Must we discuss this again? What is done is done. I doubt he will be very pleased with you once he realizes you came with me. I hope this will not cause you too much trouble, but you made that decision on your own."

"I'll be fine. I'll just tell him I came along to keep an eye on you. You, on the other hand, really need to prepare for his backlash. He's never been very fond of you."

"And I have yet to regret any of my decisions. Allow me to deal with Brandon on my own; he will hold his tongue once he comes to his senses."

"I don't think you understand the gravity of the situation. This is serious, Mahdon. This is going to cost you more than just a slap on the wrist."

"Then that will be my burden. I made the right choice. You know that as well as I."

Naliz leaned back in his chair, nodding in agreement. "I see that now, yes. I knew the instant I saw her. No matter the form we choose to take, the eyes never lie. However, not everyone will see it that way. She hasn't awakened yet and that may pose a problem. I'm only trying to protect you."

"What do you propose I do?"

"Do what you must to get on Brandon's good side. Lie if you have to. Tell Brandon you're sorry for defying him and beg his forgiveness."

Mahdon's face twisted in disgust. He made no effort to conceal his distaste with the idea, his tone bordering on amusement. "You know I will never do that."

Naliz looked saddened. Mahdon suspected the council member already knew what Brandon had in store. "Then I suppose you'll have no other choice than to face the consequences."

"So be it."

Maiya awoke to the light of the sun, feeling well rested for the first time in a very long time. It wasn't until she sat up in bed that she remembered where she was. When she laid down to sleep, she had half expected to wake and realize it had all been a wild dream. The walls around her now showcased a red and orange sunrise, the colors wavering as the sun slowly lifted from the imaginary horizon. The sound of birds' morning conversations played over the gentle hum of the ship, giving further credibility to the illusion.

As Maiya crawled out of bed and dressed, the sound and images faded, returning the walls to their former pastel blue hue. She grabbed the communicator and turned it over in her hand several times before ultimately deciding to hold off on contacting Mahdon. After all, he had said she had free reign of the ship, and she was uncertain how often these moments of alone time would present themselves. She pocketed the device and exited into the corridor.

Heading down the hallway to the right, she rounded a corner and soon found herself standing in the middle of a four-way intersection. Doors lined the walls at regular intervals along the hallways to her left and right. Directly in front of her there was what appeared to be an elevator shaft with an unusual looking symbol printed on the wall above. Curious, as the opening lacked a door as one would expect, Maiya stepped to the edge and peered first up and then down. She was immediately overcome by vertigo. Her suspicions were substantiated – the shaft did, in fact, connect to other levels of the ship – she found herself puzzled that no elevator car or platform appeared to exist within.

"May I help you find something?"

Maiya started, startled by the sudden appearance of Naliz beside her. She took a step back, trying to find her words, and feeling as though she'd been caught red-handed. Finally, she shook her head, reminding herself of Mahdon's words.

"No... I'm fine. I was just going for a walk. Trying to gather my thoughts about all of this."

"I see. Have you come to any conclusions?"

Maiya hesitated a moment, then replied with a long sigh. "Just that I don't want to disappoint anyone, but I probably shouldn't be telling you that. Mahdon is so confident. What if he's wrong?"

Maiya blushed and looked down uncomfortably. "I'm sorry. We just met. I should really be keeping this to myself."

"You may be right. On the other hand, I would like you to understand that you can trust us, so feel free to say whatever it is you think. I imagine it must be difficult for you to be away from your kind. However, I would caution you against allowing such fears to overtake your mind. Such thoughts can cloud judgment and leave you vulnerable.

But never mind that now. Shall we go find the ambassador? He has been eagerly waiting for you to wake. I suspect he will be far better at calming your nerves than I could ever hope to be."

Maiya followed Naliz cautiously into the "elevator" shaft, fully expecting to plummet downward at any moment. To her surprise, the air beneath her feet felt as solid as the floor she had just stepped away from. Maiya bent low and swept her hand past her feet, finding that it remained unaffected by the seemingly solid surface.

Naliz seemed unaware of her concern as they began to rapidly descend several floors; instead, he laughed. "I take it you are unfamiliar with gravity tunnels? I do hope Mahdon can help you remember who you are, but in the meantime, please excuse my amusement."

Their speed decreased, and they came to a stop before a hallway nearly identical to the one they just left. Maiya followed Naliz from the gravity tunnel and watched as Mahdon materialized almost instantaneously before her eyes, once again appearing in formal attire as he had on their first encounter. He looked as excited to see her now as the moment when she agreed to join him on this journey.

"Good morning! I trust you slept well?"

"Yes. Morning... so strange. Does it still count as morning when there's no sunrise? I don't even know what time it is back home. I guess it doesn't really matter, does it?"

Mahdon laughed. "Perhaps not. It can take some time to adjust to the change in environment. I do hope you found the solar simulation helpful. Shall we continue our discussion from earlier? I have much to share with you before we arrive."

"I'd like that."

Mahdon motioned for her to follow and the three headed toward the back of the ship until they reached the conference rooms. Maiya and Naliz took seats across from one another while Mahdon swept a hand over a panel on the far wall.

The room grew dim and darkened until almost no light remained. Mahdon stepped away as a pinpoint of light formed in the middle of the main table, hovering like a miniature sun. All at once, the light erupted outward, forming a slowly moving radial mass of holographic stars, planets, and cosmic debris that filled the room. Every color of the rainbow was showcased in the swirl of lights, adding to the splendor of the image. Maiya watched as the hologram then zoomed in on one of the many "arms" of stars.

"This…" Mahdon circled a finger over a section of the stellar map, "…is where your solar system is located."

He swept out his hand and the image once again zoomed out, though now a much more obvious red point of light glowed at Earth's location. He traced a finger down the same spiral Earth rested in. He came to a stop and indicated another cluster of stars.

"And this is home. Relatively speaking, the systems are very close."

Maiya raised an eyebrow. "How close is close? Time-wise."

Naliz laughed. "If we were to use the technology available to the people on the planet we just left, it would take thousands of your years. Fortunately for you, we have something much better. It will take approximately one of your lunar cycles."

Maiya couldn't help but feel a little offended by the comment… even if it was accurate. She couldn't deny that she was impressed with everything she'd witnessed, and even preferred it, but the remark only served to remind her how small she already felt. She wondered if Naliz realized that he came off as arrogant, and she was thankful that Mahdon seemed to lack that characteristic.

"And during this time, what will you have me do?"

Mahdon smiled. "We may do anything you wish. I, of course, will do my duty to teach you of our history. I will also assist you in any way I can. Naliz will be open to answering any questions you have about our society. First and foremost, I think it best we prepare you for what to expect upon arrival. It may not seem crucial at the moment, but I assure you the time will pass much more quickly than you expect."

Mahdon returned to the panel on the wall, raising the lights and causing the hologram to fade away. He took a seat next to Maiya and motioned to Naliz, who promptly rose and stepped to the head of the table.

"There are currently five members of the council - Brandon, Saren, Jo'dai, Tanin, and myself. Before we arrive, it would be good for you to be familiar with each of them. I am the only one aboard this ship; however, I can provide you with a full profile of each member. You should speak as though you have known us for your entire life - even if you do not remember us." Naliz spoke softly, but with conviction.

Each word he said flowed effortlessly like those falling from the lips of a well-trained politician. Mahdon had made reference to the council before, but it was now clear to Maiya that this was a man in a position of power. She suddenly felt foolish for ever mentioning her self-doubt to him and decided to henceforth make it a point to keep such thoughts to herself.

"At this time, Brandon is the oldest member and head of the council. He and I are the most versed in religious doctrine, though Brandon oversees all council affairs - whether they be related to religion, political considerations, or otherwise. He has held this position since before the gift."

"What about you and the other members? Were you on the council then too?" Maiya asked.

"Yes. Little has changed since then. There was a time when such term longevity was not only impossible but would have been frowned upon. When Alurine arrived, a peace followed that rendered a change in leadership both unnecessary and unwanted."

"I see." Maiya was unsure how she felt about the idea of one leader for what amounted to a hundred or more generations back home. The whole concept was unbelievably foreign and made her a little sad. But if world peace truly existed, was that really such a bad thing?

"The idea is strange to you," Naliz said. Unlike Mahdon, he had readily picked up on Maiya's discomfort. "This is not to say we don't value the input of our citizens. The ambassador serves as a representative of the people in both diplomatic missions and when advising the council. I assure you —"

"My apologies for interrupting." The familiar voice of Daera, the ship's communications expert, filled the room, cutting Naliz off.

Mahdon pressed down a button on a device that sat in the center of the main table. "What is it, Daera?"

"I've received a transmission from Brandon. He's requesting to speak with you and Naliz immediately."

Mahdon and Naliz exchanged a look. It was difficult to tell from their expressions if this was a bad thing or merely unexpected.

Naliz turned to Maiya and gave a slight bow. "You'll have to excuse us for a moment. Duty calls."

Mahdon stood and Maiya followed his cue to join him in a smaller adjoining room. It appeared to be a waiting room of sorts with several wide-armed single seater chairs and strange potted plants she'd never seen before.

"I must apologize," Mahdon said. "This is poor timing. Brandon can be…" He waved a hand in the air as if physically searching for the right word. "…persistent. I promise you this will only take a minute."

Mahdon returned to the main conference room and pressed the button on the center console, informing Daera to pass the transmission through. The wall containing the panel brightened and soon displayed a bearded man who appeared to be slightly older than middle-aged. His hair was greying, and his garments resembled those of a 15th century nobleman. He presently wore a feather trimmed fur cloak and sported a scowl on his face. When he spoke, the restraint required to steady his tone was clear.

"This is an unsanctioned mission. I am not surprised to see such behavior from the ambassador, but you, Naliz? I'm very disappointed. If you think for one second that bringing back that woman is a good idea, you are gravely mistaken. You will return her to her planet at once."

"I cannot do that." Mahdon's voice was calm. "We have run out of options; the people are dying. I will not sit idly by when all prophecy speaks of her return."

"That is not your decision to make!"

This time, Naliz spoke. "High Councilor, if I may… I have met this woman, and she is as Mahdon claims. I had doubts at first myself, but after seeing her, it is clear to me. I did not join the ambassador without careful consideration."

Brandon gritted his teeth. "You best pray you are right. Even still, this will not be without consequence."

"Understood."

The transmission was abruptly ended.

Naliz sighed and shook his head at Mahdon. "I cannot defend you forever. I find it unlikely that he will contact us again before we arrive. Perhaps his temper will have curbed by then."

The two men retrieved Maiya and continued with the prior discussion. Naliz provided her with a handheld holo-device loaded with the member information and gave a brief demonstration on how to use it. He reminded her how crucial it was to be a diligent study and then adjourned the meeting for the day. From that point forward, they met twice weekly to test her knowledge and answer any questions that arose. Maiya would see him on occasion outside of these scheduled times, but it was Mahdon with whom she found herself spending vast stretches of time.

Over the next three weeks, Mahdon met with Maiya daily for history lessons and meals. Within a week, Maiya had convinced him to try a wide array of foods from sushi to cheeseburgers and everything in-between. They soon found he had a particular fondness for cashews, and he would often be seen snacking on them outside of their usual mealtimes.

In exchange for her full attention during the sometimes-boring history lessons, Mahdon shared stories of his own past with Maiya. These many times related to the lesson itself and usually revolved around a memory Mahdon held especially dear. Maiya was surprised to find that, though their pasts differed greatly, she could often delve into her past and recall a similar memory of her own to share.

She soon grew fond of their time together and found it to be the highlight of her day despite the many wonders the ship had to offer. Much like herself, he was endlessly filled with curiosity and his excitement at the tiniest things often left her smiling. And so, it was on the twenty-fifth day of the journey that she met him outside her quarters with a smile on her face and passion for learning in her heart.

"Hello, Maiya!" Mahdon seemed especially happy this day and greeted her with a smile so large that it rivaled her own. "I have a surprise for you."

"I like the sound of that! What is it?"

Mahdon took her by the hand and led her to the bridge of the ship. Maiya gazed out at the forward-facing window and her heart skipped a beat.

"Welcome to Amertine. We have arrived earlier than expected."

CHAPTER 3

Maiya looked down at a planet that didn't look much different from her own, though being familiar with a globe, the differences were readily apparent. More obvious than the changes in the planet were the two moons which orbited it. All the anxiety and fear she had tried to suppress quickly cropped up in the back of her mind as she began to accept that this was actually happening.

"Are you ready to depart?" Mahdon stood behind her, hands folded in front of himself. He smiled when she turned away from the window to face him, unaware that she felt like running past him to hide in her now familiar room.

Calm down, it's going to be great, Maiya thought, nodding to Mahdon as she walked to his side.

They proceeded down the long corridors to the side bay doors where the shuttlecraft they'd arrived in now sat ready for their departure. Maiya closed her eyes and inhaled deeply. She exhaled slowly as she sank into the passenger seat, trying not to think about what she was expected to do once they landed.

Mahdon rested a hand on Maiya's and sent her a reassuring smile. "You will not disappoint. The people will love you… I promise."

Maiya nodded but said nothing in reply.

The large doors swept open and the craft moved out with a sharp jolt. They accelerated rapidly downward, breaking through the clouds to reveal a yellow-orange landscape webbed with rivers and mountains. They swept low over a mountain range, following a river as it cut its course down the mountains. The mountains soon gave way to a vast expanse of plains and forest through which the river flowed. Mahdon slowed the craft as they passed over a golden city nestled between waterfalls of varying heights. Tall buildings rose from the rock, glistening as precious metal does. The mist from the falls caused the city to sparkle more brilliantly in the sunlight. A deep gorge lined one edge of the city, to which the water fell to a river below.

"The capital city, Fimbira, is below us now. We will dock at the manor that will be your residence while you remain on Amertine. Should you choose to stay, you are welcome to keep it, as it was designed specifically for you."

The craft crossed over the gorge to a secluded estate. A large three-story building sat at some distance from the cliff, surrounded on three sides by thick orange forest. A significant garden with a hedge maze and central fountain stretched out behind the mansion, completing the image of excessive wealth. Mahdon brought the craft to hover within the confines of the garden, aligned evenly with a balcony on the second story.

"This whole place is for ME?" Maiya asked.

"Yes. I will, of course, stay temporarily until you become comfortable."

"Don't you think it's a little big?"

"It was my understanding that the leaders on your planet live in large residences. I apologize if I was misinformed." Mahdon frowned. "You do not like it?"

"It's not that at all. It's just not what I'm used to."

Mahdon released the side lock and climbed out of the craft, offering his hand to help Maiya out. Warm air awaited her, bringing with it the pleasant floral scents of the gardens. She paused to enjoy the fresh air, having missed it during the days aboard the ship.

"This residence is quite a bit larger than your last domicile. However, it has some features that I believe you will find quite nice."

Floor to ceiling windows ran the length of the balcony, separated only by three sets of fully-windowed doors. The middle set of doors already stood open, entering the mansion at the white marble landing of a grand staircase. The stairs split two-ways, curving down to the main floor and up to the third.

The two stood in silence for a moment, admiring the detail that had been put into the wooden railings and grand foyer below.

"It is more beautiful than I imagined. Naliz presented me with the design and map for this residence, but this is my first time seeing it in person. Though construction began before I left, it was completed during my time away. Follow me. If my memory serves me correctly, the main bedroom should be this way."

They made their way to the third floor, where they passed a lavish study before reaching the corner bedroom. The bedroom was closer to a family room in size, and Maiya thought, larger than her whole apartment back home. Even the closet was grand in size. The design of the room was a unique blend of modern and historical, unlike any Maiya had personally stayed in before. She walked the perimeter slowly as Mahdon spoke, stopping to run her hands over a hardwood dresser. The craftsmanship was remarkable.

"Tonight, there will be a welcoming ceremony held in your honor. You will have attendants to cater to your needs and free reign of the grounds as you wish. Naliz is meeting with the council as we speak to arrange any last-minute details. It would be appropriate at this time for you to rest if you are able."

"How long do I have?"

"Approximately twelve hours."

Maiya looked up from the dresser. "Twelve? And that's tonight?"

"Yes. You will find the days are slightly longer than those with which you are familiar."

"Then maybe I'll wait to rest… I'm not sure I could at this point anyway. Do you have somewhere you need to be? I wouldn't mind a last-minute lesson."

"Did you have an inquiry about something specific?"

"A couple of things…"

"I will be happy to answer if I can."

"This might seem like a strange question, but…" Maiya took a seat at the end of the bed and continued, "Brandon… is that his real name?"

"He did not always go by that name, no. The change is fairly recent — only 200 years or so. He was once known as Tribian."

"Then why does he go by Brandon now?"

"That is a mystery to me. Brandon is very private about his affairs."

"I see. I shouldn't pry then, huh? The other thing I was curious about was something you said on the ship. You mentioned that there's a whole era of unknown history. Why? What did you mean?"

"May I suggest we continue this conversation in the study?"

Maiya rose to meet Mahdon and the two walked back the way they had come. The walls of the study were lined with floor to ceiling shelves, each full to capacity with leather-bound books. A large wooden desk sat at the far end of the room, set before the equally tall forward-facing windows. Arm chairs similar to those aboard the ship sat in sets of four at two points closer to the entryway. Maiya selected one and Mahdon sat across from her on the opposite side of a low table.

"This entire room contains what you might consider folklore. These tomes are filled with stories that we could neither confirm nor deny, yet many had been told for generations when I was young. There are stories that speak of a time before the Amerti people."

"Wow. There must be hundreds of thousands of stories in here! Can you tell me one?"

"I do not know where it is located in here, and I fear I will not do it justice without imagery to accompany it. It would be easier to show you."

"How?"

Mahdon leaned forward, elbows on his knees, and reached his hands across the table, palms up. "Place your hands on mine."

Maiya did as instructed and, as their hands met, she felt flooded with unusual emotions. The room around them seemed to shift and transform until they were standing at the base of a mountain after dark. Maiya jumped back and reflexively removed her hands from Mahdon's. The scene did not change, and she found they were both now standing.

"Where are we?"

"Do not be afraid. We have not left the study. In fact, we are both sitting there as we speak. I have simply allowed you access into my mind."

Maiya bent down and picked up a rock, finding it to feel as real as the scenery appeared. "It's so realistic."

"Yes. I assure you that what we see will pose no threat to you."

Maiya looked around and could see no foliage or water nearby. The entire environment within her view consisted solely of rocks. She followed Mahdon to a small trailhead that headed up the mountain, and after a brief walk, they came to a stop beside a small encampment. Four individuals sat around a fire playing a game with rocks in the dirt. They took no notice of Mahdon and Maiya, which Maiya found odd considering the large, pointed ears atop their heads.

Their faces were nearly identical to those of humans, though their noses had the slightest bit of a unique curve to them. Their bodies were athletic and their hands flexible with long, agile-looking fingers — the kind that she had heard called "piano fingers" in the past. Much like humans, they were mostly devoid of hair, except for their long, bushy tails they had wrapped around their legs as they sat.

Beyond that, they were fully clothed and even wore jewelry. Although Maiya had never seen them before, it was clear to her which were male and which were female.

"What are they?" She regretted the words as soon as she said them. She could tell just by looking at them that they were members of an intelligent and sentient species.

Mahdon took no offense but corrected her. "The more appropriate question would be 'who?'"

Maiya blushed, wondering why this had not been shown to her in their prior discussions. "I'm sorry. It looks like I've put my foot in my mouth again..."

Mahdon eyed her curiously for a moment. "That seems a strange thing to do. I do not see your foot anywhere near your mouth. What would compel you to do such a thing?"

Maiya stifled a laugh. "Never mind... it's not meant to be taken literally. Do you miss it?"

"What?"

"Your tail."

Mahdon smiled. "You do ask bizarre questions. Truthfully, it has been so long that I do not even remember what it was like to have one."

"I bet you were adorable."

This time, Mahdon blushed. "I believe that is a compliment? Thank you."

They turned their attention back to the group where the female farthest from them was now throwing rocks aside with great annoyance.

"So, who are they?" Maiya asked.

"The creators. This is the origin story of our people. The one with the rocks is Alurine. The dark-haired male is Hokar, and the other male is Reedon. The other female is Jovienna."

Me, Maiya thought. *That completely unfamiliar woman is supposed to be me. There's no way.*

Alurine swept back her red hair with a great sigh. "I tire of this. Let us make things more interesting."

"What do you suggest?" asked the golden-haired woman to her left.

"A new game."

Hokar scoffed at the idea. "You always cheat."

"I do not! I simply add a little flavor to improve upon things!" Alurine's frown turned to a smile. "Besides, what I have in mind is no more than a friendly competition to see who the best artist is."

What happened next was nothing short of remarkable. As Alurine swept her hands through the air, the sky turned a brilliant red and waves of light ran across like aurora borealis. The three joined her, each creating something more colorful and complicated than the last. Life sprang forth across the land, transforming the landscape from one of dull grays and browns to one of gold and blue with every color of the rainbow dotted throughout.

After she finished with the sky, Alurine had broken apart the ground, creating canyons and striking peaks. Reedon followed by filling in the gaps with rivers and lakes, while Jovienna painted the land with grass and trees. Hokar was the first to bring true life to the world they created, populating the sky with little purple birds that spiraled through the air as they flew. Jovienna and Reedon followed suit, producing larger animals, though all appeared to be herbivores which mingled together in peace.

It was then that Maiya saw what Hokar meant by "cheating." For every creature the other three created, Alurine drew in a predator that turned the others into prey. She had even altered some of the plants, twisting them to turn them poisonous or unsavory. She seemed to delight in bringing chaos to everything that otherwise existed in harmony.

After some time of watching, Maiya saw Jovienna form a little figure in her hand and move it to the valley below. It resembled the four on the mountain, though lacked the extravagant jewelry and garments; it was the first Amerti. Hokar formed one of his own and set it by the first, smiling when the two mini foxlike people held each other close.

35

They all stopped and watched while the Amerti foraged for food and drank at the river. The Amerti frolicked in the fields, chased birds, and curled up next to one another to sleep. Though they looked like their creators, it was clear how very different they really were. All but Alurine looked satisfied with the work they had done, and they sat back to enjoy the scenery of the new world.

Alurine swept up the sleeping pair and whispered something over them. When she set them back down, they awoke alarmed, looking around themselves fearfully and seeking shelter in a cave.

"What have you done?" Hokar demanded.

"I told them they exist."

Not another word was spoken as the image faded away and Maiya once again found herself sitting across from Mahdon in the study. She sat back in her chair, wondering how she could be sure this wasn't just a mirage.

"That was incredible," she said at last. "But why didn't you show me this before? It would have been so much easier to teach me."

"I did not want to overwhelm you. I hope you did not mind the lessons without the added flare."

Maiya smiled slightly. "Not at all. I've enjoyed getting to know you."

"As have I. Do you have any additional questions for me?"

"Only about tonight. Where is this ceremony? Should I be wearing anything in particular? Will I be expected to do anything?"

"The ceremony will be held here at the manor; there is a ballroom and banquet hall on the lower level. Your attire will be the traditional skai'ra – in Jovienna's favored colors, of course. As far as expectations are concerned, just remember what Naliz has taught you and be yourself."

"I guess I should try to get some rest then." They both rose and walked back to her room.

Mahdon paused outside the door and bowed his head slightly. "If you need me for anything, you will find me in the banquet hall."

Mahdon departed as Maiya closed the door and fell back on the bed. She stared up at the ceiling and let out an extended sigh. "No big deal," she said to herself. "I just have to save the world."

"Tanin – economics. Jo'dai – security. Saren – culture and history." Maiya had been walking the room for at least an hour reciting council details when there came a knock at the door. "Come in."

Maiya had expected Mahdon, but to her surprise, two unfamiliar women entered with a wrapped garment and large wooden chest. They looked dressed for the evening, each wearing an ankle-length, cheongsam style dress. Maiya watched as they set the chest by her corner vanity, and then turned back to greet her with enormous smiles.

"It is so wonderful to meet you!" The first woman, dressed in green, extended her hand and shook Maiya's firmly. "You may call me Yiva. This is Aarnesi."

"It's nice to meet you. I'm Maiya."

Aarnesi pulled out the chair from the vanity and ushered Maiya over. "It will be our pleasure to prepare you for this evening's events. We have had to make some alterations for your hair and skai'ra, of course, but I hope they will please you."

"I'm sure it will be lovely."

Aarnesi ran a brush through Maiya's hair while Yiva began removing several pieces of golden jewelry from the chest. She placed before Maiya a set of golden bracelets, a gemmed necklace, and a circlet of interwoven golden strands. The circlet was especially unique in design, having two large curves which appeared to be intended for wrapping around ears atop the wearer's head. Maiya pondered how they might adjust this piece to accommodate the differences in cranial structure.

With quick, yet delicate motions, Aarnesi wove Maiya's hair into two waterfall braids which met at the back of her head. Yiva placed the circlet on her head and Aarnesi wove the dangling waterfall sections of Maiya's hair around the curves until all but a few strands framed her face. The end result was a braided up-do with two small peaks where the circlet curved.

"And now for your skai'ra."

Maiya stood as Yiva unwrapped the dress and laid it out on the bed for her. Much like the outfits the two stylists wore, it was an ankle-length, cheongsam style dress. This one, however, was primarily purple with golden trim and flower details. It seemed to sparkle in the light and had a lower neckline than the other dresses. When they finished helping her dress and adorned her with the necklace and bracelets, Maiya stared at herself in the mirror for a moment. She finally looked the part that Mahdon had asked her to play; she hardly recognized herself.

"I don't know what to say. Thank you."

Aarnesi and Yiva smiled. As Aarnesi closed up the chest, Yiva spoke. "You are very welcome. Now, if you are ready… we will summon Mahdon. He will meet you at the base of the stairs and take you to the banquet hall."

Maiya nodded and followed them to the main floor where they left her standing in the foyer. She was admiring a painting to the left of the main entryway when she heard Mahdon approach from behind. His face lit up when she turned to face him.

"You look beautiful."

"Thank you. You're looking quite handsome yourself. I like the new look." Maiya smiled, pointing out his cleanly shaven face. While she was dressed in traditional Amerti attire, he wore a black tuxedo with a violet vest and tie.

"Shall we?" He offered his elbow and the two walked a long hallway that ran along the front of the manor. From here she could see guests arriving and entering at a set of doors that she presumed entered the banquet hall. As the hallway curved, she could now see into the connecting room and hear the chatter and laughter of hundreds of attendees. Music similar to that of a full string orchestra could be heard in the background, though no instruments could be seen from here.

As they neared the entryway, a group of five individuals stepped forward to meet them. Maiya immediately recognized them as Naliz and the other council members. Brandon stood in the forefront with a tall, muscular man to his right and the others closely behind. Based on Naliz's holograms of each member, she knew the tall man to be Jo'dai. Saren, appearing as a scarlet haired woman with dark eyes, walked beside Naliz immediately behind. The last member, Tanin, brought up the rear.

"Goddess," Brandon greeted her with a broad smile, taking her free hand to kiss it gently. "It's a grand pleasure to make your acquaintance."

"Please… call me Maiya. It's good to see you're in good health and fine spirits, Brandon. I look forward to being of assistance."

"In time, yes," Mahdon said. "Tonight is for celebration."

Brandon nodded. "That it is. Come – it is time we introduce you."

Mahdon unlinked arms with Maiya and passed her off to Brandon who led her into the banquet hall. As they stepped through the double doors, the music stopped, and the room fell silent. A thousand heads turned to watch as Brandon took Maiya to a raised platform where the head table sat. Mahdon and the remaining council members followed, taking seats at the head table. Maiya sat at the center with Mahdon to her right.

Glasses filled with a dark beverage reminiscent of wine had been set at each place setting. Brandon grabbed one and stepped down before the head table and crowd, who moved to tables to gather their own.

"Friends. Citizens," Brandon raised a glass to Maiya. "Honored guest. Tonight, we do not mourn the loss of those who have fallen to the disease. Tonight we celebrate the return of life, prosperity, and the end of death. Many years have been dedicated to the study of the ancient prophecies, and it is now our great honor to witness one come to fruition. For tonight we dine with the Goddess Jovienna!"

The room filled with applause and cheers – all eyes on Maiya. She smiled slightly, trying not to blush from the attention.

Brandon stepped back up on the platform as he continued, "Please help yourselves to the many exotic tastes of Earth. For those who are less adventurous, you will find some Amerti fare as well. To the future!"

The entirety of the room joined Brandon in the toast and cheers. "To the future!"

The music and chatter of the guests started back up as Brandon took his seat immediately to Maiya's left. As if on cue, several servers stepped forward and removed the lids from the trays centered on the tables throughout the room. Being at the head table, Maiya had an individual platter set before her. She marveled at the unusual fruits and leaned to Mahdon for input.

"What are all of these? Which one do you like best? Also… I thought you didn't need to eat, so why the big feast?"

Mahdon laughed. "Always so many questions! This is a very special occasion. Some of the greatest pleasures in life come from unnecessary tasks. If you had not convinced me to over-indulge on the journey over, I am almost certain I would have caved now. I think you will enjoy all of the fruit. The lonai – the yellow ones – are my favorite; they are quite similar to your dragon fruit – perhaps a little sweeter."

Maiya picked up a lonai and moved it gingerly between her fingers. It was comparable in size and shape to a grape, but she found it had a similar texture to an apple when bitten. The flavor was particularly delightful – so much so that she found herself finishing every last one before trying anything else on her plate. The rest of the meal was consumed in much of the same fashion; she moved from one unfamiliar item to the next until the platter was clean and her hunger sated.

Brandon leaned in as Maiya sat back from the table. "The meal was to your satisfaction, Goddess?"

"Yes, thank you. It was all very good."

"Good. The Earth food I tried was favorable as well. The thing you call 'steak' was especially enjoyable. Now…" Brandon took a long swig of his drink before rising and offering Maiya his hand. "With the end of the meal comes the time for entertainment. It would please me if you join me for an opening dance."

Maiya accepted his hand and glanced back at Mahdon as Brandon led her onto the floor below. All around them people rose and moved to the edges of the dance floor to watch. Brandon lifted a hand and nodded to the band. The music shifted from slow and quiet to more upbeat and significantly louder. Maiya immediately recognized the tune as one Naliz had played for her when he spoke of Brandon.

Naliz had advised her to study a modified version of the dance that traditionally accompanied the song, and now Maiya silently prayed that she would remember the steps. She had practiced with him for weeks, but never had she felt the pressure of this moment weighing on her so heavily as she did now. She felt the gaze of every Amerti in the room as the two stepped back from one another and regarded the other with a tilt of the head. Lightly joining right hands, they moved past each other and spun back to lock eyes. She counted each movement while desperately trying to keep her eyes on Brandon and off of her own feet. As the dance progressed, the speed and proximity of the two dancers rapidly increased until Brandon lifted her upward at the final crescendo of the song.

A split second of silence was followed by an uproar of applause. Maiya felt her heart racing as Brandon brought her feet back to meet the floor. The experience was exhilarating, but she was glad it was over. Brandon kissed her hand before raising it above his head with a toothy smile.

"It has been my honor to present the Goddess Jovienna to you, the finest citizens of Amertine! Let the entertainment begin!"

Amongst the cheers and applause, Brandon hooked arms with Maiya and led her back to the head table, which had been cleared except for decanters of various alcoholic beverages. Mahdon poured her a glass of one with an oaky bouquet.

"You were a delight to watch. I imagine Naliz is quite proud."

"Thank you. I was so afraid I'd make a fool of myself."

The majority of guests returned to their seats while a group of ten or so set up a three-tiered stage in the middle of the main floor. The lights dimmed, and the orchestra began a new, calming tune. A circle of glowing orbs lit up the center stage, surrounding a tall male. As he spoke, the four corners of the stage brightened and figures resembling Alurine, Reedon, Hokar, and Jovienna came into focus. It was clear from Maiya's vantage point that, unlike the majority of the guests, the four had taken on the true form of the Amerti.

What followed was a tale similar to that which Mahdon had shown her earlier that day. Brilliant, colorful lights with no obvious source replaced the vibrant telepathic imagery, and music and dance replaced conversation. With the exception of the narrator's occasional commentary, the presentation was entirely devoid of speech.

The stage darkened, and the crowd displayed their appreciation. The music and artistic display transitioned from one story to the next, showcasing several major historical events of Amertine. The closing scene was that of Alurine lifting skyward while a dozen Amerti celebrated below. This was them bidding her farewell after they received what they now simply referred to as "the gift." The actors bowed, the banquet hall lights grew bright once more, and Maiya shared in one final round of applause.

Once the volume returned to pre-entertainment levels and the stage had been removed, Brandon once again rose to address the crowd. "It has been a grand evening, and I am certain many of you wish to personally interact with the Goddess. Allow me to introduce one more guest before we begin the social hour. Goddess, if you'll join me…"

Maiya stood and followed Brandon to the doorway where they'd entered earlier in the night. She sent Mahdon a perplexed look, but he appeared just as confused as she felt.

"Please, gather around," Brandon waved for the guests to draw closer. All but a few in attendance moved before Brandon. Maiya watched as Mahdon and the council members stepped down to stand at the perimeter of the crowd.

"You all know as well as I why Jovienna has returned to us at such a trying time. Here, tonight, let us witness the healing power we have so desperately needed!" Brandon stepped to the side of the entryway and the crowd let out a unified gasp.

A figure slowly appeared in the hallway, hazy at first, and seemed to be flickering in and out of existence. The figure solidified into that of a woman, though her movements were erratic and breathing labored. Maiya's breath caught in her throat and eyes widened; she knew without a doubt that this Amerti was dying.

Mahdon pulled Naliz roughly aside. "What is he doing? She is not prepared for this! It is too soon!"

"I assure you, I had no knowledge of this. Brandon gave no indication of his intentions for the evening."

As they spoke, the woman stumbled further into the room before collapsing to the floor. The crowd parted and backed away from her in fear, leaving her alone in the center of a large ring of onlookers.

Maiya rushed to the woman's side and knelt next to her, feeling utterly powerless. The woman opened her mouth but could manage no more than a whimper. The pleading look in her eyes nearly broke Maiya's resolve. What had only been a few seconds seemed to stretch into an eternity, and when it was over, the woman vanished in a scattering of dust. Maiya stared at where the woman's form had been only moments before and saw no trace of evidence that she had ever existed in the first place. The room felt dead all around her.

After a moment of icy silence, Brandon addressed the room. "It is unfortunate that the evening should end on such a sorrowful note. I suspect the Goddess has her reasons and will not take her duties lightly."

He gave a curt bow of his head in Maiya's direction and then motioned for the remaining council members to follow him from the room. As Brandon exited, Mahdon saw what looked to him like a glint of satisfaction in the high councilor's eyes.

Naliz paused before exiting and rested a hand on Mahdon's shoulder. He sounded sincerely apologetic as he spoke. "I warned you, Mahdon. He will not make this easy for you. Or for her."

He then exited with the others, leaving Mahdon to pick up the pieces.

CHAPTER 4

The next morning Maiya awoke to the sound of a knock on the bedroom door and then the slight creak as the door opened a crack. She sat up in bed confused, for a moment not knowing where she was.

"May I come in?" Mahdon poked his head through the opening, waiting patiently for her response.

Maiya ran her fingers through her hair and rubbed her eyes. "Oh... yeah, that's fine."

Mahdon was at her side without a moment's hesitation, a huge smile on his face. "There is something I need to show you. Come quickly!"

He grabbed her arm and pulled her out of bed, nearly tripping her in his excitement. Maiya found herself needing to run to keep up with his pace. They rushed down the stairs and through the front door, where Mahdon came to an immediate stop.

Spread out before them as far as Maiya could see, large, white flowers had grown amongst the grass and trees. The sun had just barely risen, and dew glistened on each flower. Maiya knelt down next to one and admired the seven perfect and pointed petals and spiral pistils. Each flower was nearly the size of one of her hands.

She looked up to Mahdon and smiled. "They're beautiful. I didn't see them yesterday, but they're everywhere. What are they?"

"Jovaia lilies. Never in my life have I seen them bloom. They are proof of who you are and that you have returned."

"Never?" Maiya blushed. After the events of the previous night, she didn't think anyone would ever have faith in her again. It seemed she was wrong.

"There is something else I must show you as well. It may help you remember who you are."

"Okay." Maiya stood and followed Mahdon back inside where he led her to a large room that resembled an art gallery. Large murals decorated the walls and artifacts rested on pedestals throughout the room. A large circular table made from dark marble stood in the center of the room, bare except for a single colored tile at each cardinal direction.

"This room tells the history of our people - of your people. Each of these paintings shares the stories of one of the gods, and each of these items was owned by a previous incarnation." Mahdon indicated the wall to the right of the entryway. "This is your history."

Maiya walked the length of the room, pausing briefly at each pedestal to look over the artifacts. On her second pass back to where they'd entered, one particular item caught her attention and she felt immediately drawn to it. This artifact appeared to be a golden gem-encrusted short staff, though something about it seemed incomplete.

She looked to Mahdon, wishing to examine it further. "May I?"

"Yes, of course. You need not ask permission from me."

Turning back to the staff, she slowly lifted it from its mount and flipped it over in her hands. It was roughly four feet tall and surprisingly lightweight. Upon further inspection, Maiya could see that, though at first appearing to be made from gold, the staff itself was, in fact, carved from the wood of a golden tree. Three rings of purple gems were evenly spaced at the top, midpoint, and bottom of the staff. The staff itself was otherwise very simplistic in design.

Looking at the ends of the staff, Maiya noticed that one end had a slight curvature around the edges and a dimple in the middle. Running her fingers around the curved edges, she felt a sudden surge of knowledge sweep over her, and she could see now why the staff had felt incomplete.

A picture formed in her mind as clearly as though she had recalled a memory. Image after image filled her mind, painting scenes from a life she never knew she'd lived. Atop the staff rested a silver, metallic orb. At first glance it appeared unremarkable, devoid of any seams or markings, but to the trained eye, there was much more to be seen. She replaced the staff and stepped back in silence, trying to make sense of the memories she'd acquired.

Looking up from the staff, she turned back to Mahdon. "Where's the orb? This artifact... I... remember it. I don't know how or why, but I do. There's no other way to describe it but as memories."

Mahdon smiled. "You are beginning to remember? This is wonderful news. Yes, there was at one time another part to that artifact."

"What happened to it?"

"I fear it has been lost since the Great Religious War of Arkhan... or so it is believed."

"I can see it so vividly, and I know it's powerful, yet anything more than that is hazy. What makes it so special?"

"There is no doubt that the staff once carried another piece, but what that was is the subject of much debate. One possibility is the Hokaruin orb. According to religious texts, the orb was crafted thousands of years before my own time by a smith who had hoped to capture and harness the power of the gods. It is said he was successful, but only thanks to Alurine who offered to help as a prank on Hokar."

Maiya considered this for a moment. "If it was Alurine's, then why would it be on Jovienna's staff?"

"I do not know. I am afraid the history of the orb is a bit lacking in detail."

"What exactly does it do?"

"Some claim it gives those who hold it the power to heal. Others say it can grant any wish the bearer desires. Truthfully, no one knows. There is not a single Amerti alive who knows what it looks like or if the orb described is anything more than legend."

Maiya turned back to peer down at the staff. "We need to find it. It's real. I can sense it... and I think I know where it is. Sort of. When I held the staff, I saw a cave on the edge of a town surrounded by forest. There was a statue in the middle of the town. It's a little fuzzy... hard to describe..."

"If you saw it again, would you recognize it?"

She nodded. "I think so, yes."

"Shall we take a look?" Mahdon gestured to the table.

Moving to the center of the room, Maiya could now make out details of the four tiles built into the table. The one closest was that of a dark violet lily outlined in gold. A red flower with silver trim decorated the tile on the opposite end, and blue and green flowers were displayed on the tiles to either side. As with the outfits and artifacts, the colors coincided with the god they were said to represent.

Mahdon placed his hand over the violet tile and lines of light immediately coursed out from the center connecting to the other three tiles and forming a dome of light over the table. A visual representation of Amertine rotated slowly in the middle, a translucent globe surrounded by stars.

"Show all historically relevant locations for the Felis Staff."

Roughly half a dozen pinpoints of purple light appeared on the globe in response to Mahdon's command.

"Display aerial views of each location."

The holographic display zoomed into the first location and painted a one-foot square 3-D map of it beneath the globe. The globe shifted through each location until maps of each were laid out like tiles on the table.

Mahdon swept out a hand, shrinking the globe and pushing it to the side. He reached out to pull up the first location. The 3-D map now spun slowly at eye level as the globe had before.

He stepped to the side and gestured to the map. "Care to do the honors?"

Maiya stepped forward and touched the map cautiously. She found the image responded easily to her touch, focusing in on streets and buildings as she placed her fingers over them on the map. She flipped through the first two maps and brought up the third. A small figure had drawn her attention to this particular one. The image was that of a decently sized town of basic brick structures and stone streets constructed in a circular pattern. Dense forest made up the perimeter.

"Zoom in on the center of location three."

Buildings swept rapidly past as the map followed the path of one of the main cobblestone roads to the center of town. The image slowed and paused at the town center where a large red stone statue rose from the ground.

It showed an Amerti reaching skyward with one hand to the outstretched hand of another who seemed to be floating upside down in midair. A silver orb was suspended between the two and silver and gold "flames" rose up surrounding the lower Amerti. Though visually quite similar, the orb contained in the statue did not have the magical aura that Maiya had felt radiate from the one in her memory.

"That's it. That's the place I saw. I think we need to go there for the orb. There should be a cave somewhere nearby."

Mahdon looked uncomfortable with this news. He nodded. "Yes. This is Ularia. It was, at one time, a temporary location of the high council chambers. You may find it interesting to know that this is also the city where the first case of the disease was reported. It is for that reason that the council no longer frequents that location. I know precisely where the cave to which you refer can be found. If you are prepared, it would be my honor to guide you to the site."

The two exchanged glances, and Maiya felt more at ease. "I'll go get ready."

"I will make arrangements with the council; it should only take a moment. You may join if you wish."

Maiya followed him from the gallery to the third floor and past the study to the right. A set of double doors led into a conference room similar in size and layout to the one she'd seen on the ship, though the decor matched that of the manor. Almost immediately upon entry into the room, a familiar face popped up on the wall display.

"Brandon. We were about to contact the council. What gives us this honor?"

Brandon shifted his gaze from Mahdon to Maiya. "I am happy to see that the Goddess seems to be doing well. I am terribly sorry about how the evening concluded." He gave her a smug smile before looking back to Mahdon. "Your presence is requested by the council this evening."

"Perhaps this can be moved up to an earlier time? Maiya and I have an item to discuss with the council, and it would be preferred if we could do so before the day is done."

"This is a matter between the council and the Ambassador. Any issues concerning the Goddess will have to be addressed separately."

"What is this meeting regarding?"

"All discussion will take place at the usual time."

Before Mahdon could open his mouth to protest, the screen went blank. Maiya could sense his unease as he turned his attention back to her. She wasn't familiar enough with Brandon to know his motivations, but her limited interactions with him had already left a bitter taste in her mouth.

"My apologies," Mahdon said. "It seems our trek will be delayed until tomorrow."

Naliz stood in the entryway of Brandon's study, waiting for the council leader to take notice of him. Several minutes passed while Brandon flipped through a large tome, writing notes in a separate journal. When he failed to acknowledge Naliz's arrival, Naliz broke the silence.

"What in the seven planes was that last night?" Naliz demanded.

"An executive decision." Brandon remained unfazed, keeping his eyes on his work.

"What right do you have to do that to her?"

"Every right in the world, in fact. I was quite clear that the human was not to be brought here. I told you there would be consequences."

"Yes... but this? Why punish her for our choices? I had reservations at first, but once I met her it became clear that she is who Mahdon claims."

Brandon finally looked up at Naliz. "If she's truly Jovienna, then why didn't she save the woman? It's apparent to me that this human is nothing more than a powerless fraud, and you're a fool if you believe otherwise."

"And if you're wrong, this could jeopardize everything we've worked toward."

Brandon regarded Naliz with little concern. "Everything we've worked toward or your stubborn friend? I know well what I am doing."

"I realize that Mahdon may not always obey the council's wishes, but he's only trying to help. The people will lose faith."

"Perhaps they should."

Naliz was taken aback. "Have you lost your mind?"

"I have never seen things more clearly than I do right now."

Brandon closed the journal and rose with a rolled piece of parchment. He rounded the desk and stopped before Naliz. Though the form he took had always been taller than that of Naliz, he seemed to tower over him even more so at this moment. His tone was calm, but the threat was clear as he placed the parchment in Naliz's hand.

"I suggest you remember your place."

Naliz said nothing more as Brandon walked past and exited the room. Unraveling the paper, he stared in stunned silence at the message before him. He wondered now if Brandon's plan had any place for him at all.

It wasn't unusual for Mahdon to be asked to appear before the council, but something about this "invite" felt different than most. Normally Naliz would contact Mahdon and give him an overview of what would be discussed. This invitation had come directly from Brandon, and when asked what the council meeting was about, Naliz consistently changed the subject.

For this reason, Mahdon approached the situation with caution, entering the council chambers preparing for what he believed to be the worst-case scenario. Had he known what was about to happen, he would not have entered the chamber with such confidence.

The main council hall was considerably sparse, having been built in the largest cavern of a multi-chamber cave. Five circular platforms rose roughly a foot from the ground at the far end of the circular hall and recessed lighting of glowing orbs created a single line of light along the walls. The room was otherwise devoid of any furniture or decor.

Each of the council members stood in human form upon their own platforms, with Brandon standing proudly in the center. Mahdon entered the room and stopped before Brandon, looking up at him as he had so many times before, and recited the same line he had for many years past.

"I present myself before the council, ready to aid you as you aid our people."

Brandon looked down from his platform. "Do you know why we've summoned you here today?"

"No," said Mahdon, shaking his head.

"You're aware that the council ruled not to bring the female here, correct?"

"Yes."

"Yet you did it anyway."

"It is what the people wanted. The dates and location are consistent with the prophecy; the events surrounding her rebirth are accurate. She is the one."

Brandon looked annoyed, tapping one finger against the knuckles of his other hand, his penetrating gaze causing Mahdon to shift uneasily from one foot to the other. Brandon stepped down from where he stood and stopped a couple of feet before Mahdon.

"Your service to this council is no longer necessary."

Mahdon was astounded. "No longer necessary? Are you suggesting what I think you are suggesting?"

"It's not a suggestion. Your time as a council aide has come to an end; from now on, the council will not require your opinion. You have proven incapable of following the council's orders."

Mahdon gaped in amazement at Brandon's words. "You must be joking!"

"Certainly not. I never joke about council decisions."

"It is not my duty to obey the council. The service I provide is not one of my own opinions; I speak for the people. You cannot ignore your own people! Their voices must be heard; to do otherwise destroys any hope for the future. Without her, there may not be a future!"

"We listened to the people and determined that not bringing her here was the best course of action. What the people need is stability, not some outsider masquerading as our savior. The council's decision is final."

Mahdon glared back at Brandon angrily. "Is this the council's decision or your own?"

"All council decisions are subject to discrimination. You know that as well as I. Everything we do is for the good of the people, whether you agree or not."

"This is low, Brandon. Even for you."

"I understand the point you are trying to make, Ambassador, but this is not the way to do it." Brandon made little effort to conceal his distaste for Mahdon, sneering slightly as he spoke the word "ambassador."

Mahdon looked to Naliz for support. "Surely you must see the madness in all of this? Why are you not speaking up?"

Naliz didn't respond, but instead turned his head to look away. Mahdon hadn't been prepared for such a betrayal from his closest friend but reminded himself that speaking against Brandon could only result in Naliz being removed from office as well.

"I realize that the death at the ceremony may have left some with doubts, but I never expected it from any of you. Just this morning the Jovaia lilies bloomed. I saw them with my own eyes… touched them with my own hands. And now the cure to the disease is within our grasp. We believe we know where to find the Hokaruin orb."

The council members noticeably perked up at the mention of the lilies and the orb. Even Brandon reacted with a tilt of his head and raising of an eyebrow. All eyes now fell on him.

"Is it true? Have the lilies bloomed?" Saren asked. "And what of the orb? If it were to fall into the wrong hands…"

Brandon held up a hand to cut her off. He glared at Mahdon. "What you are suggesting is that we put our faith in a myth. The last mention of that artifact was prior to the administration of the gift. What makes you so certain that it even exists?"

"She had a vision. It is the first of her memories to return. I do not believe she could have known about it otherwise."

His eyes narrowed. "And this vision was of what, exactly?"

"She saw Ularia and the old council chambers. She believes that is where the orb is and feels it can be used to help the people."

"Ularia…" Brandon frowned. "I see. You may go. It appears that the council has some new matters to discuss."

CHAPTER 5

It took Mahdon nearly twenty minutes to locate Maiya once he returned to the manor. He finally found her in a lounge adjacent to the mansion's private dining hall. She was curled up in a large chair near the fireplace flipping through an unmarked tome. She set the book aside and smiled when she saw him.

"I hope it's okay that I brought this down here. This lounge is so cozy."

"Of course." Mahdon sank down across from her on one side of a leather couch.

"Are you okay?"

"I am... fine."

Maiya frowned and gave him a sideways look. "It's okay if you're not."

"How do you deal with it?"

"With what?"

"The emotions."

"What do you mean?"

"I am not used to feeling so much. The freedom to shift from any constant form allows for freedom from emotion as well."

"So, you're like a Vulcan?"

Mahdon gave her a nonplussed look. "A what?"

"Never mind. Bad joke. To answer your question... often not very well. It's pretty common for people to resort to drinking their problems away."

Mahdon looked once again confused by her phrasing. "And that works?"

"Only temporarily. Uh… I noticed you have a wide variety of food options from Earth. Do you happen to know what was brought back for drinks?"

"I believe Lahna recommended having a large selection of 'wine, beer, and spirits', but I am unfamiliar with the third term. She said you seemed to like those beverages."

Maiya blushed. "Okay… I guess I drank more than I thought. Anyway… where might I find those?"

"I can show you." Mahdon began to stand and she motioned for him to sit back down.

"You stay here. I can get it."

"There is a wine cellar off the other side of the kitchen. The other beverages are down there as well."

She smiled. "I'll be right back."

Maiya made her way through the kitchen to a set of wood and metal double doors. The handles were designed to look like grape vines, and the doors themselves were made in such a way that she could see through to the short set of stairs beyond.

On the other side she found a cave-like tunnel followed by the wine cellar itself. Countless racks filled with red, white, and rosé wine lined the walls. Stone archways opened to the left and right where two additional rooms of wine could be found. The only exception was a six-foot-wide section directly ahead where a wet bar and half a dozen shelves sat lined with everything from grain alcohol to Chambord.

She scanned the shelves and was happy to see they had spared no expense on the quality of the selections. She grabbed a bottle and two glasses from the bar, filling them with ice from an ice bucket that seemed to almost magically produce ice before her eyes. Beneath the wet bar, she found several dozen options for mixers tucked away in the cabinets. She pulled out a clear bottle and set it with the bottle of liquor. Once satisfied with the drinks, she set it all on a tray and carried it back up to the lounge upstairs. Mahdon sat up as she handed him a glass. She sat back down across from him and raised her glass.

"Cheers."

"What is it?" Mahdon sniffed the drink. "It smells like trees and…" He paused to think of the word, "…citrus?"

"Gin and tonic. A very simple drink, but good with the right quality of gin."

They each took a sip, and Mahdon gave a pleased nod. He then proceeded to empty the glass in one smooth swig. Maiya stared at him.

"You do realize that's alcoholic, right?"

"That would explain a few things."

He set down his glass and she filled it before handing it back to him. "What happened today?"

"The council's sense of reason died. I have been removed from office as the council's advisor."

"Why? Can they do that?"

Mahdon sighed and leaned back in his seat. "Brandon has made it quite clear that he can do whatever he wants."

"So, what does that mean exactly?"

"It means that the council no longer exists for the people. If they do not agree with what the people want, then the council will freely do the opposite."

Maiya frowned. She understood too well the repercussions of unchecked power. She hoped his interpretation of the situation was exaggerated. She also wondered if the death at the welcoming ceremony had anything to do with the decision.

"Is this happening because I'm here?"

"They would have you believe so… but truthfully, this has been a long time coming. Even before the gift, the council would test their boundaries. I fear we have come to rely on them too heavily."

"Won't there be an uprising if people know this is happening?"

"I would find that doubtful. Brandon can be very charismatic. He has been council head for a very long time and the people put and keep him there willingly."

"Maybe if we have the Hokaruin orb they will see things differently."

"That would be my hope. I do not wish to overthrow the council; they have done much good for the people. They cannot, however, continue with their current line of thinking. One of the prophecies concerning your return spoke of a new era. It is my personal belief that this means you will be a leader who brings new enlightenment to Amertine. Perhaps you will lead the council in the correct direction."

"That's a lot of pressure. Let's just focus on getting that orb first…"

"Yes. Tomorrow." Mahdon raised his glass in a toast and the two emptied their drinks.

"One more?"

"Yes, please. I am quite fond of this."

Maiya poured two more and they clinked glasses. She took a sip, pondering her next question. She felt silly for even asking, but the gin had begun to loosen her inhibitions and even pointless questions had become worth asking.

"Why do you still speak so formally to me?"

He looked surprised by the question. "I do not wish to be rude."

Maiya laughed. "You'll have to try a lot harder than that to be rude."

"You would not mind if I push words together as you do?"

It took Maiya a moment to realize what he meant. He looked so serious that she tried her best not to laugh again. It made her wonder how rude she must have appeared to him. Here he was worried about using contractions, and she hadn't given a second thought to how she spoke. "Not at all. I just want you to be yourself around me. If I'm going to be sticking around, I don't want anyone to feel guarded around me. Speaking of which…" Maiya stood and moved to sit closer to him on the opposite side of the couch. "When we were on the ship you talked a lot about your life after Alurine, but not much about it before. What was that like?"

"It was so long ago. I hardly remember."

"What about your family? Or is that too personal?"

"No," Mahdon relaxed a bit and smiled. "I am… I'm… happy to share. I never knew my father. He died when I was very young. My mother raised me and my two older sisters."

"Where are they now?"

"My mother died not long after Alurine's arrival. As for my sisters, they both reside in Fimbira."

"Do you see them often?"

"On occasion. They were at the ceremony, actually. I was hoping to introduce you, but the evening ended much more abruptly than I anticipated.

Maiya cringed and took a long drink. "Yeah… I wish I could forget that altogether."

Mahdon set his empty glass on the table. "I feel funny. Is that normal?"

"That depends. How often do you drink?"

"Last night was the first time since..." He paused to think about it. "...since I do not know when. Sometime before the gift, perhaps. I suppose I have had a glass or two of wine at celebrations since, but I don't believe I have had anything this potent before."

"You may want to slow down then."

He leaned his head against the back of the couch as he looked at Maiya. "Back then I thought I would be a scientist. I hadn't decided on a specialty yet, but I knew I wanted to get away from Amertine. I never dreamed I'd be the Ambassador of Intergalactic Affairs or advisor to the council. And yet... it is how I have spent the majority of my life. I do not know what I will do now."

"You're still the ambassador, aren't you?"

"Yes, and I will continue to do whatever I can to assist you. However, any sway I had with the council is gone."

"What about Naliz?"

Mahdon made a face. "Would it be terribly rude of me to change the subject?"

"Ah. Moving on then..."

She poured herself another drink. "Do you want another or are you done?"

"I think it is best if I don't indulge further. I've nearly said things I should not more than once."

Maiya raised an eyebrow. "Oh, really? Those are the most fun things to say! Or at least for me to hear. Your secrets are safe with me."

"I do not trust Brandon. I know I said that I don't wish to overthrow the council, but there are moments when I believe that would be best. He's so..."

"Arrogant?"

"Yes. Among other things. He does not always make the logical decision and lately that has become frustrating. I think it will be better once I am free of this body."

Maiya frowned. She had hoped his confession would be one of a less serious tone. "Hopefully that will change soon. In the meantime, take a deep breath and focus on what you can do to fix it. Just sleep on it."

She stood and retrieved the tome from where she left it. "I'm heading to bed. I hope you're feeling better in the morning. Good night, Mahdon."

"Good night, Maiya."

It was barely after sunrise when Maiya crawled out of bed. She showered and headed down to find Mahdon still in the lounge where she left him. She took a seat beside him as he extended a greeting.

"Good morning."

"Morning. You didn't stay up all night, did you?"

"Sleep does not come naturally to me anymore." He smiled sincerely and continued, "Thank you for talking with me last night. I am feeling less distraught today. I hope you don't mind that I took the liberty of putting in a breakfast order for you."

Right on cue the chef brought out a plate and set it before her. Maiya wondered how he'd known to make her favorite – a sausage croissant sandwich and hash browns with a side of maple syrup. Had they really paid that close of attention to her?

"I've secured transportation to Ularia. The shuttlecraft is waiting on the second-floor balcony. I do not know what to expect once we arrive, but it may be difficult to get into the old council chambers. Last I heard, there was dark magic surrounding that area."

"What do you mean by 'dark magic'?"

"That cave may very well be where the disease originated. Anyone who has gotten close has become infected. We have performed scans to locate any biological source, but we have been unable to determine a cause. Some locals have even reported sightings of dark shadows moving through the area with no explanation. No one has ventured that way in many months."

Maiya felt a chill run down her spine. "And now we're going there..."

"Yes. I confess that this destination causes me a sense of unease, but I have faith in you. I fully believe that you will be unaffected by any forces that reside there."

Maiya kept her thoughts to herself concerning her own discomfort with the situation. She finished her meal in silence and then set the plate aside. They both stood and headed to the second floor and stepped outside to where the shuttlecraft was waiting.

"I'm guessing this will be a rather short flight?"

"We will stay within the atmosphere for this trip, but yes. Our destination is relatively close."

Maiya followed Mahdon into the craft and sat back as the ship moved up and out. They swept over the falls and past the capitol city, heading in the direction of a dense forest. As they approached the perimeter of the forest, the shuttle began to slow rapidly until it stopped altogether. It moved slowly downward until it rested on the ground. Mahdon frowned at the controls and waved a hand over the main panel. "Something is wrong. We have lost power."

"Is there anything we can do?"

"Typically, the onboard computer's diagnostic scan would report an error before engaging the emergency landing. It did not do that this time. The backup computer has malfunctioned as well. Without one of those systems online, I cannot begin to troubleshoot the issue."

"Is there someone we can contact?"

"Normally I would use the shuttle's built-in communicator. Even that appears to no longer be functioning. I've never encountered this before. The odds of such a situation occurring are only 1 in 9,155,000. It did not strike me as necessary to bring an alternate communication device."

"So, there's nothing we can do?"

"I do not believe so."

"Could this have anything to do with the council's decision yesterday?"

Mahdon turned away from the controls. He looked displeased with the notion. "That thought had not occurred to me. Though it is not outside the realm of possibility, such a premeditated act would indicate greater problems than I am prepared to admit. I am hoping this is an unfortunate coincidence."

Maiya didn't have a positive alternative to offer. Her faith in sentient beings had died long ago. Instead, she focused on the current state of affairs and gave Mahdon a reassuring smile.

"How far are we from the next town?"

He pondered the question for a moment and considered their approximate location. "Perhaps an hour walking. Ularia is through the forest ahead."

"Then I suggest we start walking."

Mahdon stood and opened the door via a manual override and the two stepped out onto the golden grass. Maiya looked around and then toward the forest ahead. Aside from the craft they just exited, there were no visible signs of civilization in any direction. The dense foliage ahead prevented visibility beyond a few feet, and the silence beyond the edge of the tree line was outstretching.

Maiya swallowed hard. Growing up in what was essentially the middle of nowhere, she had spent a significant amount of time in the woods as a kid. During that time and the years that followed, she had gone on numerous backcountry camping trips. This was the first time she felt afraid of what she couldn't see. She chose to keep this to herself.

"Let's go."

She led the way, pushing past branches on both sides. The canopy overhead thickened and what was day quickly looked closer to night. After several feet of near impassable terrain, the foliage at ground level thinned out enough to make walking easier. The silence lingered for only a few seconds before she could stand it no longer. Though it felt like summer outside, it sounded more like winter.

"Where are the animals? The birds?"

"It is rather unusual. I would prefer if we move through here as quickly as possible. I don't enjoy the sensation this place gives me."

"Like being watched."

"Yes."

They stopped for a moment and looked at each other with grim expressions. Knowing that Mahdon felt it too didn't make Maiya feel any better. It became harder to shake off the discomfort and attribute it to her imagination when someone else wanted out as badly as she did. They pushed forward once more.

"Would Brandon have any reason to stop us from doing this?"

"I cannot think of one. He and I haven't always seen eye to eye, but he always has his reasons for what he does. What would motivate him to interfere with a possible cure, I do not know. I do not believe removing me as advisor was done to prevent us from ending the disease. It does, however, limit my influence in the future."

"Speaking of which… what will you do once I've served my purpose? Will you go back to exploring the universe?"

"Eventually, yes. It was my hope that we could stir up more scientific interest amongst the people. People have become all too content to sit idly and watch their lives go by. You would think that immortality would inspire individuals to pursue endeavors they could only have dreamed of before. As it turns out, many have felt that they have all the time in the world, so they need not take up new challenges until another day. Now that that concept has been threatened, it may be easier to introduce exploratory thinking. If there is a positive side to all of this, that would be it. Once this is resolved, the difficulty will come in convincing them there's more to life than simply being comfortable."

"What about the Amerti who didn't accept the gift? You mentioned before that there were some. They couldn't all have died without having children. It's been generations, yes, but wouldn't their descendants still be alive and in favor of living their lives to the fullest? Maybe they could offer some insight."

"Some may be willing, but most have a distorted view of our society. The Zumerti – those who still embrace mortality – tend to keep to themselves and have a culture all their own. They do not reject technology, but for the large part, they do not embrace it either. Many of them were raised to believe that the gift was a curse and not a blessing. Those who are aware of the disease often say that we deserve it."

"That's pretty harsh."

"It may sound that way, yes, but it is all they have ever known. If you're told something long enough, you will believe anything. I pity them."

"I suppose that's true."

Maiya was about to expand on that thought when she saw movement in the brush to her right. She came to a stop and held up a hand, motioning for Mahdon to stay where he was. She scanned the forest, listening intently for any indication that they weren't alone. No sounds met her ears; the woods around them remained as silent as a tomb. She shook her head.

"I'm sorry. I thought I saw something. It must have been my imagination."

They began walking again, though both looked around more cautiously than they had before. It was another twenty feet before she saw it again. This time it was a flash of movement to their left. Mahdon placed his hand on her shoulder and leaned in, his voice a whisper.

"We are not alone."

Maiya felt the urge to grab his arm for security but thought better of it. This was hardly the time to show fear. Instead she nodded slowly in agreement and pressed forward in silence. Up ahead an outcropping of rock rose just high enough for them to keep their backs shielded until they could determine what, or who, they were up against. They leaned up against it and looked out in opposite directions.

Maiya squinted into the dark, and that's when she saw it. It wasn't a living creature that she saw; it was the rapid spread of death. The trees and brush wilted as the life was sucked out of them, and whatever caused it was moving in their direction.

"Mahdon…" Maiya reached for his hand. "What is that?"

His eyes grew wide when he realized what she was referencing. It could now be seen on both sides of them and stretching out to connect in the direction from which they had come. He glanced up at the outcropping of rock behind them.

"We need to move. Now."

They scrambled up the rock face as the sweeping death moved in to engulf the ground where they had just been standing. The forest on the other side remained untouched, though Maiya doubted it would stay that way for long.

"Run." Though Mahdon's voice was calm as it often seemed to be, the sense of urgency was apparent. "Do not stop."

Maiya didn't need to be told twice. She ran until her lungs burned and calf muscles began to tense. She ran without looking back, knowing she had Mahdon at her side and the silent death filling in the gaps behind them as they went. By the time they reached a break in the trees, she felt ready to collapse, the dwindling adrenaline rush the only thing keeping her moving forward.

Mahdon reached the tree line before her and came to a stop as he turned back to face the forest. While she was panting and out of breath, he hardly seemed like he had been running at all. She caught up with him and gazed back. The threat that she expected to see was no longer anywhere in sight.

Mahdon touched her arm lightly. "It's safe now. You can rest."

Maiya moved to a log further from the forest's edge and sat down. She took a steadying breath and looked up at Mahdon. "What the hell was that?"

"Klartex. It was a weapon of biological warfare used long before Amertine achieved peace."

"If you've achieved peace, then why is someone using it on us now? Why does it even exist anymore?"

"I was not aware that it still did. I am only familiar with it due to my historical studies. If the aim of the attacker was to prevent us from arriving, they have been unsuccessful. I recognize this area; we have reached the outskirts of Ularia. If they wished to keep us away, it would have been wiser to push us in the opposite direction."

"Unless they intended to herd us here." Her expression was grim.

"It would seem an odd decision to push us closer to our destination."

"Yes... especially after what happened with the shuttlecraft. Maybe they wanted to delay us." The two exchanged concerned looks. "We might as well get this over with. If someone is trying to kill us, harm us, or otherwise, I'd like to know why."

Maiya stood and allowed Mahdon to take the lead. Across the field was a pile of rubble that was overgrown in large part by weeds and crooked trees. As they approached, they could make out a collapsed stone archway and broken stone door with characters that were strangely familiar to Maiya. Though she had not seen them in this lifetime, she recognized them. A dark passageway stood open where the door had once been.

"What language is that?" Maiya asked.

"Fudarin. It is the language of the creators."

"I know it."

"Peace, prosperity, and knowledge for all." Mahdon read from an intact piece of stone.

"These are the keys to eternal life." Maiya finished, reciting the rest of the phrase from a long-forgotten memory.

Mahdon looked at her and nodded. As he moved to take a step into the passageway, he was immediately stopped by an unseen force and could go no further. He reached out a hand and tried to sweep it through the air at the same position but was once again met with resistance.

"There is an energy shield here. We will be unable to pass unless we can find the trigger to release it."

Maiya pressed a hand to the invisible shield and marveled as it first glowed a fiery red and then faded away. Her hand fell through to the other side. She swept her other hand through the air and then stepped into the entryway.

Mahdon looked at her with intrigue. "Or you could do that."

As they walked into the darkness, motion sensing recessed lights began to glow on both sides of the tunnel. Though the floor was mostly covered in broken rock or other debris, the faint bluish hue the lights provided was enough to see without issue.

Following the tunnel inward and down, the two came to a large cavernous room where the standard five platforms rose from the ground as they did in all common council chambers. Aside from some fallen rubble from above, the room appeared largely untouched by time. Three sets of double doors were built into the far wall, while tunnels branched to the left and right.

Mahdon pointed to their right. "If my memory serves me correctly, the hallways exiting here are circular and meet somewhere in the back. There will be personal quarters and separate communication rooms along that route."

"And the doors in the back?"

"The central one leads to the council's private meeting hall. I am unsure about the other two. They are atypical."

"Right-hand rule…" Maiya tried the door and shook her head when she found it locked. "I guess we're starting with the left then."

The door to the left opened easily to reveal a stone staircase spiraling downward. The same recessed lighting lined the walls, and the air grew noticeably colder as they followed the stairs down. The bottom of the stairs opened to another, smaller cavern, this one in much worse condition than the one they left. Only about half of the light orbs were still intact, leaving the room with a particularly ominous glow.

Aside from a large pit, the room was empty. They moved to the edge of the pit and looked into darkness. Neither could see the bottom, but a large cave-in on one side indicated to them that, at the very least, there was a bottom to be found.

A chill ran up Maiya's spine. "What is this place?"

"I have no idea." Mahdon responded uneasily. He clearly felt disturbed by this room. "I fear that I may not want to know."

"Something very bad happened here. I don't know what exactly, but I can sense it. At the very least, someone died here."

A cool wind blew up from the pit, causing them both to back away in surprise. A shadow moved rapidly past them and vanished up the stairs. Barely a second passed before a loud crash echoed from somewhere else within the council chambers. They looked at each other for confirmation that they had both seen and heard the same things.

Somewhat reluctantly, they followed the path of the shadow figure back up the stairs. When they reached the top, Maiya pointed a shaky hand at the rightmost door. The once locked door was now cracked a few inches ajar. Mahdon stepped over by the open door and peered inside. Another set of stairs curved down in the opposite direction from those behind the door to the left. He listened for a moment and gestured for Maiya to join him when he heard nothing.

"There must be a logical explanation for this," he said.

"I tend to agree... but what concerns me more is who else is here with us and why."

Mahdon smiled and raised an eyebrow. "I presume they already know we're here. We are not dead yet, and with you here, I'm basically immortal again. Allow me to go first."

"Let's not get too cocky!"

Mahdon led the way down the stone steps, pausing intermittently to listen for any further sounds. They continued to hear nothing beyond their own footsteps and quickly found themselves in a study at the base of the stairs. Unlike the rest of the council chambers, this room looked nothing like the cave system it had been built into. In fact, it looked entirely out of place and more fitting to be part of the manor in which Maiya currently resided.

Furthermore, the room appeared to have been hastily torn apart. Tapestries had been ripped from the walls and laid in shambles on the floor amidst piles of open tomes. The desk and shelves sat bare, every item that could be thrown to the floor laid there now. Even the desk drawers had been pulled away and tossed aside.

They dug through the mess on the floor, but both felt confident that they would not find what they had come for. Whoever had arrived before them had been thorough in their own search. After half an hour worth of rifling through the room, Maiya sat back against a wall in defeat.

She sighed. "If it was going to be anywhere in here, it was going to be here."

Mahdon was busy putting the room back together, pushing the final tomes back into place along the wall of shelves. He paused momentarily to give her a reassuring smile. "Perhaps that is not why you recalled this place after all."

He put away the last book and then bent down to pick up the desk drawers. Maiya eyed him curiously, wondering why he was bothering to clean up a mess in a room they would likely never visit again. He righted the one unbroken chair that remained in the room and leaned back in it, closing his eyes with a pleased sigh.

Maiya moved over to sit on the desk. "You really confuse me sometimes; you know that?"

"Why is that?"

"The situation hasn't changed any and yet you go from serious to happy like it's nothing. We aren't any closer to a solution than we were two days ago."

"I would have to disagree. Two days ago, we didn't know where we were going and now we're here. A couple of hours ago, we could not even get in here."

Maiya frowned, failing to see his point. "But there's nothing here…"

"Not that we can see, but there's something. No one has been down here in decades. No one has even dared get close in months for fear of falling ill. Yet you showed up, and we were able to enter without issue. It may not seem like much now, but it is progress."

"I guess…" She wasn't convinced. "Now what do we do?"

"That is your decision to make. If you wish to return to the manor, we will need to secure another mode of transportation. Unless you intend to spend more time in here, we will likely need to go into the town proper."

Maiya felt nauseated by the thought of going to the town and facing a repeat of her first night there. She had been so certain that what they needed could be found in these halls, and now her confidence was dwindling once again. At the same time, the presence of the shadow being was undeniable, as was the opening of the door to this study. Something had directed her to this place and she wasn't ready to leave until she found out why.

"I think we should stay for a few days. We can scope out the quarters for a place to sleep and see what else we can find. Maybe there's —"

She was interrupted mid-sentence by a rumbling from above. The room shuddered from what felt like a quake, and they both grasped the desk until the shaking stopped.

Mahdon frowned. "I would not advise staying here if random noises and movement such as this are common. Even if we intend to come back, we should consider staying in town."

"We should at least see what that was before we go."

They left the room and headed back up the stairs, noticing nothing out of the ordinary along the stairwell. As they rounded the corner at the top and entered the main council chambers, they noticed some additional debris along the floor, but nothing of significance. The far end of the room was another story.

The tunnel entrance appeared dark and surrounded by dust. As they approached, and the dust settled, their worst fears were quickly realized. The entrance was now sealed with rubble, removing any option they had to leave. They exchanged looks as the dark realization sank in: much like the earlier events of that day, this was no accident.

CHAPTER 6

A couple of hours had passed while the two moved aside fallen rock before they finally decided exiting via this route was not a viable option. They had only managed to clear out a few feet when they realized that the entire tunnel was potentially collapsed. Whoever had done this had no intention of them seeing the light of day any time soon.

Maiya brushed herself off and looked to the hallway left of the main chamber. "If we're going to be stuck here, we might as well make ourselves comfortable. There are beds in the personal chambers, right?"

"Of course."

"I thought I should ask since you said you don't need sleep. I assumed that applied to everybody."

"It does. However, this location was the primary council meeting location at the time of Alurine's arrival. Everything in here was designed to provide the comforts of mortal life. The food supply, on the other hand..." Mahdon shook his head. "...that disappeared a long time ago."

"So, what you're telling me is... those are some really old mattresses?"

Mahdon blushed. "I wish that I could provide something better. We perfected biologically sterile surfaces a long time ago, so if your concern is germs..."

Maiya laughed. "I'm just trying to lighten the mood like you did earlier. I don't intend to stay here very long. I'm really not that worried about the sleeping conditions."

Mahdon smiled. "And you call me confusing?"

"Anyway, I'm going to go check out the back rooms. Did you want to join?"

"If you do not mind, I would like to return to the study. I believe there may be something of use to us there that we have overlooked."

They agreed to report any interesting findings and then headed in opposite directions. Maiya entered the hallway to the left, stopping every few feet to listen and check that there was no one behind her. She had wanted to ask Mahdon not to leave her alone, but she didn't want to sound too paranoid. They had both seen and heard the same things that day; if he felt comfortable leaving her alone, she trusted his judgment.

Maiya came upon the first set of quarters on the left side of the hallway. The door was closed and similar in appearance to those in the main hall. She listened for a moment and then pushed the door slowly open to reveal a modestly sized room. A small wooden desk, chair, dresser, and single person, oval-shaped bed were the only items in the room. The walls and floor were bare, but the lighting in the room provided a warm glow that also seemed to keep the room at a comfortable temperature.

She slid each dresser drawer open slowly and pulled out neatly folded robes that had somehow survived the passage of time. Aside from the clothing, the drawers were empty. The two desk drawers were also empty. She exited the quarters and continued down the hallway.

Midway to the next room, an alcove was carved out of the wall, containing the statue of a long-haired male. He stood tall with his hands held up to chest height on either side. A small silver bird rested in one hand and a bowl in the other. Multi-colored orbs of light glowed at his feet. Maiya recognized this as a shrine to Hokar. The next set of quarters she came upon was nearly identical to the first, the only difference being in the orientation of the furniture.

Past that room was another shrine, this one for Jovienna. The statue stood tall with both hands held forward as though preparing to cast a spell. At her feet were the same glowing orbs seen by Hokar's shrine. Maiya stared up at the determined expression on the statue's face, feeling compelled to reach out and touch the statue at its base. As with the staff, when her hand made contact, she was flooded with new memories. She had not only been present for the last religious war, she had brought an end to it.

In her mind's eye she saw a battlefield littered with the bodies of the dead and dying. She had offered them a chance to lay down their arms and make peace with one another, but they had chosen to fight instead. She became aware of the power coursing through her being - the power not only to heal, but the power to destroy as well. The memories faded into the background as she took a step back from the statue.

She silently urged one of the orbs into an outstretched hand, and when it obeyed, she looked at her own hands as though they were foreign to her. She opened her hand and watched as the orb began to hover over it, then she spun it in the air and back down to the base of the statue. She smiled slightly and turned back around to head back to the study.

Mahdon was flipping through a stack of carefully selected tomes when Maiya returned upstairs. He gave her a smile and then added the current book to the top of the stack and grabbed the last one. "You have returned quicker than I expected. I am reviewing Saren's interpretation of recent historical events."

"I didn't finish searching the rooms; I only made it about halfway. What do you mean 'her' interpretation?"

"As the most recently appointed lead historian, she is responsible for recording significant events as they occur. In any case, I am nearly finished. As it is customary for religious leaders to transcribe history as they learn or experience it, I suspected many of the texts were written by Brandon. However, that does not appear to be the case."

"Why the interest in Brandon's perspective?"

"I thought perhaps we could find some greater explanation for why he would do this to us."

Maiya raised an eyebrow. "So, you do think he's responsible for everything that's happened today."

Mahdon frowned and nodded. "Yes. Despite wishing otherwise, I cannot dismiss the likelihood. Did you find anything?"

"Yes... I think." She wasn't completely sure that the movement of the orb had been of her own doing. She didn't feel any different now and felt silly trying such a thing again.

"What is it?"

"There are shrines to each of the gods in the hallway upstairs. When I touched the one for Jovienna, I saw more images from the past. And there's more..." She trailed off as she concentrated on the tome that Mahdon had just grabbed. With little hesitation it began to rise and floated to her. She took it from the air and walked it back to the desk where Mahdon was now smiling broadly.

"I don't quite understand my own power yet, but I can feel it."

"This is very good news. Once you've returned to your former self, this will seem like nothing. I was not yet born when last you visited, but I did see the miracles of Alurine. The gift she bestowed upon us was but a tiny fraction of the power you possess."

She felt drained from the minor skill she'd just discovered; she couldn't imagine doing anything more significant. "When you're finished here, did you want to finish searching the other rooms? I need to lie down for a bit."

"Yes, of course. I wish you a restful sleep."

"Thank you."

Maiya left him to finish reviewing the final tome and settled down in the first room she'd searched. The sudden exhaustion hit her like a wave, and within seconds, she had drifted off to sleep.

Hours passed without incident while Maiya slept and Mahdon made a final sweep of the remaining three council member's quarters. Finding nothing worthy of note, he once again returned to the lower study, leaving Maiya alone in the quarters above. Only a short time passed before Maiya took notice of his departure.

She shivered in the dark as an icy chill filled the room and startled her awake. The significant drop in temperature felt as drastic as stepping from a heated home out into the middle of a winter night. She stiffened as she watched a dark figure move through the room, blocking the dimmed glow of the orbs at the foot of the bed. She couldn't make out any features in the dark but could feel the presence of the shadow being as it studied her.

She stared in the dark, afraid to move, for what felt like a significant length of time. It whispered in her mind, speaking in the same language seen throughout the council chambers and in the ruins outside. At last it seemed to tire of her and vanished into thin air, leaving the cold behind in its wake. Maiya laid frozen for a moment before darting from the bed and out the door. She stopped in the hallway to calm herself, no longer wishing to wander through this place alone. Once her hands finished shaking, she ran to find Mahdon.

Maiya barely rounded the corner into the main chamber when she saw Mahdon running toward her. He was clearly concerned and placed his hands on her shoulders when he reached her. "Are you okay?"

"Yes. Just a bit shaken. She was in the room with me."

"She?"

"The shadow we saw earlier. I don't know who or what she is, but it's definitely female. I couldn't see her, but she felt familiar to me. She needs help."

"Where is she now?"

Maiya shook her head. "I don't know. She just vanished."

"Did she hurt you?"

"No."

Mahdon's expression softened slightly. "When I heard you scream, I thought something awful had happened to you."

Maiya gave him a nonplussed look as a shiver ran down her spine. "I didn't scream… I was too scared to even move."

Mahdon paled. "We should not stay here any longer. I believe I have found another exit. I suggest we leave before things escalate. Follow me."

They once again crossed the room and took the stairs down to the study. Mahdon began tracing his hands along the base and sides of the bookshelves, as if in search of a trigger they could not see. Maiya watched the stairs uneasily, expecting the shadow to make its reappearance at any moment.

"Do you know what that thing is?"

"No. But how can it possibly be good when it scared us both like that? I have never encountered anything of the sort."

"Do you think it's a ghost?"

Mahdon briefly paused what he was doing. "A what?"

"The soul of a dead person who's stuck here for some reason."

Mahdon shrugged and returned to his search. "I have heard of something similar, but not the same."

As he ran his hand along the side of one of the bookcases, an opening materialized in the wall opposite the stairwell. The two took one final look around the room and then started down the newly discovered tunnel, seeing no obvious end in sight. Unlike the one they used to enter the council chambers, this one was in pristine condition. Mahdon suspected it had been designed as an emergency exit for rare situations such as this. He waited until they distanced themselves from the study a bit before inquiring further about what Maiya had suggested.

"Are these ghost things common in human beliefs?"

"Spirits in general are widely believed in, but not by everybody. What did you mean when you said you've heard of 'something similar'?"

"There are some religious texts that speak of wandering spirits, but they are not the souls of the dead. They are something else entirely – often malevolent beings – though that is not always the case. I remember hearing stories about them as a child and they always frightened me."

Maiya frowned. "That sounds more like demons. Maybe we shouldn't talk about this now."

The feeling that they were being watched began to sweep over her again. She fought the urge to look behind them, feeling the overwhelming need for a sense of security. She slipped her hand into his as they walked in silence. He glanced down but said nothing.

They continued down the tunnel for a couple hundred yards before coming to a stone staircase leading up to an odd-looking door. The door appeared to be made of heavy wood with a large ring to one side for a handle, but when viewed from certain angles, it was translucent to a room beyond. Maiya released Mahdon's hand and approached the door. She reached out for the handle just to watch her hand slip through it.

"It's a false door." Mahdon said as he stepped forward and lightly touched a stone to the right of it. The illusion faded away, revealing another room in full clarity.

"Clearly. I totally knew that."

Mahdon gave her a doubtful look and moved into the next room. When they were both through the archway, he reached above it and the space filled in to match the surrounding walls. Maiya found it was now solid from this side. Unless someone was aware of the door's existence, it was impossible to tell where it had been.

Looking around their latest surroundings, it was clear that they were now in the basement of a different building. A set of stairs ran the length of one of the walls and barrels lined another in stacks of three. The floor and walls were all the same stone as the council chambers they just left. The basement was cool but not overly damp or musky, and they could tell it was well cared for.

Exiting the basement, they found themselves in a kitchen that housed several brick ovens, though nothing was in them now. The only light in the room came from the connection to the next room. Outside of the kitchen, they entered a much larger, open room with some low tables and cushions pushed off to one side. Moonlight shone through tall windows along two of the walls, casting light across the red-toned hardwood floors.

Maiya caught a glimpse of movement high in the rafters over the door, but she was unsure of the source. She took a step to each side in an attempt to get a better view.

Mahdon remained oblivious. "This is the town hall. I am surprised we did not see the caretaker. I would expect them to be here even now."

Maiya kept her eyes locked overhead and pointed to the region where she had seen the movement. "I saw something move up there."

"Lights." On his command, the room brightened, illuminating an Amerti's foxlike tail that dangled down from a ledge above.

"Hello?" Mahdon called up but received no response. "I'm going to check it out."

He appeared to vanish before Maiya's eyes. Moments later, an unconscious Amerti woman floated down from above. Mahdon reappeared in human form as he set her gently on the floor. Her breathing was shallow, and though she occasionally moaned in pain or twitched, she remained unresponsive.

"She's very sick. It won't be long now."

Maiya knelt by the woman's side and brushed her hair out of her face. The woman felt so warm to the touch that she seemed to be radiating heat. Maiya tried to call on the power she had felt before, but inside she was panicking.

The memory of the other night flashed in Maiya's mind and she fought to push it away. It then occurred to her what Mahdon had said previously about changing form. She tried to keep the worry out of her voice, but she had never been very good at concealing her emotions. "You just shifted and touched her. Won't you get sick now?"

"It is a possibility, yes." His tone was matter-of-fact.

This news wasn't helping her anxiety any. As the panic cropped up again, she felt herself growing angry with him for doing something so stupid and acting like it was nothing. "Why would you take that risk? What will happen when you get sick?"

"Then you'll help me."

"You don't know that! What if I can't? I haven't been able to help anyone yet." She looked back at the woman, once again feeling utterly useless. All she wanted in that moment was to disappear. "You said she doesn't have long. How long is that?"

"It varies by individual, but once it gets to this stage, it's typically only a few days. I suspect she has been this way for a while, so it is difficult to tell."

"We need to get her out of here. Is there a hospital we can take her to?"

"There should be one fairly close, yes." He bent down and picked the woman up.

Maiya opened the door for him and they emerged at the town center. The statue from her memories stood before them in a small, circular lot across the pavement. The surrounding area was raised for foot traffic with roads branching out in several directions between two and three-story buildings. Many buildings had lights on at the higher levels and a large number of Amerti citizens moved about the town despite the late hour.

Most of the Amerti they saw were human in appearance, but the occasional unique individual could be seen. There were absolutely no children to be seen. Despite her knowledge about the people's lack of reproduction, Maiya still found this to be a bit shocking. Those who took notice of Mahdon and herself eyed them curiously, whispering to one another in their native tongue.

They followed a side street away from the town center, gathering more attention as they went. Those they passed hurried to the other side of the street to avoid close contact with the woman Mahdon carried, but otherwise paid special attention to them. By the time they reached the hospital – a fairly nondescript, single story building – a small crowd had gathered that followed them from a short distance.

A dark-haired male stepped forward and called to them before they could open the hospital doors. "Some have said you are Jovienna. They say you have come to save us. Is this true?"

Mahdon spoke up for Maiya. "Yes. This is the goddess."

The man turned back to the crowd to convey the message in Pandornu. It occurred to Maiya at this time that, unlike those at the welcoming ceremony, very few of these people understood English. As they listened to the man speak, they began to whisper even more amongst themselves and most bowed out of respect.

Maiya calmed her nerves and addressed the crowd. "Please stand up. You don't have to bow to me. I will do everything in my power to stop the spread of the disease and bring an end to your fear and suffering. I promise you that."

She turned and entered the building, holding the door for Mahdon. They first entered an elaborately detailed antechamber further showcasing the wealth of the planet. Precious metals and gems decorated murals on the walls. Floating lights seemed to dance over their heads. Passing through this room, they came to a large multi-bed ward that made up much of what remained of the building. Each side of the room contained a dozen black, circular beds, many of which were occupied by Amerti men and women in various phases of the illness. Most of the occupants were curled up in their native form, but a few had taken on other appearances. A single Amerti male tended to the ill, but it was clear that all he knew to do was make sure they were comfortable as they waited to die.

Some of the ill appeared to flicker in and out of existence as the woman at the ceremony had, while others remained unconscious like the one Mahdon now carried. Still others babbled incoherently in-between groans of pain. The caretaker rushed to Mahdon, visibly distraught at the sight of the woman they brought.

"There is an open bed in the back." He led them to the back of the room where Mahdon laid the woman down on the bed. The caretaker leaned over her and softly touched her face. "Braelyn, I am so sorry. This is my fault."

"We found her like this in the town hall," Maiya said. "Do you know how long she's been ill?"

The man shook his head. "Not specifically, no. A couple of days, perhaps? The last time I saw her she was displaying no symptoms. I had asked her to come by and now, due to that, she will die."

"Not necessarily. What's your name?"

"Alaric."

"We're going to find a way to help her, Alaric." Maiya pulled Mahdon aside and lowered her voice. "I don't know what to do yet, but there must be something. I need more time."

Maiya looked back at Alaric, hoping she didn't unintentionally lie to him. After a moment, a thought came to her. "You slowed time when we first met. Can you do that again and leave us unaffected?"

"The device we used to do that is onboard the ship on which we arrived. It is only accessible from there."

"Can you get back there to use it?"

"I could request it of Daera if I can locate a subspace communicator. However, I have ethical concerns about using it on Amertine."

Maiya frowned. "Did you have these concerns about using it on Earth?"

"Of course, but the circumstances were different. It was necessary to remain undetected."

"And now it may be necessary to save lives. If possible, we could pinpoint the hospital." Maiya moved back to Braelyn's side and looked at Mahdon. "You should hurry."

"I shall try." He turned and left, hoping he would return before it was too late.

Mahdon wandered the streets of Ularia for hours in search of a shuttlecraft like the one they had used before. Though such crafts were fairly commonplace, they were often found at scientific hubs, and Ularia was not one of these. As such, he had no luck in locating one and was forced to consider alternatives.

At last he returned to the town center where he stopped outside of a large, three story building across from the central statue. Stone letters spelled out "Ularia Academy" in Pandornu. It was here that he spent countless hours, and often days at a time, studying and, later, teaching religious history. He entered the building and proceeded directly to the office of one of his past students who now taught at the academy.

A man opened the door, pleasantly surprised to see him. He addressed Mahdon respectfully in the native tongue. "Advisor! To what do I owe the honor?"

"I need to request access to one of your conference rooms. I need to contact a member of the council and, at this time, I lack even a basic communicator. A secured line would be much preferred."

The man looked puzzled. "Has something happened?"

"Yes… but I am afraid there is no time to explain. May I trouble you to help an old friend out?"

"It's no trouble at all. I believe conference room five is currently unoccupied. No access code will be required. Just promise me it won't be so long before I see you again."

"I will do my best. Thank you, Professor."

Mahdon made his way to the second floor through the familiar halls, reminiscing on old memories. Many discussions and debates had taken place in every section of this building. In fact, it was in conference room five where he had first shared his findings about Jovienna's prophecy of reincarnation.

He secured the door and activated the communicator, entering in Naliz's personal line via telepathic link. Almost immediately, Naliz appeared on screen wearing a frown.

"Mahdon. I didn't expect to hear from you again... especially not so soon. Please understand that there was nothing I could do."

"That doesn't matter now. It isn't why I'm contacting you. I do need you to do something for me, though."

"What is that? I see you are contacting me from the academy. You went forward with your plan after all.

"Yes. Whether I have Brandon's approval or not, I will not abandon my people. I hope you can understand that."

He sighed. "Yes. Of course. What is it you need?"

"I need to contact Daera, but I lack the means to do so. The only communication devices I have been able to locate are specific to use on Amertine."

"What about the shuttlecraft you took to Ularia? That should have the proper equipment."

"I no longer have access to it. It was sabotaged and failed before we even arrived."

Naliz looked around him quickly, clearly surprised. He lowered his voice. "Are you certain that is what happened?"

Mahdon wasn't expecting Naliz to be unaware, but it was clear he wasn't feigning ignorance. "I have ruled out the other possibilities. Sabotage is the most likely scenario. That is not the only problem we have encountered; I can elaborate at a later time. In the meantime, I need communication established."

"What you ask of me is extremely risky. As you well know, all subspace communication is monitored. Brandon has already begun spreading rumors that the goddess has left in shame."

"It's barely been three days since our arrival. This is absurd."

"I am well aware. However, if Brandon finds out that I'm helping you, I will be ejected from the council and we will lose any influence over him."

Mahdon nodded. "I understand. If you get me the proper equipment, I can contact her myself. It should not be difficult for you to acquire another craft."

Naliz shifted uneasily. "I will meet you outside of the academy."

"Thank you."

The line of communication was terminated and Mahdon went outside to wait.

While Maiya sat with Alaric, she was unsure what she could possibly say to soothe his emotional pain. She learned in this time that Braelyn was not only a friend but had been the equivalent of his spouse since long before the gift. Despite the widespread advice to remain in a mortal form to avoid falling ill, many of the Amerti grew restless and, no longer being accustomed to a constant form, did not always heed this advice. Braelyn was not an exception.

Alaric had been in need of some rest and had requested that she step in at the hospital while he took some time away. During this time, she had shifted several times, a risk that Alaric knew she was likely to take. Not surprisingly, she soon fell victim to the illness like so many before her. To date, Alaric had watched helplessly as more than fifty people succumbed to the disease. He was not prepared to watch his best friend die in the same manner.

"What of you?" He asked. "Do you have a mate on your planet?"

"No."

"Then you are amongst the majority here. Partnering up is a thing of the past. Those of us who have mates now are either Zumerti or had them before Alurine's time. I suppose I will soon be among the majority as well."

Maiya placed her hand on his and looked him directly in the eyes as she spoke to him. "Maybe you will. But maybe you won't. I know this isn't easy for you, but no matter what happens to her, you will survive. I won't tell you that you'll get stronger for surviving her loss... because, frankly, I don't know if you will. Only you can decide what you do after she's gone. But until that moment comes, try to stay strong for her. Talk to her. If she can hear you, maybe it will help her stay strong too."

Alaric said nothing for a moment, then smiled slightly. "I believe you are right. Thank you."

Maiya responded with a smile of her own, patting his hand lightly. And as Braelyn began to flicker in and out of existence, she begged in her mind for Mahdon's return.

It didn't take long for Naliz to arrive in Ularia. He set the craft down gently on the road to one side of the academy and released the passenger side lock. Mahdon climbed inside while Naliz called for him to hurry. They immediately took to the air and moved out away from the city.

Naliz shook his head as he navigated the craft skyward. "I don't know what I am thinking. Brandon will surely find out about this. When he does..." He rubbed his temple with a sigh. "I suppose it is too late to worry about that now."

"Where are we headed?"

"To see Daera, of course."

Mahdon wasn't expecting this. "You wish to join me? All I needed was the shuttlecraft's communicator."

"I don't know what you're planning, but I assure you it will be safer to speak with her in person. That ship is not monitored as our communications would be otherwise."

They landed in one of the ship's side bays as it orbited the planet, and then they disembarked to make their way to the bridge. Daera appeared before them almost immediately, having noticed the craft as it approached.

She gave a nonplussed look. "Ambassador? Why have you returned so soon? Is the Goddess with you?"

"No. However, she has made a request of me."

"How might I be of assistance?"

"We need to use Reedon's Arrow."

Before Daera had the chance to respond, Naliz voiced his disapproval. "Absolutely not! Had I known that was the reason for this contact, I would never have agreed to help you. This is a clear violation of our peoples' rights."

"Since when do you take issue with exercising power in a questionable manner? We are doing this to save lives. Not control them."

Naliz looked prepared to respond but chose to keep his mouth shut when he caught Daera staring at them. Instead, he shot Mahdon a look to indicate that this would not be forgotten later.

Mahdon continued, "We are only aiming to target the hospital in Ularia to give ourselves some additional time to save the lives of those infected there. Ideally, we would target all hospitals, but I have not had the opportunity to alert other caretakers of this plan."

Daera looked cautiously at Naliz and then back at Mahdon when Naliz said nothing. "Let's not waste any time then."

They exited the shuttle bay and headed to a room just off the bridge. The room looked similar to the ship's other conference rooms with one obvious exception. Where a table would normally stand, a three-foot-tall pyramid shaped object rose from the floor. It emitted a gentle hum as images of planets, stars, and planet-bound life raced and then slowed around it as if passing at different rates of time. The room itself had an unusual feeling about it, as though it, too, was experiencing jerky shifts in the passage of time.

Mahdon stepped forward, standing between the pyramid and the images which flew past. As he did so, he disappeared from view of both Naliz and Daera. Though he could still see the room around him, to any onlookers, he had simply vanished. He now saw a thousand more moments in time dance across the sides of the machine. As he held one hand toward the pyramid, he envisioned the hospital in his mind. In doing so, the side facing him revealed past and present recordings of occurrences at that location. Among the moments, he watched himself leave the building earlier that night, and he saw Maiya and Alaric as they sat at Braelyn's bedside.

"Stop." He commanded. A series of images froze before him, and he reached out and selected one shortly after his departure. He marked Maiya and Alaric with auras of light. "Return to this moment and pause here. The two selected subjects will remain unaffected and proceed in the original timeline."

The recordings of time began to play once more. He watched himself leave and Maiya and Alaric talk. He watched as every moment past his departure became a motionless backdrop to the actions of the two he left behind. He stepped back through the wall of swirling images and nodded to Naliz and Daera, indicating he had completed his task.

"We should return to Ularia at once. There is still much to be done."

"Here, take this." Daera handed him a handheld subspace communicator. "Let me know when it's time and I'll handle things from here."

"Thank you. If everything goes as planned, we may find use for it again. I am confident that the goddess has only our best interests in mind. Soon the populace will realize that as well."

Mahdon and Naliz then exited and headed back to the shuttle bay.

Maiya could tell Alaric was close to breaking down when time in the room began to rewind around them. Braelyn's form stopped fading and rapidly became solid once again. Soon after, the entirety of the room stilled. At first Alaric was alarmed but calmed when Maiya touched his hand.

She was elated by this familiar silence. "It's all right. Mahdon did it. Braelyn is going to be fine now."

She stood and hurried to the door, expecting Mahdon's return at any moment. She was not waiting long but was surprised when he did not arrive alone. Naliz gave her a small smile and nod, but it was clear he wasn't happy. It was apparent to Maiya that he was biting his tongue.

"Naliz... I wasn't expecting to see you here."

"Yes, well, I am just as surprised as you, it seems. This is not how I would have handled this situation. You had better know what you are doing."

"That's the problem," Maiya said, "You weren't handling the situation at all. That's why I'm here. And questioning my decisions right now isn't going to fix this. I know what the council did, and I know what you didn't do."

Naliz frowned and looked away uncomfortably. "You act as though I had a choice."

"We always have a choice." Maiya sighed. "Water under the bridge. I'm not saying you have to agree with me, but if you're going to be here, you need to be willing to work with me... not against me."

His annoyance was evident as he shifted his gaze from Maiya to Mahdon and back again. "Understood. Now if you'll excuse me, I have some business to attend to."

"Of course." Maiya watched him leave and looked to Mahdon. "He's angry with me."

"It's not you. Naliz isn't accustomed to taking orders, and he's been doing it often lately. I would imagine he feels quite powerless. He's torn between two allegiances, and I don't think even he knows where his loyalties lie."

"Should I be worried?"

Mahdon shook his head. "He just needs some time."

"Speaking of which... now that we've bought ourselves some time, where do we start? I expected to learn more in the council chambers, but I'm not eager to go back there any time soon. Are there any other shrines or artifacts in the area?"

"Many. Ularia is a religious center and perhaps the most historically relevant city on Amertine. The town center is where it is believed Tarn crafted the Hokaruin orb. It is also where Alurine last appeared to us. Some historians speculate that this is where you first appeared to our people before we even knew how to build homes... let alone cities."

For a moment an image of a park-like setting appeared to Maiya and was gone just as quickly. She tilted her head in thought until the name came to her. "The Klintorian Gardens... will you take me there?"

"Yes. May I suggest we wait until morning? It will be easier in daylight. I can take you to better accommodations for the night."

Maiya smiled. "Lead away."

A short walk later and they arrived at a large dome-shaped building that Maiya soon realized was a standalone house. The side street they stood on was pleasantly quiet and had similar, though not identical, homes nearby.

Though not far from the town center, this neighborhood felt much more rural.

Mahdon swept his hand over a panel on the outside of the home and the door swept open. As they stepped inside, the lights came on automatically, revealing a large open space of wooden floors and accents. To the right, several pillowy cushions around a low table served as seating on the floor. To the left, there was a kitchen area with an elegant stone counter and an inside herb garden. A staircase in the middle ran up to a loft above.

There were moving pictures on the walls much like those Maiya had seen in the dining hall on the ship, though these seemed more personal in nature. The back wall of the building was largely windows, but the night made it difficult to see what sat beyond. The room was otherwise remarkably clean with sparse furnishings.

"I know this is not what you're accustomed to, but I thought you might like to see a more common residence."

Maiya was admiring an image of an Amerti family standing at the base of a waterfall. "Whose home is this?"

"Mine. I have not been back in a long time."

"I'm honored." She looked back at him with a smile. "Is this your family?"

Mahdon seemed strangely embarrassed by the question. "Yes. The man is my uncle. That was taken when I was a child."

"It's a nice picture. And this place is immaculate. Who takes care of it while you're away?"

"I have offered my home to several friends in the past, but I do not know if any have accepted the offer. With the exception of pruning, the garden is self-sufficient. The ventilation and energy systems in the house are similarly advanced."

"Impressive. I assume the bedroom is in the loft?"

"Yes. You are welcome to it. Should you need anything, I will be down here."

"Thank you for everything. I know the past couple of days haven't been easy for you. I never meant to put you in an uncomfortable position with Naliz or anyone else."

Mahdon smiled. "You worry too much. I'm happy to be of assistance. Have a restful sleep."

The domed ceiling over the loft provided a pleasant backdrop as Maiya laid back in the large, circular bed. It wasn't clear if the constellations that she watched pass overhead were simulated or real, though she didn't recall seeing any windows on the exterior of the dome's peak.

A set of controls built into one side of the bed allowed her to control the temperature, lighting, and sound in the loft. She dimmed the lights and selected one of the many nature options from the audio choices. She closed her eyes and settled in as she listened to leaves rustling in the breeze. A smile crossed her face as the sound of distance thunder rumbled, and she drifted off to sleep.

When morning came, a brilliant reddish-orange glow filled the room and the soft sound of chimes stirred her from her sleep. As she sat up, she realized the chimes were, in fact, a subtle morning alarm built into the sleep program she'd chosen the night before. She switched off the audio and went downstairs to find Mahdon standing at the kitchen counter wearing the waistcoat that had become his usual attire. She thought it unfair how perfectly put together he always was, but then she reminded herself that he did not face the same physical restrictions. He didn't seem to notice her arrival, as he appeared lost in thought. He had one hand on the countertop, tapping lightly with his fingertips, while he held his head in the other.

"Are you okay?"

He stood up straight and gave her a perplexed look. It was a moment before recognition crossed his face. "Maiya... hello."

"Hi... what's going on? You're acting strange."

"My apologies. I was just..." He trailed off and looked around the room in confusion. "I don't remember what I was doing. Are you ready to go to the Gardens?"

"Maybe after breakfast. I haven't eaten anything in a while." She frowned. "I'd like to know you're going to be all right. I haven't seen you like this before."

"You don't need to worry about me. I have a lot on my mind, is all." He gave her a less than convincing smile.

"Okay..."

She decided to drop the subject for the time being, suspecting that he was just as uncomfortable with the memory lapse as she felt. In the meantime, she determined, it was better to focus on finding a cure than worrying about his slightly unusual behavior. She watched as he walked outside and returned with three large blue eggs.

"Paku eggs. They are similar to those from the creature you call a chicken."

He set them on the counter and fiddled with some controls on the side facing away from Maiya. What resembled a partially transparent griddle appeared on the countertop beneath the whole eggs. As he adjusted the settings, the shells from the eggs promptly disappeared, leaving only the egg whites and bright orange yolks. He turned and carefully selected leaves from two of the herbs in the hanging garden and added them to the dish.

The entire meal was thrown together and completed in a matter of minutes. Though she had only seen him use three ingredients, the dish resembled an omelet wrapped in pita bread. Mahdon grabbed tongs from a drawer and offered the hand-held egg "sandwich" to Maiya.

"It's called an eraypa. The crust is a type of dough that one would traditionally spend hours preparing. I confess that as it is one of my programmed meals, the quality of the bread has suffered a bit."

Maiya took a bite and gave him a thumbs-up of approval. The dough had a slight sweetness to it that paired perfectly with the eggs and Mahdon's choice of herbs.

"Shall we?" Mahdon motioned toward the door. Satisfied with the meal, Maiya nodded and the two headed out. They had barely left the quiet cul-de-sac when Mahdon stopped dead in his tracks and looked around in confusion. He stepped to one side of the adjoining road and leaned against the nearest building.

"What's wrong?"

"I just need to lie down for a moment..."

Maiya tried to keep the alarm out of her voice, but felt it was on the verge of breaking. "You're sick, aren't you?"

Mahdon didn't say anything.

"We have a few days at least, right? We can get you to the house, and I'll... I'll figure something out."

As she stepped over to help him stand, he collapsed to the ground. Maiya dropped to his side trying to get any reaction from him, but he remained unresponsive. With no one else around and her friend dying before her eyes, she succumbed to her fear and fell apart.

CHAPTER 7

"How did this happen?" Naliz stared Maiya down from the opposite side of the bed. Mahdon laid unconscious between them, his breathing shallow.

Shortly after Mahdon passed out, Maiya had located the communicator he held and, after several failed attempts, managed to contact Naliz. He arrived minutes later, and the two loaded Mahdon's limp body into the shuttlecraft, bringing him back to the nearby house where he would be safe from prying eyes. Up until now they had hardly exchanged words.

"Before we got to the hospital, we found a sick woman. She was out of reach, so he shifted to go get her."

Naliz sighed and dropped his head. "Mahdon, you idiot. I've told him a thousand times not to do such stupid things. But does he listen?" He shook his head and stood.

"Where are you going?"

"If this gets out, there will be chaos. However, the council needs to know. I'll only be a moment."

"Please..." Maiya reached out a hand to stop him. "Give me until tonight to figure something out."

He appeared hesitant, looking first at Mahdon, and then away. After a moment of contemplation, he relented. "One day. If he hasn't improved by nightfall, I need to alert the council."

"Understood."

Naliz disappeared downstairs, leaving Maiya to sit in silence. Truth be told, she was grateful for his departure. His presence only served as a reminder that the one individual who trusted her without question was no longer able to speak to her defense. The thought made her want to cry, but she knew it wouldn't do any good. She'd spent enough time feeling sorry for herself and it had gotten her nowhere. She took Mahdon's hand in hers and kissed it softly. She watched him for any signs of waking, but he remained dead to the world. She tried to call on the power she'd felt before but felt all but dead inside.

"I'm so sorry."

Hours passed in similar fashion, and she felt every minute as they ticked by. As the day moved to late afternoon, and then evening, the weight of all she'd failed to accomplish had become too much for her to handle. She'd requested a delay only to sit idly by while time slipped through her fingers.

"Please wake up." She begged, fighting back the tears. "I need you here right now. I don't know what to do. Help me. I'm sorry; I've failed you."

She felt a hand on her shoulder and shifted her gaze up to Naliz. He looked at her with such a sad expression that she suspected he had been watching her for a while. She released Mahdon's hand and sat up straight.

"Brandon and the others will arrive shortly."

"What will happen to him then?"

"He'll be transported to the current council chambers. We won't be able to heal him, but we can prevent the disease from progressing."

"I thought you didn't approve of my methods to do that."

"There's another way. One that won't draw any unwanted attention."

Maiya felt suddenly overcome with rage. She abruptly stood and all but yelled at Naliz. "Then why haven't you already done it for the others?"

Naliz was unfazed by her reaction. "It is in the council's best interest to keep some technology confidential. If we had a cure, we would not hesitate to use it."

"Typical."

She had held higher expectations for such an advanced society, yet continually had felt short-changed when it came to the council. Here she was supposedly revered as a god and yet she knew nothing. She questioned how much Mahdon was even aware of given Brandon's apparent dislike of him. It wasn't long before she heard the voices of the other council members as they made their way up the stairs. The moment she saw Brandon's face, she wanted to smack him for the snide smile he wore.

Arrogant as ever, he laughed. "It appears the ambassador has put his faith in the wrong people."

Naliz sighed. "Is this really necessary?"

"When you said he'd fallen ill, I could hardly believe it. I had to see it for myself. Imagine my delight now that I see it to be true. This is far more amusing than I thought it would be."

Maiya glared at him. "How can you possibly find this funny?"

"How can I not? My chief opposition just took himself out of the picture. I have half the mind to let him die. He deserves it for the trouble he's caused me over the years. Now, my dear…" He stepped closer and ran a hand down the side of her face. "There's just the matter of what to do about you."

His words, coupled with the touch of his hand, ignited something deep inside Maiya, turning it into a raging inferno. Everything else in the room faded into the background as her anger rose to the forefront and overwhelmed her senses. Before she knew it, he flew backwards across the room and collided with the wall, collapsing hard to the floor. Her hand remained outstretched, having expelled a force so great that the onlooking council members stepped back in fear.

"Never touch me again."

After a moment of hesitation, Jo'dai moved toward her only to be thrown back by a sweep of Maiya's hand. Saren and Tanin rushed to the two fallen council members, looking to Naliz for guidance. He offered no support, having not removed his eyes from Maiya since the first blast. Brandon quickly came to and stared wide-eyed at her. The fear in his eyes was evident, and for once, he had no remarks to share.

"You will keep your distance." She warned.

They watched her in silence as she turned back to Mahdon and sat by his side. Her face softened as she once again grabbed his hand in both of hers and brought it to her lips. In doing so, she felt an energy flow through her that presented itself as a warm glow as it moved outward from her form. The glow brightened to a nearly blinding light as it filled the room and then dissipated rapidly. Within seconds, Mahdon's eyes fluttered open, and he sat up slowly. He looked around the room and then to Maiya with confusion.

"What's going on? Why is everyone here?"

Naliz promptly dropped to his knees as a look of shame spread across his face. He looked as pitiful as a dog that had just been reprimanded. "I have allowed fear to prevent me from standing on the side of truth. I am truly sorry."

Maiya sighed and held up a hand. "Don't. I want all of you to leave."

The council members remained frozen with their eyes locked on her. She felt drained as she had back in the council chambers, but she wasn't prepared for them to see that. She turned to them with a threatening look on her face and refused to hold back her anger.

"Get out!"

They didn't need to be given a second warning and stumbled from the room in the uncomfortable silence that followed. A few seconds later, only she and Mahdon remained. He looked frightened by her tone and said nothing. Her face softened as she held back tears.

"I thought you weren't going to make it."

"Why would you think that?"

"You were sick. I didn't know what to do, so I contacted Naliz... but then Brandon showed up and made things worse. He even threatened to let you die."

Mahdon looked appalled. "He did WHAT?"

Maiya moved aside as Mahdon adjusted to sit next to her on the edge of the bed. He looked to the stairs and shook his head with a sigh. He turned back to Maiya and gave her a slight smile in an attempt to lighten the mood. "I don't know what you did, but he's clearly afraid of you now."

Maiya chuckled. "I have to admit, it did feel pretty good to put him in his place."

"What exactly did you do to him? I have never seen him unable to speak like that."

"I may have sent him flying into the wall..."

Mahdon laughed. "You 'may' have? This is a significant development. I suspect that there will be some major changes after what happened here tonight."

Maiya's expression shifted back to one of concern. "He really hates us."

"Perhaps. That may no longer be of any consequence very soon."

"What do you mean?"

"The council has witnessed your abilities firsthand. No one has ever recovered from the illness. That makes this a miracle and puts you in a powerful position."

"What will happen then?"

"You will take your rightful place as head of the council."

Maiya's breath caught in her throat as her face grew pale. "Excuse me? I don't know how I feel about that. I thought I was here to help find a cure and then go home."

"The prophecy of your return was unrelated to the disease. That was unforeseen, and we were fortunate that it aligned somewhat with your rebirth. You are meant to bring about a new era."

"How do you know that it hasn't already begun? So much has already happened in my short time here."

"It has, yes, but without new leadership, change may not last long. Does this information upset you?"

Maiya shook her head slowly. "No. It scares me."

"Are you afraid you won't do well?"

"Surprisingly, no. It's not that at all. I don't know how qualified I am for such a title, but I've already done things I never thought possible. Regardless of that, it's clear a change is needed. I'm more worried about the backlash. Even if Brandon doesn't have the power to stop this, I'm afraid his supporters will be more than happy to cause trouble during the transition period."

"Even Brandon cannot deny what has occurred." Mahdon offered her a smile and stood slowly. "There will always be opposition to change, but it is inevitable. When the change is for the best, you should never back down."

"To be clear, we're just going to pretend he didn't threaten your life?"

"Not at all. It was foolish of him to say such a thing, and it won't be easily forgotten. The council members are still downstairs; we should address them while we have them here."

Maiya exhaled slowly and steadied her nerves. She rose and nodded to Mahdon, following him downstairs. With the exception of Brandon, the council members stood silently at the base of the staircase. They said nothing, looking sheepishly at Maiya as they waited for her to speak.

As Maiya gathered her thoughts, Brandon's voice came bitterly from the front door. "I believe they're here for you."

After exchanging a look with Mahdon, they moved to where Brandon stood and peered out the window. Hundreds of Amerti had gathered in the streets, patiently waiting for someone to come outside.

"Why are they here?" Maiya asked.

Mahdon shook his head. "I do not know. Shall we find out?"

Maiya took the lead, followed closely by Mahdon and then, momentarily, by Brandon and the remaining council members. A dark-haired woman rushed through the crowd and dropped down at Maiya's feet. Maiya quickly knelt to check if she was okay but was pleasantly surprised when she was met with a smiling face as tears of joy streaked down the woman's face.

"Thank you, Goddess!" The woman threw her arms around Maiya, nearly knocking her over in the process. "I thought they would not survive the night."

The woman released Maiya and turned back to the crowd. She motioned with one hand and two men, who could have been carbon copies of one another, stepped forward to join her. They had both taken on the appearance of long-haired blonde men with the slightest hint of facial hair.

"My father and brother were on the verge of death. They had not woken for days, but then your light came to us. I knew it was a miracle and we had to see your face for ourselves. It isn't much, but…"

The man standing to Maiya's left stepped closer and presented her with a small box. He opened it to reveal a seven-pointed gemmed hair clip resembling a Jovaia lily. "This belonged to my mate, Zahna, before the disease took her life. Please accept it as a token of our gratitude."

Maiya blushed. Her natural reflex would be to refuse such a thoughtful gesture, but her interactions and cultural discussions with Mahdon had taught her to react differently. Instead she held out her hands and smiled politely as the man gently handed her the gift.

"It's beautiful. Thank you."

As the three stepped away, more men and women stepped forward to offer their own thanks. These were followed by yet more people until the last of those present shared their personal story, leaving Maiya surrounded by hundreds of gifts. At some point during all of this, music had risen in the streets and laughter and dancing soon followed. Brilliantly colored lights flared upward and flickered over the mass of celebrating people like silent fireworks. The Amerti began to once again shift freely, no longer fearing the repercussions.

Collecting what she could, Maiya slipped from the spotlight and back into the house. Mahdon and Naliz followed, each carrying armfuls of the tokens of appreciation. The remaining council members followed suit, though all seemed to do so out of shame rather than respect. None had dared to speak since Brandon had drawn attention to the throngs of people. It was this grand display of faith in her that gave Maiya a newfound confidence.

Once they were all gathered in the main living area, she spoke. "I know this doesn't make you happy, but it's time for a change. I freely admit that I didn't have much faith in myself when I first started the trek to Amertine. Naliz and Mahdon can both attest to that.

But rather than work with me, you chose to challenge me and make my task more difficult. As you saw today, that didn't work out so well for you. I will never claim to be the solution to all of your problems, but I promise that I will never intentionally add to them."

She set her gaze on Brandon, expecting an objection, but he remained silent as she continued. "I ask now that you resign your position as council head. If you are willing to cooperate and recognize your own shortcomings, I will keep you on as an advisor."

Brandon scoffed at the idea. "How very gracious of you. I suppose you expect me to be grateful for the grand opportunity to be at your service?"

"On the contrary... This is exactly the kind of response I expected from you. You're far too narcissistic to ever admit your own faults."

Brandon glared at her and began pacing the length of the room. He stopped before the council members, his rage quickly escalating as they looked away from him. "Why are you all standing here silently while this woman attempts to overturn our very way of life? You will regret this."

Brandon shook his head and stormed off. The sounds of celebration briefly grew louder as he exited the building, then returned to a reasonable level as the door shut. Naliz looked embarrassed by the behavior, but the tension amongst the council members was visibly lessened with Brandon's departure.

"I'm truly sorry for all of the trouble you've faced. He'll come around; I'll make sure of it," Naliz said.

Mahdon smiled and nodded to him. "Thank you."

Maiya's annoyance toward the council hadn't yet dissipated, but she chose to keep this to herself. If she could get through this transition period without any further drama, she was happy to bite her tongue. She smiled politely instead.

"I think we've all had enough excitement for one day. Shall we reconvene in, say, three days? It will give each of us some time to process our own emotions and move forward with a fresh start."

They each sheepishly agreed, leaving the house to Maiya and Mahdon as they went their separate ways in the early morning hours.

CHAPTER 8

The following two days passed without any contact with the council, and Maiya was glad for it. For the first time since she arrived on Amertine, she felt she could truly relax. Though Mahdon was eager to discuss their next steps, he had given her the full two days to explore, free of any expectations. It was on that second day that Mahdon gave her a proper tour of Ularia, including the university where he both studied and taught, and a leisurely walk through the Klintorian Gardens. Not surprisingly, many Amerti stopped them along their way to show Maiya their admiration for her other worldly abilities.

Though it was nice to feel appreciated, Maiya soon found the attention exhausting and began dodging glances to avoid any more of it. Mahdon took notice of this during their stroll through the gardens and casually pulled her aside.

"Is something troubling you?"

Maiya shook her head, feeling embarrassed by her introversion. "No... I'll be fine."

He tilted his head to look in her eyes. "If you are unwell, we can return to my home. You're under no obligation to be here today."

"It's nothing like that. I'd just prefer some time alone."

"Oh. I can leave you be if you wish."

"Oh, no... I don't mean completely alone! I mean that I'd prefer some time alone with you. I think I'm drawing too much attention to myself."

Mahdon smiled slightly. "I see."

He looked around to ensure no one was watching and then grabbed her hand and nodded to a grouping of trees and bushes to their right. "Follow me."

Maiya ducked her head and held his hand as they pushed through to a small dirt and brick path hidden amongst the trees. "Where are we going?"

"There is an area of the gardens that was closed off during Alurine's time on the planet. It was never reopened."

"Is it dangerous?"

"Not at all. Overgrown, perhaps, but not dangerous. It was one of her favored locations for privacy, so it was left as such for a long time."

They continued along the winding path for another fifty yards until they broke through the trees into a small clearing. Despite the path being almost entirely overgrown in some spots, the grass where they stood now was strangely well maintained. A lone tree stood in the middle, surrounded by a bed of bright red moss. A crumbling brick wall stood in a semi-circle on the opposing side, covered in red and violet climbing vines.

Mahdon led Maiya onto the soft moss, and they took a seat near the base of the tree. "I came here often in my youth to meditate. It has changed so much, and yet it still brings me peace when I'm distraught. This tree is a seedling from the one that grew here in Alurine's time. Prior to that, there was a wall that ran the perimeter and no tree at all."

"I can see why you like it. It's so calm here. It reminds me of a place from my own childhood."

"May I ask what your childhood was like?"

"Of course; you can ask me anything. I don't think it was anything special, though. It was sad sometimes, happy other times. I got lonely a lot. We moved all the time, but other than that, I think it was fairly typical. What about yours?"

Mahdon didn't say anything for a moment, then shook his head and looked at her. "It was so long ago that I can hardly remember. As you know, my father died before I could ever know him. My mother was an engineer and was intent that we be constantly learning, so she introduced us to new ideas regularly. I was usually happy."

"You do seem to be happy more often than anyone I've ever met."

"I have had many years to find what makes me happy and many, many more of freedom from emotional distress that would threaten that happiness."

"When you're not in a physical form like this, do you feel anything at all?"

He nodded. "Some, yes, but nothing comparable. Content may be the best way to describe it. No anxiety or fear. No sadness. It is much easier to focus on the most logical solution rather than the most emotional reaction."

"I wish I felt that way. I tend to think of myself as a fairly logical person, but sometimes the anxiety gets to be too much. It's something I've struggled with for a long time now. A few years ago, I never would have done anything as spontaneous as getting on that ship. I'm still not entirely sure why I did." She shrugged and then smiled. "Anyway... despite the drama, I'm glad I did. And I'm glad I met you. You've been a good friend to me."

"Likewise. I have not had many close friends in the past."

Maiya was surprised. "Really? It seems like everyone likes you."

"Perhaps many do, but not everyone. I've spent so much of my life focusing on my studies and the next great historical event that I rarely found time for socializing. Naliz and I bonded over our shared love for religious history, but he would be the only one I'd consider to be a close friend. There was another when I attended the university, but as with my parents, she has since passed."

Maiya frowned. "I'm sorry to hear that. What happened?"

He shook his head. "We never found out. One day she was here, and the next she didn't come to lecture. It was late in the day, and no one had heard from her. That was unlike Mira. All attempts at contacting her failed, and when another day went by, search parties were formed. Her favorite tail ring was found in the woods near the university, but she never was.

"For years I'd look for her whenever I could spare a moment, but I never found anything that would lead me to believe she was still alive. After that, I put all my energy into my research and eventually Naliz came along."

"That's so sad."

"I mourned her for a long time. I don't think I even realized until she was gone how much I loved her."

Maiya put a hand on his and squeezed it gently. "I shouldn't have pried. I'm sorry."

Mahdon gave her a slight smile. "It's not a problem. She's no more than memories from a distant past. If not for the heartache, I believe I would have become a very different person."

The two leaned back against the tree and sat in silence for a moment. Maiya was unsure how to follow up such a heavy conversation and feared saying the wrong thing should she ask anything further. She tilted her head just enough to watch him as he closed his eyes and let out a relaxing sigh.

Another moment passed before she spoke. "Back aboard the ship, on the day we first met, you asked if I would join you for further exploration. I would love that."

Mahdon opened his eyes again and leaned forward. "I am very pleased to hear that. It will, of course, be a while before we can do that. We need to make certain the political situation on Amertine has stabilized. Are you sure this is what you want?"

"Yes."

"What has made you decide to stay?"

"I think I just needed a reminder of how difficult it is to find good company. I'm not quite ready to give that up yet."

Mahdon laughed. "You flatter me. Shall we continue our walk?"

They both stood and followed the path around to the other side of the brick wall. The clearing came to an end only a few feet beyond and led back into dense foliage. The path wound through the trees down an incline that gradually grew steeper, at which point a set of stone stairs replaced the packed down dirt. The light that filtered through the canopy of the forest was minimal the further they walked, but spherical lights lined the steps and provided a soft blue glow to the surrounding area. The sound of a gently bubbling stream met their ears as they reached a large outcropping of rock at the bottom of the steps. Roughly ten feet further down, clear water coursed by.

Mahdon and Maiya sat on the edge of the rock and watched as various birds flitted between the trees and critters gathered along the rough banks below to drink their fill. The animals hardly took notice of the two, looking briefly before returning to their respective tasks. Mahdon pointed from one grouping of birds to the next to share the species and any unique facts that came to mind. One species of bird that he was particularly fond of was a pale orange and known for flying backwards at high speeds to confuse and escape predators. Of the animals gathered below, the most numerous resembled a small, antlerless deer.

Mahdon continued to share his wildlife knowledge throughout the afternoon and into the evening as the last of the diurnal species wandered off for the night. Maiya drew comparisons to those she knew from her own life, but largely listened. She enjoyed hearing him speak with such passion in his voice, as though every aspect of life ignited a spark inside him. It was refreshing to see a love for life and learning that could turn the simplest subject into one of utter fascination. In her short lifespan, she had failed to hold onto that excitement and appreciation that he managed to retain after a multitude of lifetimes.

Once the sun had fully set and the only visible light came from the lights bordering the path, they returned to the clearing above. The sky was clear apart from a few wispy clouds drifting past the sliver of moon that hung over the planet. Maiya gazed skyward, admiring the plenitude of stars that stretched across the heavens.

"The stars are beautiful. I rarely look at them anymore. And now I have a whole new set to admire. At least, I think they're different stars. I imagine there's some overlap in there. Do you have names for any of the constellations?"

"Yes — there are approximately seventy-five official constellations. Do you see those seven stars in an arc just above the tree line? Those form Cygneb — the Great bird. The four that look like a diamond overhead form 'The Explorer.' That one may take some creative interpretation. Your planet cannot be seen without aid, but it resides in the Great bird."

"It's so strange to think about. I wonder if I ever looked toward Amertine the same way. The number of planets my eyes have passed over without me seeing them must be immense. I always suspected there was more life out there; the universe is so vast that it would be foolish to think otherwise."

"Soon you will be able to visit more of them."

Maiya smiled. "I can't wait. But first I need to make it through tomorrow."

"I will be there to assist you. You need not worry."

Maiya shifted her gaze from the sky over to Mahdon. "Is there anything I should know beforehand?"

"It will primarily be an introduction to your new role and will require nothing significant from you. In two days, there will be a swearing-in ceremony."

"Should I be concerned about backlash at this point? I'm worried there will be bitterness with an outsider taking on this role without a vote."

"There may be some, but you already have the support of the majority. You may regard yourself as an outsider, but you are not. I hope in time you will feel more comfortable in your role."

Maiya nodded. "I think I will. I won't deny this is something I've thought about a lot in the past. I mean, not this specifically, but who doesn't want to do something that matters?"

"I believe you already have."

Maiya wasn't convinced that she had. Though the people had been healed, she didn't believe this was entirely of her own doing. It was still unclear to her *how* the light had come to manifest itself on the occasions that it had. If anything, she felt more like a witness than an active participant. She decided it was best to change the subject as quickly as possible.

"It's getting late; maybe we should head back for the night."

"If you wish."

They followed the overgrown path back to the main garden walkway which was now aglow with the same spherical lights as the steps down to the creek. A few citizens milled about but by and large, the gardens were noticeably less populated than during the day. In the dark of night, Maiya noticed that a whole new array of flowers had blossomed. Bioluminescent in nature, they emitted light of varying hues from red to violet and everything in-between.

Maiya half laughed as she admired the night-time flora. "Seriously? Is everything here beautiful?"

"We take great pride in our surroundings. Anything that sparkles, glows, or grows is popular."

"I can't even keep flowers alive. The only thing I can grow is weeds."

"It is my understanding that weeds are more difficult to avoid than to grow."

"Exactly."

"Oh," Mahdon chuckled. "I may be able to teach you if you ever wish it."

"That wouldn't be the worst thing in the world. Another time."

The two returned to Mahdon's residence and Maiya settled into bed for the night. Mahdon waited until he knew she was asleep and then returned to the old council chambers via the hidden door in the town hall. On the way, he came upon Braelyn who was now in perfect health and high spirits. She had returned to her posting as caretaker and had restored the town hall to a more cheerful décor. She regarded him warmly when he arrived, recognizing him as the council advisor and Ambassador, though she did not recall seeing him only days earlier.

"I am happy to find you well," Mahdon said.

"To what do I owe the pleasure?"

"I have some council business in the archives."

"Archives?"

She gave him a puzzled look, at which point Mahdon realized she had no prior knowledge of the hidden entrance. He found this a bit unusual, but then again, this location had not been used in centuries. He saw no harm in her knowing of it now.

"The back entrance to the prior chambers is in this building."

Braelyn looked suddenly uneasy. "That explains it."

"Has something happened?"

"I saw a dark figure on several occasions before I got sick. Being this far from the cave entrance, I had assumed it could not be the same thing that made others ill. It seems I was mistaken."

"Have you seen it since you returned?"

"No. I pray I never do again. If you're going in there, you'd better be careful."

"I appreciate the warning. I should not be gone long."

Braelyn watched him enter the basement but did not follow. Mahdon went to where he had previously sealed the opening and traced a hand across the wall in a pattern he had learned long ago. The doorway was revealed once more. He took one last look around the room and down the hallway before stepping through to the other side. He had felt a sense of unease the last time he walked this hallway but now it was amplified by the solitude. He steadied his nerves and proceeded to the study. He half expected to find the room once again in disarray but was pleasantly surprised to find it as organized as he had left it.

Mahdon walked to where he shelved the books on council procedures and civil law and grabbed the most recent versions. Though he was well-informed on such matters, he suspected Maiya might appreciate the texts for review. He briefly considered looking upstairs to see if anything had changed after their hasty departure but thought of Maiya back at the house. He hadn't told her where he was going, and should something happen, he was unsure if she would be informed in a timely manner. He pulled out one last tome and headed back down the hallway. He resealed the door and returned to the house without incident.

CHAPTER 9

As they walked to their transport the following morning, Mahdon presented the books to Maiya one at a time. He gave a brief description of the contents of each but neglected to mention where they had come from. He decided that, at this point in time, it was an unimportant detail that would only serve to worry her. Maiya took the stack of books and nearly toppled from the weight. Mahdon had made them look unreasonably light and she found herself envying his seemingly unlimited strength.

Maiya let out a nervous laugh. "It looks like I have some studying to do. I hope I don't need to know all of this today."

"Not at all... only the first book or two."

Maiya paled. "Please tell me you're joking."

Mahdon laughed. "You can relax. Great leaders are not made overnight. Think of these as reference material. You do not need to memorize them. You do not even need to carry them."

He reached out to her and she happily handed the books back to him. When they got to the shuttle, Mahdon climbed inside while Maiya walked around it for a quick inspection. Much like the last craft, there didn't appear to be anything obviously wrong with it.

"Are you sure this one isn't sabotaged too?" Maiya asked, half-jokingly.

Mahdon smiled and held up not one, but two handheld comm devices. "I imagine our luck would need to be very poor for that to happen. In addition to these, I took the liberty of personally inspecting this one and have both Daera and Naliz tracking our position."

Maiya laughed and climbed into the passenger seat. "Fair enough."

The shuttle doors closed, and the craft began navigation to Fimbira. As was customary, there was a formal headquarters for most council affairs in addition to the separate closed-door meeting chambers. Unlike the more secluded chambers, the headquarters had remained in the same location for thousands of years, and again, unlike the chambers, the headquarters was easily the most visible building around. It was the tallest building in Fimbira and stood at the edge alongside the falls. The building itself was rounded and appeared to have tendrils that stretched out laterally and down the cliff-face. Two large balconies stuck out over the cliff's edge - one at the base of the building and another toward the top. Several smaller ones wrapped around the midsection of the building.

The ship came to rest on the lower balcony where the council members were patiently awaiting their arrival. Brandon, however, was nowhere in sight. Maiya was unsurprised, imagining that he would likely avoid her until absolutely necessary. She counted this as a minor blessing. Naliz greeted them warmly and led them inside. The remaining three members each gave a respectful bow of the head and waited for Maiya to enter the building before following suit.

The main floor of the building resembled that of a large office building or luxury hotel. Large pillars stood in the corners of a high-ceilinged room filled with various decorative plants and pieces of lounge furniture. The floor was a black marble and the walls a reflective gold. In the center stood a single gravity tunnel. They stepped in and began moving almost immediately.

As they ascended the tower, Naliz spoke. "There are ten floors dedicated to housing – one floor per council member with the exception of the council head who is allotted a two-story domicile. The remaining four floors are for visiting dignitaries – or rather, they were. We have not had much use for them in some time now."

"Do you still have leadership at lower levels of government? Cities or states?" Maiya asked.

"Well... yes," Naliz said with some hesitation.

"You say that like you aren't sure."

Naliz shook his head. "It's not that. It's a unique situation at this point that any leadership is necessary at that level. We've come to realize that community decisions rarely face opposition when there's no competition for resources. If not for the need to preserve our culture and prevent the degradation of our society as a whole, I imagine the council would no longer exist."

They came to a stop and exited into another large, open room. The walls at this level were primarily glass and far above the rest of the city. Maiya had never been afraid of heights, and yet the view was dizzying. She had never been in such a tall building, and now she was on the top floor of one that overlooked not only the city, but the sheer face of a cliff.

"Most public government decisions are announced on this floor," Mahdon said. "It is here that citizens can express their dissent or approval. There was a point where we would hold weekly meetings to hear from the people, but attendance has dwindled over time. If we are to further advance as a society, I believe we should bring back these sessions. It will, of course, require some finesse to garner sufficient interest."

"Is this something that all of us would attend?"

"You may if you like, though often times I held these sessions alone and recorded and relayed all concerns."

"That seems strange to me. Maybe I'm wrong, but I'd think that part of being a good leader involves directly interacting with those who disapprove of your decisions. You can get a pretty good idea of another person's stance indirectly, but to really understand, I think it's important to make time to listen and ask follow-up questions."

Mahdon smiled. "I tend to agree."

The group moved out onto the balcony and Maiya looked out at the city. She had previously taken note of how the city appeared to be made of gold but had not noticed the older looking architecture spread throughout. Large stone pillars were common amongst the structures, reminiscent of ancient Greece. Saren moved alongside Maiya and spoke for the first time in Maiya's recollection. Her voice was soft and sweet-sounding.

"Many of the stone buildings date back to the Reedon era. It was a time before the High Council was formed and much smaller city-states ruled across Amertine. Fimbira was one of the most powerful with a great strategic advantage given its location. However, it was not always the capital. When the nations united, Ularia was given that designation."

"Why the change?" Maiya asked.

"It all came down to location in the end. Though the leaders at the time had no expectations of a future insurgency, they could not deny the militaristic advantage. Given its rich history, Ularia remained the cultural hub."

Maiya nodded in acknowledgment. "The mix of time periods is fascinating to see. Maybe you can show me some of the more relevant ones up close sometime?"

"It would be my honor, High Councilor."

Maiya once again felt awkward hearing herself being referred to by a prestigious title. She contemplated suggesting that they call her by name, but quickly dismissed the idea. She liked the way it sounded. This title didn't presume she was anything more than mortal, yet it commanded respect. Maiya turned back from the city and looked to Mahdon.

"What else would you like to go over today?" She asked.

"Your first duties will begin after the swearing in ceremony tomorrow. At that point you will be shown to the primary council chambers. Today we will focus on the procedural aspect of council affairs. You'll be introduced to your security detail and granted full access to this building."

"Security detail? I don't recall seeing one previously."

"It is rare that you will. Though they haven't been needed in some time, we keep them as a precaution. They often scout ahead, create a perimeter around, and search buildings. It's become a relatively simple task with our current technology. Speaking of which…" Mahdon motioned for Naliz to come over. "I believe the council has knowledge of some things – perhaps many things - that I do not. I admit that I am envious of the knowledge to which you will be given access."

"There will, of course, be some preliminary security screenings before any confidential information is released," Naliz said. "Standard procedure."

Maiya wondered what these screenings would entail. It wasn't as though she had anyone she would be able to, or want to, tell. Except, perhaps, Mahdon. While it made sense in some regards, it made less sense when coupled with the knowledge that they were making her a leader within a month of her arrival. It almost gave her the impression that they wanted her as a figurehead more than anything. They were happy to freely hand her the keys to the car so long as she didn't drive on any major highways. Regardless, she saw no reason why she wouldn't pass.

"Will they take long?" She asked.

"No."

"Is this something we can do now?"

"Anxious to get started, I see."

Maiya smirked. "I've never been very good at waiting."

"Very well. I see no reason to delay. Follow me."

Naliz headed back to the gravity tunnel and both Maiya and Jo'dai followed. Mahdon gave a slight wave but stayed behind with the two remaining members. They moved down rapidly, passing the ground floor and going several stories below ground. When they came to a stop, it was on the solid surface of what Maiya realized was the lowest level. A short hallway with three doorways was all that sat on this level. The one straight ahead appeared to be some sort of vault, while the two doors on either side of the hallway were windowless and metal, but otherwise typical.

Jo'dai stepped forward and stopped before the 'vault' door. He reached one hand to the door but did not appear to touch the door and did not speak. In reality, it looked like he had done nothing at all. Despite this, the door split in the middle and each side slid into the adjacent walls as lights switched on beyond it. The room ahead contained a bizarre collection of unfamiliar contraptions and large heavy-duty security enclosures. In the middle of the room there was a slightly raised metal circle protruding from the floor. By Maiya's estimation, it was approximately ten feet in diameter. There was nothing within the perimeter of the circle other than bare floor. Jo'dai stepped into the room and off to one side. Immediately after Maiya entered with Naliz, the large door closed behind them.

"Please," Naliz gestured toward the circle. "Step inside and take a seat."

Maiya took a hesitant gaze around the room before complying.

"We already know everything we can about your external affairs. Research and observance have shown us all of that. What we don't know," he tapped the side of his head, "is what is up here. This will be more of a psychological screening. As head of security, Jo'dai will administer the test."

Maiya nodded and watched as Jo'dai ran a hand over a panel near the wall. The room immediately vanished. She stood alone on a rocky embankment, watching as ocean waves crashed into the rocks far below. Apart from a single strand of hair that caught in the salty breeze, her hair stayed firmly in a donut bun under a combat helmet. She brushed the stray hair away from her face and stepped back from the edge. Though she would never admit it, she was anxious about this mission. She didn't know where her head had been. This was not the time to be daydreaming. The sun was nearly gone on the horizon, and she had to get back to her unit. They were only twenty meters away but not visible from her current position.

"Lieutenant?" A uniformed man stood waiting when she turned around.

"Yes, Sergeant Morrison?"

"All squads are in position and ready to move out, ma'am."

They returned to where the squad leaders waited near some brush on the crest of a rocky hill. Looking out at the terrain before them, a large stretch of tall grass sat between them and a rocky crag. The occasional tree or large patch of brush rose above the grasses to the right. Maiya surveyed the land one last time before relaying orders.

"First squad, overwatch from this bluff. Second squad, move behind first and await orders. Third squad will move through the scrub on the right to the opposite end of the field. Establish an overwatch on that outcrop and signal when in position. Once we get the signal, we'll move up with the first and second squads to give the next orders." She looked to Morrison. "Sergeant, position to the left of first squad. I'll position my machine gun team to the right of first squad."

The troops moved to carry out the orders. Maiya got into position and watched the field while third squad skirted the edge. It wasn't long before a pinpoint of light flashed twice in the distance. Maiya motioned for the squad to move out and started across the field. If their intelligence was correct, the compound shouldn't be far now. As if to confirm her suspicions, a round of gunfire sounded ahead of them. They continued their advance on the compound without casualties, though encountered frequent reminders that the other side was not so fortunate. Absolution for those sins would have to wait.

It wasn't until they began closing in on the main building of the complex that things shifted out of their favor. By the time she saw it, it was too late. She recalled an explosion and fire, but everything beyond that in her memory was blank. When she woke, she was lying in the back of a truck with her hands restrained. Her head was pounding, and her arms were bloodied. Two men sat near her with assault rifles in hand speaking in an unfamiliar language. Everything felt jumbled. She didn't know where she was, why she was here, or how she'd come to be in such a predicament. The truck came to a stop, and the men stood and pulled her roughly from the vehicle. The darkness made it difficult to see, but Maiya could tell they were in a wooded area. They led her into a squat brick building and left her in a small, concrete cell.

Her head eventually cleared, and she pieced together where she was and what happened. Maiya listened for the guards and other prisoners. When she heard none, she surveyed the cell and the surrounding area for any structural defects or tools that may aid in an escape. The cell itself was 6-by-6 feet and windowless. The metal bars that made up one of the walls proved sturdy when she grabbed them. The hallway outside was bare and no immediate exits could be seen from her position. She suspected any escape would prove difficult.

It was at least a day before she saw another person again. At which point, they passed her a meager serving of stale bread and left without saying a word. Time soon became a blur without any reference for day and night. She spent her time pacing the length of the cell or digging at the floor beneath her mattress. Despite her best efforts, this proved fruitless. Never once did she become aware of the presence of other prisoners. With only her thoughts to keep her company, she devised elaborate schemes for an eventual breakout. During this time, she had lost nearly one-quarter of her weight and grown weak, making these plans impractical.

Once every other day or so, the same man she saw the first day would drop off a plate of what typically amounted to table scraps. On one of these days, the man was accompanied by another who appeared to be older and of higher military standing. They unlocked the cell door and the older man stepped inside.

"Your comrades won't be coming for you. My men have made sure of that," he said.

Maiya said nothing and refused to react.

"There's still the matter of the other troops. I need you to tell me what they have planned."

"What makes you think I would know?"

"I know you're an officer. You've had communication with other officers."

"I only know what they tell me. That doesn't include future movements outside of my platoon."

"Do you want to go home? I can make that happen or prevent it from ever happening."

Maiya once again didn't respond. The man stood in silence for a moment before stepping back out and relocking the cell.

"You'll change your mind."

By Maiya's estimate, it was only a couple of hours before anyone returned to see her. This time it was the younger man and two others in similar attire. The familiar guard unlocked the cell and the other two stepped inside. The two of them grabbed her arms while the third produced a switch. With one swift hit to the back of her legs, he brought her to her knees. Her bare feet now exposed, he repeatedly struck the bottom of them until they began to bleed. Not quite satisfied, he instructed the men to remove her shirt and then turned his attention to her back until that too was red and raw.

Through all of this, Maiya grit her teeth and squeezed her eyes shut trying desperately to not give them the satisfaction of her crying out. Once they left, she remained curled up on the floor as tears ran down her face. Over the course of the next three days, the men would return every few hours to deliver more beatings. By this point, she had little fight left in her and struggled to keep conscious. The blood loss was enough to impair her but not to kill her. At last their anger seemed to subside, and Maiya was once again left to ponder her situation in solitude. A week passed. Then two. The older man finally returned, once again accompanied by the guard who always seemed to carry the keys. He walked into the cell and moved to stand in the far corner, leaning against the wall casually. Both he and the guard had guns strapped at their side but neither looked particularly secure.

"Have you considered my offer?" He asked as he flipped open a lighter and lit a cigarette.

"You never made an offer. You only made threats."

He took a drag on his cigarette and exhaled slowly. "Let me be clear: you will denounce the atrocities committed by yourself and your men and you will provide us the intel we need to take back our country."

"Those are some pretty big demands from a guerilla terrorist." Maiya watched the guard from the corner of her eye. He had left the cell door open and seemed to be relaxed and looking away, uninterested in the happenings here. These men were cocky and failed to realize she still had some fight left in her.

"You're arrogant for a woman. Consider yourself lucky that we've treated you like a man. We're not the monsters you make us out to be, but we will be if that's what it takes to break you."

Maiya mustered all the strength she could manage to stand and face him directly. The pain in her feet had improved but was still very much present. She stared him down, ready to get one last word in but knew it was now or never. As he brought the cigarette back to his lips, she bolted to the right, knocking the guard off-balance and pulling the gun from his side. Both men were taken by surprise, obviously less prepared than they should have been. She ran down the hall to the left and rounded the corner as the two men gathered their wits and took off after her. She quickly reached the front exit of the building and pushed it open into the blinding light of day. Four men with assault rifles sat at a wooden table playing a round of cards. They jumped up upon seeing her and called out for her to stop.

Maiya ran into the forest and crouched in the thicker brush before they caught up to her. She watched as three of the men ran past her position. She didn't see the fourth or the two men from inside. She suspected there were many more of them forming a larger perimeter. Time was more critical now than ever before. She scanned her surroundings and listened intently for movement. When she was confident that there were no longer eyes on her, she continued distancing herself from the building. It took several hours of low and slow movement, but she eventually found herself clear of all enemy influence.

She continued moving through the night until she reached what she determined was a safe distance and then settled in for a short rest. As uncomfortable as the outdoors could be for sleep, it was far better than the cell from which she fled. At the sign of first light, Maiya began moving once again. If her estimates were accurate, she would be closing in on her company's location. It wasn't long before she found herself flanked on both sides by friendly forces. Her anxiety finally began to dissipate as they led her back toward the temporary camp, but she remained on high alert.

Unfortunately, that would not be enough this time. Maiya caught a glimpse of something unnatural in the tall grasses to their right, but by then it was already too late. The surrounding friendly troops engaged with the enemy as Maiya dropped to the ground. She felt like she'd been punched in the chest. A strange numbness washed over her followed by a burning pain. It all happened in a matter of seconds. She saw a medic coming to help her, but he seemed so far away. She closed her eyes to try to calm her mind and focus. It was getting harder to breathe. She felt so light-headed...

When Maiya opened her eyes again, her heart was racing and her hands were shaking. She wasn't outside or lying on the ground anymore, and the unusual sensation no longer overwhelmed her. She looked around the room feeling a slew of emotions. Naliz and Jo'dai stepped away from the control panel. They didn't appear to be alarmed or otherwise concerned.

Maiya looked around in horror and confusion. "What the hell just happened?"

"Your screening is complete," Naliz said. "It can be a bit disorienting at first. The simulations are those of your brain's own making. They differ for everyone, so not even I know what you saw. We can measure how you would react when facing various stressors even when you are not consciously aware of how you'd respond."

"Is it normally unpleasant?" She asked.

"I haven't had one in a very long time, but if I remember correctly, yes, very much so."

Maiya was still shaking. "A little warning would have been nice."

"It wouldn't have made a difference. In any case, you passed."

If that's passing, I don't want to know what failing is like. Maiya thought to herself.

Jo'dai motioned for her to remain seated. "Stay there for a moment. We need to collect your biometric data. This will only take a few seconds."

Jo'dai stepped back to the panel and passed his hand over it. Maiya felt a warm, tingling feeling sweep over her body. If not for the residual emotions felt in the simulation, it would have been almost calming.

"You may exit now," Jo'dai said. "I've added you to the system and granted you top security access. The only item left to do is to test it. That will be simple enough. If you're ready, we will head back upstairs."

Maiya stood and followed them out of the room and back down the hallway to the gravity tunnel. They ascended rapidly and came to a stop just shy of the top floor. A hallway curved to the left and right with no visible windows or doors. Upon stepping into the hallway, what had appeared to be a wall vanished to reveal a row of windows into a room filled with holographic images. Some of these were clearly video of the exterior of the building while others appeared to be infrared images of the same locations.

The surveillance room stretched the length of the building and curved around along the outer wall.

"Hello."

Maiya was startled by the sudden appearance of a woman to her left. She didn't think she'd ever get used to their propensity to do that.

"High Councilor, this is Aveen," Jo'dai said. "She will oversee your security detail."

Aveen smiled politely and gave a slight nod. "It will be my pleasure to be of service to you."

Maiya smiled. "It's nice to meet you."

"There are six members on my team, excluding myself. All are assigned to your protection. There are many others assigned to building and chamber security as well." She nodded toward the holographic displays. "As you can see, we have the vicinity well-covered."

"Your setup is rather impressive," Maiya said.

"Thank you. We haven't had a security breach in quite some time. Is there anything I can do to assist you while you're here?"

"An introduction is all for now," Jo'dai said.

"I will see you at the ceremony tomorrow," she said with a nod and then vanished as suddenly as she'd appeared.

Maiya stepped into the gravity tunnel alongside Naliz and Jo'dai.

"I think that will be all for today," Naliz said, "Unless you have further questions?"

Maiya was about to shake her head when she remembered the security access. "What about testing the security?"

"Security is proximity based," Jo'dai explained. "You would not have been able to enter the surveillance floor without proper access."

They returned to the ground floor and stepped into the lobby.

"After tomorrow you are welcome to take up residence here if you wish," Naliz said, "In the interim, I would advise you to return to the manor and familiarize yourself with tomorrow's proceedings. The shuttlecraft outside is yours to use as you wish. I know Mahdon would be more than happy to instruct you on its operation."

"Thank you." Maiya watched them disappear as Aveen had done, and then she stepped outside to wait for Mahdon.

CHAPTER 10

Shortly after Maiya exited the building, Mahdon materialized in front of her next to the shuttlecraft. He always seemed so happy to see her and was especially so this time.

"Seriously," Maiya said, "Someone has got to teach me how to do that."

"I have been told you were granted security clearance."

"It looks that way," Maiya said as they climbed into the transport.

Mahdon navigated the craft over the gorge and down to the nearby estate. They landed in the back just as they had when they first arrived on Amertine.

"How was the screening?" He asked as they disembarked. "I imagine mine was different. I only have access to the most basic of private affairs."

Maiya frowned, thinking back on how powerful the emotions had been. "It was unpleasant. I hope I never have to repeat it. I think... I think I died."

Mahdon stopped in his tracks and turned to look at her. "What?"

"I don't think there's any other way to describe it."

Mahdon looked confused and a little concerned. "What exactly did they do?"

"I'm not entirely sure. I sat where I was told, and then I suddenly wasn't me anymore. I mean, I was me, but not who I am now. It was like I existed in a completely different reality, unaware that I was ever part of this one. Naliz said it tested my subconscious response to various stressors."

Mahdon was clearly uncomfortable with the prospect. "I do not believe I am familiar with that technology. It sounds invasive."

"What was yours like?"

Mahdon shrugged. "I think I was asked a dozen questions. Perhaps fewer."

"Oh, come on!" Maiya grumbled. "This better be worth it. Do you mind grabbing the books and meeting me in the study?"

"Not at all."

Mahdon stepped back to the shuttle to retrieve the books while Maiya went inside and down to the bar in the wine cellar. She grabbed a bottle of gin and a bucket of ice. As she recalled, there were already several glass tumblers available on a side table in the study. She returned upstairs and found Mahdon already waiting for her. She sat down and poured herself a glass of gin on the rocks.

"Tomorrow," Maiya said. "What have I done to deserve this role?"

"Politics are not always about what you've already done. This is more about what you can do if given the proper authority. Think of it as an opportunity to make an impact on the future."

Maiya took a sip of her drink. "How do you fix apathy?"

Mahdon said nothing in response. He shook his head and shrugged.

"Will I see you much after today?" Maiya asked.

"That depends," Mahdon said.

Maiya took another sip of her drink and leaned forward in her seat. "On what?"

"Officially there are no longer any council advisors. My clearance was never revoked, but if you choose to enforce Brandon's decision, that would be your right. Of course, if you wish to reinstate me, that is also an option."

Maiya laughed. "Well, duh. I am definitely not going along with his petty power tactics."

"In that case," he said, "I will see you at all open council meetings. I am not permitted in the closed-door sessions except under special circumstances."

"Do you know the reason for that?"

"It is my understanding that those are the meetings where the primary discussion and decision-making takes place. If there are other undertakings at that time, I am not privy to them. I am a representative with no formal vote."

"I guess that makes sense. I'm looking forward to continuing to work with you, however that may be."

Mahdon smiled. "If our time together is any indication of future interactions, it will be quite the adventure."

"I hope so," she finished her drink and set the glass aside. "If it's okay with you, I'd like to go to bed now. Today was far more draining than I expected it to be."

They both stood and walked down the hallway to her room, stopping before the door.

"I wish you a restful night. I will return in the morning."

"Thanks," Maiya said, "Have a good night, Mahdon."

Morning came fast and all of Maiya's anxiety came rushing back. Every little detail was beginning to cause her stress: what to wear, what to say, and everything that could go wrong. Unlike her introduction to Amertine, she wasn't provided specific attire for the event. The one thing she was sure of was that Mahdon would do his best to help her get ready and keep her informed. She put on a slimming, yet modest pant suit and hoped it would be acceptable. As promised, Mahdon was waiting on the main floor to meet her.

"I wasn't sure what I should wear," Maiya said.

"That will be appropriate," he said and then smiled, "You look nice. Are you ready to depart?"

She nodded. It only took a few minutes to fly across to the headquarters where they met up with the council members. She could already tell that a large crowd was gathering at the base of the steps in front of the building. She wondered how many more she couldn't see.

"The perimeter of the building has been secured," Jo'dai informed her.

"The swearing-in ceremony will be relatively quick," Saren said as the group walked into the building. "You will take an oath before you assume the full power of the office. This is typically administered by the current individual holding that position. After the oath has been completed, there will be a symbolic transfer of power."

"Will I need to give a speech?" Maiya asked.

"It is not required, but some have chosen to do so in the past."

"Would it be better if I do?"

"Only if you feel there is something that needs to be said."

Maiya couldn't think of a single thing to say that wouldn't feel awkward or sound trite. She already felt like she was going into this unprepared. She didn't need to stress herself out over a last-minute task. They walked through to the front entry and paused before the large, windowless doors. Saren stepped off to the side with Maiya.

"We will go out first and Mahdon will direct you when it's time for you to join us. You should proceed down the middle of the path and come to a stop at the top of the stairs."

Maiya stayed to the side while Mahdon opened the door and the four members walked outside. The response from the crowd was immediate as the sound of clapping and cheers filled the air. Maiya suddenly felt overwhelmed by her nerves. She leaned against the wall to try to steady her breathing.

"Are you unwell?" Mahdon asked.

"I think I'll be fine. It's just nerves. Being in the spotlight isn't exactly easy for me."

"Did you feel similarly when you were first introduced?"

Maiya nodded. "Very much so."

"Was there something specific that helped last time?"

"I don't know."

"May I?" Mahdon held out his hands, palms up.

Maiya stood up straight and placed her hands on his. They now stood on a beach as the water rushed to shore and back again. A wave of tranquility washed over her, quickly replacing her anxiety. The imagery faded away, but the calmness did not. She looked in Mahdon's eyes and smiled.

"I believe they are ready for you," he said.

Maiya removed her hands from his and he opened the door for her. Mahdon stopped just outside the door while she continued forward. Saren and Naliz stood to her right, and Tanin and Jo'dai stood to her left. Directly ahead stood Brandon. Saren had made reference to the current holder of the office, but Maiya was still surprised to see him. She suspected he was only doing this for show to avoid looking bitter and disrespectful. He smiled and greeted her with a slight bow of the head, and she forced herself to do the same. She walked forward until they were facing each other at the top of the stairs with the crowd to her left.

"Do you present yourself before the council and your fellow citizens prepared to take on the role of High Councilor and all the obligations that go along with it?" Brandon asked.

"Yes."

"Will you execute the will of the people to the best of your ability even when it conflicts with your own?"

"Yes," Maiya said. She knew with confidence that she would be better at that than Brandon had been.

"Will you strive to preserve and protect our culture and history, now and in the future?"

"Yes."

"If you are sincere in your intentions, hold out your hand and recite the oath after me."

Maiya held out her hand as Brandon removed a pin from where one might expect a lapel pin to be worn. As ornate as it was, Maiya was surprised she'd never noticed it before. The design was that of a lily surrounded by flames. A bird with outstretched wings rose above the lily. He placed it in her hand and straightened his clothes.

"I solemnly swear, on this day and each day henceforth," Brandon said, pausing after each line so Maiya could repeat, "That I will keep the promises asked of me today, and I will faithfully execute all duties that the position allots."

Brandon took the pin from her hand and fastened it on the left lapel of her suit jacket. "In taking the oath and wearing this as a symbol of your loyalty and dedication, you are now entrusted with the office of High Councilor. I hereby relinquish any and all claims I previously held."

Music began to play as the crowd applauded and each of the council members came forward to congratulate her. Brandon even retained his smile while he did the same. Maiya waved to the crowd and followed the rest of the council members back inside as directed. She hadn't been sure what to expect and was relieved by how quick and simple it had been. It was no wonder Mahdon never prepped her for this.

"We'll go directly to the council chambers," Naliz said.

All but Brandon exited out the back and boarded a shuttlecraft to depart. The craft descended into the gorge and flew along the falls until the entrance of a cave came into view on the opposing wall. They landed just outside the mouth of the cave and stepped out into the waterfall mist. Maiya looked up but couldn't see the city from here. With the surrounding mist, she wondered if they were even visible from above. She turned back to the group and they followed a path into the cave until it opened into a large cavern. A single set of double doors could be seen in the back. The room looked very similar to the one she had been in outside of Ularia, though it lacked the hallways and extra rooms that were part of the older location.

"I know it doesn't look like much, but it has served us well over the years," Naliz said, "Those without clearance can neither see nor enter where we did. Temporary access may be granted as required, but those situations are rare."

Maiya walked across the room to where the middle platform stood. She found it rather amusing that they'd been placing her on a figurative pedestal for weeks and now she would be expected to stand on a literal one. She stepped onto it and looked down at the others. She found it strangely satisfying to stand above the rest. She stepped down and followed Naliz to the set of doors.

"This is where we will discuss all matters of the highest importance," he said as he opened the doors and walked into a room which looked like nothing more than a standard conference room.

"If I may ask," Maiya said, "what's the point of standing in a circle out here?"

"In one sense, it's symbolic," Naliz explained. "It symbolizes a higher level of knowledge and authority. It also makes it easier for all council members to readily interact with visiting advisors."

Maiya didn't see why this couldn't be accomplished at the table but saw no point in pursuing the question further. Saren and Tanin walked past her and took seats in the private meeting hall.

"There are important matters to discuss," Jo'dai said as he followed them into the room.

Mahdon looked at Maiya and spoke for the first time since they'd arrived. "If I am not needed, I will take my leave."

Maiya nodded. "You may go."

She had spent nearly every waking minute with Mahdon since leaving Earth and felt somewhat anxious when he disappeared and left her alone with the others. She took a seat at the head of the table and waited for Naliz to close the doors and join them. Once everyone was seated, they looked to Maiya. She suddenly felt very awkward for not knowing the proper procedure for calling the meeting to order. She made a mental note to review the books Mahdon had given to her. She hoped that no one would judge her too harshly for winging it this one time.

"Jo'dai," she said, "please share with the council what it is you'd like to discuss."

"I have received word from some of the outlying cities," he said, "and it seems that while the disease has been cured in all regions within several hundred miles, it has not been eradicated."

Maiya tried not to let the fear show on her face. She had yet to fully understand her own abilities. What if she was unable to perform such a miracle again? She knew well that time was limited, and every second led the afflicted closer to death. To her relief, no one in the room appeared to share her concerns.

"Fortunately," Jo'dai continued, "those who have been previously healed no longer seem to be susceptible to infection."

"That is a relief," Naliz said with a sad smile.

"How many people have been reported ill?" Maiya asked.

"I have only been made aware of a few hundred, but they are scattered throughout the cities. It could be thousands."

Maiya nodded somberly. "Jo'dai, can you provide me a map showing all known centers of infection? I will need to visit as many as possible until it's gone for good."

"Of course," he said as he swiped his hand over a small set of controls on the table before him. Maiya hadn't taken notice of them previously, but now she saw that each seat had its own panel.

As she had seen before, a holographic representation of the planet began rotating over the table. A green pinpoint of light denoted their location, and many small red dots began to pop up around the continent. Even as they watched, new points of light would flicker into existence. She was thankful that, while they continued to appear, they were not doing so rapidly.

Jo'dai manipulated the hologram as he spoke. "The map is current. Security units stationed all over Amertine continuously update it as they become aware of existing cases. We should start in the north and work our way around. It will not be a quick or easy task."

Maiya sighed. She knew the mass healing in Ularia had been too good to be true. She reminded herself that it had still been effective, just not to the extent they had all hoped. If she had to travel to every location, she feared it would take her a lifetime. If she was lucky, the next visit she made would have similar, if not better, results than the last one.

"Has there been an increase in cases? Or were these existing but not yet reported?"

"Only a few cases are known to have occurred over the past few days. As most are aware, they will not become ill if they stay in form. To my knowledge, the disease has not spread any more quickly than usual."

Maiya nodded in acknowledgment. "That's good news, at least. Can you make this map accessible when we're away from here?"

"It already is," Jo'dai said and then went on to explain the many functions of the pin she now wore. As it turned out, the so-called "symbol" of power was rather powerful itself. Not only was it a communicator, it also had all the same capabilities as the meeting room computers. Once he completed going over the functionality, he concluded by offering his assistance should she decide she needed it after they adjourned.

"I will be joining you when visiting the more remote villages," Saren said. "It will be beneficial to have a travel companion who is familiar with the local language and customs. Those who reside further from the capital are unfamiliar with your native tongue. There are some who are still unaware of your presence here."

Maiya was surprised to hear this, but after considering it for a moment, she concluded that it would be ridiculous to assume an entire planet would be fixated on a single prophecy. Narcissistic, even. She wondered if her time spent with Saren would be anywhere near as pleasant as her time spent with Mahdon. Aside from Mahdon and Naliz, these people were all strangers to her. She knew their names and much of their personal history, but this wasn't the same as knowing them personally.

"Understandable," Maiya said at last. "Is there anything else we need to discuss today?"

"There is one thing," Naliz said hesitantly. "Brandon has expressed interest in becoming an advisor. He cannot do that without your vote."

Maiya stifled a laugh. "He didn't seem too keen on the idea when I suggested it."

"He's a stubborn man, but he can be reasoned with when given the opportunity."

Maiya seriously doubted Brandon's capacity for reason. In every unpleasant encounter she'd had with him, he allowed his ego to get in the way of better judgment. The thought put a bad taste in her mouth, but she couldn't afford to make any enemies at this time. She had yet to prove her worth as a leader. If she could learn to rein him in, perhaps he could provide valuable insight.

"I'll consider it. I'm not deciding that today."

Maiya was returned to the manor with the intention to pack in preparation for an early departure the next day. She would be accompanied by Saren and her personal security team. The others would stay behind to monitor the overall situation and provide aid as needed. For now, she was left to her own devices.

Determining that she would be of little use if she didn't understand how to use her abilities, she decided that there must be something in the manor that could help her with this. She first went to the gallery in the hopes that an artifact there might trigger a memory, but she was met with disappointment. Though she did gain some memories, none of them were of consequence. She then recalled how Mahdon had described the books in the study as unverified folklore and thought that, perhaps, these might uncover some deeply buried knowledge. The task before her would prove daunting.

Some of the tomes had names on the spine but many were untitled and identical to the rest. She picked a book at random and began flipping through the pages. She checked another and then another. All were in Pandornu. Some words were familiar as though she'd learned them before, but most were not. She dropped down into a chair with a sigh. She thought about Mahdon and how she wished he was here to translate. Though he was always happy to help, she worried that she relied too heavily on him. She struggled to think of an alternate option outside of asking one of the council members to give her lessons on the language. Finding this option utterly unappealing, she finally relented and used the pin to contact Mahdon.

"Hi."

Maiya turned to see him standing in the doorway. She couldn't help but smile when she saw him. He smiled in return, but she thought he looked a little sad in the eyes.

"Shall we begin?" he asked. She nodded, and he sat down across from her. "I believe this will be relatively easy for you to learn. It does not have the same tonal complications or complex rules that many of Earth's languages possess. However…"

"What?"

"I've spoken with Naliz," he said.

"And?" Maiya regarded him intently. She wasn't sure where he was going with this.

"While it is possible to study remotely, it is not always ideal. Naliz has informed me that you will be traveling for some time. It may be more beneficial for you to study with Saren while you are away."

"Oh. Would you rather I wait until I meet up with her then?" Maiya hoped she didn't sound as disappointed as she felt. She didn't know what she was expecting, but it wasn't that.

"Not at all. I have always enjoyed our lessons. I do not want to be responsible for slowing your learning."

"Why don't you come with?"

"You haven't grown tired of my constant company? I thought you might prefer some time to become acquainted with the other council members."

"I wouldn't say I'd prefer it. That's not to say I don't want to get to know them." She sighed and opted to be completely honest. "I know I ask a lot of you, but it's a lot of change all at once. I'd feel more comfortable if you came along. That said, please don't feel pressured to join if you'd rather not."

He smiled. "I would be honored to accompany you once again. Let us begin your first lesson."

Mahdon began by presenting her with the alphabet and teaching the sounds for each letter. They spent the next several hours reviewing these basics and going over some introductory words and phrases. Maiya found the language fairly easy to grasp and proved to be a quick study. She was confident that with daily practice she would be able to hold simple conversations in no time. As they wrapped up the lesson, Maiya felt re-energized and hoped Mahdon would be up for spending more of the evening together. The way she saw it, this could be the last carefree day for a while.

She opened her mouth to make yet another request of him, but he beat her to it. "There is a game that I've always enjoyed playing. Would you like to play it with me?"

"What sort of game?"

Mahdon thought for a moment on how to best describe it. "It is a combination of a board game and a puzzle."

"Sure, I'll give it a try. Hopefully I won't embarrass myself too terribly."

"It is a rather simple game," Mahdon said as he made his way to the desk and pulled out a stone slab and a small pouch. "It is called 'Tane Kaut.' Directly translated it means 'Refractive Illumination.'"

He set both items on the table in front of Maiya, removed a small token from the bag, and placed it in an indent in the middle of the slab. What had at first appeared to be a plain stone board now showed a large, holographic, multistory maze. Four little lights glowed in the bottom corners of the maze: one red, one green, one blue, and one purple. On the top level there was a miniature floating sphere.

"The objective is to reflect your beam of light to the orb before all other players."

He poured out the contents of the bag to reveal a large number of mirror-like objects of varying shapes. He went on to explain gameplay. Each time the game was played, the maze was randomly generated to avoid memorizing and regularly using the same route. This was not enough to convince Maiya that she stood a chance against him.

They took turns placing or moving pieces to redirect their beams of light from the bottom of the maze to the top. As she suspected, Mahdon won easily. The second time around, she came closer to the goal, but lost once again. As she had always liked a good challenge, this only increased her determination to win. Mahdon waited patiently with a wry grin while she contemplated her next move in game three. She glanced up at him and narrowed her eyes.

"I think you're enjoying this a little too much. Just you wait…"

"Isn't that what I am already doing?"

She glared at him, and he smiled sweetly back at her. She finally placed her piece and leaned back with a satisfied smirk. When Mahdon looked back at the puzzle, his smile faded.

"You blocked my path."

She shot him an evil grin. "Not so cocky now, are we?"

"By the time I complete an alternate route, you will already have made it to the goal. Well played."

"Thanks. I had fun. We should do it again sometime."

"That would be nice. I'll bring it along if you would like."

Mahdon was happy to see Maiya so relaxed and carefree. He knew she'd been particularly stressed lately with all that had happened in such a short time. The change in her demeanor was welcome. He intended to continue to be there for her until she no longer asked it of him. It was a commitment that he saw no difficulty in keeping.

Having taken up residence at the council headquarters in Fimbira, he returned to the manor with Saren the next day. Upon meeting up with Maiya, he was pleased to see that she was still in high spirits. She greeted them warmly as she stepped into the transport. This would be the furthest they traveled on the planet in terms of both time and distance. They would begin at the most remote locations and then make their way back toward the capital over the coming weeks.

Maiya hoped that this initial flight would give her enough time to tap into what she'd felt the times she'd previously felt the magic in her veins. It had been an energy like none other, and yet, had felt so natural. In-between language practice and discussion topics, she focused her attention on attempts to channel this into moving small toiletries she'd carried along. It seemed the harder she tried, the lesser the results. Concentration was certainly required but not in the way that she thought. The entire practice was tied more to emotion than to thought. It was almost instinctual in some ways.

She found it difficult to conceal her delight when floating a brush from one hand to the other began to become effortless. At this point in time, they were traveling over an especially barren landscape, and Mahdon looked over at her with a bemused look when she let out a brief cry of excitement. Catching his stare, her face flushed with embarrassment.

"I was just practicing," she said.

"I take it that it's going well?"

"So far. How much longer until we arrive?"

"Three or four more of your hours. We'll be stopping briefly in a few minutes. There's a beautiful overlook up ahead."

They landed on a red rocky plateau that overlooked miles of grassland and rock formations. The only sound that could be heard here was that of the wind blowing through the grass. Maiya sat on the edge and looked out in silence until Mahdon and Saren joined her. She had yet to see the security detail, but Saren assured her that they were within the vicinity.

"Most of the north is prairies like this," Mahdon said. "I don't come this way often, but if you like lightning storms, you will see many around here. The town we're heading to now is along the Maerez River."

"We need to go."

The voice came tersely from behind them. All three turned to see Aveen with a neutral expression on her face.

"Is something wrong?" Maiya asked.

"The situation is being handled."

Maiya and Mahdon exchanged confused looks but stood and headed back to the ship with Saren. None of them said a word as they lifted off. Maiya looked out as they flew away, but by then Aveen had already vanished. Once the plateau had faded out of sight, Maiya broke the silence.

"What was that about?"

"There are rumors of an unstable woman in these parts," Saren said. "It is my suspicion that they spotted her. We would not want to risk putting you in danger."

"What makes her so dangerous?"

"She holds radical ideologies."

Maiya wasn't satisfied with this answer. She wasn't sure if this meant different beliefs from the norm or if it was specifically those against her. She also found it disconcerting that a warning hadn't been given prior to their departure. She shot Mahdon a look and the one he gave in return indicated that this was the first he was hearing of this.

"What has she done that makes her such a threat? And why wasn't this mentioned before?" Maiya asked.

"I have not been provided the details, High Councilor," Saren said.

Maiya sighed. "Of course not. I suppose I'll have to discuss this with Jo'dai."

CHAPTER 11

No one said much for the remainder of the journey. Mahdon could sense that Maiya was annoyed, and Saren was her usual quiet self. He thought it best to focus on their arrival and leave the subject untouched until another time. He did, however, share in Maiya's frustration. The more time that passed, the more secrets the council kept. The populace had become complacent, completely unaware of the power grab that had taken place. The political environment had grown increasingly worrisome, but Mahdon had faith that all of that was about to change.

Saren broke the silence as they landed next to a modest structure. "We've arrived."

Maiya brushed her hair away from her face and picked up her bag. She gave Mahdon an encouraging smile. Now was not the time to dwell on things that couldn't be readily fixed. She needed her focus and her energy to be on their current mission. She exited the shuttle and stopped to take in her new surroundings. The town they were in now looked nothing like the two she'd visited previously. There didn't appear to be any discernible town center and a single line of buildings lined each side of the river. Larger plants flourished on the river banks, but the region was otherwise grassland.

It was early evening and several residents had come outside to see what was going on. A few eyed them suspiciously from a distance, unsure what to make of their unusual appearance. Mahdon said something in the native tongue while Saren shifted form, and the tension visibly lessened. Two of them approached Saren, frantically leading her away as they spoke in heavily accented Pandornu.

Mahdon glanced over at Maiya. "We should follow them."

They trailed behind Saren, moving at a more casual pace as the remaining residents followed them with their eyes. Maiya looked around at all the staring faces.

"Do they know why we're here?"

"Yes," he hesitated and gave an indecisive shake of the head. "And no."

"What do you mean?"

"They know that we came to help, but they don't know who – or *what* – you are."

Maiya stopped walking and Mahdon followed suit. "How is that possible? You obviously have a communication network around the planet. If they accepted this so-called 'gift' then it stands to reason that they would be similarly technologically advanced. If not, after thousands of years, that's kind of depressing."

"You are correct that they are equally advanced. All citizens have access to the same technology. Most do not choose to use it to gain knowledge or stay informed."

"I guess our people aren't so different after all. I'm not gonna lie… I think that's a bit disappointing."

Mahdon raised an eyebrow. "You would prefer we differ greatly?"

"I'm learning more every day that I have a lot of misconceived notions about what the future could look like. That's all. It's sad to think that some things may never change."

"They will," he said confidently.

The exterior of the building they entered was drab, but the interior was modern and brightly colored. The setup was open-concept like that of Mahdon's in Ularia, but there were two sets of stairs along the back wall that led up to separate bedrooms. A large holographic video – that Maiya would later learn was essentially a television – played in the middle of the room. They went up the left set of stairs and saw an Amerti man unconscious on the bed. Saren spoke and gestured toward Maiya.

Maiya sat on the edge of the bed and looked at Saren. "May I have a moment alone with him?"

She nodded and relayed the message. Once Maiya was alone with him, she closed her eyes and thought back on that day when she saw Mahdon in the same state. The fear, the sadness, the anger, and the intense need to save him had overwhelmed her. It all came rushing back and she allowed herself to succumb to the flood of emotions. It was from this that she drew the energy to revive the man. She felt the warmth envelope her as it emanated from her core as it had before.

The result was almost instantaneous. The man opened his eyes, and when he saw Maiya, he sat up abruptly and began speaking rapidly. Hearing the commotion, the others quickly re-entered the room. Maiya and Mahdon exchanged smiles as the man's family ran to his side, and the three shared in a joyful reunion. It had been so easy and yet, so rewarding. Maiya had never felt so sure of herself. What followed was a toned-down celebration from that in Ularia. Though their city had no children to speak of, the revelry was playfully childlike in many ways. They played in the river and sang cheerful songs from higher branches of the trees that ran along it. Maiya watched others dance while she enjoyed a glass of sweet wine from a bottle she'd brought along. Even Saren took part in the festivities, laughing and regaling Maiya with tales of her own travels. This was a side of her that Maiya hadn't yet seen, and she suspected the drink might have had something to do with it.

They stayed through the night and reviewed the updated map the next day. Much to their relief, the spell had a similar radius, so the healing effect was widespread. Based on their current estimates, they would be able to complete the planned route in roughly a year. The three soon fell into a comfortable routine, filling their days with travel or visits to new communities and their nights with games and language study. Tane Kaut became a regular fixture in the evening with all three having their personal winning streaks. They spoke primarily in Pandornu during these game sessions to give Maiya practice without forcing her into more serious discussions. As the days turned into weeks, Maiya gained noticeable proficiency in the language and demonstrated this in her interactions with the locals.

During this time, Saren had opened up significantly. Maiya soon became aware of Saren's unique sense of humor, and the two came to appreciate one another's company. Saren inquired more about Maiya's life before and shared details of hers as well. As it so happened, Saren was not only well-versed in culture but in technology as well. While most Amerti were educated in the use of advanced technology, she understood the intricacies and was knowledgeable in much more than functionality. This led to some interesting conversations regarding the potential for future advancements. Though Maiya often felt out of her depth, Mahdon assured her that he was in the same boat.

On the rare occasion, they would have a day with little to no obligations, and Mahdon and Maiya often spent this free time together. Mahdon had never been to many of the cities where they stayed, so this gave them ample opportunity to explore. When Saren wasn't furthering her anthropological knowledge, she would join them as well. Most intriguing to them was how commonplace the consumption of food was in the region they now visited. While those in the south had quit almost entirely due to the work involved in collection and preparation, people in the north saw the lack of a permanent form as an opportunity to overindulge. As it was no longer a necessity, much of what they chose to produce provided little to no nutritional value. This was both a blessing and a curse, as it gave Maiya the chance to try a much wider variety of treats than she already had, but it was largely empty calories. She tried her best to try it all in moderation. Mahdon, on the other hand, was taking full advantage of his limitless metabolism.

"Phenomenal!" Mahdon took another bite of a mini cake as he plopped down on the ground next to Maiya.

She was sitting alongside a lake and had been creating little figures out of water and making them dance across the surface. Four months had passed with them on the road, and her abilities had grown considerably. She stopped the spell and eyed Mahdon enviously.

"When we first met, you showed no interest in eating and now I swear it's your favorite pastime. Is it even possible for you to gain weight?"

He paused a moment to think about it before eating the final bite of cake. "I do not believe so. If you prefer, I can make it appear as though I have."

She sighed. "No, I'm just jealous that I have to actually watch what I eat. The day I figure out how to do your little shape-changing trick, watch out world."

"Have you finished practicing for today?"

"For now, anyway. Why?"

He smiled and stood up. "I have a surprise for you."

"Oh?"

She stood and followed him away from the lake. They boarded the shuttlecraft that sat outside their temporary residence, and Mahdon flew it into the upper atmosphere. Maiya hadn't been up this high since they first arrived, so it struck her as odd. When they docked on the ship above the planet, she gave Mahdon a confused look. Now familiar with the look, he gave her a reassuring smile.

"Do you remember your assigned quarters?"

"Yes. Are we going somewhere?"

"On the ship, yes, but nowhere else."

They walked through the ship until they reached her old quarters. He stepped aside to allow her to open the door. Her heart skipped a beat and her eyes lit up when she entered the room. She immediately ran to the bed and laughed out of sheer surprise. Her two furry companions looked up at her, content as ever. They had obviously made themselves at home.

"MeowMeows! Kevin!"

Mahdon gave her a quizzical look. "I am by no means an expert on animal names, but those strike me as peculiar. Isn't Kevin a human name?"

"Yep."

"May I ask why you chose the name?"

Maiya shrugged. "He looked like a Kevin."

Mahdon wasn't sure what she meant by that. He didn't know what a 'Kevin' looked like. Maiya stood to give him a big hug and then returned to the cats. She picked up the one she'd called 'MeowMeows' and walked over to him with a huge smile. She handed him the cat and then retrieved the other one.

"When did you send for them? We've been together almost constantly."

"During your first council meeting. I figured that if you were going to stay, you might miss them."

She smiled again. "Thank you. Do you think Daera would mind watching them a bit longer? I don't think it would be fair to them to change locations every day."

"I imagine she wouldn't mind at all."

The cats had never been very big fans of strangers and often hid or watched anxiously when they were near. However, that was not the case with Mahdon or Daera. Even on the day she met them, the cats had given no indication that anything was out of the ordinary. She wondered if they gave off a calming sense to animals in general or if the cats simply viewed

130

them differently from humans. Either way, she was glad that they seemed to like Mahdon. From that point forward, they would spend a little time every day or so to visit and play with the cats.

This presented the perfect opportunity for Mahdon to give Maiya flying lessons that didn't interfere with their regular transit. Her first day at the helm, she hadn't been expecting to fly. She'd made an off-handed comment about how normal it had become to fly so high above the planet, and he suggested they make it "more interesting." Before she knew it, he was directing her on a set of controls that had always appeared non-existent from her perspective in the passenger seat. He had certainly achieved the goal of making things more interesting. She imagined he must be the most patient driving instructor ever with the way she initially accelerated far too rapidly. Even when she thought her own maneuvering was terrifying, he'd laugh as though they were on a carnival ride. In time these flight maneuvers became intentional as she gained skill and could control the craft without thinking about every action she made. Though she never felt the need to take advantage of it, she was happy for the new freedom this afforded her.

Maiya had settled into her new role with ease and the feelings of doubt she once felt now seemed so foreign to her. The need for escape was no longer a persistent cry in the back of her mind. She couldn't imagine her life being any other way. They'd already completed over half of the planned route, and there had been no resurgence of the disease in any of their prior locations. This boosted her confidence further which, in turn, increased her spell efficiency. She was learning new magic and techniques every day and, in some cases, calling on knowledge from long-lost memories.

The more she used it, the easier it became for her to identify different classes of magic and refine her skill in each. She could even sense the presence of others and was rarely caught off guard. Whenever one of them changed form, it was as if the magic filled the air around them. Despite all of this, the art of shapeshifting eluded her. It seemed to be a more unique form of magic that she had yet to see in any of the spells she mastered. She was attempting to break into this new class of magic when Saren approached her in the field. Maiya turned her focus to Saren with a smile and a wave.

"Good afternoon, High Councilor."

Maiya laughed at the formality. No matter how many times she said the title wasn't necessary, others continued to use it. She recognized, at least in part, that Saren now said it half-jokingly because she knew it made Maiya smile and shake her head.

"Hi. What's up?"

"Has Mahdon told you anything about the Alarien Festival?"

"It doesn't sound familiar. What is it?"

"I'm surprised he hasn't mentioned it. It's one of our most important holidays. It's an annual, three-day festival to celebrate the cleansing and renewal of the soul. Many refer to it as the 'fire festival' for good reason. Fire cleanses all and allows for transformation. I thought you might like to participate in one of our largest cultural events."

Maiya's face lit up. "I'd love to. When is it?"

"It begins tomorrow. The city we will be visiting continues to take part in all traditional aspects of the holiday. I would be happy to explain the significance of each event when we arrive. I think you will enjoy it very much."

"Thanks. I'll look forward to it."

The two returned to their local residence and met up with Mahdon. Much to their mutual surprise, he had been collecting supplies for the following day. Saren had believed he'd forgotten all about the holiday when, in fact, he had been making preparations in the hopes of surprising Maiya. There were several recipes commonly prepared for the holiday, so the counter was covered in a wide range of ingredients that he'd spent the day gathering. He hadn't cooked in ages, making the task before him a large undertaking. He smiled sheepishly when he noticed their arrival.

"I apologize in advance if the food doesn't turn out."

Maiya smiled. "Would you like some help?"

"Yes, thank you. That may be wise if I want any of this to be edible."

Maiya looked over the selection of fruits, vegetables, and other items on the counter. She wondered where he found it all considering stores weren't a thing that seemed to exist on this planet. Mahdon divided the ingredients up by recipe and stepped back to run each recipe through his head to confirm he had everything they needed. Maiya began prepping produce as instructed while Mahdon went through the kitchen and collected all the tools necessary for making six types of finger foods. Unlike most meals that could be completed in a matter of minutes using preset recipes via the kitchen controls, these traditional food items required more finesse in the cooking process.

Several hours and many taste-tests later, the kitchen was a mess, but they now had three savory and three sweet options to choose from for the holiday the next day. All of the foods played on the fire theme in one way or another. One of the sweeter treats was made up of bits of fresh fruit and candied nuts inside of red and orange edible flowers. Maiya was most proud of how these ones turned out and had eaten quite a few of them already.

Tired and excited about the celebration to come, Maiya headed to bed while the other two got the kitchen back in order. She was awakened by Saren before the break of dawn and groggily questioned if something had happened. Saren shook her head.

"Please accept my apologies for waking you, High Councilor. The sun is preparing to rise; it's tradition to be outside to greet it on the first day of the festival. I should have mentioned this yesterday."

"That would have been nice," Maiya grumbled. "Give me a second to get dressed and I'll meet you downstairs."

Mahdon was chipper as ever when Maiya stumbled down the stairs half awake. She was not a morning person, especially when the sun had yet to rise. The fact that the other two had no need for sleep made her even grouchier. She gave a half wave of acknowledgment but said nothing. The air outside was already warm, and it was evident it would be a hot day. This only strengthened Maiya's desire to go back to bed, but the walk to the edge of town and the sight of the gathered crowd perked her up a bit. It looked as though the entire town had come out to see the sunrise. The general energy was overwhelmingly positive and boosted her mood considerably.

As the sun rose above the horizon, she felt it had been worth the early morning. The vibrant colors that crossed the sky and reflected across the dew speckled field made the day feel welcoming. Once the sun was fully risen, the crowd dispersed, and they headed directly back to load the shuttle with the previous night's cooking and head to the larger city. The flight only took about an hour, but the celebration was already well underway. As Saren explained, the festivities began immediately after sunrise. The main plaza and many of the surrounding streets were abuzz with citizens singing, dancing, sampling foods, and participating in other activities.

One of the adjacent roads had been converted into an obstacle course that people raced through, two at a time, each protecting their own little flame. The task was a challenge meant to reflect the difficulties of keeping the flames of faith, passion, and ambition alive throughout life's struggles.

Another street was dedicated to demonstrating courage in the face of adversity. There were fires to jump over and tasks to complete while surrounded by it. Maiya wondered if any of this held any real meaning anymore now that their lives no longer shared the difficulties humanity still faced. It seemed far more playful to her than it would be if courage was actually needed. Nonetheless, it was amusing to watch, and she contemplated attempting the obstacle course.

Saren led them to the center of the main plaza where a large fire burned. Throughout the festival, it would be tended to burn nonstop. There were tables covered with pieces of papery bark nearby that people would write their regrets or negative thoughts on in order to toss them into the fire and burn them away. Maiya found the idea pleasing and chose to participate by burning a laundry list of her own negative ruminations. She found it strangely satisfying, like lifting a weight from her shoulders that she didn't even know she'd been carrying.

Along the perimeter of the plaza, individuals lit candles for various reasons. Saren indicated that this could be done for a prayer, as a symbol of hope for the future, or for any number of reasons if it was healing for the soul. Maiya grabbed a candle of her own and lit it with a flick of the wrist. A few onlookers stared at her wide-eyed, to which she responded with a smile as though it was the most normal thing in the world. These people, in turn, pointed her out to others.

Mahdon leaned in to whisper in her ear. "You seem to be drawing quite a bit of attention to yourself. I thought that you didn't care for that."

Maiya grinned. "That was before I knew what the hell I was doing. Now it's fun to see the looks on their faces. If it bothers you, I can stop."

He laughed and made a slight sweeping gesture with his hand. "By all means, enjoy it while you can."

They spent the better part of the day sampling foods and sharing those that they'd made. They watched others compete and indulged in a locally brewed beverage which was the closest thing to beer Maiya had tasted to date. Saren referred to it as 'alusha.'

"It's an extremely potent beverage brewed once a year specifically for this event," she explained. "Be careful that you don't drink too much of it. We can free ourselves from the intoxicating effects before it gets too extreme. Unfortunately, you cannot, and I assure you that isn't a pain you want to be feeling."

Maiya could see how it would be easy to overindulge. The flavor was misleading about the alcohol content, as any hints of it were barely noticeable. She limited herself to one glass and left the rest of the drinking to Saren, who delighted in trying every variety available. During their travels together, Maiya had learned that in all their years working with Brandon, Saren and the other council members had rarely taken on any physical form for more than a few minutes at a time. Brandon insisted that doing so would threaten logical decision making by bringing too many emotions into the equation. Saren now took full advantage to make up for all the years without.

They stayed well into the night until Maiya determined she needed to get some sleep before another day of celebration. The party had only grown livelier as the night grew later, and once Maiya was asleep, Saren and Mahdon returned to it. When she woke before dawn, they still had not returned. Feeling unusually wide awake and her mind suddenly racing, she decided to leave a note and go for a walk. The city had a walking path that went up and along a series of small hills that overlooked the town center. She sat beneath a tree and looked out into the night. She could see a hundred pinpoints of light from the fires that lined the streets below and the one larger one in the middle. Overhead the sky was clear, and thousands of stars twinkled in the dark. For the first time in a long time, she felt alone.

It wasn't long after her departure that Mahdon and Saren returned expecting Maiya to still be asleep. When Mahdon saw the note, not knowing how long she'd been gone, he went to look for her. A brief walk later, he found Maiya sitting alone atop a small hill, head tilted back as she gazed up at the stars. She seemed unaware of his arrival at first, her face revealing that she was lost deep in thought, a troubled look resting distantly in her eyes. He considered saying something but thought better of it and planted himself beside her on the golden grass.

A moment passed before Maiya broke the silence, leaving her eyes fixated on the sky above. "Sometimes I have these stark realizations that I'm completely alone, that no one is thinking of or missing me, and that I could very well die alone. I know they don't actually know I'm gone, but still, it can be a bit overwhelming."

Mahdon frowned. "You know that's not true, don't you?"

"I'm sorry. I didn't mean it like that. I know I'm not alone; I should be clearer. I mean the family and friends back on Earth. Realistically, I haven't been away very long, but some days it feels much longer. And now I'm billions of miles away from even the worst of my kind. I never thought I was the type of person who gets homesick. Maybe I've just never been far enough away. People have always been so good at upsetting me and yet, thinking about the holidays makes me miss them. It feels... I don't know. I can't adequately explain it, but I feel completely alone."

Another moment passed in silence while Mahdon tried to find the words to say, though nothing came to mind that he felt could comfort her. He wrestled with his thoughts, failing to understand how she could possibly feel as she did. In a sense, she was right; Maiya was completely alone in anything she had ever known. Mahdon could no more sympathize with her feelings of exclusion and loneliness than she could understand his fear of being confined in a mortal form.

Finally, he spoke. "I'm here with you now."

A smile crept across her face as Maiya turned to face him and placed a hand atop his. "I'm glad you are. I'm not sure I could do this without you."

Mahdon shook his head and delivered the most dubious look Maiya had ever received. "Do you have any idea how many people are alive because of you? That was all your doing. You're a lot stronger than you think. I'm just along for the ride."

"Maybe," she said as she moved closer to him and leaned her head against his shoulder. "Maybe not. I'm lucky to have you here either way. It's strange, really. Even though these down moments exist, I don't think I ever felt as happy back home as I have in my saddest moments here. I think what makes me feel the worst is that I don't miss it like I should; it's only on these rare occasions that I do."

"Why now?"

"I'm not sure, exactly. The holiday maybe. Everyone here seems so happy, so fulfilled. I've never felt that way," Maiya tilted her head up to meet his eyes, "but I think I'm starting to. And it scares me."

Mahdon had never felt so close to Maiya before, and for once he found his own human form becoming comfortable. She smelled like flowers to him and the feeling of her hand on top of his made his heart race. It was a feeling he hadn't known for a long time. He felt a sudden urge to put his arm around her but was unsure if it would be appropriate. He had avoided considering how he'd feel if she ever chose to return home, but now the thought of her leaving saddened him. He didn't want her to go.

"Why should happiness scare you?" he asked.

"Because of what it means."

"I'm not sure I understand."

Mahdon felt every second as it ticked by, his eyes still locked onto Maiya's. Had Maiya always been this beautiful to him or had he stayed in this form for too long? Had he drunk too much and failed to recognize the effects? He pushed away those thoughts; he knew that wasn't it. He'd only had the one hours ago. He feared that what he felt was no more than a chemical response that only existed due to the form he had chosen. He feared that he had misread the situation. He feared that he would offend her. But most of all, he feared that this moment would never come again. As he pondered what she must be thinking, she made it clear with her next move.

When Maiya's lips met his, he felt it — that sense of fulfillment that he knew she so desired. That which he had feared for so long felt undeniably right. More than anything, he hoped that she felt it too. After their lips parted once more, silence lingered in the air around them, and Mahdon could see her blushing in the moonlight.

Maiya felt immediately embarrassed and backed away. "I'm sorry. I shouldn't have done that."

Mahdon smiled slightly. "No, I liked it. I would be lying if I said I haven't thought about that before. Is that wrong?"

She returned his smile. "Not at all. I've been wanting to do that as well. I was afraid that I might upset you or that I misinterpreted our friendship. I never want to hurt you."

Mahdon was delighted by her words; this was more than he had dreamed.

Maiya let out a nervous laugh and moved close enough to rest her head back upon his shoulder. "It's hard for me to believe how much has changed since I've known you. We come from very different backgrounds, and," she gave him a smirk and wink, "you're so old."

Now Mahdon blushed. "Thanks for that reminder."

"Maybe it should bother me, but it doesn't. When I look at you, I don't see it; I just see you. And technically… I'm older than you… or so I hear."

"I don't know what to say. I never expected this."

"Now what happens?"

Mahdon shrugged. "I don't know, but I am happy that I finally got to be this close to you. Even if it was only a one-time thing."

"It doesn't need to be. That is, unless you want it to be..."

"I was hoping you'd say that."

The two exchanged smiles and embraced once more, each feeling luckier than the other. For the first time since she had arrived on Amertine, Maiya felt this was where she belonged. Though everyone she had met held her presence here to a greater purpose, for her, it had all led up to this single, seemingly insignificant moment. She finally felt she'd found her home.

CHAPTER 12

When the golden sun kissed Maiya's skin at morning's first light, she was happy to find Mahdon still held her close in the golden grass. She lifted her head from his chest and was surprised to find he had his eyes shut. Excluding the time when he had been ill, never had she seen him sleep. She watched as the light filtering through the leaves of the lone tree danced across his face, and she smiled at the memory of the pre-dawn hours. Had someone told her a year ago that her life would lead to this, she would have thought them crazy.

He looked so peaceful that she didn't want to disturb him, but she didn't want to worry Saren either. As she sat up, he opened his eyes. He looked around confused for a moment and then got up and brushed himself off.

"Did I fall asleep?"

"It looked like it."

She could tell this alarmed him but was unsure why. Not wanting to pry, she didn't ask him about it.

"We should get back," Maiya said. "Do you have any idea how long we've been gone?"

"I do not."

He stood and offered his hand to pull her up as well. They began the walk back, holding hands but without speaking a word. Everything felt surreal and neither knew what to say. When they reached the residence, they exchanged looks and released their hands before entering. They hadn't discussed how this might affect their group dynamic and were in silent

139

agreement to keep it to themselves for now. Walking inside, Maiya determined this would be a lot harder than she initially thought. She felt like a school girl with a secret crush and found she was smiling to herself and looking in his direction more often than usual. It was unlikely that Saren took notice of this, but it made her feel she was being obvious just the same.

Over the next couple of weeks, Maiya kept longer hours to allow for more alone time with Mahdon. They typically walked or flew to places far from the busiest streets of whichever town they were visiting at the time. There they would hold one another and share the thoughts and regrets they kept from everyone else. One of these days, Mahdon had attempted to write her a sonnet, as he once read that this was considered a romantic gesture amongst some humans. While the act itself was thoughtful, the poem was more humorous than romantic. Maiya loved every entertaining line of it.

Three months after their first kiss, they found themselves absentmindedly holding hands as they walked through town. They'd been discussing what they might do after the healing circuit was complete, as that time was quickly approaching. They stopped in their tracks when they sensed her arrival and turned to see Saren. She looked from their joined hands up to their faces with a brief laugh and shake of the head.

"I suspected it might be something like this. I considered trying it out myself before we go back to business as usual." She grinned. "What do you say?"

Maiya felt her face turn red and looked at her dumbfounded.

Mahdon simply stared. "What are you asking?"

"Uh…don't worry about it, Mahdon. Thank you, Saren, but I think I'll have to decline," Maiya said.

Saren shrugged. "That's quite all right. I'm sure I can find someone around here who shares my curiosities."

"Is there something else?" Maiya asked.

"Yes. I've been in contact with Naliz, and the rest of the council has chosen to join us for the remainder of our journey. They are already in transit and will meet us in Muldira tomorrow."

Maiya tilted her head to one side, eying Saren with suspicion. "That's odd. Is there any particular reason why?"

"It was somewhat unclear, but by the sound of it, they want to be present for the official eradication of the disease. At this point, that will be within two months' time. Now, if you'll excuse me, I have one last night to explore." Saren smiled and disappeared.

Maiya sighed, shook her head, and looked at Mahdon quizzically. "I'm not sure I want to know what she means by 'explore.' She used to be so reserved."

"I believe this is a more accurate representation of who she used to be," Mahdon said. "I don't recall her being so jovial in recent centuries past, but it is my understanding that she used to be quite the partier."

The rest of the council was already waiting for them when they arrived in Muldira mid-morning. During their travels they'd gone from heavily forested land to plains, tropics, back through more temperate forest, and now to a desert region. As they disembarked, they took on much more serious expressions, as though the vacation was over, and it was time to get back to work. Though they'd done nothing wrong, the presence of the others made them all feel a bit awkward. Naliz met them outside, leaving Jo'dai and Tanin to their own devices elsewhere.

He gave them a broad smile when he saw them. "Mahdon, my friend! It's been too long." He then nodded to Saren and Maiya. "Of course, it's wonderful to see the both of you as well. I hear, and have personally seen, that this has been a resounding success."

"That it has," Mahdon said. "Have you been updated on the status of Maiya's abilities?"

"The healing, yes. Has there been another development?"

"The High Councilor has proven her birthright in countless ways," Saren said.

Maiya smiled. "Would you like to see?"

Naliz nodded. Maiya bent down and picked up a handful of sand from the dry desert floor. Holding her hand open for him to see, she transformed the lifeless sand into rich soil from which the beginnings of life sprouted. She set it on the ground, and they watched as a small oasis spread out and grew up around them. Mahdon and Saren had gotten used to such demonstrations, but Naliz watched in wonder.

"Fascinating," he said. "I think the others will be equally impressed. Regarding that, I was hoping we might begin regular council meetings. In particular, I would greatly appreciate it if we could settle the matter of Brandon."

Maiya had to restrain herself from rolling her eyes. It had been nearly a year, and she hadn't heard from either Naliz or Brandon, but it seemed every time she saw the one, the other came up. She reminded herself that it was silly to hold a grudge for so long, especially when he held no real power. It was perfectly reasonable to give him a second chance at this point.

"After all this time, why the urgency now?"

Naliz sighed. "I tried to convince him to wait, but he insisted on coming along to personally make a formal request of you."

"He's here now?"

"He's inside, yes."

Maiya looked to Mahdon and Saren to catch their reactions. She looked back at Naliz with a slight nod. "I suppose there's no harm in listening to what he has to say."

The building Naliz selected for their stay was quite a bit larger than they'd become used to and thus, provided ample room for privacy. Brandon was in the main living space watching a holographic projection. He switched it off and stood to meet them as they entered the room. They were immediately taken aback by his current appearance. Though he kept the same general physical traits, he had cast off the ridiculous nobleman look and looked instead like a clean-cut man in business casual attire. Naliz later told them this new look had come about a month or two after their departure.

"High Councilor, Ambassador, council members." Brandon bowed his head respectfully to each in turn. "I must give you my sincerest apologies. I allowed jealousy and distrust to guide my actions. I am truly ashamed for letting such negative emotions influence me. I ask nothing of you but your forgiveness and understanding that I only want what's best for our people. Please allow me to make amends for my actions."

Maiya could easily understand distrusting a stranger. Even now she was wary of Brandon's motives and ability to be humble. She eyed him suspiciously, searching for a hint of the ploy he might be pulling. Counter to her expectations, she found none. The glint of arrogance he typically had in his eyes wasn't present, and his tone sounded sincere. Had he finally observed the situation from a logical perspective? She wasn't so sure.

"How do you intend to do that?" she asked.

"I am at your service however you wish it. I have many connections all over Amertine. They are now at your disposal should you choose."

"What type of connections?"

"Whatever you want. Top scientists, the best chefs, locals in every city imaginable who know everything you could possibly want to know."

Maiya looked over at Mahdon. He nodded. "Brandon is well-known and very well-liked. It could be advantageous."

Eyes and ears everywhere, Maiya thought. It was better to have them with you than working against you. "Okay. Assuming the rest of the council is onboard, you may advise on a trial basis. Any intel you should receive beyond that of council security should be reported immediately. The council will use their discretion in what to do with that info. Agreed?"

"Yes. Thank you for your consideration, High Councilor."

Brandon wasted no time in keeping up his end of the bargain. The council was presented with almost daily tidbits of information: from the simplest things, such as the best place to view each city, to details about the local leaders and other respected members of the community. He was such an extrovert that it was rare for him to return without new knowledge. One thing was clear: he knew how to make people like him.

After a while he seemed far less threatening and far more eager to please. At various times, Maiya was almost convinced that he might even be attempting to flirt with her. She never went out of her way to spend time with him, but he always seemed to know where she was and would show up randomly to say 'hello' and attempt to make small talk. Maiya was relieved when Mahdon indicated that he had picked up on a similar vibe; it reassured her that she wasn't imagining things. She even joked that she was the new hot commodity that everyone wanted.

With only two larger cities left to visit, Mahdon told Maiya that he would need to go away for a few days. She was curious as to why, but when she asked, he simply told her that he'd explain when he returned. This left her with plenty of time alone with the other council members. She didn't talk to Jo'dai much beyond security updates, and she didn't talk to Tanin at all. In fact, she couldn't recall a time she had ever heard him speak. She decided to inquire about this when she had a moment alone with Naliz.

"He's a man of few words," Naliz said. "He and Brandon have been close friends for at least two millennia now. Beyond that, he tends to keep to himself."

"Then the chances I'll ever get to know him are slim."

Naliz nodded. "In all likelihood, you are correct. He's even more secretive than Brandon, and Brandon loves his secrets."

"Speaking of secrets," Maiya hesitated a moment, but her curiosity got the best of her, "do you happen to know where Mahdon was going? He was very vague."

Naliz was clearly surprised. "I wasn't even aware that he left. When was this?"

"Yesterday after we all split up for the day."

"Interesting. I wondered this morning when he didn't join us, but I assumed he was running an errand for you. Thinking back on it now, it would have made more sense for Brandon to be doing those tasks. I'll see what I can find out."

"Thank you."

The following day would typically have been a transit day, but unsure of where Mahdon had gone, the council thought it was best to remain until he returned. Naliz contacted past colleagues of Mahdon's in an effort to locate him more quickly but to no avail. Maiya remained at the residence much of the day discussing the latest scientific breakthroughs between rounds of Tane Kaut. By the third day of Mahdon's absence, she began to worry and could no longer remain idle in the house.

Anxious and in need of an escape, she wandered the city for hours. She eventually found herself lost in an older part of town with cobblestone streets. This part of town was surprisingly vacant, and only a few others could be seen walking here. Maiya felt this to be somewhat unsettling and began back the way she'd come. As she headed down the main road, she saw the remaining Amerti disappear as she drew closer to them. It was then that she became aware of the person walking up behind her. She turned to see a middle-aged woman who appeared human staring at her wide-eyed. She was wearing a rucksack on her back and carrying a basket of food in one hand.

"You don't belong here," the woman said forcefully, her voice growing louder with each word. "Leave now."

Maiya held up her hands and backed away slowly. "I'm leaving. There's no need to get angry."

The woman looked like she was about to speak again when two members of the security team appeared and flanked her. They began dragging her away as she fought to break free. Brandon showed up next to Maiya and began to rush her off in the opposite direction. The woman began yelling when Maiya turned to look back.

"If you stay here, you'll die! Leave! Leave!"

"She is unstable," Brandon said. "She would rather not have outsiders on Amertine and may become violent. It's very sad."

"Where are they taking her?"

"They'll return her to her home and give her something to calm her down. She'll forget she ever saw you, and everything will be well."

"How did she get like that?" Maiya asked.

Brandon shook his head sadly. "Nobody knows."

Maiya wondered if there was a way to help the woman or if she was merely a xenophobe. In which case, she may already be beyond help. She chose to put these thoughts out of her mind and come back to them later. After the encounter, Brandon took her to see a man who had perfected 'Veris.' The local delicacy was made from the boiled root of a water plant that grew in the region. Mixed with various spices and then baked over a wood fire, the ability to make it with the proper texture and complex flavor was a rare art. It wasn't at all what Maiya was expecting when she heard the word 'root' mentioned. She could think of nothing to compare it to but agreed with Brandon's assessment that it was one of the best things she'd ever taste.

On the way back to the house, Maiya unexpectedly found herself in a pleasant conversation with Brandon. He told her about the other foods and drink she should try. In his time, he'd visited every past restaurant, chef, and baker around the planet. He'd sampled every drink possible, alcoholic and non-alike. He had truly been a glutton. He also shared his interest in exploration. Brandon didn't speak as passionately about it as Mahdon, but he craved adventure as well. He told her that though he loved Amertine, he was fascinated by what else was out there. For the first time, Maiya thought she could grow to like him despite his egotistical tendencies.

On the fourth day, Saren and Maiya were out walking when Mahdon returned. Maiya stopped mid-sentence to run to greet him. She'd never been so happy and relieved to see him. She'd also never been so annoyed at someone for not explaining where they were going. It wouldn't have been so bad had he at least told Naliz. He smiled and hugged her but seemed a little off to Maiya. She couldn't put her finger on what it was exactly. Saren didn't seem to notice anything.

"Ready to tell me where you were?"

"Yes, but I need to speak with Naliz first."

Maiya's curiosity was piqued. What could he possibly need to discuss? It wasn't something for the council, or he would have told her directly. She nodded her understanding and sent him off to have his talk. She looked to Saren to see if she had any clue what was going on, but she simply shrugged. Mahdon hurried back to the residence and found Naliz alone in the living room. He walked over to the window and stared out for a moment, then exhaled slowly and spoke.

"I was hoping to talk to you about something that's been weighing on my mind. As my oldest friend, I was curious what you might think."

Naliz sat down, prepared to listen. "Of course. What is it?"

Mahdon tried to collect his thoughts and choose his words, but Naliz found them for him.

"You've grown fond of her, haven't you?"

Mahdon turned away from the window. "Yes."

In his hand Mahdon held a small purple flower that changed colors in the light when viewed from different angles. Naliz let out a small gasp at the sight of it.

"Is that a Scifta Calia?"

Mahdon nodded. The flower was amongst the rarest in the world and was impossible to cultivate. They were exceedingly difficult to find, growing only under very specific conditions. Years ago, they were one of the most expensive items an individual could buy.

"Mahdon, you know I can't condone a relationship with her."

Mahdon frowned. He wasn't expecting that. "And why is that, exactly? There are no religious doctrines or laws forbidding it."

"Nevertheless, Brandon..."

Mahdon narrowed his eyes at Naliz. "Why are you so afraid of him?"

"I'm only trying to keep your best interests in mind."

"I don't understand why he would even care."

Naliz sighed. "I know you don't... but he does. This could be very bad for the both of you. If you care for her, I advise you to keep your distance."

Mahdon began pacing the room. He didn't understand where this was coming from. Brandon had been nicer to him in the last couple of weeks than he ever was in the past. He thought things were progressing in the right direction. Now it seemed Naliz was suggesting otherwise.

"I don't care what Brandon thinks. Neither should you. He is no longer the head of the council, so any influence he had over my decisions is gone. In the past, he has done everything in his power to cause trouble for me."

"Not everything," Naliz shook his head bitterly. "It may not seem like it, but he is still a very powerful man, Mahdon. You don't want to be on his bad side."

"I was under the impression that I already was. He's never cared much for me."

"It will get worse. There are things you don't know about him."

Mahdon stopped and looked Naliz directly in the eyes. "Is he a threat to Maiya?"

"I don't think so."

"Then whatever it is, it doesn't matter."

"I can see there is no dissuading you. Is there nothing I can say to make you change your mind?"

"Do you personally object?"

Naliz thought for a moment and then shook his head. "No."

Mahdon left to return to Maiya. Saren excused herself when she saw him approaching to give the two of them space to talk.

"Do you mind if we go somewhere else?" He asked.

The question made Maiya nervous given the recent odd behavior. She didn't know what to think. She nodded. "Sure."

They walked to the shuttlecraft he'd borrowed and flew out to a large red rock formation that sat on the edge of town. They landed and walked for a bit over the rocky landscape until Mahdon was satisfied with the privacy of the area. They sat in the shade where the towering rocks rose up on all sides of them and the wind made a pleasant whistling sound when it blew through the surrounding formations. They had both been relatively quiet on the walk over, each facing their own set of nerves. Once they were seated, he took both of her hands in his and looked her in the eyes.

"Are you all right?" Mahdon asked.

"Yes," Maiya said unconvincingly. "Just tell me what's going on. Should I be worried?"

"Not at all. Had I known I'd make you feel that way, I would have gone about this differently. I'm sorry, Mai."

He reached into his pocket and pulled out the carefully wrapped flower. Maiya regarded it with a mix of admiration and confusion as he placed it in her hand. She gave him a puzzled look while she waited for him to explain.

"This is why I left. I went to find it for you."

"It's beautiful," she said, "but why go to all the trouble for a flower?"

"It's much more than that. It's also known as the 'first flower.' According to mythology, obtaining one promises a blessed union."

Maiya looked up sharply. "What are you saying?"

"I wasn't certain at first. I thought I knew, but I feared that I might be wrong." He smiled at her. "I know how I feel now. There's no doubt in my mind. I love you."

Maiya felt frozen for a moment and simply stared at him. They'd been dancing around the subject for months, but she wasn't prepared for the actual words. She felt the same but never had the nerve to say it, as though saying the words would somehow break the spell. Her heart leapt, and she felt the excitement of their first kiss all over again. She smiled and leaned over to kiss him, unable to fight off the giddiness any longer. The feeling was almost electric.

Mahdon smiled when they broke the kiss. "Is it safe to assume you share the feeling?"

Maiya laughed. "Do you really need to ask?"

"If I remember correctly, you did call me adorable," he said playfully, "so maybe I don't."

"You remember that?"

"Of course. I remember everything you tell me."

"That proves nothing. Puppies are adorable."

"Are puppies not loveable? If adorable equals loveable and I am adorable, then by the transitive property of adorableness, I am also loveable."

The look Maiya gave him was nothing short of perplexed amusement. "You are so weird."

"That's why you love me."

She smiled and gave him a little kiss. "Fair enough."

CHAPTER 13

It was late by the time Mahdon and Maiya returned to the others. Unsurprisingly, everyone was present and awake when they walked into the house. Maiya had used a preservation spell on the Scifta Calia shortly after receiving it and now openly carried it in her left hand. Saren sent them a devilish grin when she noticed Brandon was fixated on this. Taking notice of this, Naliz cleared his throat and broke Brandon out of his stupor. Neither Maiya nor Mahdon had given this a second thought.

"Did you have a pleasant evening?" Naliz asked.

Maiya nodded. "Yes, thank you."

"We were discussing departing tomorrow morning for Kauria. We should arrive before mid-day. Will this be acceptable?"

"Of course. I should probably get some sleep. I'll see you all in the morning."

Maiya retired to one of the bedrooms only to be visited by Saren a few minutes later. Saren smiled as she sat on the edge of the bed.

"There's only one reason one would give another such a gift. I didn't realize it was that serious. The very fact that he's developed such strong emotions says a lot about how much time he's spent in that body. I enjoy the emotional intensity from time to time, but this is a far too confining existence for me. I don't know how he does it. He must really love you." She paused a moment, mulling over a thought. "I wouldn't be surprised if he gives up his immortality for you."

This was the first Maiya heard anyone mention such a thing. The prospect of him living forever while she faded away hadn't even occurred to her. The concept of mortality was so deeply ingrained in her being that she once again failed to see the bigger picture.

"He can do that?"

"Our existence isn't permanent. Not if we don't want it to be. I am only aware of a few who have gone through with it, but yes, it is possible."

That wasn't something Maiya could ever ask of him. Experience had taught her all too well that nothing lasts forever. It would be cruel to have him give up so much only to have it all fall apart later.

"Why are you telling me this?" Maiya asked.

"It was merely an observation. I was surprised when I saw the flower, and I wasn't certain if you understood the full significance of it. I've enjoyed getting to know you over the past year and I'm happy for the both of you. Such things are rare. I'll let you rest now."

Saren smiled again and departed for the night. Maiya eventually drifted off to sleep, but when she woke in the morning, her mind was already pre-occupied with overanalyzing Saren's remarks from the night prior. If Mahdon was willing to make such a major commitment, what could she possibly offer him in return? She tried to brush the thoughts aside by reminding herself that she hadn't asked anything of him, and he had yet to offer. There was no sense in dwelling on the possibilities. She'd cross that bridge if the time came for it.

The flight to Kauria was typical with one glaring exception. Though Brandon had made a point of being at Maiya's side almost constantly, he now rode separately with Tanin and Jo'dai. Naliz suspected this was in large part due to Mahdon's declaration. He knew Brandon well enough to know that he would only maintain his silence if he distanced himself for the immediate future. Brandon's motivations weren't yet clear to him, but Naliz could tell he'd developed a bit of an obsession with Maiya. While in the beginning his disdain for her was obvious, now his fascination with her greatly outweighed any purely negative emotions.

The city they visited now was one of the largest on the continent and, while it didn't have the same opulence, it was architecturally very similar to the capital city. This was the first time they would be staying in a high-rise building since they left Fimbira. Unlike their other destinations, the building where they stayed was a proper hotel. Saren explained that the city had a large Zumerti population whose livelihoods continued to depend on providing services to others. The system of currency used for exchange of these goods and services was a credit-based one. The council had a longstanding relationship with many generations of a few families and thus had ongoing arrangements that took the place of said credits. Nonetheless, their in-person interactions had always been limited.

Aside from the obvious, the biggest difference Maiya noticed about the Zumerti was how their displays of emotions were far more muted than the others. From what she understood in her discussions with Mahdon and Saren, the regular lack of emotion made the experience of them far more extreme. Some were better than others at mastering control over them, but many others — such as the hundreds of festival goers she'd seen — felt intense euphoria, as though the feelings themselves were a drug. While the shapeshifters thought the Zumerti were foolish for their choices, the Zumerti viewed the inability to effectively control emotional reactions as a weakness. There didn't appear to be any real animosity between the two groups, but it was clear that they still heavily judged the other to this day.

They were shown to the presidential suite and given a rundown of the services the hotel provided. Maiya unpacked her travel bag and then returned to the lobby ahead of the group.

"You are not like the others," the woman working the front desk said when Maiya emerged from the gravity tunnel. "They are from here. You are not."

"Is it that obvious?" She knew that the others could sense an individual's specific energy, but she wasn't aware if that ability extended to the Zumerti.

"Perhaps not obvious, but I can tell. I could easily have been wrong in my assumption, but you don't strike me as Numerti."

Maiya hadn't heard the term before, but she could only assume 'Numerti' was the term applied to those who were no longer mortal like them.

"What makes you say that?"

"You don't have the same flawlessness as the others."

"Um, thanks?"

Maiya wasn't sure if she should be offended, but the woman had a point. Beyond the Zumerti and the woman who had yelled at her to leave, she had yet to see anyone who didn't maintain a nearly pristine appearance. If a single hair fell away, they could simply will it back into place. Maiya's hair wasn't a mess, but it was far from perfect.

"Is it true that you came from another world?"

"Yes."

"I heard that they brought you here because you can do strange things — magical healing and other unexplainable things. Can all of your kind do the same?"

"No."

"Is it only the women?"

Maiya wondered where this line of questioning was going. She didn't want to be rude, but she suspected that there was more behind the curiosity. "No. It isn't common at all. Is there something that you needed?"

"You're not the first I've seen, so I thought maybe it was common for your people."

Maiya knew that, outside of the council, there were many others who had made themselves appear human as well. She had already seen many during their short time in Kauria. The woman must have been mistaken in her assumption.

"A lot of others have taken on a similar appearance."

"Recently, yes. This was a long time ago."

The statement caught Maiya completely off guard, and at first, she wasn't sure how to respond. What did the woman consider to be 'a long time'? She had been told she was the first to be brought to the planet. She knew Mahdon hadn't lied to her when he said that, but she also saw no purpose in this woman lying to her.

"When?"

"The first time was forty years or so ago. The second time perhaps another twenty after that."

Maiya just looked at her, trying to read her facial expressions. Now the woman looked surprised.

"You were not aware? I thought they might be friends of yours."

Maiya shook her head. "No. I was very young twenty years ago. Are you sure about this?"

"Yes. I —" she paused, looking away for a moment, "it appears that your travel companions have returned."

Maiya thanked her and walked over to meet up with the group. Brandon was noticeably absent again. Saren led the group from the centrally located hotel through bustling streets to a small restaurant. They drew a bit of attention on their walk due to their unique appearance, but by and large, people were focused on their own activities. The attention came primarily from the children who Maiya was equally distracted by given they were the first she'd seen in a year. Pushing through the throngs of people, they walked through the restaurant to a back door. The door unlocked when Saren moved a hand past the sensor, and she was greeted by name by an automated voice. She waved them through the door into a secluded patio area where there was only one large table and no other patrons.

A man came out as they took their seats and introduced himself as Rarn. Rarn was the oldest member of one of the families that continued to hold an arrangement with the council. He was well-acquainted with the members and had familiarized himself not only with their current appearances but with Maiya's as well. Though she never saw anything that resembled a camera, Maiya's face and name had been all over their news feeds for months now. She made a mental note to speak with Saren and Jo'dai about the technology so she could be better aware of when it was present.

"We have prepared a menu in anticipation of your arrival. We hope that it will be to your liking," Rarn said as he nodded for the kitchen staff to bring out the first course.

Throughout the meal, he would return for the delivery of each course to describe the dishes and then disappear again to give the council privacy to discuss their own affairs. Jo'dai ran over the security measures that had been taken for visiting such a large city and then Naliz went over the intended schedule for the coming days. Nothing stuck out as differing from their usual plans. Maiya contemplated whether or not she should bring up the conversation she had earlier that day, then ultimately decided this was as good a time as any.

"I was told that I was the first person to be brought here from Earth. Is there any chance that isn't true?"

Everyone at the table simultaneously stopped what they were doing and looked at her. They had varying looks of confusion and curiosity on their faces. Mahdon looked mostly confused by the randomness of the question. Maiya felt the rest looked more curious and maybe even slightly nervous that she was asking.

"Why is everyone looking at me like that?" She asked.

"You're the first," Naliz said. "The question was surprising. What has spurred such a question?"

"The receptionist at the hotel seemed confident that she'd seen humans in the past."

The tension at the table visibly diminished. Maiya wasn't sure what they were expecting her to say, but they were clearly relieved by her answer.

"Oh," Naliz said, nodding. "I'm sure many have taken on similar appearances at this point. That must be the case here."

"She said this was decades ago."

"Preposterous."

All heads turned to look as Tanin spoke up for the first time in Maiya's recollection. He didn't sound angry or annoyed. His voice was calm, but the fact that he had chosen now to speak up drew Maiya's suspicion. When he had their attention, he continued.

"Excuse my bluntness, High Councilor, but if you are to govern effectively, you should not humor such outlandish claims. Put no stock in the words of a Zumerti."

His comment hit a nerve. Maiya sat back and did her best to respond with a steady tone. "I welcome everyone's input, Tanin, but I will not tolerate isolating an entire subsect of the population."

"Perhaps if you understood the reality of this world, you would not be so foolish."

Naliz stood and looked down at him. "You're out of line, Councilor."

"I've said my piece." He stood and left.

"That was unexpected," Naliz said, shaking his head. "I have no idea what's come over him."

"Yes," Saren agreed. She was clearly uncomfortable. "That was highly unusual."

They went about the rest of their day without much deviation from the original schedule. Now that she'd mastered the healing magic, the task was no more complicated than standing in a central location and holding the intention in her mind. This made for a very easy day. Maiya did, however, find herself much more aware of the interactions she saw between the two groups of people. For the most part the Zumerti weren't treated poorly, but far too often she could tell through the subtle actions of others that they were looked down upon. It was no wonder that they were bitter and thought the disease was well-deserved. She concluded that this was an issue that they would need to address in an upcoming meeting. She wondered if she would be met with any resistance when broaching the subject.

In the meantime, she intended to see if the woman's claims had any truth to them. The next morning, she went straight to the front desk in the hopes of inquiring further about what the woman said she'd seen. Unfortunately, she didn't appear to be working that day. When Maiya asked the man who was now working the front desk, he admitted his surprise that she wasn't already there. This immediately set off warning bells in her head, but she didn't want to jump to conclusions. There were plenty of reasons one might be late or miss a day of work.

She asked Mahdon if he could keep an eye out for anything unusual and then met up with Saren to go see some of the more popular sites in the city. On the itinerary there was both a museum of sculptures and one of technology to visit, which Saren expected to take the better part of the day. This gave them ample time to discuss Tanin's bizarre reaction amongst other things when they weren't actively looking at the exhibits. Saren told her that he'd always been very to the point and forward about his opinion, but she'd never seen him show such blatant disregard for authority. Whatever the reason was for it, she shared in the curiosity.

The last exhibit of the day was one on gravity tunnels. Maiya was pretty confident that it was intended for children, but she found it fascinating. She was playing with an interactive demo on gravity shifting when she realized she was being watched. She caught sight of the person out of the corner of her eye but couldn't see anything more than that. They had been peeking through a doorway into the room but were obviously focused on her and what she was doing. She told Saren she'd be back and went to investigate.

Once she was out of the room, she hurried in the direction she thought they'd gone. It didn't take long to realize the culprit had exited through a back door. Maiya exited into an alley alongside the building and found that the woman was already waiting for her. She wasn't carrying anything or yelling at Maiya this time, but there was no doubt that it was the same woman Maiya had seen the day Brandon came to usher her away. It was obvious now that she was on edge, as she was constantly looking around anxiously.

"We don't have much time," the woman said. "They're always following me. I managed to lose them, but they'll find me again soon."

"Who are you?" Maiya demanded.

"Lydia. I was surprised when I saw you. I'd heard rumors, but I didn't think they could be true. It wasn't so easy for me."

"What are you talking about?"

"You walk around freely, and they treat you well. Is it true you came here willingly?"

"Yes."

Maiya wasn't sure what Lydia's point was in all of this. She wondered if the claims of instability were warnings she should have heeded. So far everything that was said sounded like nothing more than random babbling to her, and now Lydia suddenly looked very emotional.

"Why? Why would you do something so reckless? If you value your life, then find a way to go back." She was practically in tears at this point, and it dawned on Maiya that these were not the pleas of an angry woman. Maiya immediately felt pity for her.

"What happened to you?"

Her eyes glazed over as she stared off at nothing, and her voice grew slower and quieter. "I trusted too much, and then I lost everything. I'm sure my family mourned me a long time ago. Yet here I am – trapped."

She shook her head as if to bring herself out of the daze and then wiped away a stray tear. "I'm sorry I'm such a mess. I never meant to yell at or upset you. I'm not normally like this. I told myself I would be okay, but it's been so long. There were others before me, and I began to relive it all when I saw you. I couldn't bear the thought of it happening to another. I lost it. I'm sorry."

Maiya felt a tightness in her chest as a feeling rose up in her gut. The longer she listened to Lydia talk, the stronger the gut feeling became. She knew her assumption could be wrong, but it felt too right not to be said.

"You're human, aren't you? You don't just look it. You're actually human." Maiya asked the question, but she wasn't sure she wanted to know the answer. It would only bring about more questions.

Lydia nodded. "Yes."

CHAPTER 14

Maiya's head was spinning as she processed the new information. Lydia cautioned her against believing anything she was told. She explained that she had been brought here against her will and had spent almost half her life in solitude. She'd been subjected to experiments and though she had managed to escape several times, it was only within the last year that they lost enough interest in her to leave her alone. Not long after that final escape, she learned the reason why – another had been publicly brought to the planet and drew attention away from her. They still followed and watched her but no longer cared who saw her.

When Maiya asked who had done these things to her, she didn't have a clear answer. She said the faces were always changing and often times she never saw the offenders at all. She only heard their voices and their questions. Whoever held her captive had incorrectly assumed she had the power that Maiya possessed. She'd talked to others through holes in her cell walls who had been brought before her for the same purpose. None of them ever proved to have what they were looking for. This meant that Maiya had been the real target all along. She felt sickened by the thought.

All of this was shared in a hurry before Lydia expressed concern that they had been talking for too long. She promised to find Maiya in Fimbira if they were both still on the planet and then took off running. Maiya had grown so comfortable and thought she had made some real friendships, but now she wasn't sure what to think. Had they been playing her all along? For what purpose? She knew she had to regain her composure before returning to Saren or there would be no way to keep the conversation to herself. She had always worn her heart on her sleeve and had never been the greatest of actors, so the task took every ounce of focus she could muster.

"Are you ready to go?" Saren asked upon Maiya's return.

She nodded and they began walking back to the hotel. Maiya chose to make small talk about the exhibits in an effort to appear as she always had. She couldn't help but look for clues to any ulterior motives, but she doubted any look would betray Saren. If they were prepared for it, they could be deceptive far more easily than any human ever could. They reached the hotel without any indication that anything was out of the ordinary. The real challenge would be when she saw Mahdon. She didn't believe for a second that he could be capable of such atrocities, but she couldn't ignore a warning due to her own feelings. She would have to keep her silence until she knew he wasn't part of the threat.

Upon reaching the room, he pulled her aside and asked if they could talk. His voice was more serious and urgent sounding than usual. She wondered if he had followed her and knew she'd spoken with the aforementioned "unstable" woman. She agreed, and Mahdon gave the group a cheerful good-bye, telling them that he and Maiya would be out for a walk. The change in tone came off as odd to Maiya, as it was clear he didn't want anyone else aware of the urgency. They walked a few blocks before his demeanor turned serious again. He waited until they were in a crowd of people, confident no one could hear, before saying anything.

"I kept an eye out today as you requested. Two of the staff members were discussing the other employee's absence. They described it as highly unusual, so I decided to investigate some. Long story short, I got in contact with her mate who told me she never came home last night. He knew she had planned to spend the evening with some friends after work, so had not even begun to ask around until this morning. It appears she's missing."

Maiya frowned at the confirmation of her suspicions. "That's convenient."

"Given how he reacted to yesterday's topic, I have every reason to believe Tanin had some level of involvement in her disappearance. I don't know why, and I have no proof to offer you, but it is what I suspect."

"And if he did?"

"If he did, I would like to know the reason for it. At first, I thought his reaction was one driven by growing resentment, that perhaps he felt he is a more qualified leader, but now I'm concerned about what he may be hiding."

Maiya desperately wanted to tell him about her earlier conversation, but what if he already knew? What if this was all a ruse to draw out a confession of what she'd learned? She'd been so happy and now she was consumed with doubt.

"And what do you think he's hiding?"

Mahdon looked down, as though he was uncomfortable with the thought he was about to share. "This may be a ridiculous notion, but you may not be the first human he's seen. The implication being that he has done more than see."

Maiya wasn't surprised by this, as it was the first thought she had when Tanin called the idea of others preposterous. If the situation wasn't so worrisome, she would have found Mahdon's apparent naivete amusing. She was never quick to trust, and he was always giving people the benefit of the doubt. She silently prayed that he really was as clueless as he seemed.

"What do you think we should do?" Maiya asked.

"Normally I would ask Naliz for his assistance or suggest that you have Jo'dai assign a security team to watch him."

"But?"

He shook his head and sighed. "Though it saddens me to think it, if Tanin has classified knowledge of misdeeds, the rest of the council may as well. Until we have more information, I do not think it is wise to trust them with this concern."

"I agree. Once we get back to Fimbira in a few days, we can spend more time on this."

Mahdon and Maiya went to dinner before returning to the hotel for the night, where they found that everything was as it should be. Saren and Naliz welcomed the two back as they normally would and even Brandon was coming back around. The trip in the morning would be the last they were making before their focus would shift to long-term goals for the future. It had been a long time since she was last at the manor, but Maiya craved being there alone after so much time spent with the others. She hoped that having the place to herself would allow her to properly process her thoughts. In the meantime, she kept a close eye on interactions between the others and any tension that had been present before was gone. It was as though the uncomfortable luncheon had never happened.

On the evening before their return to Fimbira, Brandon asked if Maiya would be up for a walk and expressed his desire to discuss what might happen over the following months. She agreed, and the two walked along the river in the city while he apologized for any awkwardness he had caused. He admitted his jealousy and told her that he worried the past contentions between him and Mahdon would hinder any developing friendship he could have with Maiya. She told him she understood and that she wouldn't let that happen unless Brandon did something truly egregious. She wasn't sure if she could take his word at face value, but she firmly believed in the concept of keeping your friends close and your enemies closer.

Mahdon was understandably curious what was discussed, though he assumed it was regarding Brandon's standing as an advisor. When Maiya shared Brandon's true intention for wanting to talk, he simply laughed. He had no interest in letting the past define his current interactions with others. Maiya could be Brandon's best friend for all he cared; managing her friendships wasn't something he had any desire to do. She was, after all, her own person, and he trusted her judgment.

Their arrival at the council headquarters came late in the day, but Maiya was eager to begin her personal research on how Lydia had come to be on Amertine. She decided she'd begin by reviewing the procedural texts Mahdon had provided her to see if they could offer any clues as to what records the council typically kept or where classified activities might take place. She knew it was a longshot, but she didn't want to leave any stone unturned. She informed the group that there would be a formal meeting in three weeks' time and then left them to fly over to the manor.

She spent the next two weeks completely absorbed in learning the intricacies of council protocol and hardly slept. Mahdon stopped by each day but mostly kept to himself unless Maiya needed him to be available to answer questions. When he wasn't with her at the manor, he was doing his best to determine if there was anyone else he could trust with his concerns. By the time of the first post-trip council meeting, Maiya was well-versed in both current procedures and archaic laws. She knew that if they had been following their own protocol, there should be records of every decision the council made as well as their dealings with the Zumerti. Much like they had found in the Ularia council chambers, these records were left behind in whichever locale was used at the time. The frequency in which locations changed was not a set number, so the total number of locations to search was unknown. She would need to rely on one of the others for this information.

Maiya arrived shortly before the others and chose to sit rather than stand awkwardly on the pedestal. She thought she might reserve that for a day when she wanted to feel powerful. For now, all she wanted was answers and progression in the right direction. She called the meeting to order and allowed each member an opportunity to give any reports they had. Jo'dai was pleased to announce that the status of the disease had not changed. From what they could tell, it had been officially eradicated. Naliz shared that he and Mahdon had begun receiving feedback from citizens who wanted to do more with their lives than they had been. The close encounters with death had been enough for many to request that they be given guidance in how to better put their skills to use. Maiya thought it was sad that they had no idea what to do with themselves, but then again, she never did know what she wanted to do with her life either.

After a brief discussion about organizing an event to work with these individuals, Maiya moved onto her topic regarding the treatment of the Zumerti. She wasn't sure how attitudes could be improved, but something had to change. Saren suggested that it might be best to become familiar with the current customs and culture and educate the populace. That is, if they could get anyone to listen. Though they all shared the same heritage historically, their modern-day beliefs had changed quite a bit and no longer aligned with those of the Numerti. Naliz admitted that he wasn't certain if they even shared the same religious beliefs anymore. Maiya tasked him with gaining that knowledge. Tanin chose to keep his thoughts to himself this time. All in all, she felt they were starting in the right direction.

After the meeting wrapped up, Tanin immediately departed while the rest remained behind. Maiya was anxious to return to her own planning and bid them farewell shortly thereafter. Mahdon appeared at the entrance as she was leaving and informed her that he was on his way to meet with Naliz but was glad he caught her before she left. Now that she had finished the texts he gave her, he was hoping they might begin to spend more time together again. She had yet to clue him in on the next step of her plan. In all her caution, she had distanced herself a bit and was missing him as well. She wished she could confirm that he knew nothing of the abductions so that she could confide in him and allow things to return to normal.

The sky was already darkening when Maiya returned to the manor, but she still noticed Lydia as she stepped out from the surrounding forest and into the back garden. Lydia hurried over to her, and Maiya led her inside to the lounge on the main floor. Once they were away from any windows, Lydia sat back in a chair and relaxed a bit. Maiya looked at her and waited for her to speak. When she still said nothing, Maiya did.

"Would you like something to drink?"

Lydia nodded. Maiya went to the kitchen and returned with several options. Lydia's eyes went wide, and she immediately perked up.

"You have wine?"

"Yes," Maiya smiled. "Would you like some?"

"Please," she picked up a glass and waited for Maiya to open the bottle. "I don't remember the last time I even saw it. This house and everything else they've given you is unbelievable. They might actually like you."

Maiya filled their glasses and then sat back down. She didn't have a good response to Lydia's statement. Good intentions didn't always accompany good treatment. It's much easier to trust a person who treats you well than one who treats you poorly.

"Where are you living now?" Maiya asked.

"There are well-maintained buildings in most cities that no longer have occupants. I don't know who maintains them or why they're no longer used, but it allows me to move from place to place as it suits me."

It suddenly occurred to Maiya that she should have offered something to eat, but despite Lydia's transience, she didn't appear malnourished.

"What have you been doing about food?" Maiya asked.

"I usually stay in places where the other mortals are; it makes it more accessible."

"They don't find your presence odd?"

Lydia looked down at her drink, swirling it in her glass. "They don't exactly lock their doors around here. I don't expect you to understand, but I'd rather not be seen if I don't have to be."

Maiya nodded her understanding. "You said that you're always being followed. Did they follow you here?"

"They saw me enter the city earlier. I don't think they know I came this way."

"Why don't you stay here? This place is way too much for one person."

Lydia smiled. "You mean until we return home, right?"

Maiya swore to find a way for Lydia to go back, but she remained on the fence about her own future. She wasn't willing to condemn an entire race for the actions of a few, and she wasn't yet convinced that the ones she'd grown close to had anything to do with what happened to Lydia.

"You said there were others," Maiya said. "When you escaped, were any of them still there?"

"One. I never found out if she got away. I don't even know if she's still alive. I was too afraid to go back."

"Do you know where you were kept?"

Lydia shifted uncomfortably. "Vaguely."

"Maiya?" Mahdon's voice echoed as he made his way down the stairs.

Maiya wasn't expecting him, but she had always told him he could visit at any time. That possibility had slipped her mind when Lydia arrived. She was standing to intercept him when he appeared in the doorway. He stopped abruptly, looking from Lydia to Maiya and back again. His face was masked with confusion.

"I don't understand," he said after a long moment of simply staring. "Who brought you here?"

Lydia said nothing as she stared back at him. He turned to Maiya.

"Is this why you've been so distant lately? Why didn't you say something?"

"He doesn't know," Lydia said flatly. "He's just as surprised as you were."

He looked back at her and then sat down across from her. "Please explain this to me."

"You brought her here," Lydia said. "We didn't know if you were part of bringing me here as well. We had reason not to trust you."

Mahdon frowned. "Harsh but understandable."

"I'm sorry," Maiya said as she sat back down. "I wanted to trust you. This is Lydia."

Mahdon leaned back in his seat and nodded his understanding before addressing Lydia once more. "I assume you are the secret Tanin has been hiding. I gather you didn't come here willingly."

"Nope."

Mahdon sighed and dropped his head into his hands. "What is happening? Were you told why?"

"They were convinced that I had super powers or some crap." She shook her head and took a long drink.

"Do you have any idea who brought you here?"

"Nope. I didn't even realize that I left Earth until I'd already been here for close to a decade."

Mahdon was shocked by this revelation. Though Maiya said the receptionist indicated it had been a long time, he incorrectly assumed that this had all happened within the past couple of years – possibly during the first few months of their travel. It was hard to believe that Lydia could be here so long without drawing more attention to herself. She would have stuck out as being peculiar looking.

"How is it that you've remained hidden until now?"

Lydia had finished her first glass of wine and was pouring herself a larger one now. "It wasn't entirely by choice. I was a prisoner until less than a year ago."

"I was hoping we could find out where she was kept," Maiya said. "That could give us some indication of what to do next. We were talking about it when you showed up."

Mahdon nodded. "I may be able to help with that. Saren would know more about specific structures and where they would be located."

Maiya and Lydia simultaneously shot him nervous looks. It was clear neither of them was comfortable with the idea of expanding the number of people who knew about them talking. The greater the number, the higher the risk that there would be negative ramifications. Mahdon recognized this and offered clarification.

"I'm not suggesting that we tell her about you, but I know now that we are not the only ones with plans to investigate Tanin."

"Oh?" This was news to Maiya.

"When I arrived after the meeting, the other members were already discussing it. They each have their own concerns about his motives and prejudices. They did not mention humans specifically, but it was evident that they distrust him."

Lydia was still frowning. "Maybe he has dirt on them. How do you know that they aren't afraid he'll rat them out about something?"

Mahdon looked at her with confusion, and Maiya realized she hadn't yet used that idiom around him.

"Why didn't they say anything to me about this?" Maiya asked.

"I believe it was their intention to. They were hesitant to say anything while there was risk of him being in earshot. Jo'dai has already arranged to place a covert security team on him. He didn't want to swap out the primary detail; he thought it would raise suspicion. They asked me to relay this information as it would not appear unusual for me to visit at this time."

"This definitely makes things more interesting. Let me know if you hear anything else. Help them with their investigation, but don't mention anything about Lydia."

Mahdon nodded. "Of course."

Maiya replenished her drink, poured one for Mahdon, and then sat back. She looked at Lydia. "Are you comfortable moving forward with this?"

Lydia took a deep breath and nodded. Over the next two hours, she slowly recounted every detail she could manage. She didn't recall an attack or being taken aboard a ship or anything between her last day on Earth and the day she awoke somewhere underground. She had suspected she was being followed for several days before she was abducted, but every time she tried to get a good look at who was watching her, they'd be gone. She remembered seeing at least half a dozen men but never more than one or two at a time. She described them as having a very stereotypical government agent look – almost as though they were pulled from a movie set. She assumed that's what they were until Maria, the woman being held in a cell next to hers, told her that they weren't what they appeared.

Maria told her that she'd already been there for over twenty years and that the woman who used to reside in Lydia's cell had already been there for forty when she arrived. Maria didn't know what became of the previous occupant; she had been there one day and gone the next with no warning. All of the women were around the same age when they arrived, and all were well-educated with little to no connections where they previously resided. All of their birthdays fell during the same two-week time span, and the similarities didn't stop there.

When they weren't locked in their cells, they were escorted to a darkened room where they could never see the face of the man who commanded the others. Here they would be individually questioned or harmed in an effort to get them to "awaken." None of them understood what this meant until one day when one of the captors grew irritated and intensified Maria's torture while demanding that she use her powers to defend herself. It took her four days to recover enough from that session to be able to move again.

After that incident, three of them made their first escape attempt. It was then that they began to become aware of the true nature of their situation. They were all three out of their cells at the time and made a break for it. An exit was in sight when two men appeared before them seemingly out of thin air. Two more appeared when they turned back the other way. This all occurred prior to Lydia's arrival, and they no longer permitted more than one of them to be out at any given time.

Lydia wouldn't witness this appearing and disappearing act as clearly until she'd been there almost a year. She'd grown to hate the men with such ferocity that her own escape plans developed with murderous intentions. She never heard any names, and they never showed emotion beyond the occasional bout of anger, so this made it easier for her to silence her conscience. The accommodations were clearly quite old and were literally falling apart. Lydia's cell was littered with rocky debris that had fallen from both the ceiling and walls, so she chose to use this to her advantage. She spent days sharpening one end of a chunk of rock until she knew it would draw blood. When one of the men came for her again, she lashed out at him in a rush of adrenaline, stabbing him repeatedly in the neck before he had time to react. He fell backwards grasping at the wounds as she pushed past toward the door. Almost immediately, he appeared in front of her again, completely unharmed and prepared to strike her. She took a hard blow to the head and was on the floor where he should have been. She was moved to a less dilapidated cell at that point.

Having her perception of reality flipped upside-down, she remained shell-shocked for a while after that day and didn't even bother fighting back. A year passed, and then another. No new prisoners arrived, but over time Maria and Lydia became convinced that they were the only two left. They didn't know what became of the others, and neither of them knew if they wanted to know. A few more years passed, and then a year came where they were no longer taken from their cells for the interrogations. Whoever was holding them captive no longer had the same intense interest in them that they had before, and both women had become so docile that the guards began loosening their security.

After seven years, the two finally met face-to-face. Every few days they were allowed out of their cells and able to spend time together. The guards never spoke to them except to tell them to return to their cells when they grew bored watching them. Beyond the opening and closing of the cells, Lydia never saw the guards, but she knew that they could appear anywhere without a moment's notice. During this free time, she and Maria began to test the limits of how far they could make it away from the cells before being given any indication that they would be stopped.

The first time that they made it out of the building, they were apprehended directly outside and lost these free-range privileges for a few months. The second time it was late at night, and they made it fifty yards from the building and into the forest. Once again they were penalized for months. However, both of them had taken note of the lack of any obvious outside barrier. There were no guard towers, fences, or walls. If there were any at all, they were much further away. The only visible entrance to the building itself was a door in the side of a rocky hillside. The third time they made it out, there was only one guard present. He caught Maria as they ran out, but Lydia managed to remain hidden through the night.

This is when she discovered that even if she kept running, she would never have anywhere to go. After receiving her undergraduate degree, she did a year of backpacking around the globe and the majority of that time was spent camping under the stars. She'd become so familiar with the constellations in both the northern and southern hemispheres that she could easily navigate by them. The sky was clear this night, and it was all wrong. She searched the sky in all directions but remained baffled. When they found her in the morning, she was lost in her thoughts, unable to reconcile herself to the fact that she may never see her home again.

This time when they locked her back up, the drive to escape was lost. She wondered if Maria knew how futile their efforts really were. She'd been fueled by anger for so long, and now she felt empty. Any hope for a future had been crushed in a fraction of the time that she'd survived on that hope. The change in her demeanor was readily apparent. The next day, she did nothing but sleep and had no interest in eating anything for a few days. When she still hadn't said anything, Maria expressed her concern and demanded to know what happened to her. Lydia explained what she saw and was met with disbelief. Maybe she didn't know the sky as well as she thought she did.

Lydia knew that it was far more likely that Maria was right, but she didn't want to fool herself either. She had assumed the unfamiliar food was from a part of the world she hadn't yet visited, but now she began to question that. For years, each time she saw the guards, she would ask them why they were still being held there, and she wouldn't receive any acknowledgement. Still she persisted. Until one day, one of them finally gave her an answer.

"Do you think this is where I want to spend my life?" He asked. "If you came across an unusual creature, would you keep it to yourself or would you inform others? Releasing you would do more harm than good. You cannot survive out there."

The remaining years went by in similar fashion. Then finally, within the past year, Maria and Lydia made the final escape. They ran in separate directions with the hopes that at least one of them might make it. Lydia knew she was being watched, but this time she wasn't stopped. She wondered if it had been the same for Maria or if she was pursued by more dutiful guards. Wherever she was, and whatever the case may be, Lydia was determined to remain free.

She didn't care how great the cost.

CHAPTER 15

Lydia remained hidden away at the manor, happy to keep the cats company while Maiya and Mahdon searched for evidence of Tanin's indiscretions. Mahdon provided Maiya with a list of the council chamber locations from the past 500 years and spoke with Saren about possible bunker and prison locations from before that time period. She didn't ask why and happily obliged. They got to work immediately, traveling back each night to ensure they were regularly seen in Fimbira.

Months passed without much progress. Maiya reviewed records of major events, Zumerti deals, and the council's activities at each location she visited. She'd already been through 200 years' worth of records and everything appeared in order and airtight. Mahdon was having similar results. Feeling frustrated, Maiya chose to pause her own investigation and join Mahdon in his. She let Lydia know that they would be gone for a week.

"Do you think we'll find the building?" Maiya asked as the two of them headed out.

He shrugged. "I don't know. There may not be anything left to find."

"And if there isn't?"

"If one person knows you weren't the first, it's likely that there are others. I thought we could start there. If we can find out why she knew, perhaps we can find someone who will talk."

"That's a good point. What are we going to do about Lydia?"

He looked over at her with slight hesitation. "I wanted to talk to you about that."

Maiya frowned. "Okay, nothing positive ever starts that way."

"I think we should take her back to Earth. Keeping her here longer increases the risk that something will happen to her."

"Makes sense to me."

He sighed. "That means we will need to trust others with this secret. Leaving with a ship will not go unnoticed. It would be easier if we could send her on her own and remain here to distract from the departure, but if I were in a similar position, I don't believe I would be comfortable with that."

"I know she wants to go home, but that's going to be a tough sell either way. Are you sure we can trust anyone else with this?"

"I don't think we have much of a choice."

Maiya took a moment to think about this and nodded. "We'll talk to her when we get back."

They landed in Kauria late that night and checked into a room at the same hotel as before. Mahdon already had the necessary contact information for Allonis – the mate of the woman who had gone missing, so they contacted him early the next day and asked if he would be willing to talk. Since Mahdon last saw him, he had taken significant measures to search for Lanys, and her name was all over the local media. Maiya felt embarrassed that she hadn't learned her name up until now. So far all leads came up with dead ends, and any hope for finding her was running dry.

When they arrived at Allonis', they had the opportunity to speak not only with him, but with her immediate family as well. If her family suspected anyone specific to be guilty of foul play, they weren't talking. Maiya got a clear sense from them that they were uncomfortable with her presence, and she suspected that they knew more than they were saying. As Maiya was aware, Lanys came from a prominent family that had close ties with the council, so she decided it was time to use this to her advantage. They were hesitant at first, but it was easy to convince Allonis that any additional or incriminating information he could provide would be kept private. Her mother was more reluctant, and it was clear that this reluctance was driven by fear. Maiya pulled her aside to speak in another room while Mahdon stayed with the others.

"You know something, don't you?" She asked. "Is there a reason you're afraid to tell us what it is?"

She looked down at the floor nervously. "My apologies, High Councilor. I did not mean to offend. We have honored the arrangements; she should not have said anything. If this is a test, I…"

Her voice cracked and trailed off. It was obvious she was on the verge of tears and fighting them off as best she could. Maiya reached for her hands and tilted her head to get a look at her face.

"No test," Maiya said. "I don't know how things were handled in the past, but that's going to change. I'm only looking for the truth."

Maiya spoke with her for a while before returning to the rest of the group.

"I think this has been helpful. Thank you for taking the time to meet with us." She gave Allonis a small smile and then turned to Mahdon. "Mahdon? Do you need anything else before we go?"

Mahdon stood and thanked the family again. Maiya waited until they got back to the hotel to say anything about the conversation she had.

"I don't know if you noticed, but that woman was traumatized. When you spoke with the rest of her family, did you get the same impression?"

He nodded. "I'm unsure of the reason for it, but it was clear that they do not trust us. Allonis was the exception."

"I know why, and it isn't good. There really isn't a nice way to put it."

Mahdon took a seat and sat back to listen. After Maiya left the room with Lanys' mother, he didn't gain any additional useful insight. Allonis mentioned some people with whom Lanys had less than positive interactions but nothing stuck out as worth investigating. He wasn't sure what to expect.

"It seems the Zumerti deals with the council aren't as mutually beneficial as we've been led to believe. It's true that they do receive some benefits, but the cost for them is extreme. If they step out of line," she paused and sighed, "she said that the council is not above threatening them. She assumed we were there to punish them for what her daughter told me."

"What?" Mahdon's face twisted in disgust. "Why would they do that?"

"It gets worse," Maiya said.

"I pray that I'm wrong about what will make this worse."

"The day Lanys went missing, two men paid her family a visit and told them that they wouldn't be seeing her again. They were told that if they didn't take their contract more seriously, there would be dire consequences. I was going to ask her what the men looked like, but we both know that knowing that wouldn't make a difference."

"What kind of contract could that possibly be?"

"I asked that too. Along with many others, her family was hired to work on the construction of a craft for transporting goods from off the planet. Several of them offered to join the crew once it was ready, but they were told that their presence would require too many resources. So, since they couldn't go along, a couple of them decided to build in some hidden recording devices for the sake of living vicariously through those who got to go. Of course, that meant that they saw more than they bargained for, the council found out, and they were given an ultimatum."

Mahdon sighed. "This is a lot to process."

His eyes glazed over as he sat in silence, trying to determine how they should proceed. Though the entire council was being accused of these transgressions, he thought it unlikely that they were all aware of the wrongdoings. Whether or not it was denial, he wasn't sure. What could he do to stop them if they were all responsible? They were already in power, and no cage in the world could hold them. However they chose to handle the situation, there would be risk involved.

"I think I know Naliz well enough to tell if he's lying," Mahdon said. "At least, I hope that I do. I will do my best to figure out his level of involvement."

"Maybe there's a way for us to find out about them all at the same time. We'll have to include Brandon as well."

"What do you suggest?"

"You aren't going to like it," she replied. "You can slow time, and you can pause time. What else can you do with it?"

"Changing time can be messy. What exactly did you want to do?"

"Is it possible to look back without going back?"

"Yes," he nodded, "but you need to know exactly when and where you want to look. If you look in the wrong place, there are serious privacy concerns to consider."

Maiya smiled. "Then I guess we'd better find out where to look."

Thanks to the latest information they obtained, Maiya had a better idea of which records she would need to review. They were able to narrow down the search to two previous council locations, and both were relatively close to their current location. The first site they visited was conveniently located at the base of a crater a few miles outside of town. Despite going unused for more than two centuries, the chambers were immaculate. All of the records were easily accessible, so it didn't take long to find financial notes that struck Maiya as suspicious.

Every trade, arrangement, and other exchange with the locals was thoroughly documented up until a point. The documentation went from including details such as the names of those involved and the exact payment accepted, to providing only vague descriptions. Most of these entries were simply labelled as "negotiated worker" or "essential materials."

Maiya held up the log for Mahdon to see. "I think we have our when. Now it's just a matter of where. Unless that decision was made right here."

"We cannot discount that possibility. It would certainly make this easier."

"Do you mind if we check now? I really want to see this thing firsthand."

Mahdon smiled. "You're the High Councilor. How we handle this is your decision. If my estimates are correct, Daera should be overhead shortly. We should make our way back outside."

Maiya felt they were on the verge of something crucial and was filled with renewed energy. She didn't expect to solve this in a day, but after months of dead ends, the progress they were making was astounding. She wanted to press forward while her motivation was still high. She practically ran to the shuttlecraft, barely allowing Mahdon to get seated before she took it skyward. Daera wasn't expecting them when they docked but was pleased to see them as usual.

"This is unexpected," she said. "To what do I owe the pleasure?"

Maiya grinned. "Official council business."

She leaned over to Mahdon to whisper in his ear. "I always wanted to say that."

Daera smiled. "What can I do for you?"

"We need access to Reedon's Arrow," Mahdon said.

Daera nodded. "Of course."

They made their way to the front of the ship and Daera opened the room for them. They stepped into the room and Maiya nearly fell over from the sudden shock of the minor time shifts. She reached for the wall to balance herself and watched with fascination as the images moved around the pyramid.

"Wow," she said, "I feel funny. How does this thing work?"

"It's largely thought controlled. You need to get close to use it. I can show you."

Maiya stepped through the images with Mahdon and watched as he reached out a hand toward the pyramid. The images displayed on the side facing them changed to those of the council chambers outside of Kauria. Maiya found the mosaic of the thousands of moments in time to be dizzying. The moments that played before them narrowed until only those spanning the first few days of the vague logs were displayed.

"Stop," Mahdon said, and the scenes froze before them. "You hold an image of the location in your mind. If you know what was happening at the time, it makes for a more efficient search, but in this case we only have a rough time period to go on. The more exact you are with your timing, the fewer scenes you will need to review. We can now watch each of these individually as we choose. This can also be used to reverse time at the selected location, but that should only be done close to the present time."

"Why is that?"

"If you aren't careful or inclusive enough with what to leave unaffected, the results can be unpredictable."

He pulled up one of the frozen moments and allowed it to play out. Maiya felt like she was watching security footage and couldn't help but wonder how the 'camera' angle was decided.

"Is it safe for me to interact with it?"

Mahdon nodded. "Yes. Verbal commands are necessary to do anything beyond viewing, so feel free to review."

Out of curiosity, she reached out a hand and found that she could, in fact, change the perspective as well as zoom in and out. She watched as five individuals materialized in the meeting room. Though they didn't appear human, they bore some resemblance to the leaders she knew. It was strange for her to see them this way; she felt like she was spying on a group of strangers. She watched as the meeting began and listened to their discussion on the notes they'd received about some religious prophecy.

"Interesting," Mahdon said. "I remember providing that information to them at the open meeting prior to this. This was regarding where we might find you. It was the first time we broached the subject."

Maiya found this surprising. "This was hundreds of years before I was born."

"Yes, but it is when we first started to notice the signs that your time was approaching."

As the meeting went on, the council decided that they wouldn't be allocating any time or resources to investigating the claims further. Mahdon shook his head as he listened, remembering all the times he presented evidence only to be ignored. It had been a very frustrating time for him. He eventually got Naliz on board when he finally took the time to properly analyze everything Mahdon told him. The meeting was wrapping up when Saren stopped the group to bring up one last topic.

"I have spoken with the Lorian family, and they expressed interest in taking part in our latest venture," she said. "I don't believe I am aware of any new arrangements."

"Have they mentioned any details of what this might be? The last agreement we discussed was regarding housing, was it not?" Naliz asked.

"That is correct. They seemed to think there is a new, unrelated opportunity. They did not give specifics; they assumed that I knew what they were referencing."

Brandon looked over to Tanin. "I presume you have informed the rest of the council on the status of our current relations with the Zumerti?"

"There is nothing to tell, High Councilor," Tanin said. "I will have someone speak with them and clear up any confusion."

Brandon smiled. "Excellent. We will reconvene at the usual time. This meeting is adjourned."

They all disappeared as quickly as they had appeared, and time continued forward with nothing new to be seen.

"When was this?" Maiya asked.

"This took place after the first unusual transaction. No more than a day or two after the date in the log."

Maiya nodded. "I thought so. I think it's safe to say that he lied, but that doesn't mean they didn't find out about this later."

"True. Still, it is a relief to know that they were not complicit in the initial planning."

"I wish we knew the dates when those women were actually brought here. I'd like to see who took part in the actual transport. Any idea what could have happened to this ship they were building? It's not this one, is it?"

Mahdon shook his head. "No, this was constructed very openly. The records have long been accessible to the public. Perhaps we can find more useful information at the next site."

They spent some more time reviewing the meetings that followed the one they'd just watched, but they found nothing of interest. If the rest of the council was aware of the project, they never discussed it in their most private interactions. Determining that there would be no more useful information gathered from this location, Maiya and Mahdon decided to call it a day. Daera was surprised when she finally saw them again several hours later, but she didn't pry into what they has been doing.

"Thank you," Maiya said as they headed out. "Our activity here is to be kept private. We may be back in a couple of days."

Daera nodded and bid them farewell. The next day they left Kauria and dedicated the entire day to flying to the second site. They made several stops along the way to enjoy the scenery and spend time together away from the frantic pace that had become their day-to-day life. Maiya was content to do nothing but sit together and watch the day go by in silence. When they did talk, it was about their future and the goals they hoped to accomplish. Mahdon hadn't asked much about what she intended to do about the life she had back on Earth, but now that the topic of returning for Lydia's sake had been brought up, he found it difficult not to ask.

She'd already expressed her intention to stay, but it was never clear if that was a decision for the short-term or one for life. He wondered if she would change her mind once they went back. He'd spent minimal time on her planet and was admittedly hoping to see more of it. He would even be willing to live there if she asked it of him. He also wondered how Lahna was faring given her extensive stay on an alien world. It would be nice to catch up with her after they dropped off Lydia. He casually mentioned this, and Maiya laughed, joking that she hoped Lahna hadn't died of boredom.

All discussion about the trip ceased there, and they returned their attention to the task at hand. They stayed in a smaller town that night and retrieved the records the next day with plans to go through them when they got back to the manor. While she didn't expect anyone to have stopped by, she was anxious to get back and check on Lydia. Mahdon had already planned to get Naliz alone to talk when they returned and was similarly anxious for their arrival. Upon their return, Maiya found Lydia in the lounge, and Mahdon went off to meet with Naliz.

Lydia's response to their travel plans was enthusiastic, but as expected, she was less than thrilled when Maiya indicated that it would be better to have more people on board with the plan.

"I don't get why you can't just say you're going back," she grumbled.

"They know I'm in the middle of an investigation; I think the timing would be considered odd to them."

"So what?"

Maiya sighed. "Would you put your faith in a leader who ran off to take a vacation whenever anything important came up?"

"Leader? Give me a break. You can't seriously be planning to come back. What could you possibly want to stay here for?" Lydia was pacing the room, clearly annoyed.

Maiya thought it was better to let her air her grievances than to try to argue. She had every right to be concerned about the level of risk they'd be taking. Lydia was mid-rant when Mahdon returned from his own discussion. She stopped to look at him and then broke out laughing.

"That's why," she said with a shake of the head. "It is, isn't it? You're going to throw your whole life away for a man?"

Maiya sighed. "Are you done?"

"I just don't get it. All I want is to get away from this place."

"Given your experiences, I don't blame you. I'm sorry that happened to you, I really am, but this isn't as black and white as you're making it out to be. Please try to understand that." She looked over to Mahdon. "Do you have something for me?"

"Yes."

She left the room with him, and they went upstairs to talk in the study. Mahdon sat down, and Maiya could already tell that he was worried about what her response would be to what he was about to tell her.

"The conversation went a little differently than I intended."

"Meaning?"

"He knows me too well. He could tell that I knew something before I had a chance to ask him anything."

Maiya sighed. "What did you tell him?"

"I know what you're thinking. He doesn't know that Lydia is here."

Maiya's tension eased. She was in no mood to get into another dispute with Lydia before the current one had time to pass. "I love you, but you really need to work on that tell of yours."

He looked confused but continued. "He knows that we saw someone and that we reviewed some records. He asked what we found, and now he wants to confront Tanin. He was not pleased about being lied to. He isn't convinced that the records are related to a ship, but he agrees that they wouldn't be kept secret if the council would have approved of them."

"When was he planning to do this?"

"He agreed not to say anything until he's discussed it with you. He wants to stop by later."

"Oh," Maiya frowned, "That complicates things a little. Now I have to figure out what to tell Lydia. She's already annoyed with me."

"I saw that. Is there anything I can do to help?"

"I'm pretty sure she views every single one of you as an enemy. In her current mood, she's more likely to throw something at your head than to listen to you."

He shrugged. "The day we met, you asked if I was going to kill you. Stranger things have happened."

"Your optimism is sweet, it really is." She sat down and sent him a challenging smile. "If you think she'll be nicer to you, be my guest and go talk to her."

"Challenge accepted." He returned her smile and left the room.

Maiya envisioned Lydia yelling at him and was already planning her 'I told you so' speech. She knew it was childish, but she was feeling salty at the prospect of him being a better negotiator than her. It took approximately twenty minutes for him to return, and when he did, he was not alone. He had a very sheepish looking Lydia in tow.

Lydia sighed. "I'm sorry for going off on you earlier. I know you're not trying to screw me over."

Maiya stared at her dumbfounded and then looked at Mahdon who was looking irritatingly proud of himself.

"What in the actual hell?" She exclaimed.

He shrugged slightly, as though he had no idea why she was responding as such.

"Um, okay," Lydia said. "Did I miss something?"

Maiya turned back to Lydia and shook her head. "Nope. I appreciate you saying that. Thank you."

"Anyway," Lydia continued, "I'm tired of hiding. If it's okay with you, I'd like to be here when you talk to your friends. Nothing's going to change if I keep expecting you to put off the inevitable."

"Are you sure?"

She nodded and took a seat across from Maiya. Mahdon contacted Naliz and let him know that it was a good time to come by if he was ready. He arrived almost immediately thereafter and brought Saren along. Mahdon met them outside and led them up to the study to meet with the others. It took them a moment to notice Lydia, at which point Naliz gave her a very similar look to the one that Mahdon had when he first saw her. Saren smirked and said nothing.

"Mahdon," Naliz said slowly, "a word, please."

The two stepped back out of the room and closed the doors. Naliz opened his mouth to speak and then waffled over what he wanted to say. He took a deep breath to calm himself before saying anything.

"This is not what we discussed. Why is it that you always wait until I arrive to tell me what's going on? I was not prepared for this. A private ledger is one thing, but this," he shook his head and sighed, "this is something entirely different. If she didn't come here of her own volition, which, given the secrecy, I gather she did not, then what we have here is a serious crime. People used to pay with their lives for similar offenses."

"I am well aware. Maiya has had her reasons for not divulging this information."

"As well she should. There's no telling how many may be involved. I do not like surprises, Mahdon. I hope the High Councilor has a plan."

When they re-entered the room, Maiya was explaining their intentions to Saren. Naliz waited for them to finish and then went to introduce himself to Lydia. She looked him up and down and then interrupted his introduction.

"I know who you are," she said scornfully. "You're another one of the politicians who did nothing to prevent this from happening."

Saren laughed. "I like this one."

Naliz shot Saren a glare. "I'm very sorry for what happened to you. Had I been aware of the circumstances, I would have done my best to prevent it. It's too late for that, so now all we can do is remedy the situation."

"We need you to keep the focus on cultural relations for a while," Maiya told him. "As far as anyone else is concerned, Mahdon and I are tying up some loose ends back on Earth and will address any concerns and act as mediators upon our return. Naliz, you will serve as High Councilor during our absence."

"I will not disappoint. When will you be departing? Jo'dai will want to make sure you have adequate security to accompany you."

"I'm sure he will, but if there's going to be anyone else joining us, they need to be thoroughly vetted. I don't want anyone along who is good friends with Tanin or who may have been a guard at this facility... wherever that may be."

Naliz sat on the arm of one of the chairs. "To what facility are you referring?"

"Why the hell do you think I was brought here?" Lydia asked. "It wasn't to hang out and get to know everybody."

"Truthfully, I had not thought about the reason why. The fact that you were is reason enough for concern."

Lydia began sharing her story all over again. Maiya watched Naliz and Saren's faces to better read their reactions. Saren's expression shifted from amused to appalled, and Naliz looked increasingly uncomfortable. By the time she had finished the retelling, Naliz looked livid. Seeing this increased Maiya's confidence that neither of them were involved.

Naliz stood and paced around the room. "I'm going to kill him. As soon as we can prove his guilt, he's finished."

"That may be a while," Maiya said. "Everything we have is circumstantial. There's obviously someone responsible, but we can't conclusively say it was him. How do you expect to find out?"

He stopped pacing to meet her gaze. "There are ways."

CHAPTER 16

Naliz indicated that he and Saren would use every resource at their disposal to search for evidence while Maiya was away. He informed Maiya that Reedon's Arrow and the Hokaruin Orb were but two of four powerful artifacts. Two of these artifacts had been lost and two had not. In addition to Reedon's Arrow, the council had access to the Seed of Revelation. This allowed an individual to pose a question and learn the truth they most feared. Though what they were shown was the absolute truth, it was always the most negative answer that suited the question. Given the dark nature of the artifact, it had seldom been used unless the questioner already knew the answer wouldn't be good.

Naliz intended to use this to their advantage, but it would require something from Tanin to be of use to them. There was a point in time when they could have used something as simple as a strand of hair. While this would still be possible with a human or Zumerti, it was no longer a feasible option for the others given the dynamic nature of their form. This meant that they would need to get their hands on something he valued if they wanted an accurate answer. The first challenge would be determining what, if anything, he valued. The next challenge would, of course, be acquiring it. Mahdon and Maiya wished them luck with this task and then made preparations for their own objective.

They took a roster of who was currently onboard the ship and had those leave who were not along for Maiya's initial transfer. Though the plan was to keep Lydia out of sight – a seemingly easy task given the size of the ship – Mahdon felt he could trust the remaining crew should that prove to be a problem. It took a couple of days for Naliz and Maiya to convince Jo'dai that a security detail wouldn't be necessary off-planet, but he ultimately relented. The ship was stocked with supplies, and then Lydia and the cats were taken aboard shortly before the intended departure.

They were closing in on the two-year anniversary of Maiya's arrival when they left Amertine behind. Maiya watched as the planet shrank to a speck in the distance and felt the same level of anxiety and anticipation that she had on that first day. This time, however, the fear was replaced with indecision about what to do once they arrived. Lydia had been gone for so long that she would no longer have a home or job to go back to. They could return her to her hometown, but then what? What would she tell her family? 'Abducted by aliens' hardly seemed the correct answer.

In all this time, Maiya had only learned the most basic details about Lydia's life on Earth. She hadn't asked because it felt too much like rubbing salt in the wounds. Now that they were safely on their way back, she was more comfortable with the idea. Lydia had become much less hostile as well and freely opened up about where she'd left off with her life. She'd just completed her master's degree for Atmospheric and Oceanic Sciences, had informed her family, and was preparing to celebrate. She already had a job waiting, so everything was looking up. As with Maiya, she had been fully engaged in her studies and had little in the way of local friends. Her last night was spent with several of her classmates; they had dinner and a couple of drinks but nothing significant. Despite this, she didn't recall ever making it home.

Prior to all of that, she'd grown up in the Midwest with her parents and younger brother. Her brother had recently gotten engaged, and the wedding was planned for the following year. She now wondered if he was still married and if she had nieces and nephews who'd grown up without ever knowing her. The thought had fouled her mood for years, but now the prospect of meeting them made her smile.

"Where will you go?" Maiya asked her. "What will you do now?"

"I guess I'll go back to see my parents. That's assuming that they're still alive."

"What are you going to tell them?"

Lydia furrowed her brow. "Don't you have a plan for that?"

"What were you thinking would happen?"

"I don't know. I never expected to get home, honestly."

"Think about it, and I'll discuss the options with Mahdon and get back to you."

Maiya had intended to give Lydia an answer that same day, but coming up with a solution wasn't as simple as she'd hoped. In all likelihood, Lydia had already been declared dead. This would make getting her life back even more of a hassle than it was already going to be. They would need to explain her missing time, and her return would draw a lot of attention. Another option was to come back with a new identity. Mahdon assured them that he could get the appropriate documents to achieve this. This would be easier to arrange, but it meant that Lydia could never see her family again. She made it clear that she'd rather take her chances with her real identity.

This left them with the original problem of explaining where she'd been for so long. Though Lydia remained amused by the idea, it didn't seem practical to Maiya to play the amnesia card. Not only was it rare, but it would be difficult to maintain the charade. The only idea that remained plausible to Maiya was to fabricate a long-term abduction by somebody else. The questions grew from there. Where had this person been keeping her? Why did they abduct her? How did she escape? And, perhaps most pressing, who abducted her? Maiya toyed with some possibilities for how this could be managed, but it would require a bit of compliance from Mahdon or one of the other Amerti on this voyage.

It would require a bit of time, commitment, and willingness to deceive. She wasn't yet comfortable with her approach on how to make the suggestion. It was, however, the one idea she thought they could flawlessly pull off. When Maiya finally presented her idea to Mahdon, he was initially reluctant. It would require someone to take on the role of captor and act out the repulsive personality. Lydia fully supported the plan; she had, in fact, stated that it would be like playing a part in a movie. Mahdon wasn't so sure. He likened it to lying and was uncomfortable with the notion of playing the part himself. He wanted to help as needed but would rather someone else do it. They agreed to check with Lahna upon arrival and discussed additional details in the interim.

The trip back went by relatively slowly at first, but as they began to occupy their days with arrival plans, the time seemed to fly by. They played games and listened to Lydia share her excitement about the future she could now have. She was already talking about the book deals she could get to share the harrowing story of her captive years. Mahdon was especially confused by this. If she did this and avoided the truth, she wouldn't just spend a few years sharing her story; she'd spend the rest of her life living a lie.

It wasn't until midway through the trip when the crew became aware of Lydia's presence. She'd spent the majority of her time either in her quarters or in one of the conference rooms playing with the holographic displays. Maiya typically brought her meals to her there, which she never seemed to mind. After two weeks, she'd grown bored with walking the same routes day in and day out. She decided to explore in the opposite direction when she happened upon the bridge. Within seconds of entering, a man appeared near a console to her right. He was clearly surprised but also pleased by her arrival.

He smiled. "There are two of you. I was unaware the goddess brought a friend."

"Heh. Goddess?" Lydia stopped herself just short of laughing and muttered to herself. "And here I thought the whole super power thing was farfetched."

"You must think me terribly rude. I should have introduced myself when we came to your planet the first time." He extended a hand. "My name is Klydin."

Lydia looked at his outstretched hand and then shook it awkwardly. "I'm Lydia."

"Why haven't we met yet? It must have been a difficult adjustment for you."

"Yes, that's why," she said as she meandered to the forward-facing window and watched the stars streak by. "I wish I could have seen this before. At least then I would have known something beautiful."

"Have you known the goddess a long time?" Klydin asked.

"No." She walked back from the window. "Can we please just call her by her name?"

"I do not wish to be disrespectful."

"Trust me, she won't mind. What's your role in all of this?"

"I'm the navigations expert."

"Cool. Do you know where we are?"

"We are nearing the star you call 'Bellatrix.'"

She stared at him, waiting for him to explain further. After a while, it was clear he didn't realize she was expecting more from him. She sighed. "I have no idea where that is."

"It's part of the constellation you call 'Orion.'"

"Ah, okay. Thanks. At least I can see that from home."

Klydin watched her as she stared out the window. "May I ask what has brought you to the bridge?"

Lydia made a face and waved a hand in the air as if she was physically searching for the answer. "Just bored. I'm not sure where Maiya or Mahdon went, and I haven't been up this way. The view is great here. Do you ever tire of it?"

"I have not yet. I've mapped out large stretches of the galaxy, but I've only visited a few locations. You can see them here." He brought up a holographic map and pointed out three stars closer to Amertine. "Perhaps I can explore your planet when we arrive. I was not given the opportunity last time."

Lydia smirked. "Good luck with that. Most humans never have that opportunity."

As Lydia was about to leave, Daera was returning to the bridge.

Daera smiled. "Oh, hello! I don't recall seeing any mention of you on either manifest. You must be important if they're keeping you a secret."

Klydin looked at Daera in surprise. "You haven't met before?"

"No. I don't think we were supposed to either."

"Well, this was fun," Lydia said and exited the bridge while the two crew members stared after her in confusion.

When Maiya woke the next day, Mahdon was already waiting to talk to her. After meeting Lydia, Daera contacted Mahdon to inquire about the situation. He had been vague in his response and wanted to let Maiya know before he said anything further. Fully aware that Lydia would likely be discovered, they had discussed their options about what to tell the crew. They eventually decided that the truth would be easiest and reasonably safe considering the journey was already underway. They agreed to inform them all at once to prevent any further random encounters should Lydia wander off. Maiya called for the crew to report to the dining hall, and when everyone was assembled, she stood to formally introduce Lydia.

"As some of you are already aware, we have a guest onboard who, like me, came from Earth. This is Lydia. The purpose of this mission is to take her home. Given the nature of the events that brought her here in the first place, any knowledge of her is privileged information. Those who need to know about her have already been informed. Likewise, there are others who shouldn't know, so keep it to yourselves. Understood?"

Each crew member acknowledged their understanding as they left to return to their posts. Daera stopped Maiya on her way out.

"Why all the secrecy?" Daera asked.

"There's an ongoing investigation," Maiya said. "That's all you need to know for now."

Daera nodded and filed out of the room with the rest of them. During the time that remained, several crew members talked amongst themselves about their theories surrounding the situation, but no one said anything to suggest they knew more than that. Much to Maiya's relief, the next two weeks passed without incident, and she once again found herself gazing down at the planet she had called home. The thought of returning felt increasingly odd to her, as she contemplated what she would tell her family if she dared to visit them at all. Meanwhile, Lydia was anxious to get to the surface and pick up where she'd left off.

"Are you ready to go?" Mahdon asked.

He met Maiya on the bridge and drew her out of her daze. She nodded and walked with him to the shuttle bay. "Yeah. Did you talk to Lydia?"

"Yes. She's quite stubborn, but she understands."

Maiya and Mahdon would be going down to meet up with Lahna before putting their plans into action. Daera contacted her ahead of time so she'd be prepared for their arrival, but neither was familiar with what had been discussed in regard to Lydia. As they were boarding the shuttlecraft, Daera showed up to deliver one final message.

"High Councilor, my apologies for not mentioning this sooner, but there's something you should know."

Maiya stopped and eyed her suspiciously. "What?"

"When I came to collect your cats, I spoke with Lahna to see how things were going here. It sounds like not much has changed since then, but as far as your life goes, she's made some… changes."

"Meaning?"

"It may be better for you to see for yourself, but you'll need to be careful. She doesn't live alone anymore."

"Wait," Maiya said. "If she doesn't live alone, then should I even be going down there? Won't they mistake me for her?"

"She has that covered. I've already activated the time perimeter, but you'll want to land away from the apartment since she isn't alone."

"Thanks."

Mahdon landed the craft on the opposite end of the apartment complex. Much like the last time they were here, the time change on the surrounding environment would affect anyone else who entered the perimeter while leaving them unaffected. As they approached the apartment, Maiya wondered what else Lahna could possibly have changed. She hoped that being alone on the planet hadn't harmed her sanity. Before knocking on the door, she looked to Mahdon for support and he gave her a reassuring smile. The one who answered the door was a sandy-haired man with glasses and a bubbly personality. He shook each of their hands as he introduced himself.

"Wow, the resemblance is uncanny. You must be Maiya's cousin. I'm Liam. It's nice to meet you."

Maiya smiled politely. "It's nice to meet you too."

"I'm sure Maiya told me already, but I have an awful memory for names."

"Oh, um, I'm Marie," she pointed at Mahdon, "And this is Mark."

Mahdon smiled. "It's nice to meet you."

"Please, come in. Maiya should be out in a moment. She was wrapping up arrangements for the sampling tomorrow."

"Sampling?" Maiya asked.

"The wedding venue is putting together some options for us to try. Their selections sound amazing; it should be a pretty good menu. Can I get you something to drink? If you're into beer, I have a lager that I made. If not, that's cool too."

"That sounds great."

Maiya and Mahdon took a seat on the couch while Liam disappeared into the kitchen. She looked at Mahdon wide-eyed and tried to keep her voice down as she shared her surprise.

"I'm engaged?! What the hell happened while I was away?"

Liam returned with a glass for each of them and was describing the flavor profile when Lahna joined them. Her hair was considerably shorter than Maiya's at this point and was now a natural looking wavy blonde. She sat by Liam and smiled sweetly.

"It's so nice to see you again. Will you be in town for long?"

"We're just passing through," Maiya said. "It will be nice to catch up. I was also hoping we could discuss a family matter if you have a chance."

"Of course."

Maiya took a sip of the beer and was pleasantly surprised. "This is really good. Thanks for sharing. Do you brew regularly?"

"This is only my third batch, but you have to start somewhere. I'm glad you like it."

Maiya looked back to Lahna. "I hear that congratulations are in order. Getting married, wow. That's a big commitment. Planning to stay in the area?"

"For now," Lahna said, fully understanding the true meaning behind the question.

Maiya leaned forward, activating her communicator while doing so. "We really need to talk."

Liam now sat frozen mid-drink, courtesy of Daera. Per a last-minute decision, she was to be ready to act should the roommate cause a delay in Maiya's plans. Though Maiya could have easily waited for an opportunity to take Lahna aside, she found herself growing impatient with not knowing what 'she' had been doing for two years. Lahna glanced over at Liam and then back to Maiya.

"I was wondering if you might do something like that."

"It looks like you've settled in nicely. Does he know what you are?"

"No. Maybe I'll take him back with me someday, but I'm happy here now. From my understanding, you've made quite the life for yourself as well. Am I mistaken in sensing something between the two of you?"

Mahdon smiled. "Did Daera tell you?"

"She only mentioned the change in the council head. If you ask me, it's about time. Brandon has always been power hungry."

"What have you been doing since we left?" Maiya asked.

"Well, 'you' are graduating early. I upped my course load and have been spending most of my time outside of that working on a research project. I met Liam at a physics symposium that first year. I never intended to make this permanent, but I'm useful here. Every old idea I have is new here. The hardest part is pretending I don't know as much as I do."

"You're really happy?"

Lahna smiled. "Yes. Of course, if you want it back, I can start again. I would miss Liam, though. He's a very sweet man."

Maiya was happy for Lahna and relieved that things were going well, but she couldn't help but silently mourn her old life. If she didn't, no one else would. Lahna really had been a better version of her.

"Have you seen my family?" Maiya asked.

"I haven't seen them, but I have spoken with them. They're doing well. Will you be visiting them?"

"I don't know. I should, but I'm afraid it will make this harder."

Lahna nodded her understanding. "You aren't staying then."

Maiya shook her head. "No."

"Then why are you here? I would have happily sent a report had one been requested."

"We need to return a woman, and we were hoping that you would be willing to help with that."

A bemused look crossed Lahna's face. "Return a woman? What do you mean by that?"

"She was abducted," Mahdon explained. "We do not know who all was involved, but she's been missing for quite some time. We cannot leave her without an explanation for where she's been all this time."

"Who would do such a thing? Why?"

"The evidence suggests that they were trying to find Maiya – or someone like her. There were others, but we do not know what became of them."

Lahna frowned. "Despicable. What can I do to help?"

Mahdon filled her in on the specifics of the plan, and Lahna readily agreed provided they could wait until Liam was away at a conference later that week. She said it was the least she could do given the extent to which she'd taken over Maiya's life. They already had the completed documentation prepared for their captor's persona, so now it was only a matter of getting everything in place. Though there had been many details to iron out to cover their tracks, the plan itself was simple.

They would come collect Lahna in two days' time and bring her and Lydia to a location predetermined by Maiya. Lydia would 'escape' and be found by unsuspecting strangers along the closest roadway. Ideally, the authorities would waste no time in locating and apprehending her kidnapper. They would collect her fingerprints and DNA which would conveniently match those they had planted in the FBI database. After a couple of days of media coverage, the kidnapper would seemingly disappear without a trace. The alter ego would be on the most wanted list, and Lydia would be free to tell the tale of the woman who insisted she was keeping her safe from the apocalypse.

After they finished detailing the plan for Lahna, Maiya looked at the still frozen Liam and then down at her empty glass. "I think I'm going to need another one of these. It might look a bit strange if my beer is suddenly gone."

Lahna laughed and refilled it for her. "As amusing as that might be, your point is valid."

Maiya thanked her and took a swig. "Daera, we're good here."

When Liam returned to the standard flow of time, he managed to spill his drink on himself and Maiya nearly choked on her own while fighting back a laugh. She wondered if the shift in time had any lingering side effects or if he was otherwise aware of it. Liam commented on his clumsiness while Lahna brought him a towel. They made small talk while they finished their drinks and then Maiya and Mahdon thanked them for their hospitality and returned to the ship. Lydia was already in the shuttle bay when they landed. She walked over to Maiya before she even had a chance to stand.

"Well? How did it go?" She asked.

"You'll have to wait a couple of days, but she agreed."

The look on Lydia's face shifted from one of anxiety to pure glee. She hugged Maiya and when she walked, she had a noticeable bounce in her step. The next day, she finished working through the minor details of her story, and when the time came to execute the plan, she had a difficult time containing her excitement. Daera had been able to confirm that Lydia's parents and brother were alive and well, and she had twin nieces to meet.

They picked Lahna up as planned and dropped her off at the remote, and currently uninhabited, cabin in the Southern Rockies. They provided her with a complete set of used survival gear, and she took on the appearance of an older, athletic woman with crudely cut greying hair. They thanked her and promised to keep an eye on the news until she performed her disappearing act. Next, they dropped off Lydia closer to the highway.

Lydia hugged them both. "If you change your mind and decide to come back, look me up."

"Will do," Maiya said, "but then it will be your turn to supply the wine."

Lydia smiled and laughed. "Deal."

They wished her well and said their goodbyes. Mahdon positioned the cloaked shuttlecraft overhead so they could witness her rescue firsthand, and when they were confident that she was in good hands, they returned to the main ship. As promised, they monitored the media and watched the tale unfold over the coming days. Lahna played her part well and raved about the end of days while Lydia enjoyed a tearful reunion with her family. Watching Lahna on the news, Maiya couldn't help but wonder how much of her life was nothing more than an act based on Maiya's old one. She'd made adjustments that Maiya never would have, but had her personality changed drastically from her true identity? Whatever the case may be, she nailed the performance that she was putting on now. The day that Liam was scheduled to return from his conference, the breaking news hit that 'Selma Packerman' had mysteriously vanished, and Lahna was back home in time to meet her fiancé.

Their job complete, Maiya hesitated to leave. She hadn't seen her own family in years and felt she owed it to them – and herself – to give a proper goodbye. The reality was that they would never know that's what she was doing, and the whole idea felt grossly awkward. She realized that if she thought too much about it, she'd break down and cry, but staying didn't feel right either. She'd become a woman torn between two worlds, and neither would leave her feeling complete. She had a sense of purpose now, but it wasn't here.

Reedon's Arrow made it possible for her to watch her family from afar, and she did so for a couple of days before making her final decision. She put together a care package that included a long, sentimental, and she later decided – rambling – letter and shipped it to them from her old town in Colorado. She vowed to return for a visit once the investigation was concluded and relations stabilized on Amertine. She took one last look and bid the planet farewell.

CHAPTER 17

Maiya didn't say much about their short visit to Earth. Instead, she chose to focus on what awaited them when they made it home. They limited their communications during this time in an effort to reduce the risk of a security breach. Any contact with Naliz was done over a secure line and kept as brief as possible. They informed him that their trip was a success and he indicated that a development had been made on his end as well. Maiya stopped herself just short of inquiring further, then thanked him for his help. At the very least, the progress sounded promising.

Mahdon took notice of her inability to relax and be patient, and thus, did his best to distract her with less serious matters. He told her of popular tourist destinations on Amertine and of the planets they could visit without an extensive time investment. While this certainly served its purpose, it became more difficult to calm her mind the closer they got to their arrival. He worried that this might negatively impact his own ambition, but ultimately, it was more important to him that she be happy. When it came within a week of their arrival, he allowed himself to at least present his idea to her.

"There will be a total lunar eclipse the night of our arrival," he told her, "it will be one unlike any other. It is rare that both moons exist in syzygy with the planet, but that will be the case that night when they're both full. It would delay our landing a bit, as I believe this will be best seen from our closer moon. If you're interested, I would very much like for you to join me."

Maiya was intrigued. "Sure, why not? But won't we miss out on seeing the moons align if we watch from there?"

"We can return to the planet's surface in time to watch them shift from their alignment. At the point of totality, it will present itself as a total solar eclipse from the moon. I thought you might enjoy experiencing both a lunar and solar eclipse in one night."

Maiya smiled. "That sounds great."

When they entered the planet's orbit again, Maiya had Daera contact Naliz to inform him of their arrival and nighttime plans. He welcomed them back and let them know that he would be stopping by the manor early the next day. Seeing this as her last opportunity to relax before a potentially tumultuous day, Maiya suggested they turn their eclipse viewing into a dinner date. She commandeered the kitchen for an hour and put together her personal version of fettucine alfredo to take along. She met him in the shuttle bay, and though he was always well-dressed, she thought he looked extra nice that day. She couldn't put her finger on it, but something about him was different and her heart melted when she saw him.

She smiled. "Well, don't you look dapper?"

The eclipse was well underway when Mahdon flew them down to the surface, but it was far from totality. He opened a bottle of chardonnay while Maiya set up their meal on the little table they placed in the shuttle for the occasion. The quarters were cramped, but the view was perfect.

"Have you witnessed this before?" Maiya asked.

"Once, but not from up here. I hope you won't be disappointed."

"Are you kidding me? I've already seen things that most people never will. Simply being here is amazing."

"I still remember the first time I saw Amertine from up here. It was surreal. I stared for a long time thinking about how small my world was when it had felt so big before. Yet there I was, able to see it all from the confines of a ship. It's a bizarre feeling to feel both trapped and free all at once."

Maiya nodded. "I know exactly what you mean."

As they wrapped up their dinner, Mahdon set down his fork and nodded toward the front window. "Have you noticed how much darker it's gotten? It's getting close now."

Maiya turned her attention outward and watched as the surface of the moon around them took on an orange-red hue and nothing but a red ring surrounded the planet. She'd never seen anything like it and sat mesmerized by the totality.

"Every sunrise and sunset," Mahdon said.

"It's beautiful."

"There's an old fable that says that if one is to stand in the light such as this, they will be granted eternal life and will know only happiness throughout those days."

"It looks like you're a little ahead of the game on that one," Maiya said.

She was still fixated on the eclipse and didn't notice when he reached into his pocket and pulled something out.

"It may not be eternity," he said, "but I would be honored if you will allow me to spend what time we have with you by my side. I understand that there is a tradition in your culture to symbolize this intention and commitment."

Maiya looked back to him now and gasped as he produced an amethyst and diamond ring. The band itself resembled vines that flowered where the gems were set. Her hands began to tremble as her heart picked up the pace.

"This has been at the forefront of my mind for months now. Waiting for this moment has been difficult, but it was important to me that you be less stressed when I ask. Will you do me the honor of walking by my side?"

Maiya sat speechless, questioning if this was really happening. She knew her answer, but the words evaded her. She didn't think she would ever understand how he could look at her with such love and admiration. A happy crier, she nodded as she felt herself begin to tear up.

"Yes."

She held out her hand for him to slip the ring on her finger and then leaned across the table to kiss him. Upon returning to the manor, they laid out a blanket amid the flower garden and watched the eclipse from the other side. So much of Maiya's life had been focused on what she was lacking and how she fell short, and now the pendulum had swung so far in the opposite direction that it hardly felt real. Though Naliz was due to arrive in a few hours, Maiya found herself too high on dopamine to sleep.

By the time Naliz arrived, she had barely slept, but the giddy school girl feeling from before had her smiling nearly non-stop. She wondered if

Mahdon had shared his intentions with him. They met at the front door and proceeded to the lounge.

"Welcome home, Mahdon. And you as well, High Councilor."

"Thank you," Maiya said. "How have things been going here?"

"They are," he paused as he often did when debating his word choice, "progressing in the right direction. I have taken the liberty of scheduling a meeting for this afternoon under the guise of a status update due to your arrival. I believe we have what we need to confront Tanin, and I think we should do so today."

"What did you find?"

"The question was posed, and what we witnessed took place in orbit around your planet. I was neither familiar with the ship nor the crew. They all took on the same likeness, and they gave no indication of who they might be. Tanin was giving them orders to bring back the woman who met the criteria he provided to them."

"What sort of criteria?" Maiya asked.

"He told them that she should be 'the same as the last ones,' but that the coordinates differed. He remained off planet, and several of them returned with an unconscious woman. I do not claim to be an expert on human aging, but she resembled the one you took back."

"Can you show me?"

"Yes, of course. I thought you might like to, so I came prepared."

He unwrapped what looked to Maiya to be nothing more than a misshapen hunk of rock. Whatever it was, she could tell that it had been broken in some way.

"What is that?"

"What remains of his most precious possession."

Maiya eyed it curiously. "How do we use it?"

"It will require us to go elsewhere if you wish to see it firsthand. The Seed was planted not far from here."

The three walked out the back doorway of the manor and headed through the garden to the back woods. Naliz had suggested that they walk to avoid any unnecessary attention. He explained that where the artifact was buried, a spring had formed that now contained the power required to answer inquiries. The spring was hidden away in a secluded woodland clearing, sheltered within a small cave. To the untrained eye, it appeared as no more than a shallow pool with a mound of rock rising out of it.

Up close, Maiya could see the top of a hole at the bottom of the mound from which the water flowed. Naliz told her that they would need to go inside; this meant she would need to slip under the water to swim to the other side. She wished he had told her this beforehand so she could have at least adjusted her clothing choice. She took off her shoes and removed her outer-most layer of clothing to swim over, and when she made it through the gap, she watched Naliz and Mahdon appear completely dry on the rock in front of her.

"I was unaware that this existed," Mahdon said. "Has it been here long?"

Naliz nodded. "Centuries at least."

They helped Maiya up and she took a look around the small cavern. The hole she swam through was the only large entrance, though there was a smaller opening roughly twenty feet up near the peak. They currently stood on a relatively smooth rock floor that split the main pool from the point where she'd come in. The entire cavern glowed blue, and thousands of droplets of teal light rose upward from the primary pool like glitter falling skyward. Naliz handed her the item he'd brought along. Maiya looked at it more closely and could now tell that it was a piece from a horse-like sculpture.

"Strange," she said.

"Place it over the spring."

Maiya didn't see anywhere she could set the sculpture above the spring. As she stepped closer, she could feel the intensity of the magic emanating from the water and how it drew her forward. She held out her hand and watched as the piece rose upward to hover in midair. She felt compelled to move closer and walked into the pool.

"Hold the question in your mind and allow yourself to slip under the water," Naliz said, "but be careful. That magic will consume you if you let it."

Maiya was mildly alarmed by his statement, but the spring was welcoming. She leaned back in the water and watched as the sculpture dissolved overhead. Though she wasn't sure how to word the question, the artifact seemed to know what she was asking. She soon found herself surrounded by fragments in time that coursed around, above, and below her. After this dizzying display, a scene formed before her, not unlike when Mahdon had shown her the images from his mind.

It was as Naliz described, albeit more upsetting when viewed directly. The unconscious woman was indeed Lydia, and Tanin showed no remorse as he confirmed that she met the necessary criteria to be 'Subject 15'. It was all very methodical. Maiya continued watching until she was pulled from the water by Mahdon. She knew Naliz had mentioned something about going underwater, but she didn't recall actually doing so. It wasn't until her head broke the surface that she realized she'd gone under. It turned out that if the viewer didn't keep their mind somehow tethered to their physical reality, they could accidentally drown themselves. This was a feature credited to Alurine, their very own trickster god.

Maiya was nearly dry by the time they got back to the manor. She could tell that the heat of the day was leading up to an evening storm and thought it fitting to match the one that had been brewing inside herself. She wasn't sure how the confrontation would turn out, but she had no intention to keep the matter private afterwards. If they had no real way to imprison him, she at least wanted society to know that he'd fallen from grace. As the hour of reckoning rapidly approached, Maiya sent Naliz to make sure Brandon was present for the meeting as well. Though he was no longer on the council, his status at the time of the events was troubling.

When the time came, she found herself unexpectedly calm. Whatever the outcome, she was ready to face it; even if that meant more than one person would need to be brought down. Tanin was alone in the council chambers when the rest of them arrived. He stood tall on one of the pedestals and let out a derisive snort when they entered as a group.

"I know the true purpose for this meeting," he said. "I am no fool. It seems I have been robbed."

After these words, it became evident that neither Jo'dai nor Brandon had been enlightened on the situation. They simultaneously looked to Maiya for an explanation. She chose to leave them hanging and allow Tanin to continue. Their apparent confusion seemed to amuse him. Every word he said was dripping with condescension.

"Oh no, High Councilor, have I spoken out of turn? You come to shame me for my secrets, yet you keep your own. Are you picking apart their lives as well?"

"Should we?" Maiya asked.

"Whatever you intend to do, I suggest you get it over with."

"If you know what this is about, then this is your opportunity to explain yourself," Maiya said.

Tanin's tone remained unchanged. "I have no desire to explain myself to you. Nor will I."

"What, pray tell, is the meaning of this?" Brandon demanded, having quickly grown frustrated with being left in the dark.

"There are only a few who have security access to my home. Khalei's sculpture has conveniently gone missing, so one of you is to blame."

"For what purpose?"

"There is only one I can think of," Tanin said.

Understanding crossed Brandon's face. He looked to Maiya. "What has he done?"

Maiya nodded to Naliz, who then stepped forward to declare the charges made against him. Tanin would give an occasional nod. At one point, Maiya could have sworn he almost smiled, as though he was proud of the allegations. Once Naliz concluded, Tanin was given the opportunity for a rebuttal and to make a plea. He chose to do neither.

"Is it true?" Brandon asked. "Have you brought shame upon us all?"

Tanin looked at him briefly, said nothing, and then looked back at Maiya.

"I do not know what you saw," he said, "but you know. Do what you will with it."

Maiya sighed. "Very well. If you accept the charges as truth, I have no choice but to strip you of your title and formally remove you from the council. The public will be informed of your crimes and a new member will be appointed."

Tanin nodded and stepped down. "It won't make a difference. You can't lock me away."

"I'm well aware. When the time comes that I can, you'll be stripped of your immortality as well."

Tanin looked at Brandon before he left. "Enjoy your new master."

Once they were sure he was gone, Naliz spoke. "It was the right thing to do, but he will fight us on this. He'll do his best to spread fear about you. He may even succeed."

"Lucky me," Maiya said. "If we can't force him to give up his immortality, then what do we do?"

"There may be a way," Brandon said.

They all turned to look at him.

"Are you offering to help? You aren't worried about yourself?"

"I have nothing to hide, and I do not like being betrayed. I will not stand for it."

Maiya wasn't so sure that he was innocent, but if he knew of a method, then the knowledge was valuable. "What do you suggest?"

"The Hokaruin orb. I believe we can use it to our advantage."

Saren and Naliz immediately exchanged a look. Even Jo'dai's attention was caught.

"I thought it was lost and its function unknown," Maiya said.

He nodded. "Yes, but what is lost may be found. Most theories suggest it could be used for our purposes."

Mahdon wasn't typically one to go along with Brandon, but he nodded in agreement. "I believe it is worth the time to search for it."

"Okay. If everyone agrees, let's move forward with that."

She waited for a confirmation from the remaining members and then instructed Jo'dai to revoke Tanin's security access upon his return to the headquarters. Naliz would be delivering a prepared statement to the central media hub, and they would move forward from there. Maiya dismissed them all and headed back to the manor with Mahdon as the sky began to darken. She could already see lightning in the distance and wondered where Tanin would go. It felt wrong to relieve someone of their home in the wake of a storm, but she knew this would hardly affect him.

"Do you think we can trust that Brandon wasn't involved?" Maiya asked. "I couldn't really get a read on him."

Mahdon parked the shuttle and waited until they were inside the house to reply. "While it is possible that he was, I don't think we have the means to prove it. He would have covered his tracks, and it's unlikely that he would have gotten his own hands dirty. If he orchestrated all of this, there won't be records of it."

"Can't we ask the question like we did with Tanin?"

Mahdon shook his head. "There is nothing that Brandon values or loves more than himself. I've been in his residence many times, and I've never seen a space so bare in my life. If there's anything he cares about, it's well hidden."

Maiya frowned, but the comments seemed an accurate depiction of him. Thinking about the missing reagent reminded her of Tanin's reference to the one used against him. Naliz hadn't provided any specifics about the item and now her curiosity had only grown. They proceeded to the study where they watched the oncoming storm.

"How well did you know Tanin?"

"Not overly well. Why?"

"He called the item 'Khalei's sculpture'. Do you know what he meant by that?"

"Yes."

"And?"

He pursed his lips. "I don't think you'll like the answer."

Maiya had a guess but wanted to hear him say it. "Tell me anyway."

"Khalei was Tanin's son. The two had a falling out a long time ago. One of them chose to accept immortality; the other did not. Tanin watched from a distance as his son grew old and died."

Maiya felt a wave of guilt wash over her. "We destroyed a gift from his dead son?"

"Khalei was a craftsman. I imagine he made it specifically for his father."

"I had no idea. If he didn't hate me before, he definitely does now."

"If he blames anyone for that, it's Naliz."

Maiya tried to push the thoughts aside, but it was difficult to imagine being safe from his wrath. He had been clear that he held no respect for her, and their perceptions of him were inconsequential. She moved closer to Mahdon and leaned against him as he put his arm around her. Nothing further was said on the topic as the storm raged on through the night. The next day would bring another kind of storm, and she intended to steer clear of it and allow Naliz to field any questions from the media. His political prowess and long-standing relationship with Tanin would prove beneficial.

When Maiya woke the next day, the city was already abuzz with rumors and stories about the disgraced councilor's misdeeds. The knowledge of his removal had spread like wildfire overnight. Ambitious youth – though in no way young per Maiya's definition – were already talking election and preparing their campaigns. Maiya soon learned of a well-known Zumerti from Kauria who intended to run and had a rather large following. This would be the first time any of them would witness an election of this scale in their lifetime. It would be especially appropriate for a mortal to fill the role that dealt largely with their own relations. Maiya had reviewed election procedure when she first accepted her role, but it had been so long that one had been held that the rest of the council found themselves in need of a refresher. The whole situation was rather peculiar to Maiya. Late or not, at least things were heading in the right direction.

Maiya ensured that all interested parties were aware of the protocol they would need to follow, and the election was scheduled to take place in just under a year's time. This would give the populace time to become familiar with the candidates. In the meantime, as a long-term advisor to the council, Mahdon would be holding the position. In reviewing the candidates, Maiya learned that the popular Zumerti man was none other than Allonis, the missing woman's mate. His campaign was largely centered around economic transparency and equality – two things his people were clearly lacking. The more Maiya learned about the top contenders, the more confident she was that he was the best choice. She couldn't, however, do anything to show this support, as it would create a conflict of interest. It took her by surprise when Brandon not only voiced his interest in Allonis but offered to campaign for him as well.

He expressed regret in not working with the mortals sooner, citing his past disinterest in doing any real work. He swore up and down that his greatest goal now was to make up for his selfish failings. He met up with Allonis, publicly declared his support, and flashed his smile for the media whenever possible. He began rallying support in the capital, and Allonis' popularity soared. Mahdon saw the benefit in all of this, but he was quick to remind Maiya that Brandon was likely only doing it to keep himself in the spotlight. He simply couldn't bear to go without attention.

In their personal lives, Mahdon and Maiya had been quietly making arrangements for an intimate wedding ceremony. A few days after the news about Tanin came to light, they took Naliz and Saren aside to share their own. Later that same day, they shared it with Jo'dai and Brandon as well. All expressed their happiness for the couple, but one – namely Brandon – was more reluctant to do so. He wished them well, but

Mahdon could tell that he hated seeing him so happy. Everything had become a competition to him, and Mahdon was winning. It was only after this announcement that Brandon felt the need to run Allonis' campaign.

They opted for a short engagement and chose to combine traditions from both of their cultures. There would be no need for legal documents, so all they had to concern themselves with was the ceremony itself. Though Mahdon had family and friends he could invite, neither of them wanted the added attention when exchanging vows. There would be an open celebration at the manor afterwards. Two months after announcing the election, on a nearly idyllic day, the couple met in the clearing beside the spring where Saren and Naliz soon joined them. Maiya wore a primarily white, off-shoulder, bell sleeved dress with violet lace hemming the base and end of her sleeves. Mahdon had traded in his usual suit for what Maiya could only describe as a delicately embroidered sherwani. She thought he looked princely and once again questioned what someone like him could possibly see in someone like her.

Her heart raced and her hands went clammy as she looked at the man who stood before her, and she contemplated the immensity of the commitment that laid before them. She felt much like she had on that first day when Mahdon had asked her to take a leap of faith and join him on the journey that started it all. She almost didn't believe it was really happening. On Amertine the two making the commitment were tasked with officiating the wedding, and as the recipient of the proposal, it was her duty to begin.

Maiya smiled up at him, looking him in the eyes and fearing that the words would catch in her throat. "You coming into my life is the best thing that's ever happened to me."

She exhaled and let out a nervous laugh before continuing. "I know that may sound cliché, but I don't know what else I can say to adequately describe how I feel. I've never been very good with words. You're amazing in every way, and every moment I've spent with you has been surreal in the best possible way. It's like I entered a dream, and I never want to wake up. I don't know what I did to deserve someone as wonderful as you."

Mahdon smiled and took her hands in his. "You flatter me."

"I wasn't looking for this to happen, but it did, and I really couldn't be happier. I may not always be the easiest person to deal with, but I promise you that as long as I live, I will strive to be a better person for both of us. I promise that I will never lose faith in you, and I promise to love you as best as I can." She paused again to fight back the overwhelming emotions. "I love you, Mahdon."

Mahdon gave her a moment and then spoke. "I do not think it is wrong or bad to have fallen in love with you so quickly. I knew long before I said it. I realized that when I walk – when I go, whether in space or in time, in any direction, by any method – I want it to be with you. I love listening to you talk about your dreams, thoughts, and anything else you become inflamed with passion about. I love how you can look at me and make life feel worth it all. I promise to always be there for you so that you never have to face your battles alone. I love you, Mai."

He took a step to the side where one tall glass and two smaller ones stood on a stone pedestal. In one small glass was a sweet liquor and in the other, a more mellow, but slightly tart liqueur. Individually they had both always been popular drinks, but together the flavors melded to make the most loved drink the region had ever known. Mahdon picked up one of the smaller glasses, and Maiya the other. They poured them into the central glass and then took turns drinking the concoction. Maiya had always been fond of the unity symbolism used in wedding ceremonies but was particularly so when it meant she got to enjoy a drink. This one was unlike any she'd tried before, and she immediately understood how it had become so well-loved.

They turned back to face each other, and Mahdon opened his hand to reveal a red gem roughly the size and shape of a marble. Maiya gazed down at it, not understanding the significance. Both Naliz and Saren audibly gasped when they saw it.

"This is a remarkably precious stone," he said. "It's known as the Ruby of Ar'ta. I have lived a far longer life than I ever imagined possible. I would rather spend my remaining years with you than see all the centuries without you."

Maiya recalled what Saren had told her when Mahdon first told her that he loved her, and she finally grasped what was happening. *I wouldn't be surprised if he gives up his immortality for you.* She wanted to tell him not to do something so drastic for her, but all at once she found herself struck speechless by the gesture.

"Though I am afraid, I am prepared to let it go."

He began to utter some words in Fudarin, and as he did so, the gem began to emit a bright light. When he completed the final phrase, the gem glowed brilliantly and radiated a powerful magic. For the briefest moment, Mahdon looked as though he'd been zapped with a jolt of electricity. He placed the gem into Maiya's hand and closed her fingers around it. He looked a bit anxious, but happier than ever with his decision. He then guided her to the edge of the pool where a sapling rested beside a hole that Naliz had dug earlier.

"If there should come a time when you unlock the secrets of eternal life, I will accept it once again to stay by your side. Until that day, let it remain hidden away."

He knelt down and Maiya followed suit, gently placing the gem in the open ground. They lifted the sapling together and planted it to conclude the ceremony. They shared a kiss and then accepted congratulatory hugs from their two friends and only witnesses. Maiya could no longer feel the same magical energy from Mahdon as she had before. She could sense the permanence of his human form she'd come to know and was shocked that he'd actually gone through with it. She imagined Naliz felt similarly, as the surprise had yet to fade from his face.

Hand in hand, the couple returned to the manor with Saren and Naliz trailing behind. Neither knew what the two council members spoke of, but neither cared while they were soaking in the afterglow of what transpired. The celebration back at the banquet hall was bigger than either of them had expected, and they were met with awe when his family learned what Mahdon had done. Between the dinner, the music, and chatting with the guests, the rest of the evening was a blur. It wasn't until the next morning, when they woke up beside one another, that reality set in. And as it turned out, they were more than happy with that reality.

CHAPTER 18

The day after the wedding, they departed for a small island off the coast where they had an oceanside residence and white sand beach to themselves. Maiya was typically one for more adventurous trips, but they had traveled so frequently that all she wanted was to spend some time alone with him. Each morning before they climbed out of bed, they'd gaze into each other's eyes until one of them blinked or otherwise broke the serious look on their face. It had started out as the usual, sappy admiration of the other and progressed into a game of who could stare the longest without laughing. Even still, Maiya truly was mesmerized by the fierce blue of his eyes and though she would never admit it, the way she felt when their eyes met made her heart flutter.

"Your eyes are a darker brown when you're tired," he said with a small smile. "They look extra nice."

"You do know this means I win, right?"

"I think I can live with that."

She put a hand to his face, and he closed his eyes and turned his head to kiss it. The slightest touch of her hand sent pleasant tingles down his spine. It was a sensation he hadn't experienced before. At least, not to his recollection. Mahdon had some difficulty adjusting to his new body, but since making the transition, his sense of touch had increased exponentially. He felt very exposed without the ability to shift on command, but he enjoyed the newfound intensity of feeling – both physically and emotionally – that he incorrectly assumed couldn't get any stronger. Though strange at first, feelings of hunger and the need for sleep were becoming familiar again. To his own surprise, his largest hurdle wasn't any of this so much as it was keeping his image as sharp as he had before. He had always prided himself on his appearance and now it actually took work.

Maiya had a much easier time adjusting to the marriage. The hardest part for her was coming to grips with the fact that she was now the wife of an ex-immortal alien. Or rather, that she was the alien. Though they'd been together for some time now, the whole idea was still amusing to her when she took the time to think about it. She didn't know if it was fact or simply her perception, but it seemed to be more often that he'd pull her close just to hold her in his arms. He'd kiss her neck and smell her hair, and the world would fade away until all that existed was the two of them. They spent hours lying on the beach and listening to the waves while talking about everything but the political matters. They spoke of their childhood dreams, and Mahdon asked more about human customs, expressing his desire to one day celebrate them back on Earth as they had celebrated his here. At night they paid little attention to the time as they danced under the stars or laid intertwined in one another's arms.

It was a two week break from reality that they both so desperately needed, and neither was in a hurry to return to the public eye. When the day arrived, Maiya was awoken well before sunrise by a whisper. She jerked awake and looked over to see that Mahdon was still fast asleep. Looking around, she saw no evidence of anyone else in the room but was unable to fall back asleep. She slipped out of bed and stepped outside to listen to the waves. As she sank her toes into the sand, the voice came again – louder this time. As before, she heard it clearly in her mind, a woman's voice that spoke in the language of the gods.

Do not be afraid, the voice told her. We have met before. Do you remember?

Maiya could sense the familiarity, but when she searched her mind, the reason for it moved just out of her grasp. She shook her head slowly.

We are sisters, you and I. You were not ready when last we crossed paths. Now you are.

As if flipping a switch, the memory of the first night in Ularia returned to her. She saw the shadow and heard the voice, but she hadn't understood it at the time.

"You need my help," Maiya whispered.

Yes.

"For what?"

Vengeance.

Maiya wondered if the woman was referring to Tanin. Now that she knew what he had done, she could understand the plea. She knew nothing of this during the previous encounter. She was about to ask if her suspicions were correct when Mahdon came up behind her and surprised her with a hug. She jumped reflexively, half expecting it to be the woman she couldn't see.

"I'm sorry. I did not mean to startle you."

She wrapped her arms around his and leaned back against him.

"Is everything all right?" He asked. "You're up so early."

"Yeah, I'm fine. I just couldn't sleep."

She listened while they stood on the beach, but the voice of the woman never returned. Maiya considered sharing what happened, but she instead chose to leave their final day unmarred by such things. It was a bittersweet moment when they left the island behind. Henceforth, they would be spending more time together than they had before the union, but they still had their duties to attend to. When they landed at the manor, Brandon and Naliz were already there waiting for them. Maiya frowned when she realized this meant there would be no settling in before those duties resumed.

"Welcome back, High Councilor," Brandon smiled. "I trust you had a relaxing time?"

"It was nice, thanks."

He glanced over at Mahdon with a disingenuous smile. "Ambassador, you appear to be adjusting well. How fortunate." He returned his focus to Maiya before continuing. "Please excuse our timing. I wanted to be the first to share our progress. Naliz and I were able to narrow down the search to a few key locations. I believe Mahdon will be familiar with them."

"All locations are now accessible on your comm device," Naliz said. "The rest of the council is willing to assist as well, but I suggest," he stopped and looked at Brandon. "Would you give us a moment alone?"

Brandon frowned and disappeared. Naliz motioned for Mahdon and Maiya to follow him inside. He sighed. "It feels strange to say this, but I suggest that one of us accompany you. Having you both in mortal form comes with its disadvantages. Should a situation present itself where you require assistance, I would hate for there to be a delay."

"If you insist," Maiya said.

Naliz's relief at her answer was evident. She wanted to make a snarky comment about how they were perfectly capable of handling themselves, but she had no reason to refuse the help. She could always use her magic when things got difficult, and Naliz knew full well that she was far from helpless. She suspected this had more to do with his concern for Mahdon's safety. Mahdon wasn't exactly known for being cautious and now that personality trait of his had become riskier than ever.

After agreeing to his terms, Maiya dismissed Naliz and requested that no one disturb them until the next morning. She wasn't sure what to make of the sudden reappearance of the shadow woman and didn't know how to address the subject. If she found Maiya when in such a remote location, surely she could find her at her publicly known residence as well. Mahdon had noticed her presence the first time, but now he was clearly oblivious to her visit in the early morning hours. Was she the only one who could hear her?

While Maiya contemplated the ramifications of assisting a ghost, Mahdon went over the list provided by Naliz. He'd been to each of them at one time or another as part of his studies. He went to the gallery to review these locations on the larger map. He hadn't been to any of them in quite some time and wanted to have an idea of where they could possibly look once they arrived. He put together a basic travel plan with notes on potential hiding places and then returned to Maiya with his findings. He found her in the study, pouring over a text written in Fudarin. The language was only ever used for religious purposes. He had studied every religious text he could get his hands on, and this one didn't look familiar to him.

"Where did you get that?"

Maiya put a marker in the book and looked up at him. "It was sitting open on the desk. This wasn't one from you?"

"No." He stepped over to check for any markings on the binding, but it had none.

"Do you think Naliz left it here for some reason?"

Mahdon shook his head as he flipped through the pages. "Is this what I think it is?"

"I only recognize bits and pieces of the language, but it seems to be some sort of spell book."

"That is certainly what it looks like. I'm fluent, and the sentences are mostly gibberish to me. They don't even list what they're to be used for; how are you to know what the effect will be?"

"They feel different," Maiya said. "I don't know how else to describe it. There's an energy to them that I can sense when I look them over. They almost come off as using magical energy that's the polar opposite of what I've done so far. I don't think they're all dangerous, but I think many of them are intended for destruction."

Mahdon was flustered. "Who would want you to have this?"

Maiya could only think of one who would want her to study magic of this sort. She hadn't wanted to say anything yet, but if this was the doing of the ghost – or whatever she was – then there was no telling what would happen next. Maiya didn't perceive it as threatening, but it was certainly persistent. If not the woman, then who?

"Well, so here's the thing…" Maiya hesitated while Mahdon watched her expectantly. "I know it was a while ago, but do you remember that shadow figure in Ularia?"

"Yes. How could I forget? It was quite unsettling."

"I think she's following me. If not that one, then another."

Mahdon was instantly alarmed. "What do you mean she's following you?"

"That's what woke me this morning. It spoke to me. Well, not exactly 'spoke.' It was a voice in my mind, but it wasn't my own."

Mahdon dropped his head to one hand. "Why didn't you say something earlier?"

"Honestly? I didn't want our trip to end on a bad note, and frankly, I know it sounds crazy."

"This isn't good. Though I've never dealt with one personally, spirits are rarely described as anything but self-involved. Stories tell of them tormenting people."

"Are they all bad?"

"I don't know."

"Then what's the harm in listening to it?"

He sighed. He couldn't explain why, but the notion of invisible beings put him on edge. "Did it say what it wants?"

"Vengeance."

Mahdon threw his hands up in the air. "Maiya, that sounds unfriendly to me."

"Not necessarily. It's only a guess, but I think it might be the spirit of one of the women who was held captive. Could you really blame her for wanting that?"

"No, I couldn't, but you don't know that's what it is. Negative energy is dangerous to be around. If it wants vengeance, then how do you know it won't harm you if you get in the way of that?"

"And what if what we want is the same thing? Why wouldn't we help then?"

Mahdon was frustrated with her response but knew better than to argue with her. "You're too stubborn for your own good. I don't want you to get hurt."

Maiya smiled. "You don't need to worry about me. I can handle myself."

"I know you can. That doesn't mean I don't worry about you."

Maiya stepped over to him, put her arms around his waist, and looked him in the eyes. "I promise to be careful. And if she visits me again, I'll let you know. There's no reason to worry if that never happens."

He pulled her close and held her tightly. He was quickly learning that the ability to feel more was a double-edged sword. He didn't enjoy the way he felt right now, but holding her made him feel a little bit better. He thought back on all the times he had been upset or concerned in the past and was thankful that he didn't have to face the full weight at the time. He had a newfound respect for Maiya's ability to maintain her composure when he didn't know if he could have. It would take some time, but he wondered if she realized how difficult the adjustment was for him.

That evening, he looked over the book with her and they attempted to decipher the meaning behind the unusual phrasing. They paid special attention to the pages that were showing when Maiya stumbled upon it. Mahdon's best guess was that the spell's purpose was to turn something off, though he had no idea what. And while Maiya could understand some of the words, her pronunciation was greatly lacking. Mahdon helped her with this until she could recite the entirety of the spell without pause. When she was confident that she executed it correctly, and even thought she could feel it, she was disappointed to see no results. She sat back with a shake of the head and a sigh.

"Nothing happened."

Mahdon looked over the text one more time and shrugged. "You said it correctly. Perhaps there's more to it than a verbal component."

"Or it worked, and I have no idea what I just did."

"That is also a possibility."

She closed the book and pushed it aside. "I probably shouldn't be messing with something that I don't understand."

He thought her observation sounded an awful lot like what he had been getting at all along, but he didn't see the good in mentioning that. Instead, he reassured her that she'd figure it out when she needed, just as she always seemed to do. By the next morning, the disappointment had passed, and she was back to her usual self. Saren stopped by to inform them that Jo'dai would be staying behind to focus all his efforts on security while Naliz continued to monitor the election process. She would be assisting them with their search and, she added with a sly smile, anything else they might like. Maiya laughed it off while Mahdon remained naïve on the topic.

The first place they visited from the list was a seemingly unimpressive field in the Arkhan province. Maiya recognized the field from another life; it was a place of death where hundreds had come to fight over differing ideologies. Very few survived. Bones of the dead could still be stumbled upon when rain softened the ground, making it a sobering experience. Before the war, homes bordered the field, but now all that remained was the barest of ruins. Based on what Saren knew of the area, she said it was most likely the artifact would be on the edge of the battlefield if it was there at all. Maiya was skeptical that they would find it when there had been people searching for years with no success, but they assured her that she would be able to sense it if she came within close proximity. They walked the perimeter, occasionally pausing to check out the ruins, but nothing drew their attention for long.

Not here.

Maiya stopped as the woman's voice spoke up in her mind. She looked around at Saren and Mahdon, but they remained oblivious to the message.

"Is something wrong?" Saren asked.

Maiya shook her head and began walking again. She wanted to ask if "not here" meant this particular spot or the whole location, but the idea of speaking up now felt awkward. She didn't mind mentioning it to Mahdon, but she wasn't prepared to have the whole council aware of the unexplained voices.

Not here, the voice persisted.

"I'll be right back," Maiya said and then stepped off into the woods. She glanced back when she thought she was far enough away and was pleased to see that her companions were distracted and engaged in conversation with each other. "You're going to need to be more specific."

Her remark was met with silence. She sighed and wandered back. "I don't think it's here."

"Are you certain?" Mahdon asked.

"As much as I can be."

They meandered back to the shuttle, covering as much new ground as possible without going too far out of their way. For the remainder of the day, Maiya heard nothing more from the voice. She told Mahdon about the incident before they turned in for the night, and he suggested that it might be worth the risk to share the information with Saren. He understood Maiya's hesitation, but given Saren's area of expertise, he speculated that she would be familiar with any legends that spoke of such things. He reminded her that the only stories he knew were negative, so if Saren had knowledge to suggest otherwise, it wouldn't be such a bad thing. If she could confirm it wasn't positive, well, then they'd know that before it was too late. Maiya slept on it and chose to take his advice during a morning walk with Saren.

Saren's interest was instantly piqued. "You've met a faulite?"

"Um, I wouldn't say we met. What is that exactly?"

"It's a type of incorporeal being. I'm surprised Mahdon hasn't heard of them. Some religious sects view them as another form taken on by the gods."

"Are they dangerous? The first time I encountered her, I saw a shadow figure and it got very cold. It scared the crap out of me."

Saren smiled. "You have no reason for concern. They have a tendency to be a bit theatrical, but they can only work through others. They're completely harmless on their own."

She sounded confident on the subject, but doubt still crept into Maiya's mind. "You're sure that's what it is?"

Saren stopped walking to look Maiya in the eyes. "You said it spoke to you while we were together yesterday, yes?"

"Yeah."

"If it were a spirit as you suspected, I would have detected its presence. He may not be able to anymore, but in the past Mahdon would have as well. Energy signatures of that sort are incredibly difficult to miss. That leaves us with two possibilities. Either you are suffering from a mental ailment, or a faulite has chosen to reveal itself to you."

Maiya laughed nervously. "That's... reassuring."

"There must be a reason why she came to you specifically. Did you recognize her?"

"Sort of. She felt familiar and called us sisters."

For the briefest moment, there was a flash of fear in Saren's eyes, but it was gone so quickly that Maiya thought she must have imagined it. Of all the things she'd shared, it hardly seemed likely that Maiya's latest disclosure would be the one to bring about apprehension.

"Interesting. I will be curious to know anything else she says. That is, if you do not mind sharing."

"Of course. I'm not sure she'll say much at all, honestly. She isn't very talkative."

They met back up with Mahdon and shared Saren's insight on the situation. He was satisfied with the explanation but embarrassed that it hadn't occurred to him as a possibility. He had learned of faulites in passing but largely brushed the subject aside during his studies. He had always assumed they were no more than an unverified myth. He was clearly mistaken. Apparently more than one of the council members had encountered them in the past.

Over the coming weeks, the 'faulite' communicated with Maiya each time they visited a new potential orb location but was always brief. This mostly consisted of similar statements as those she made at the battlefield, though at times she made references to the past.

Do you recall the last time we were here? She would ask. Maiya never did. Every time Maiya asked the faulite her name, she would fall silent again or tell Maiya that she already knew. Maiya eventually grew tired of the lack of answers and quit asking. She started to reconsider if she really was crazy and the voice was one of her own making. As the election grew nearer, they put their search on pause, and Maiya stopped hearing from the woman. While she was grateful for this, Maiya was simultaneously concerned that this could be confirmation that she had imagined it all along. Saren once again reassured her that she had nothing to worry about; being such fickle creatures, the faulite had likely grown bored with her. Even still, Maiya remained on her guard so as not to be surprised again.

Time continued on, and the council met to go over the questions that would be asked of the candidates at the first scheduled debate. The questions ranged from those regarding basic conflict resolution to how they intended to maintain economic stability for the Zumerti while also creating positive relations between the two groups. In addition to the primary questions, both Saren and Jo'dai provided a couple of their own. They were mostly interested in seeing how knowledgeable the contenders were on their own history and technology. Naliz didn't have any specific questions of his own, but he offered to moderate.

After the meeting adjourned, Mahdon took Maiya for a picnic dinner along the falls. When they arrived, he surprised her not only with the meal but with a bouquet of the Jovaia lilies as well. They continued to grow in abundance all around the manor, so he had taken some time to put them together for her. She wasn't sure when he had the opportunity to do all of this considering how they were nearly always together, including every meeting, but it made her smile that he somehow found the time to do such things for her.

"What's the occasion?"

"Does there need to be one?"

"I guess not."

Maiya took a seat on the blanket as he handed her a glass of wine. She sat back and took a sip as he laid out plates with various proteins, fruits, and breads. He'd even taken the time to prepare various hors d'oeuvres that he knew she liked. With the sound of the falls in the background and no one else in sight, the romantic gesture turned into a late night affair. They watched the sun fall below the horizon as they finished the bottle of wine and then went for a stroll along the cliff's edge.

"I spoke with the lead astronomer and some of the new engineers today," Mahdon said. "They've selected a planet well within our range for travel. Our preparations to send an initial research team are presently underway. I believe the only remaining formality is to receive the council's approval. I can have a proposal prepared and present it at the next meeting."

"Wow," Maiya was surprised to hear of this so soon. "That's good news. Will you be going with?"

Maiya knew they already had large swathes of the galaxy mapped and there was no denying that they had the capacity for such a trip, but she had always assumed this would happen when she was available to go along. He had recently partnered with Saren and taken on the responsibilities of organizing teams for future interplanetary exploration. As the most versed in all areas of engineering, Saren was best suited for recommending and selecting crew members. She was well-connected, knowing all the best and brightest in every tech sector. Mahdon was the more diplomatic of the two and had off-planet experience.

"It was not my intention." He tilted his head sideways and gave her a playful grin. "Are you wishing to be rid of me already?"

She was about to say something clever when they were interrupted by Brandon. They both frowned at his arrival, wondering how long he had been watching them. He always showed up at the most inopportune times, and it was never anything that required immediate attention. It was almost as though his intention was to inconvenience them. The only positive thing about his unexpected presence was that he didn't sneak up on them from behind. He walked up to them as casually as though he'd been out on a walk of his own.

"This is a pleasant surprise," Brandon said with a smile.

Maiya had to resist the urge to roll her eyes. She had been giving him the benefit of the doubt for some time now, but randomly showing up in the middle of the night on a cliffside was a stretch. Even Mahdon had a hard time pretending the occurrence made any sense at all.

"Brandon," Maiya put on her best 'nice to see you' face. "What brings you out here at this hour?"

"I enjoy some introspective time whenever I may, High Councilor. I mean not to be rude, but if you recall, I do not require an adjustment to my personal schedule for a rest period."

Mahdon felt an unusually strong desire to call Brandon out on his not-so-veiled self-indulging commentary. He had always wanted to speak his mind to Brandon, but now his irritation with the unwanted intrusion and casual remark left him doubly tempted to do so. He bit his tongue on the off chance that Brandon had something useful to say.

"As long as I have your attention," Brandon continued, "I wanted to talk to you about the upcoming debate."

"What about it?" Maiya asked.

"You haven't spent much time in front of the people. I thought it would be a good gesture if you were to formally meet and introduce the candidates."

Maiya had a momentary flash of anxiety at the thought, but his suggestion was sound. Since the official transfer of power, she had stayed largely out of the spotlight. Naliz and Mahdon interacted more with the populace than she did, and that had never been her intention. She forced a small smile and nodded.

"I think that would be appropriate. I'll have Naliz arrange it."

"I will see you at the debate then." Brandon smiled and gave a slight bow of the head before disappearing.

The day of the debate came quickly, and Maiya was scheduled to meet the five remaining contenders within the hour. The event was to be held at the Temple of Alurine, one of the oldest venues in Fimbira. The capital had a historical temple for each of the gods, and Saren had given Maiya a tour of them the day prior. They were all similar in style, having stylized columns and large outdoor seating areas. It was rare that they were used anymore, but the occasion called for a unique arena. Several podiums had been set up between the columns of the entrance, facing the main outdoor space. Another podium stood to one side, angled specially for the moderator. A separate seating area was set behind this podium for the council members to sit.

The crowd had already grown large when Mahdon and Maiya landed at the opposite end of the temple and proceeded inside. The other council members were already present with four of the candidates, but Brandon and Allonis were yet to arrive. Naliz greeted them and formally introduced the four. Maiya had met each one briefly in the past but only in passing. They were all eager to present their ideas to her personally. She got the impression that they were hoping she'd sway the election in their favor, so she'd done her best to remain distanced during the election process to avoid any appearance of a bias.

Brandon didn't arrive until the last minute, allowing only a few minutes for Maiya to welcome Allonis and reacquaint herself with him. Brandon went outside to sit amongst the audience while Allonis apologized for the tardiness. He explained that he was delayed in securing transit for his family. He wanted to ensure they would be in attendance and intended to show them around the city after the debate concluded. Once they were all assembled, Naliz showed them to their positions and took a seat with Saren and Jo'dai outside. Maiya would go out last, introduce each of them, and then take her own seat alongside the other members. She had prepared statements for each that included basic biographies; now her biggest concern was that her mind would blank once she was out there.

"Remember to breathe," Mahdon told her. He squeezed her hand, gave her a smile, and went out to join the others.

Maiya waited a moment for everyone to get seated before walking out with a wave to the crowd. She barely made it outside when the applause of the audience was drowned out by the sound of an explosion. Before she had time to react, dust filled the air and the old stones fell down all around her. The ringing in her ears was the last thing she heard before she lost consciousness.

CHAPTER 19

Panic swept through the crowd as the front of the temple crumbled from the blast. The five standing at the podiums scrambled to get out of the way but were quickly surrounded by rubble. A thick cloud of dust and smaller stones blew out away from the building, carpeting the area in a mess of grey. Mahdon coughed from the debris that filled the air as he tried to wrap his head around what had just happened. As the dust settled, the pile of destruction came into view and he felt light-headed and horrified all at once. The understanding of what happened sent him into a frenzied attempt to remove and throw aside the pieces of collapsed stonework.

Naliz stood in wide-eyed shock as people ran by all around him. He was able to locate Brandon and those who had been sitting next to him, but Maiya was nowhere to be seen. Four of the five candidates could now be seen working to remove debris alongside more than a dozen others. They had thankfully shifted in time to avoid being trapped or crushed by the weight of the building. Lacking this ability, Allonis had not been so lucky. Naliz hurried forward to help in the rescue efforts, calling for the aid of heavy equipment. Mahdon persisted in his own attempts even after help arrived, digging feverishly until his fingers bled. Naliz had to physically pull him away to get him to stop and leave the rescue efforts up to those better equipped.

Jo'dai was working with his security teams to determine how anything so intentionally deadly could have happened. They were always very thorough, and yet, something had clearly been missed. They swept the area for additional explosives but found nothing else suspicious. When at last the final stones were being removed, Mahdon feared the worst. Naliz kept him away from the building until Saren could get confirmation on the status of any victims. She returned to them with the grimmest expression either of them had ever seen from her, and she shook her head slowly. Mahdon felt a wave of nausea come over him but felt a spark of hope once she spoke.

"She isn't under there. It appears as though her body's been taken."

Naliz nodded and breathed a sigh of relief. "She could still be alive. What of the Zumerti?"

"He did not make it. His family will need to be informed."

"Who would do this?" Mahdon asked. "There hasn't been a terrorist attack in centuries."

"Jo'dai has already begun assigning teams to investigate," Naliz said.

"How did they allow this to happen in the first place? There's no reason for them to have missed this."

"I don't know."

"Can we even trust them?" Mahdon could feel himself getting worked up. "If Maiya is still alive, then we need to find her before it's too late. She could be seriously injured."

Naliz crossed his arms, looked down, and nodded. "I understand that you're upset. We all are. I'm going to do everything I can to find the culprit, but in order to do that, I'm going to need you to trust me."

Mahdon was swelling with emotions that he knew Naliz couldn't possibly understand. He struggled to keep them in check, knowing that allowing them to consume him would only serve to worsen the situation. He needed to think clearly if he had any hope of locating her. This didn't make him any less frustrated with his friend's response. He bit his tongue and looked away before heading in the direction of the shuttle he brought.

"Where are you going?" Naliz asked.

"I can't stand idly by while she's out there somewhere. Let me know if they find anything."

Maiya awoke on a damp, stone surface, and found she could neither see nor stand. Shackles restrained her to the floor, pressing hard and cold against her wrists and ankles. Any shift in movement only served to remind her that the restraints were fit too tightly, as the metal cut into her flesh, rubbing her skin raw. She tried to conjure a spell but was met with no more than a spark of energy before feeling nothing at all. She silently panicked, questioning in the darkness if she was blind, where her captors were, and why she was here. Maiya fought to calm her mind, relying on her other senses to evaluate the situation.

The air smelled stagnant and she shivered in the chill of the room, both unpleasant sensations that were strangely calming in their reassurance that she was not blind, but rather, underground. The sound of water dripping from above met her ears, but the room was otherwise silent. It felt like several hours passed before she heard anything else, at which point the sound of footsteps approached from what she assumed to be the opposite side of a door. The sharp grinding of metal against metal was immediately followed by a rectangle of light as someone opened the door into the room.

Maiya squinted into the light and noticed three men standing in the doorway. As her eyes adjusted, the man in the center came into focus, and Maiya's heart stopped. Once again dressed in his preferred attire, Brandon smiled down at Maiya.

"Oh my, what have we here? I'm terribly sorry about all of this." Brandon snapped his fingers and pointed from the two other men to Maiya. "Gentlemen? Care to help our guest up?"

"Brandon? You're responsible for this? I should have known better."

As commanded, the men, who Maiya could now tell were his guards, stepped forward, knelt down, and removed Maiya's bonds. They pulled her to her feet, and she rubbed her wrists, eyeing Brandon suspiciously. They led her out of the room into a narrow hallway carved in stone, and she observed that the door she just exited appeared to be one of several in sight. Maiya now followed behind Brandon with the two guards directly behind her.

"I don't understand," she said. "What the hell happened? Why did you bring me here, and why was I chained up?"

A slight smirk crossed Brandon's face, but he remained silent and continued walking. The memory of what she only briefly saw and heard played through Maiya's mind, and she wondered about the extent of the damage back at the temple. How many people had been hurt? Had he taken other prisoners? Was she the sole target?

"Where's Mahdon? Did you hurt him?" Maiya stopped in her tracks. "I'm not going anywhere with you until you tell me he's okay."

Brandon continued walking, turning only the slightest bit to respond. "The ambassador is fine. You should be much more worried about yourself. I have eyes and ears everywhere, dear. You stepped on my toes. What did you expect to happen?"

Brandon's guards nudged Maiya, forcing her to move forward once more. They continued in silence, rounding corners and traversing long hallways until at last they came to a "T" intersection where large, ornate, wooden doors stood tall before them. Maiya tried to mentally retrace their steps to recall if they had passed any hallways that might lead out, but the circuitous route had succeeded in confusing her sense of direction.

Brandon held up a hand and the doors swept open, revealing a very rich looking study beyond. Brandon entered the room as the guards stepped to either side of the entryway, watching Maiya closely. She tried once more to call on the magic, and once more she found herself powerless. She briefly considered making a run for it, but quickly thought better of it, suspecting that she'd likely only become lost amid the maze of hallways if she even managed to outrun Brandon's guards.

"What have you done?" She demanded. "Why can't I cast?"

Brandon stopped at a small, round table roughly in the center of the room. He picked up what appeared to be a crystal brandy decanter and matching glass, poured himself a drink, and turned to face Maiya.

"Won't you join me?"

Brandon did not appear fazed by Maiya's reluctance; he simply smiled broadly in her direction. The way he looked at her sent chills up her spine, though she couldn't quite place her finger on why. When she still failed to budge, Brandon set down the drink and casually went to pour another.

"This one," He paused briefly as he filled the glass midway, "Is for you."

Stepping toward her, he reached out a hand to offer Maiya the glass. After a moment's hesitation, she stepped forward and accepted it, but waited for him to drink before indulging in it herself. Brandon raised his glass as if in a toast, took a sip, and nodded to the guards. Maiya kept her eyes on Brandon as she heard the doors close and lock behind her.

The beverage had a surprisingly sweet bouquet, closer to roses in scent than that of alcohol. She took a cautious sip and was immediately impressed and pleased with the taste, finishing it much more quickly than she had intended. She handed the glass to Brandon, stopping herself short from asking for more.

"Another?" Brandon asked.

Despite her taste buds craving more, she cautioned herself against accepting anything else he had to offer. "No, thank you."

Brandon frowned, pacing alongside the bookshelves hugging the walls closest to the doors. He ran the fingers of his right hand across the spines of several books, while lightly grasping his drink in his left. For a moment he said nothing, taking shallow swigs of his drink as he turned back to face her.

"There's a natural metal in these stone walls that can dampen those abilities of yours. At least, that is what legends said. This is the first time I've witnessed the effects. It was a risky move bringing you here, but now that I have proof, I'm glad that I did. I have to admit, I have a bit of a curiosity about your kind and you in particular. There was a time when I believed that every member of your species must have magic. I only needed one of them to show me, but they were so stubborn."

He waved a hand in the air as he paced. "I tried and I tried. Believe me, I did. They all proved useless to me. Imagine my surprise when I first saw what you can do. The things I've seen you do are fascinating."

"What is it you want with me?"

"Isn't it obvious? There is only one thing I've ever really wanted. I may look like your kind now, but as you're well aware, biologically we're very different. I no longer need to eat or breathe. I don't even require eyes to see. At any given moment, I can leave this form and be untouchable. You see," Brandon finished the final drops from his glass with a smile, "you can never hurt me. But I'm quite certain that I can severely injure you – trapped in such a fragile body."

Maiya was puzzled by why he was telling her this and felt an even deeper sense of unease. "Are you threatening me? I've seen your people suffer and die; you aren't invincible."

Brandon stopped his pacing and set down the glass on the central table. He approached Maiya with a smile, tracing a finger slowly down the side of her face as she turned away.

She shuddered from his touch. "Just tell me what the hell you want."

"Cooperation. Answers. I want to know what one of my own could possibly desire in a creature such as yourself. What did you do to him that drove him to give up his own nature? I knew you were powerful but not to that extent."

"I didn't do anything to him."

Brandon laughed, nodding like a madman. "Yes, I'm sure. Just as you did nothing in Ularia. And as you did 'nothing' in Kauria and nothing in Muldira. Need I go on? I've seen what you can do... but how? And what else are you capable of?"

He spun his fingers through a lock of her hair and moved his face within inches of her own, his voice no more than a whisper. "What other secrets do you hold?"

She slapped him hard, and he backed away slightly. "I thought I told you never to touch me again."

He smiled broadly. "What will you do to stop me?"

"You're insane."

Maiya took a step back, but with each one she made, he matched her until she found he had her flush against the wall. Maiya shifted uneasily, her mind dizzy from the thoughts of what he might do to her. She swallowed hard and inhaled deeply, trying to prepare herself for what she feared would come next. Maiya tried to push him away but was quickly overwhelmed by his strength. Brandon easily grasped both of her wrists in one hand and tightened his grip until Maiya let out a yelp from pain. The more she struggled, the tighter his hold on her became until she became afraid he'd do serious damage.

"Please just leave me alone," she said, barely managing more than a shaky whisper.

"The saddest part about all of this is that you think you have a say in what happens to you."

Maiya tilted her head toward the door and let out the best yell she could muster. "Help! Someone help me!"

Brandon laughed. "Scream all you want, woman; no one is going to save you. You're nothing more than an animal to them."

Maiya was taken aback by his comment. She'd been called many things throughout her life, but never an animal. The weight of Brandon's words seemed to have the desired effect, as her strength waned. He was right, Maiya realized; when the most powerful man in the world holds you captive, no one is going to save you.

When the doors opened once more, the guards briefly exchanged a look with Brandon before looking to the floor. The woman lying there now hardly resembled the one they'd brought here. She appeared bloody and broken, her eyes distant and dull.

Brandon was unmoved by their looks of concern. "Take her back to the cell. I've finished with her for today. You will tell no one of her presence here, or I'll find a way to do the same to you."

The guards nodded and moved past, dragging Maiya from the room as she closed her eyes and slipped into unconsciousness. When Maiya opened her eyes again, she found she was back where she had started. Though she was no longer restrained to the floor, she could feel the walls closing in on her far more tightly than before. Knowing who her captor was and what horrors he had in store for her proved to be far better shackles than the irons ever could be.

Maiya spent great stretches of time plotting her escape, yet each moment when Brandon returned for her, she found her hopes for freedom exponentially diminishing. Every time he came for her, the pattern was the same. He'd have her brought to the same room and restrained in a small alcove in the back. He assured her that this was a special space and that she would be able to defend herself there.

The first time he did this, the meaning behind his words was readily apparent the moment she was chained to that wall. She could always sense the magic when she used it, but it wasn't until that moment that she realized how much a part of her it truly was. She went from feeling drained to alert and refreshed; the difference was like that between night and day. She felt compelled to use it, but every fiber of her being told her not to. Brandon radiated an energy she had never noticed before and did his best to goad her into fighting back. After this initial taunting, he prepared himself a drink.

R.T. Smeltzer

Before Maiya there stood a square pedestal, roughly three feet tall and a foot wide at the base and top, though slightly narrower in the middle. Brandon took a sip of his drink and then stood before Maiya. He pulled a silver orb from his robes and set it upon the pedestal. It seemed to be glowing faintly and emitting a slight hum. Maiya immediately recognized it as the source of the unusual energy and knew it to be the Hokaruin orb. How Brandon had come to acquire it or how he intended to use it, she was unsure.

"Now, where were we?" Brandon asked with a smile. "Oh, yes. I believe you were going to free yourself. That is, if you know how."

Don't. The voice returned to Maiya in force. No matter what he does to you, you cannot do as he says.

"What can I do?" Maiya whispered.

I must go now, but I will return for you.

"Don't leave me."

Brandon had been watching her the entire time and was staring at her now. "Who are you talking to?"

She looked away and didn't say anything.

"I'd like to play a game," Brandon told her. "You have all this power locked away. What must I do for you to show it to me? The rules to this game are quite simple: I will test various techniques to evoke a reaction from you, and you will ensure I am pleased with your response. If I am displeased, the game will continue. If you make me happy, then the game ends and you can go home. Shall we begin?"

Maiya watched as he keyed something into a previously unseen panel on the pedestal, and then she saw nothing at all as every cell in her body experienced a sudden and intense burning sensation. She unleashed a scream like none other, but clung tightly to the faulite's words, resisting the instinct to attack her captor. She wasn't certain what would happen if she gave in, but she suspected that it wouldn't work to her benefit as intended. No matter the personal cost, she couldn't let him win.

Without fail, each time when Brandon had finished with her, Maiya would find herself waking up in the damp cell. She didn't know how long she was out or how long he'd kept her locked away. Whether it was days or weeks, Maiya was unsure. Everything had become hazy; brief glimpses of reality or fantasy intermingled with long periods of darkness had become routine.

226

She had seen several faces and heard voices of others between bouts of consciousness, but they had all become a blur with only Brandon's sticking in the forefront of her mind. As time went on, she came to appreciate the great lapses in memory, having only bruises and raw flesh to remind her how Brandon preferred to spend their time together. The last time he came to collect her, she would not be so lucky.

Three weeks passed between the time Maiya went missing and when Naliz received word that one of Jo'dai's security teams stumbled upon something that struck them as odd. Shortly after meeting with the council, Brandon was observed meeting with Tanin before entering an old bunker several miles out of town. With the exception of those who tracked Tanin, no one was ever spotted within the vicinity of him – until now. Accompanied by the security detail, Naliz went to investigate. The entrance to the building was tucked away behind a large fallen tree, but was otherwise left unguarded.

It wasn't until they started down the hallway that they crossed paths with Brandon's personal security team. Naliz was familiar with the two men who stopped them, as were the members of his own detail. They'd stuck with Brandon when he was forced to resign, effectively terminating their own security clearance.

"Where is he?" Naliz asked.

"He's asked not to be disturbed."

"Will you at least tell me what he's doing here?"

"If Brandon wants you to know of his affairs, I'm sure he'll tell you himself."

Naliz sighed. "Enough of this."

He waved to his team to keep them occupied while he went on ahead. Regardless of whatever service the guards provided to Brandon, they couldn't realistically keep Naliz away. He wondered if their sole purpose was to alert Brandon should anyone discover this hideaway. After turning down a series of hallways, Naliz approached another set of guards who stood outside of a large set of doors. As if on cue, Brandon stepped out to meet him, leaving the door cracked open.

"This is unexpected," Brandon said, though he didn't seem overly surprised.

"It's been brought to my attention that you've been consorting with the traitor. Is he here now?"

Brandon looked down at his nails, as though he couldn't be bothered to entertain such a question. "I haven't the faintest clue what you're referring to."

"Do not talk down to me, Brandon."

"If you're looking for Tanin, then the answer is no. He isn't here."

"Not now, perhaps, but he was."

"I'm sure he's been many places," Brandon said. "What reason would I have to keep him hidden?"

"I won't play these games with you any longer. Care to explain why you're spending time in a place such as this?"

Brandon smiled and stuck a hand into an inner pocket to reveal a silver sphere roughly the size of a softball. Seeing it was enough; it required no explanation.

"That doesn't belong to you," Naliz said plainly. "Where did you find it?"

Brandon passed it back and forth between his hands, pausing briefly to admire his own reflection. "It was never missing."

Naliz shook his head in disbelief. "All these years? You don't even know how to wield it. What reason could you possibly have to…"

He trailed off and grew dizzy as he recalled the last time Brandon presented this same artifact. He stepped closer to peer through the crack in the door, paling when he saw Maiya across the room. She was still chained up, but on the floor and unconscious. He pushed past Brandon and dropped down beside her. Failing to rouse her, he looked back at Brandon with a mix of shock and anger.

"What have you done?"

Brandon shrugged. "Whatever I wanted to do."

"Is this a joke to you? This is nothing short of treason. Torture, Brandon?"

Brandon laughed. "You are not without sin. Will you tell them what you've done?"

Naliz glared back at him. "How dare you compare the two. I've made peace with my past. Unchain her at once."

"I'm not going to do that."

"Then I suppose I'll have no choice but to do it by force."

Brandon continued to be unimpressed. "You have no leverage. You can't bring me down without taking the council down with me."

Naliz stood back up and walked past Brandon. "I am done protecting you."

After Naliz reached the end of the hallway, Brandon addressed his guards. "See that he's delayed. I can't imagine it will be difficult to cause a disruption. Have someone wake the woman and return her to her cell. I'll finish with her later today."

Naliz barely made it outside when he realized he had already been sabotaged. His communicator ceased to function, and the transport he brought was conveniently missing. The security detail was still present but had been occupied keeping tabs on Brandon's men. They each reported having the same communication issues, leaving Naliz with no other choice but to head back to the city at a much slower pace. He cursed.

"If anyone leaves this building, follow them."

His men nodded, and he headed toward the city. The sight he saw when he finally made it to the edge of town was heart-wrenching. Flames rose up, consuming buildings throughout the historic district. Everything in Fimbira was frantic, adding to the time it took for Naliz to locate Jo'dai. Once he finally made contact, he learned that there had been simultaneous attacks in every major city across the continent. Security teams had already been deployed to investigate and provide aid, leaving them stretched thin. Facing a major setback, Naliz was left with no other option than to wait until a new team could be assembled.

Only a couple of hours passed before the door to Maiya's cell swung open again. She shrank back out of the light as the two guards stepped in to grab her. Maiya tried to kick them away but was still recovering from the last assault and quickly weakened. As with each time in the past, they dragged her to the door to meet Brandon's waiting smile. They shackled her wrists and in-turn affixed those to a large chain.

"Please," Maiya begged, "leave me alone."

Brandon brushed a hand down the side of her face as he shook his head slowly. "My dear, you should know by now that isn't how this works."

He turned and headed down the corridor, and his guards followed with Maiya in tow. Every few feet she stumbled and fell, only to be tugged sharply upwards by the men. Neither would look at her any more than they had to, and she wondered if they felt any remorse for their actions. The familiar doors to Brandon's study came into focus and Maiya tried to brace herself for what was to come. She told herself that no matter what Brandon had in store for her, she would not cry. He received far too much satisfaction from what he did to her; she would not allow him this as well.

"Back wall." Brandon said. He set the orb on the pedestal and then poured a drink.

As had become the routine, his guards led her to the small alcove opposite the door and strung the chain through rings along the wall so that Maiya's arms were outstretched above her head and her feet just barely reached the floor. The guards checked that the bonds were secure and then excused themselves from the room.

"Now, what do I want to do with you today?"

Maiya stared straight forward and said nothing.

"Look at me."

Brandon stepped closer and Maiya jerked her head away from him. She could feel his breath on her neck and sense his growing frustration with her. He grabbed her chin and forced her to face him.

"Look at me! I will not ask you again."

Still Maiya refused and soon felt the sharp sting as the back of his hand struck her face. The taste of blood filled her mouth. Maiya glared at him and spit in his face.

"You want me to look at you? Fine. I'll look, but that's all I'll do for you. The next time you see what I'm capable of, I'll be killing you."

Brandon wiped his face clean and laughed. "Words. Only words. You can't even defend yourself. Or won't. It's time I finally break you."

Maiya watched as Brandon walked to the central table and set down his empty glass. He then moved to a large desk and pulled something from a drawer, though she could not make out what from her present location. Brandon returned to the alcove and held up what appeared to be a thorn from a rose.

"Do you know what this is?" Brandon asked.

"Should I?"

"Once you feel it, you'll never forget, my dear. This is a thorn from the Naeret bush. The poison it contains is a rather potent hallucinogen. The tiniest scratch can have a remarkable effect." Brandon smiled. "It's time you make a choice: give up your power for your freedom or spend the rest of your life with me and this little gift I have for you. But first…"

Brandon held her head against the wall, "…a taste." He scratched the thorn sharply across her neck until he drew blood and then stepped back to admire his handiwork.

The effect was almost immediate. Maiya's entire body began to shake violently and her head pounded in agony. The room seemed to swirl around her until all she could recognize was the sound of Brandon's voice.

Dark, amorphous beasts with bodies like molten lava came for her. They had no visible eyes, but countless teeth flashed when they moved. Worse yet were the sounds they made as they approached – deep, guttural, and reminiscent of demonic laughter. She flailed wildly at their many heads and rows of razor teeth as they drew closer, but found she was unable to escape as they ripped at her flesh.

Maiya watched helplessly as they tore the skin from her bones, sending wave after wave of pain throughout her body and streaking blood down her arms and legs. The slightest touch of their bodies against her own burned her flesh with such intensity that she couldn't help but cry out in pain.

Maiya looked to her hands, trying to free her wrists from the shackles, banging them hard against the wall in her panic. Another of the beasts came at her and bit at her torso. She screamed in horror for it to stop; she was going to be eaten alive.

Brandon's laughter became clearer as the room stopped spinning and the monsters faded away. Maiya could see now that her flesh was intact, though the blood and bruising remained. The pain resonated so strongly through her being that she could not fathom how such a thing could be merely a hallucination. Maiya tried to focus but couldn't stop shaking.

"Not again… please, no more." Maiya felt on the verge of tears and worried she'd break the promise she'd made to herself.

"You haven't done anything for me yet. Until then, we're only getting started."

Maiya's voice cracked. "What do you want from me?"

"I thought I'd made that clear. As you're unwilling to show it to me, you've left me with no other choice. Give me what I want, and this will all be over."

Maiya felt the sharp sting as Brandon dug the thorn into her left arm and the beasts returned for her. She clenched her eyes tightly shut, but still she could see them as plain as day and hear them as they bounded toward her.

"They aren't real. It's all in my head." Maiya said. She recited this over and over again, but it did not stop the intense fear or pain that she felt. Each time the hallucinations dissipated, Brandon increased the dosage, forcing her to face the beasts for longer and longer stretches until she felt she had no fight left in her. Maiya dangled limply from the shackles as the final wave dug their claws and teeth into her broken body.

The vision again faded, and she waited for the next onslaught to begin, but it never came. Brandon looked furious. He paced the room in a rage, sweeping everything within his grasp to the floor. He grabbed the decanter from the central table and threw it at Maiya. The glass shattered against the wall, barely missing her head. Brandon kicked over the table and glared at her.

"Guards!" The doors opened and both men stepped into the room. Even in her current state Maiya could see the shocked looks on their faces. They must have seen Brandon angry before, but never as angry as he was now. "Get this thing out of my sight! And then clean up this mess."

Brandon grabbed the orb, turned, and stormed out of the room. The guards moved quickly to release her from the shackles, only to watch her fall to the floor once freed. Though still conscious, Maiya was far too weak to walk. One of the men bent down and lifted her over his shoulder. She watched as blood began to trickle down her arms and drip onto the floor. From her new perspective, she could see blood pooling in the alcove.

The trip back to the cell was the first Maiya remembered, and the first time she felt comforted to see it. The man dropped her roughly to the floor and exited without a word. The familiar silence and darkness that followed were strangely calming as Maiya closed her eyes and waited for death.

No more than twenty minutes had passed before Maiya was awakened by a light that filled the room. Her first thought was that Brandon had returned for her, but the room remained silent and the door closed. Slowly the figure of a woman formed before her eyes. Not made of shadow, but rather, one surrounded by a magnificent aura of light, as though she herself was made of light. She placed a hand upon Maiya's, and though Maiya felt no pressure, she felt warm from the touch.

It will be okay, the familiar voice whispered, though the woman's lips did not move. I can help you if you let me. Open your heart to me and let me in. I can free you from this pain.

It was at that moment that Maiya believed she must have died. She was dead and the one Saren had called a faulite was some sort of angel who had come to put her out of her misery.

There's no other explanation, she thought.

Maiya's voice came out weakly. "Yes. I'm ready."

And then it all went dark.

CHAPTER 20

Mahdon had just laid down for the first time in days when he was woken by Saren. She looked as serious as she had on the day Maiya went missing. Mahdon was so emotionally and physically exhausted that he didn't know if he was prepared to hear what she had to say. He knew she wouldn't have stopped by if it wasn't urgent. He sat up in bed and leaned back against the headboard.

"I'm sorry for waking you, but there are some pressing matters of which you should be made aware. Naliz would have come himself, but there have been numerous attacks that he's addressing."

His heart sank further. It had been weeks since the first attack and he had been hoping it was an isolated incident. They had yet to determine who was responsible for the initial assault, and now the situation was only worsening.

"How bad is it?" He asked.

"Very. The attacks were highly coordinated and widespread, but that isn't why I came to see you. He told me they've located Maiya."

Mahdon instantly felt his adrenaline spike. He'd been searching for weeks without so much as a hint that she was even alive. Saren's lack of enthusiasm told him that it wasn't the miracle he'd been hoping for; there was more to the story that she was hesitant to share. He climbed out of bed and threw on a shirt he'd left hanging over a nearby chair.

"Is she…?"

"She was alive when he found her, but she wasn't alert. It did not sound promising."

"Where is she? Why wasn't she brought here?"

"Mahdon," she looked him in the eyes and her tone grew graver. "Brandon has her locked up. Naliz didn't have the support he needed to free her. When he came back to get it, our security teams were already stretched too thin."

Raw anger flooded his veins. "Take me there."

"It isn't safe. He'll kill you."

"He can try."

He walked past her, headed outside, and made a beeline for the shuttle. Saren followed him as she sent a message to Jo'dai alerting him that they were on their way. She requested that he have everyone he could spare meet them at the bunker. She was nervous about how it would all go down and completely unprepared for navigating through a hostage situation. As they rose over the manor, they could see the fading towers of smoke from the blaze that moved through the city. Two-thirds of the historic district had crumbled or been permanently scarred with char marks. Mahdon frowned and shook his head when he saw the devastation. It was unfathomable to him how anyone could do such a thing intentionally.

"What could he possibly gain from doing this?"

"Brandon is always scheming," Saren said. "We may not know what it is, but I assure you there's an end goal."

The flight away from town was uncharacteristically long from Mahdon's perspective. Realistically it was around ten minutes by air, but it had taken Naliz nearly two hours to get back and another before he established contact. That left them with at least three hours of undocumented time where any number of things could have happened to Maiya. Not surprisingly, they were the first to arrive at the bunker. There didn't appear to be anybody outside for Brandon's sake or otherwise.

Not interested in wasting time, and far too angry to think clearly, Mahdon jumped out immediately upon landing. Saren practically had to restrain him to get him to wait for backup. He was none too pleased with her, but as she so bluntly reminded him, he wouldn't be of any use to them dead. He found himself regretting his decision to leave without temporarily re-establishing his immortality, but quickly decided this would be contrary to the vows he had made when he and Maiya had sworn to spend their lives together. Either way, he didn't think he could ever forgive himself if she died due to his inaction.

He paced outside the door, growing more anxious by the second. When help finally arrived, he escorted them inside and did his best to stay in the back and out of the way. Despite all of the other challenges, they had managed to get a dozen security professionals together for this highly unusual rescue effort. They carried with them several bags that Mahdon imagined must be tools to aid them should Brandon continue to refuse to comply. They moved through the building, checking each room in turn, only to find no trace of Brandon, Maiya, or anyone else who was left behind when Naliz departed earlier. The study where he confronted Brandon had been ransacked, or so it appeared. Once they declared the building empty, Mahdon insisted on running through it one final time to check if they'd missed anything. Other than the devastation in the study, there was no evidence to suggest that anyone had been there recently.

"Naliz instructed his men to follow if they moved her," Saren said. "It is probable that they will contact us when their communicators are back online."

Mahdon wasn't satisfied with that scenario. He turned to the group that was now gathered back outside. "They could still be close. Spread out and check the vicinity. If they left on foot we can find them."

Saren found it highly unlikely that Brandon would make it that easy for them. However, Mahdon was so worked up that she didn't want to be the one to tell him that. If searching made him feel better or kept him from doing something rash, she was more than happy to assist. They moved out in four directions, some scanning from above while others stepped through the brush below. They found many things – remnants of old buildings, the homes of forest critters, and evidence of overgrown paths – but nothing that matched what they were looking for.

Mahdon instructed the security forces to expand the search outward from this point and then slumped down against a tree. He was running on fumes and his mind was cloudy from exhaustion. He dropped his head to his hands and then sighed as he tilted his head back to look up at Saren.

"What am I going to do?"

She sat down beside him, unsure how she could answer that. "I don't think there's anything you can do. You need to sleep. I promise you that when they find her, I'll let you know immediately."

Mahdon scanned the trees one last time and then returned to the shuttle with some reluctance.

A warm breeze ruffled Maiya's hair, and her eyes fluttered open to find she was staring up through the canopy of towering trees. Her head throbbed and neck ached. Both, she initially assumed, from lying on her back on the not-so-soft forest floor. Sitting up to observe her surroundings, she realized she had no idea where she was or how she got here.

Her wrists ached, and she rubbed them to find it only made the pain worse. Thinking back, she had no idea how they had become so badly bruised. Her lapse in memory was, in her opinion, much more frightening than the pain itself. What could have possibly happened that caused such trauma to her brain? Was all the blood she saw her own or someone else's? As Maiya stared down at her arms, the wounds disappeared before her eyes and the pain quickly faded.

Regeneration… Maiya thought.

She stood up slowly. Immediately feeling light-headed and dizzy, she leaned against a tree until the world came back into focus. The sharp snap of a branch caught her attention.

"Mahdon? Is that you?"

She was answered with silence and the gentle rustle of leaves as wind moved through the trees. It was no more than a small mammal making its way through the underbrush. Maiya moved slowly toward the edge of the woods, pausing to balance against the occasional tree each time the dizziness returned.

As she reached a small clearing, she looked up to the sun and around in an aim to get her bearings. She gathered it was early evening, but nothing else she saw was familiar. Forest spread out to both her left and right, while a smaller band of trees stood another fifty feet in front of her. Was that water she heard up ahead? Maiya listened intently until she was sure of it.

She rushed forward through the line of trees and onto an outcropping of rock. The falls stretched before her, and though not too keen on the journey ahead of her, Maiya couldn't help but admire the view. She had never been at this point of the canyon before – never stood at the top where even the city was far below. Across from where she stood – parallel with the falls and several hundred feet lower – sat Fimbira. The city seemed small from this perspective, like a golden gem nestled between the falls. Directly across the canyon from the city stood the mansion she'd come to call home. She gathered it would take her at least a day to make it that far, likely closer to two in her current condition.

"I guess I should start moving." Maiya said to herself.

She didn't make it very far before she needed to stop to rest. She felt as though she hadn't eaten in days, but try as she might, she couldn't recall where she was last. She was going to introduce the candidates at the debate, wasn't she? Had they gone the wrong way and somehow crashed? The more she thought about it and tried to summon the memories, the more intensely her head hurt. Whatever had happened, she needed to get back to check that everyone else was okay. It suddenly occurred to her that she should be able to contact them. She reached for her pin and frowned when she realized it was gone.

Of course, the one thing I really need right now is missing, she thought.

Maiya sighed and sat down near the edge of the cliff. She looked out across the canyon and back toward the woods. The sun was setting far more rapidly than she anticipated, and she had no desire to travel in the dark. It wasn't the most comfortable place to make camp, but it was better than getting lost somewhere amongst the trees. She gathered a pile of sticks and smaller brush and then set it all ablaze. For whatever reason, this simple task was even more draining on her than usual. As helpful as it might be, there wasn't much point in using magic if it was only going to make her weaker.

She was pondering this thought when she became aware of a shuttle landing not far from her makeshift camp. She walked to the edge of the fire's light and was waiting for her eyes to adjust when Mahdon stepped forward. He looked in rough shape and appeared even more weary than she felt. He looked at her like he couldn't trust his own eyes. His voice was softer than usual, almost fragile sounding.

"Maiya?"

She moved closer to him and he pulled her so tightly to his chest that she thought he might never let go. She hugged him back but with a certain level of confusion.

"Are you okay?" she asked.

He held her a moment longer before taking a step back to return her confused expression. He didn't understand why she was concerned about him considering what she'd been through. Even though he wasn't sure what exactly had happened to her, he imagined any amount of time spent as Brandon's prisoner wouldn't be pleasant. The amount of dried blood on her arms and clothes served as confirmation that something undeniably terrible had taken place.

"Are you? Where is he?"

"Who?"

Mahdon looked back at Saren, who had walked over just in time to catch the tail end of the brief interaction. She shrugged at the response, just as baffled as him.

"Do you know what happened?" Mahdon asked.

Maiya shook her head. "No. I assumed there was an accident."

"We should go," Saren said. "We can discuss this somewhere more secure. I can take care of the fire."

She headed toward the fire while Mahdon led Maiya in the other direction. They sat down in the back of the shuttle and waited for Saren to return. Maiya wanted to press for details but could tell that Mahdon wanted to do the same. She was specifically curious why he was being so clingy. They went straight to the manor when Saren returned and were immediately met by Maiya's original security detail plus several others. They had each been thoroughly vetted after the first attack. It was determined that those involved lost security clearance when Brandon, and subsequently Tanin, were removed from the council.

"The building and perimeter are clear," Aveen, the team lead, told them. "We found nothing suspicious."

Saren smiled. "Thank you."

The security returned to their posts while the others went inside.

Maiya started upstairs. "If it's all right with you, I'd like to take a shower and change before we talk about this."

Mahdon nodded. "Of course."

Saren could tell that he was hesitant to leave Maiya alone again. She placed a hand on his arm to get his attention and try to reassure him. "She'll be fine. They're keeping a much closer watch now."

He nodded slightly in acknowledgment and then went to wait for Maiya in the study. Saren soon joined him with three glasses and a couple of bottles. Mahdon raised an eyebrow when he realized that both bottles were hard liquor. Taking notice of this, Saren smiled.

"You both look like you could use a drink. I wouldn't mind one either. It could be a long night."

It wasn't long before Maiya showed up running a brush through her hair in a fresh set of clothes. She gave them a similar look to the one Mahdon had just given Saren. She sat beside him and waited for one of them to say something.

"What's the last thing you remember?" Mahdon asked her.

"We were heading to the debate."

"Is that all?"

"Then I woke up in the middle of nowhere with bruises and blood everywhere," she looked down at her arms as she said this, "but that seems to have all healed already. Did we crash somehow?"

Mahdon took a drink as he considered how to tell her the truth. She was far less troubled by the missing time, and her understanding of what happened could explain why. How could he prepare himself for shattering her reality? He shook his head.

"We made it to the debate, but the debate never happened. There was an explosion."

She sat up sharply. "What? Was anyone hurt? Why was I so far away?"

"Allonis was killed, and you were abducted."

Maiya was sickened by the news. "By whom?"

"Brandon."

"And he just dumped me there after the attack?"

Mahdon glanced over at Saren and then back again. "Mai, you were missing for three weeks. I don't know what happened after you disappeared or how you got there."

She suddenly felt that she needed air. Her mind went foggy as she struggled to comprehend what he was telling her. "Why don't I remember any of this?"

"I don't know."

"I need to lie down."

She stood up slowly and walked away with a vacant look on her face. She couldn't keep her hands from shaking and didn't want anyone staring at her while she tried to figure out how to recover the lost memories. It was hard for her to accept as fact, but he had no reason to lie to her. If anything, he would rather not have told her at all. He wanted to know what Brandon did just as much as she did, but it was almost unfair. He had the benefit of never losing his freedom, and she had to live with the knowledge that she may never know what occurred during her lost time.

Mahdon moved to follow her. "Is there anything I can do?"

Her fear and anxiety quickly boiled over into rage. She hated that she didn't know where Brandon was or what he did. She hated that he continued to get away with doing anything he desired. Most of all, she hated herself for granting him a second chance and allowing all of this to transpire. Wrath filled her voice as she exited the room.

"Find that bastard."

Mahdon waited until Maiya fell asleep and then went to visit Naliz at the headquarters. Saren hadn't yet alerted him of Maiya's return, and he hadn't contacted them, so Mahdon doubted that he had been informed by anyone else. This was also a good indicator that Brandon was still on the loose and unaccounted for. Here was a man who always fancied himself a god, and now it seemed he was nearly as untouchable as one. Mahdon stood in the doorway, waiting for Naliz to notice he'd arrived, but he was clearly engrossed in whatever work he was doing.

"Maiya's back."

Naliz halted what he was doing and looked up. He looked tense and his questions came cautiously. "How is she? Has she said anything?"

"Physically she's okay. I can't speak to her mental state. She told me that she doesn't remember anything. She didn't realize she had been gone so long."

Naliz's demeanor relaxed slightly. "I'm happy she's made her way back. That memory loss, however, is rather alarming. What about Brandon?"

"She was alone. As far as I am aware, he hasn't been located yet."

"Where is Maiya now?"

"Resting. I was almost afraid to leave her alone, but I thought you should know."

Naliz nodded. "Yes, it was good of you to tell me. Keep me updated. I'd be interested in hearing what she has to say should her memory return."

Mahdon nodded and returned to the manor for the night. Maiya was usually a light sleeper; it was different this night. She was out cold and remained as such when he crawled into bed. He laid awake watching her sleep until even his desire to keep her safe wasn't enough to keep him conscious. The next time he opened his eyes, she was already up for the day and he was alone in the bedroom. He searched for her in a mild panic but calmed when he found her in the manor's conference room along with the rest of the council.

"You're just in time," Naliz said as he gestured toward a chair. "We were about to discuss our options. I believe Jo'dai has an update for us as well."

"Apparently Brandon has the orb we've been looking for," Maiya told him.

This was troubling news. If the artifact was as powerful as they suspected, he could potentially use it against them. They had no way of knowing what chaos he could unleash upon the world. This was not what Mahdon wanted to hear first thing in the morning.

"Does he know how to use it?"

Naliz answered with uncertainty. "I believe he has an idea and thinks he can, but I find it unlikely that he has figured it out yet. If he has, and we're correct about what it can do, then we will need to proceed with extreme caution. He could do to us what we planned to do to Tanin. Which means..."

He looked over at Maiya, who was reluctant to share what she knew would be met with Mahdon's disapproval. She didn't see much point in avoiding the inevitable either. "I may be our only weapon."

There was no masking Mahdon's displeasure. "He already held you captive once. If you couldn't fight him then, what makes you think you can now?"

"This will be on our terms, and I won't be alone."

Mahdon didn't believe for one second that it would be that simple and refused to drop the subject. "Do you know how he managed to keep you locked up for so long?"

Maiya sighed. "No."

"Do you remember anything that he did to you?"

"No."

"Until we know what happened, I can't support you going anywhere near him. He could do the same thing again."

Maiya understood his point but was too stubborn to admit it. She wanted a resolution to the problem and didn't have the patience to wait for it.

"I must have escaped somehow. Either that, or he let me go. I'm sure I can do it again."

"Maybe he wanted you to get away. Why else would he have taken your memory? This could all be an elaborate scheme to catch us off guard. We might be playing right into his hands."

"Mahdon is right, High Councilor," Saren said. "You cannot underestimate Brandon. It would be unwise to assume you will be safe."

Maiya frowned. "I guess it doesn't matter much unless we find him." She looked over to Jo'dai, "What's your status update?"

"We are continuing to monitor Tanin. We have yet to locate Brandon or any of his security team. Those who were directed to keep track of him have not contacted us, and thus far, we have been unable to get a trace on their position. It would appear that communications are still down for that team."

"Are you sure they haven't joined him?" Maiya asked.

"It is a possibility. However, I believe it is unlikely. Our additional screening was very thorough."

Maiya was finding it more and more difficult to see the silver lining with all the bad news. The more they discussed the situation, the more negative outcomes occurred to her as being real possibilities. "If they're still our allies, then it's possible that they're being used as test subjects. He may be even more prepared for us. Great."

"Please excuse the interruption," Aveen appeared at the door. She waited for acknowledgment before entering the room and then addressed Maiya directly. "There's been a development. One of Brandon's men has delivered a package to Tanin. We believe it to be the item you've been looking for."

"That's convenient," Maiya said. "And Brandon?"

"He did not accompany him."

"Okay," Maiya nodded. "I'm done playing fair. We have the tech to effectively freeze him in his tracks, and that's exactly what we're going to do. Send someone with Naliz who can provide his exact location. He should know what to do next."

She looked over at him for confirmation that he understood. She expected some dissidence like she had received in the past. Given the recent acts of treason and terrorism, he offered no objections. Jo'dai informed Aveen to send a secondary team and offered to meet them once he checked in with the other security forces. Naliz and Jo'dai then headed out with Aveen.

Mahdon could see the spark reignite in Maiya's eyes and questioned her intentions. "What are you going to do, Mai?"

"Nothing yet. I need to learn how to use that thing first. I'm probably going to have to look at that book again."

Saren tipped her head to the side at the mention of this. "Book? What book?"

Maiya stood and motioned for her to follow. "I'll show you."

They went to the study where Maiya handed the book to Saren to look over. She flipped through the pages in silence, pausing to read the occasional sentence. After several minutes, she slowly closed the book and set it back down.

"Where did you get this?"

Maiya shrugged. "I have an idea, but I don't really know. It was just sitting here one day."

Maiya could almost see the wheels turning in her head. Eventually Saren nodded slowly. "There is something I need to review."

Maiya and Mahdon watched her leave before sharing a look.

"That was unusual," Mahdon said. "Perhaps she's seen this before."

CHAPTER 21

Saren notified Naliz that she needed to speak with him and would be waiting for him to return to the council headquarters. He could hear the urgency in her voice and hurried back right after completing the task that was requested of him. She was walking the length of his private balcony when he arrived. He stopped just inside the balcony doorway and eyed her inquisitively.

"This is unlike you. What is it you know?"

Saren slowed her pacing but didn't turn to face him. "Did either Mahdon or Maiya speak to you about the faulite?"

Naliz's jaw tightened and he blinked several times. He'd grown tired of being left in the dark. "They did not. Please elaborate."

"Not only was it speaking to Maiya when we were searching for the orb, it also referred to her as 'sister.' At first I thought it was a strange coincidence. When I learned Brandon had it and that Maiya's memories are gone, my suspicions grew. Now Maiya has a spell book in her possession that is uncomfortably familiar."

"What are you suggesting?"

"Brandon may be toying with us," she stopped and walked over to him, fear apparent on her face and in her voice. "But what if he isn't? If the package that was delivered is the orb, I think it will be in our best interest to keep it to ourselves."

Naliz gave no regard to her concern. "I don't think we should jump to such outlandish conclusions."

"You know I'm not one for drama."

Naliz looked down and sighed. "I know."

"It's not what I want to believe either, but if I'm correct, then we all need to be alert. None of us can be in denial. You knew as well as I that a day might come when we would need to watch our backs."

He said nothing as he turned and walked further inside. Saren followed him and sat across from him in the main living space. He looked as troubled as she felt. She watched him silently, hoping he could understand the warning she had given. She could sense that he was trying to work through a problem for which there was no definitive solution. Right or wrong, what they decided would have a lasting impact and require more secrets that neither of them wanted to keep.

Naliz met her gaze, failing to conceal the sorrow that rested distantly in his eyes. "I want to move forward. How can I if we keep playing these games? We can't keep this from her. Doing so would be treasonous. It may not even be possible to gain access without her knowledge."

"I'm not suggesting that we keep it from her permanently. It's merely a precaution until we can confirm one way or the other."

"I'll help with this only if we can agree on one thing: the moment we know these are no more than mere coincidences, we end this."

Saren nodded and stood to leave. "Agreed."

"I'll contact Jo'dai and see what we can do."

Maiya agreed to let Jo'dai do a sweep of the premises before going anywhere near it. Once she was given the all clear, she rode over with Mahdon to meet up with the others. Aside from her own people, Tanin was the only other person present. Seeing him so vulnerable in stasis was more pleasing than she cared to admit. He sat frozen in time and unaware of their presence. He had been preparing to compose a message, and there was no doubt as to who the intended recipient would be. To his left there was a small, unimpressive looking wooden box.

"Is this it?" Maiya asked.

"That is the box that was delivered," Jo'dai confirmed.

Maiya picked it up with ease. She wasn't quite sure why, but she had expected more heft to it. She examined it more closely and then shifted her eyes to look at Jo'dai. "It's safe to open?"

He nodded. She opened it slowly to reveal a silver sphere with faint, thin lines running across the surface. She lifted it from the box and turned it over in her hands. A frown crossed her face and she shook her head.

"This doesn't feel right."

"What do you mean?" Mahdon asked.

"This is a knockoff. There's not even the slightest hint of magic around this thing." She dropped it back into the box. "What was the point of misdirecting us to here? Do you think he still has it?"

Maiya suddenly winced and moved both hands to the sides of her head. Mahdon placed a hand on her shoulder and looked at her with concern.

"Are you all right?"

"I have an awful headache all of a sudden. I can't deal with this right now. I need to go back and lie down."

Mahdon glanced over at Jo'dai. "We'll need to continue this another time. I'll check back in with you once I know she's okay."

Jo'dai nodded in acknowledgment as Mahdon led Maiya back outside. He hoped the headache was no more than evidence of her exhaustion and frustration with the situation. She held her head in her hands and didn't speak another word as they flew back. She laid down in the darkened bedroom, and Mahdon gave her something to take for her head. He'd never seen her afflicted by an ailment so suddenly and it worried him. Each unusual occurrence was a reminder that only Brandon knew the whole truth and likely still had the upper hand.

He decided to go for a walk through the gardens to clear his head and see what ideas sprang to mind to beat Brandon at his own game. He didn't enjoy being outsmarted by a man who not only hated him but showed obvious pleasure in displaying it. Being alone with nothing but his own thoughts and the sounds of the natural world around him had always helped to center him and guide him toward a solution. He was thankful that this practice of solitude was just as effective at bringing him peace now as it had ever been. He walked for about an hour before something caught his attention and gave him pause. He bent low and plucked a lily from the ground. The edges of the pedals were turning a bold red, something he didn't recall seeing in the flower's description. Looking across the surrounding land, every lily within his line of sight had taken on the same colorful change. Wanting to investigate this further, he took the flower with him and went straight to the study.

Maiya was seated behind the desk when he arrived, once again flipping through the spell book. He hadn't been expecting her to be up and moving about so soon. This time she was focused with such intensity that he didn't receive so much as a tilt of the head. This determination was paying off as the first fruits of her labor began to make themselves known. The tiny traces of a smile appeared on her face as the air surrounding her hand grew thick with an inky dark energy. The space held a darkness so deep that it gave the impression that it was consuming the very light around it. Maiya sat mesmerized by it, admiring the stream of magic as it revolved around her hand. The appearance alone was enough to unsettle Mahdon.

"I'm happy you're feeling better," he said, "but is it safe to be doing that?"

She looked up sharply, closing her hand to instantly kill the flow of magic.

"There's no need to worry," she said. "I remember it all now. I'm feeling much stronger. Why have you come here?"

Mahdon thought her wording was peculiar, but nothing had been normal lately. He held up the lily for her to see. "The flowers are changing. I intended to review the folklore to determine the significance."

She leaned back in her chair and gave a slight tilt of the head. "What do you think it means?"

"I don't know. Perhaps it's a sign of things to come or maybe it correlates with the evolution of your abilities. Maybe it's simpler than that, but I want to understand if there's a reason."

"Does it really matter why? Everything changes or will change with time. It's the way of this world and every other."

Mahdon narrowed his eyes at her and sat on the edge of the desk. "Are you well? You've never turned down an opportunity to gain knowledge."

She shifted uneasily and looked down before looking back with a thin smile. "You're right. I must not be feeling myself quite yet. I should get some air. I'll let you focus on that. Let me know what you find out."

She stood and exited. Mahdon watched her go and then turned to look at the still open book. As with the last time he read them, he found the sentences to be nonsensical. The most he could decipher from her latest accomplishment was that its purpose was to conceal. It made clearer what he'd seen her do earlier. He doubted there existed any technology that could pierce a magical darkness. He wondered, if no one else could see through it, could she? What was it she planned to do? As much as his curiosity tried to get the better of him, he reminded himself that her practicing may not have an end goal at all. Since she'd begun to master her skills, she had continuously strived to expand them further. More than likely, that was the case here as well.

Mahdon cast these thoughts aside and returned to his original reason for visiting the study in the first place. The collection was so vast that he didn't know where to begin. He knew that there was some semblance of order to it all, but if it was by time period or topic, he couldn't be sure. With each book he picked up, he grew increasingly frustrated that he hadn't at least retained his ability to speed read. The life he had grown accustomed to had come with many benefits, several of which he had taken for granted. He located a few books that looked promising and set them aside. With any luck, one of them would provide him with an answer and spare him the trouble of paging through another thousand tomes.

When he determined he had reviewed enough for the day, he left the study and once again crossed paths with Maiya. This time she was in a much bubblier mood and hugged him when she saw him. In fact, it was the happiest he'd seen her since they reconnected.

"Hey you," she cooed.

"This is a pleasant surprise. It's good to see you smiling again."

"I'm feeling so much better. I think I'm ready to go back and question Tanin now. I doubt he'll be any more helpful than he was last time, but it's all we've got to go on right now. I already contacted the others to set something up. Are you ready or would you rather wait a bit?"

"Now is acceptable."

"Cool."

They returned to where they'd left off earlier in the day and met up with Saren. Several security members lined the room where Tanin still sat frozen. Maiya explained to Mahdon that the other two would be joining them but had their own tasks to perform before they could proceed. They only had to wait a moment before Jo'dai showed up at the entrance to the room and gave Naliz the go ahead to move forward. Tanin came to life with a start. He swept his eyes around the room and let out a contemptuous laugh.

"We're back to this again, are we?" He shifted and soon reappeared at the perimeter of the room. He glowered at Maiya. "You must think yourself awfully clever."

As much as she appreciated his snide remarks, the truth was that she was disappointed with herself for not thinking of the option sooner. She wasn't exactly sure what had reminded her of the energy shield outside of Ularia, but she was glad that she did. It only took a quick message to Jo'dai to put it in place. Now all that remained was the unpleasant business of once again interacting with Tanin. Now that they stood face to face, she could only hope his desire to be set free outweighed any loyalty he held for Brandon. That was, of course, assuming that he cared more about himself than he hated her.

"If this is regarding your holiday with Brandon, I had nothing to do with it."

Maiya wanted to comment on his use of the word 'holiday' but was unwilling to give him the satisfaction of a reaction. "You did know about it though."

His lips curled maliciously. "It was the best news I'd heard in days."

"I know what you're doing," Maiya said.

"Of course you do. You know everything, don't you?"

"You're trying to get a rise out of me. It won't work. I don't know what you hope to gain by using this approach, but I can tell you now that it's a waste of time."

"You act as though I care. I have all the time I'll ever need. It's only your time that is wasted."

Maiya sighed. "Fine. Have it your way. I don't mind emptying this room and leaving you here to think about it. Maybe you'll be less snooty in a few years."

She was about to signal Naliz when he begrudgingly spoke up. "I am perfectly willing to talk. Just not to you." He then eyed Mahdon up and down. "And not that race traitor either."

"This isn't a negotiation."

"You can keep me locked away your entire life, and it won't get you any closer to what you want. The day you die will be my victory. No threat of boredom can take that away from me. It will be worth the wait."

"You're lucky I don't anger easily." She nodded to Saren. "He's all yours. I'll be back in an hour or so."

Maiya had Jo'dai lift the shield long enough for her and Mahdon to exit and then informed Naliz that he now had the chance to speak privately if he so chose. She had complete faith that should Tanin say something of use, at least one of them would let her know. Mahdon had trouble understanding why she caved to his demands but figured she had her reasons for it. Even if they learned what they'd come for, the unfortunate downside was that Tanin's attitude would likely only grow more infuriating.

After they'd gone, Tanin returned to where he'd left the recently delivered package. He opened it, stared a moment, and then burst out laughing. He was still enjoying the humor in the situation when Naliz arrived.

"I see you took it for yourself," he said. "What have you done with it?"

"That is no longer your concern," Naliz said.

"Does your master know?"

Naliz shrugged off the gibe. "What were you doing with it? It's my understanding that Brandon had it for some time. If he had succeeded in his goals, what would you stand to gain? We've been down this road before. Wasn't once enough?"

Tanin held a steady gaze with him as he sat back down. "Don't you crave more? You know as well as I that what we got is merely a taste."

Saren frowned. "What more could you possibly want? You're playing with fire. You're going to get us all killed."

Tanin snorted. "Do you honestly believe that human has it in her? The idea is laughable."

"It isn't her that I'm worried about."

"Do you have any idea how long we have been searching for another one of them? If there was a threat, we would have encountered it by now."

Saren gave Naliz a look to encourage him to speak up.

"You see nothing wrong with what you're doing?" he asked.

Tanin shrugged and sank back in the chair, propping his feet up on the table in front of him. "Of course not. Why would I?"

"She's not a piece of property that you can use as you please."

He shook his head with a bitter laugh. "That didn't bother you last time."

Naliz went from calm to outraged in an instant. Tanin had struck a nerve. "Do not presume to know how I feel."

"Brandon is right. You've gotten soft. You allowed that woman to get in your head. I didn't take you for a sentimental one."

Naliz was about to offer a rebuttal when Jo'dai stepped forward and interrupted them. "This is counterproductive. Do you know where Brandon is?"

"I did, but you did as well. If he is no longer there, then no, I do not."

"Are there any additional attacks planned?"

"None to my knowledge."

Tanin was much more receptive to being questioned by Jo'dai. As much as he enjoyed taunting the others, he admired and respected Jo'dai's ability to emotionally detach himself from any situation. He knew from experience that there was no point in trying to provoke him. He was as even-tempered as they came and had never been prone to emotional outbursts. As long as Tanin had known him, Jo'dai had an unwavering calm about him. By the time Maiya returned, they'd extracted all the information that they could from him. They met outside of the energy shield and agreed to provide details once they were back at a more secure location. All were in agreement that it would be best to post security and keep him in stasis until they could determine the best course of action.

Maiya was anxious for an update and didn't waste a second to inquire once they were all reassembled back at the manor. In light of recent events, and the increase in security around her home, she had chosen to conduct all meetings there for the time being.

"What did he have to say?"

"He claims to not know where Brandon is," Naliz said. "but he admitted that this has been the plan for years now. In fact, it's been their intention since well before we met you. The woman you took back was amongst the last of them, but there were at least a dozen others. They were willing to do whatever it took to get to you."

Mahdon was shocked, to say the least. He had never been on the best of terms with either of them, but these actions were beyond his comprehension. He desperately wanted to believe that there were only a couple of victims and that it was short-lived and quickly regretted. How could these men, who he had known for so long, be so cruel? Maiya felt a pang of guilt thinking about everyone who had suffered because she existed – or because she was prophesized to exist. She could already feel the weight of the lives lost.

"And Allonis?" She asked.

"His death was more than an unfortunate accident. It was their hope that if they targeted you there, they could just as easily eliminate what they saw as an inferior candidate for office."

Maiya was filled with mixed emotions. She was angered and confused by how someone could not only be so prejudiced, but have such blatant disregard for life. This had already gone on for far too long and yet she continued to feel powerless to do anything about it. He was always one step ahead of them, and they were always one task away from making a positive change. Mahdon could see her struggling to put her thoughts into words and shared in her frustrations.

"It was only a matter of time before they were found out." He thought a moment and then looked from Naliz to Saren and then to Jo'dai. He suspected they knew something that they weren't sharing. "What justification could they possibly have for doing such things? What were they expecting to gain that would make it worth the risk?"

"They want what she has, and they feel they are entitled to it as superior beings," Saren said. "Tanin doesn't recognize our authority. He fully trusts that Brandon will come back into power. As for Brandon, he's too cocky to care. He likely believed he'd never be caught."

It hadn't been a secret how either of them viewed themselves or how they felt about others. What Mahdon still didn't understand was why such extreme measures were being taken in the first place. To his knowledge, they already had everything that they needed to get whatever they wanted. As ruthless as they'd been, he couldn't imagine that they'd waste their time with such elaborate schemes unless they felt it was necessary.

"If the orb is as powerful as texts would suggest, then what did he need Maiya for? If he views her as a threat, then why not kill her outright like he did Allonis?"

"I know you're familiar with the more common legends and the writings in religious texts, but what about those shared by word of mouth?" Saren asked.

He shook his head. "I'm afraid those stories aren't my specialty."

"There are those who say that in order to grant power the orb must first steal it. Without a source, it would be useless to him."

"What if he had succeeded?"

Saren shifted her focus to Maiya. "My assumption is that she would be dead. I don't think he ever intended for her to survive."

Mahdon looked over at Maiya, but he couldn't read her expression. She was still alive, and her power continued to grow, so either Brandon was wrong about the orb, or he had been unable to use it. Either way, it meant he hadn't achieved his goal and thus, remained a threat. He wondered what she thought about all of this and if she had suspected it all along.

"With all of these theories, is there anything to suggest that it's ever actually been used?" Maiya asked. "If none of you know how it works, then maybe none of you can use it."

Naliz and Saren exchanged a look. It wasn't as subtle as either of them thought. It was the kind of look that indicated they knew more than they were saying. Maiya had already spent time reviewing council documents for any references to the orb, but there were none that weren't already available to the public. Whatever they continued to withhold was newly learned or something they had no desire to share.

"What aren't you telling me?"

Naliz sighed, uncomfortable with the direction of the conversation. "We have reason to believe that anyone can use it. At the very least, Brandon knows how to activate it and has the ability to do so."

"What makes you say that?"

Naliz had avoided discussing his own unpleasant memories. Though he knew questions might arise, he still hadn't been prepared for this eventuality and chose his words carefully. "I've witnessed him do this in the time he's had it. The place where he kept you was designed to disallow the use of certain abilities. Specifically, the ones you possess. It was when he presented the orb to me that I saw he had you restrained in the one place where you would be capable of using them. I can only conclude that he activated it in receiving mode in an attempt to siphon your magic should you fight back. It was clear from your condition that you never did. Beyond that, there is no evidence to suggest he can use it once it has been fully charged."

This came as a surprise to Maiya. She hadn't thought to ask how they knew Brandon was the one responsible for the abduction or how they found out he had the orb. She assumed someone had seen him grab her. She hadn't considered that anyone had seen her during the time she was missing. What else had he seen? Had anyone else been with him? So many questions swirled through her head, but she didn't know how to ask them. She tried to refrain from saying anything, but as usual, her curiosity won.

"What condition was I in?"

Mahdon leaned forward on the table. "Mai, are you sure you want to hear this?"

Though he asked her the question, he wasn't so sure that he wanted to hear about it. The thought of Brandon being anywhere near her made him feel sick and upset. She inhaled deeply and nodded.

"Tell me."

"You weren't conscious," Naliz said.

"I'm well aware."

"When Mahdon first told me of your physical condition, it was surprising, to say the least. I could hardly believe it until I saw for myself. Seeing you completely unmarred now is nothing short of a miracle. I thought you were dead when I found you. Your face was heavily bruised and swollen. Your arms and legs were similar with crisscrossing cuts on them. The fact that you have no broken bones is remarkable. He even had a machine aimed at you that's sole purpose is to emit electrical current. I don't know the details of what he did to you, but I know that he didn't hold back. You're lucky to be alive."

Maiya thought back on the bruises she'd seen when she first woke in the forest, but they were nothing along the scale that he described. Was it possible that she'd healed these before waking up?

"Did you talk to him?"

"No more than was necessary."

"What did he have to say?"

Naliz looked away and replied with an unhappy murmur. "It was mostly a threat to ruin my life."

"Is that why you left me there?"

She hadn't meant to make such a passive aggressive insinuation. Though he hadn't been the one to free her, it was possible that his discovery was the only reason she was still alive. She could see that he was displeased with the comment, but he let it slide.

"We were outnumbered, so I did the only thing I could. I would have done more if possible. It was a relief to hear you'd been found safe."

"Is there anything else I should know?"

He shook his head. "We will continue to monitor the situation, and I will keep you informed."

"Thank you. In the meantime, we need to let things get back to normal. I think that's enough for today."

Everyone filed out of the room except for Mahdon and Maiya. They sat across from each other while Maiya stared down at the table in silence. She'd stopped herself just short of asking what he thought had been done to her. It might have sparked a memory, but she was more afraid that it would only hurt her more than not knowing.

Mahdon gave her a moment before saying anything. "Are you going to be okay?"

"Yeah. Nothing has changed since this morning. I just want to forget this whole thing. What could Brandon do to ruin his life?"

"They've known each other very closely for a long time. It would not be unusual for Brandon to know Naliz's well kept secrets. There's nothing I personally know that I would consider capable of ruining his life. It may have been an empty threat to put him on edge."

She finally looked up and over at him. "And if it wasn't?"

"Do you distrust him?"

"I don't know what to think. I don't think he's helping Brandon, but I don't think he's being completely honest either."

"Politicians rarely are. Despite that, he's my friend, and I trust him."

Maiya nodded. "Okay. That's good enough for me."

Over the coming days, things slowly returned to normal with the exception of their primary objective. Each of the council members visited the bombing sites to aid in the recovery efforts and issue statements of reassurance. Tanin remained in stasis and under guard, and neither Brandon nor his men made an appearance. Maiya began regular practice in preparation for her anticipated future encounters, and Mahdon continued his research into the changing flowers which were progressively getting redder. Outside of this, they met almost daily with the council to touch base and get back to working on the future election.

When they weren't meeting with the council, Mahdon and Maiya made every effort to set aside their work to spend time together.

This was complicated somewhat by the increase in headaches and nightmares that Maiya began to experience. It soon became a nightly occurrence. She'd wake suddenly in a cold sweat and be unable to fall back asleep. She never remembered the dreams but always remembered the feelings of fear and despair. Any attempt to calm her mind would typically fail, and she'd walk around the house or read a book in the study until she inevitably passed out. Perhaps most troubling to her was how she always seemed to wake up in her bed with no recollection of returning to the room.

Though Mahdon was aware of the headaches, she hadn't told him about the nightmares. He routinely slept through the night, and she didn't want to worry him. That changed one night when Mahdon woke in the middle of the night to find Maiya absent. He laid in silence waiting for her to return, and when she did not, he slipped out of bed to check on her. It didn't take long to locate her in the study where she was curled up in a chair sobbing uncontrollably.

He immediately knelt by her side and pulled her close. "What's wrong, Mai?"

She silently wept a moment longer and then choked back her tears. "I'm so tired. The nightmares are getting worse. I can't sleep no matter how hard I try."

He held her while she cried and stroked her hair. "How long has this been going on?"

"I don't know. Most days over the past couple of weeks."

Mahdon was unhappy that she'd kept it to herself for so long, but didn't think calling her out on it would do any good. Once she calmed down a bit, he said the first thing that came to mind. "Will talking about it help?"

"I don't even remember them. I just want to sleep."

"I know something that might help with the sleep. There's a root that my mother used for insomnia. It comes from a flowering plant that we may have in the garden."

Maiya sat up and wiped her eyes. "And it works?"

"It's worth a try if you're willing."

She nodded. It was still dark, but he stood to go look. Maiya followed him out and then he put his arm around her as they walked silently through the maze of plants. They found what he was looking for and harvested the root. Any hope for sleep had faded for the night, so they sat outside to talk and watch the sun come up.

"I know that I said we should wait to leave, but I've changed my mind," Maiya said.

"Leave to where?"

Maiya smiled. "Where are you sending your research team?"

The suggestion was unexpected, but Mahdon was happy to hear it. It would be good for her to be around at least until the election was finished in a couple of months, but it would be better for her safety and sanity to get as far away as possible for a while.

"Are you sure that's what you want?"

"Yes. I think it's what I need. They have things handled here, and I'm not sure I feel comfortable waiting around for something else to happen."

"I think that's a good idea. They're scheduled to leave in a few days. Will you be ready by then?"

She gave him a playful wink. "I'm always ready for an adventure. Are you?"

He smiled. "Always."

CHAPTER 22

When they had their council meeting later that day, Saren immediately agreed with the decision to spend some time away. Naliz was initially reluctant but mostly due to the existing political climate. They reached an agreement to maintain daily contact and give regular reports in the event that the mission would need to be cut short. Jo'dai was more than happy to regain some of his security to put toward finding Brandon rather than protecting them from him. Mahdon thought they were a bit too enthusiastic to see them go, but he was realistic enough to realize that it would free up some valuable resources.

Later that day, while Maiya made her preparations for the voyage, Mahdon prepared the root for her to try. She headed to bed before him, and he soon found her fast asleep. He kept watch over her through the night in the event that she suffered from another nightmare that left her awake and in tears. When the moment came that she woke, the hour was late, but she did not appear to be distressed. She looked at him in the dark until he said something.

"Did you have another dream?"

"No." She climbed out of bed and brushed her hair away from her face. "There was something I forgot to do. Why are you awake?"

"I wanted to make sure you wouldn't need me."

She looked at him briefly and then smiled. "I am doing fine, thank you. You may go to sleep."

He watched her leave the room and then settled into bed. He didn't know if she ever returned to sleep, as she was gone when he got up in the morning. He showered and dressed and then went to find her. As was often the case, he found her in the study. This time she was dressed in semi-formal attire with a lily in her hair that was almost entirely red. She was looking out the front window, but glanced back at him before returning her gaze to the front of the house.

"It looks like Naliz is on his way. I believe he is upset about something. Did he inform you of this?"

Mahdon walked over to look out. "No, he didn't."

Naliz had landed in the front – which was unusual by itself – and was walking quickly toward the house. They hurried down to meet him and opened the door before he had the chance to knock. He was frantic and insisted that they go to the lounge to speak privately. He closed the doors behind them and dove right into the news he came to share.

"Tanin is dead."

"What?" Mahdon thought he must be mistaken, and the skepticism showed in his voice. "How is that possible? He was being guarded."

"The guards are missing, but I suspect they have met the same fate."

Mahdon sighed. "Not that it's a good thing, but maybe they left and took him with them."

Naliz stumbled over his words as he struggled to calm himself down. "There is no way that happened."

"How do you know?"

He sat down slowly, and his voice trembled when he spoke. "I have never seen a scene so brutal in my life. Whoever did this prevented him from fleeing somehow and made sure he was awake so he could feel it."

Mahdon paled at the thought. He looked at Maiya, who was frowning and fixated on Naliz.

"How do you know he was awake?" She asked.

"The wounds he sustained could only be delivered out of stasis and prior to death."

Mahdon stood and began pacing. "They would have needed access to Reedon's Arrow. Do you think Brandon could do something like this? Maybe he was upset that he talked."

"I had considered that possibility. Whoever did it wanted to send a message… a very angry and bloody message. How he could prevent Tanin from escaping, though, that I do not understand."

"Why don't we look?" Maiya asked. "We know where it happened, and presumably when, so we can see who did it."

Naliz shook his head and dropped it into one hand. "We can't. The moment I learned of this, I went back up to do just that. Reedon's Arrow is no longer there."

Mahdon quit his pacing. He feared what this meant. "Is the crew still alive?"

"Yes. Thankfully none of them got in the way. In fact, none of them were even aware it was missing until I arrived."

"That would be a difficult task without anyone noticing," Maiya said. "Perhaps you should question them again."

Naliz stood back up as he nodded his agreement. "I may just do that. Please keep yourselves safe. I need to check on the others. Jo'dai made this disturbing discovery on his own, but I have yet to speak with Saren. I think it would be best if we go underground for a while. You should do the same."

They walked him back to the front door and were saying their goodbyes when Naliz noticed the flower in Maiya's hair. "Is that a Jovaia lily?"

"Yes."

He peered outside and moved his eyes over the sea of lilies that he previously failed to give his attention. "But… they're red."

"They've been changing slowly for a couple of weeks now," Mahdon explained. "I didn't realize they would do that."

"I think red suits me," Maiya smiled at Naliz. "Don't you think so, Naliz? It's been so long since I wore red."

The blood drained from his face as he took a step back and gave a hesitant affirmation. "Yes, of course. I really must go now."

He hurried back to his shuttle and flew back across the river. That was the last that they saw of him for several days while they laid low and waited for any new information to surface. The more Mahdon thought about the murder, the more shaken he was by it. Naliz had been intentionally vague, but even the few words he used painted a vivid image in his head. By contrast, Maiya was uncharacteristically calm and quiet on the subject. After the day they received the news, she never once brought it up, and he didn't want to spoil her mood with the negativity. It wasn't until Maiya brought up the research trip that he mentioned it again. At the time, they were taking a stroll through the gardens and enjoying some ripened berries straight from the bushes.

Maiya held up a perfect berry with a smile. "I wonder what kind of fruit they'll have where we're going. I can't wait to try some new ones. Well, assuming they aren't poisonous."

Mahdon put his hands in his pockets and looked down with a frown. He was kicking around a pebble when Maiya placed a hand on his arm. She looked at him with a furrowed brow.

"What's wrong?"

"I've been meaning to talk to you about that." He turned his head up just enough to make eye contact and continued. "I know it's probably safer to not be around right now, but I really think we should postpone the trip for now."

"Why?"

"What if the killer isn't finished and targets someone more publicly next time? There's been so much violence lately, and it's creating more questions that need answers. If we leave now, it will feel like we're abandoning everyone."

Maiya tilted her head and her eyes narrowed. "What are you talking about? What killer?"

Mahdon tensed up. He questioned if this was a bad joke, but she sounded serious. He straightened up and shifted angles to face her directly. He searched her eyes but found nothing beyond confusion.

"Mai, I'm not sure what to tell you. You really don't know what I'm referring to?"

She shook her head but felt the fear creep up inside. Whatever it was, she hoped he had simply forgotten to tell her. "Are you sure you remembered to tell me about this?"

"You were present when Naliz told us. Have you been having many blackouts since your return?"

Maiya backed up slowly until she came to a tree and slowly slumped down against it. She felt light-headed as a knot tightened in her chest. "I... I don't know. I remember going to bed, I remember waking up, and I remember spending time with you. There aren't any obvious gaps. What happened?"

He moved over and sat down beside her. "This can wait. You don't need any added stress right now."

"Please, Mahdon. Just tell me. I can't keep wondering. I don't know what's wrong with me, and it's freaking me out. I need to know what's going on."

He held her hand and squeezed it tightly. "Tanin is dead. Naliz said that whoever did it did so in violent fashion."

Her hand trembled in his, and her face grew ashen. "Why?"

"We don't know, but it may be a not so subtle threat for all of us."

"When did this happen?"

"Three days ago. It was either early that day or the night prior."

"And what day did we meet to discuss the trip?"

"The day before that."

Maiya relaxed the tiniest bit. "At least I'm only missing one day this time. I went to bed early the other day and woke up like normal two days ago. Do you think it had anything to do with the sleep aid?"

"I've never heard of that happening before. Human physiology is similar enough to ours that I wouldn't expect it to react that much differently. However, you didn't sleep through the night, so maybe."

"I didn't?"

"No. You said you forgot to do something, and I went to sleep. I didn't see you again until morning."

Maiya felt woozy all over again. Someone was murdered, she was unaccounted for when it happened, and she had no explanation for the lost time. She didn't think she was capable of something so twisted, but she couldn't say with certainty that she was home at the time. She still hadn't mentioned the common occurrence of falling asleep in one room and waking in another. She assumed this was either him moving her or her sleep walking. She'd heard stories about people having full conversations and walking while asleep – particularly when using sleeping pills. As scary as the idea was, it was better than being responsible for something that she didn't even remember.

Feeling defeated, she looked at Mahdon. "I think maybe I shouldn't go to sleep tonight. If my only choices are nightmares or forgetting whole days, then exhaustion might be better."

"I know you're frustrated, and you have every right to be, but I don't believe that's the proper solution. You remember the past two days, correct?"

"Yes."

"How did you sleep?"

"Surprisingly well, actually."

"It is possible that you experienced an adverse side effect that first night. If you would prefer, I will stay awake with you tonight, but it would be unwise to make it a habit."

Maiya looked away and didn't say anything for a while. Once again, he had a valid point, and she was reacting based on emotions. Part of her wanted to return to Earth and resume the boring, adventure free, but ultimately relatively safe life she had before. The idea wasn't exactly appealing, but the stress of not knowing what horrible thing would happen next was beginning to take its toll.

This too shall pass, she reminded herself. Finally, she nodded. "Okay, that's fair. Why haven't we heard from the rest of the council since then? Is anyone investigating this further?"

"They're all trying to stay hidden for a while. If I wasn't confident that we'll be safe here, I would have suggested that we do as well. As far as investigating goes, I'm afraid we're out of options until we can think of a new approach. It would be useful to look back, but that tool is no longer available to us."

Maiya assumed he meant one or both of the artifacts they'd used in the past and made a mental note to ask him more about it later. Right now, she was more concerned with the fact that nothing had come up for two days, and they hadn't heard from their closest advisors.

"Wouldn't it be more helpful for everyone to be here, then? We need to discuss our options."

"Ultimately, yes. However, if someone is targeting council members and those who are near us, then I believe it is best to remain somewhat separated for a while."

"If we haven't kept in contact, how do we even know they're still alive?"

"We should hear something in a day or two. If not, we can have one of the security teams here connect with them wherever they are."

"Do you know where they are?"

He shook his head. "Not conclusively. I have an idea of where they may have gone."

Maiya stood back up and Mahdon followed suit. "I hope they stay safe. We need to start working on an actual plan. We've already wasted too much time."

Walking back to the house, they ran through the facts for what they already knew. They agreed that no matter how gruesome the details were, they needed to know more about how and when the murder occurred. They called for Aveen to get them the official report and began putting together a timeline of events since the day of the scheduled debate. There was still no news on Brandon or most of his lackeys, but the one who delivered the package continued to be monitored. He had returned to the bunker where Maiya was kept only to remain outside making failed attempts to contact his own allies.

When it came to the crime itself, the evidence spoke for itself. The culprit got in and out without being seen and knew how to both locate and operate Reedon's Arrow. They had either prevented Tanin from shifting or convinced him not to despite the torture that would follow. Lastly, they killed him in such spectacular fashion that it could only have been done by someone who had a personal conflict with him. Unless the individual had truly dark desires and access to confidential information, there was no way it was a hired assassin. Each of the council members held some level of enmity toward him, but none so great that would inspire murder. While no one could speak on behalf of Brandon, it had become obvious that the man had no qualms with inflicting pain upon others if it served his interests.

In addition to Brandon and the council members, there were several Zumerti who had motive to be rid of him given his past interactions with their families. However, to the best of their knowledge, none of them had the means to pull off the crime. This left Brandon as the primary suspect, but Maiya wasn't so sure that she should be ruled out given her own lack of an alibi. She was too afraid to make the suggestion to Mahdon, as she felt that she was most likely overreacting and didn't want to face a reality where she wasn't.

As nightfall approached, they devised various activities that would assist in keeping them awake through the night. Maiya thought that if she could remain awake long enough, that pure exhaustion would take over and even nightmares wouldn't be enough to disrupt her night. If the nightmares wouldn't keep her awake, then she wouldn't need to rely on other options for getting rest. If it was the root that caused the memory lapse, then choosing not to use it would be an easy enough fix. As the night wore on, she discovered that this tactic was not as simple as she'd thought it would be.

They were on their third round of Tane Kaut, and she was wide awake when she began thinking about the words that must have been exchanged prior to Tanin's demise. Was he given a chance for redemption? Did he ever display any remorse, or was he just as stubborn and heartless up until the very end? Much like before, when she began to question recent events more intently, her head began to hurt. The more she pondered this, the worse the headache became. She was coming to realize that it wasn't sleep deprivation that would send her to bed, it was the need to gain some relief from the pain.

She closed her eyes and dropped her head to her hands. "Another headache... I'm going to lie down, but I need you to promise me that you'll keep an eye on me when I wake back up."

"Okay."

She stood slowly and then he walked with her to the bedroom. After a brief hug, she made her final request of him. "Every day when I wake up, can you tell me what day it is? I want to know right away if I lose time."

"Of course."

The increasing frequency of headaches on top of everything else was alarming. Mahdon had already convinced her to have a scan done shortly after they found her, but nothing came back as unusual. Whatever was causing her symptoms wasn't a form of visible brain damage. The best way to get an answer, he felt, was to speak with Brandon directly about what he'd done. Seeing as that was unlikely to happen, he considered the options that the Seed of Revelation offered to them. Given the nature of the artifact, he didn't think it would be right to do so without her permission. He also thought she should be given the opportunity to see for herself before he did.

The next morning, he honored his word and did what she'd asked of him. Though she wasn't accustomed to having constant company, she was grateful that he stuck to the agreement. Feeling somewhat relieved, she told him to resume his regular routine the next day but to continue sharing the date with her. Two days passed with no recurrence of the previous issues and no word from the others. Maiya spoke with Aveen and shortly thereafter received confirmation that they'd made contact and were actively working on their own investigation. Maiya relayed this information to Mahdon who then brought up his suggestion for reviewing her time in captivity.

She looked away, trying to put into words how conflicted she felt about knowing. She feared that if she knew the whole truth, she would suffer more for it. However, if anyone else knew and she remained oblivious, they might view her differently and she'd never understand why.

"Can we maybe not talk about this anymore? Maybe there's a good reason why I don't remember. Maybe it's better this way."

"Aren't you worried about the headaches and blackouts you've been experiencing? If there's something more serious going on, we should try to stop it before it becomes permanent. Knowing what he did could aid us in doing so."

"I'm fine," she lied. "Things are getting better already."

"It's only been two days, and we have no idea what triggered that. What about the next time it happens?"

"It won't."

"How can you be so certain of that?"

Maiya had quickly become exasperated with the conversation and took no measures to hide it. "Let it go."

Before he could say another word, she began to walk away. He wanted to respect her wishes but felt she was being unreasonable. Perhaps he hadn't given it enough time, but he wondered how long was too long to wait if something needed to be done. Later that day, Maiya apologized for her reaction and he apologized for pressing the subject. After that exchange, he chose to refrain from bringing up the topic again. If she displayed more out of character behavior or showed additional signs of memory loss, he would take matters into his own hands. He prayed it wouldn't come to that.

Only two more days would pass before he witnessed something else unusual. As they still hadn't heard from Naliz, they once again sought out Aveen for an update. She again confirmed that they were alive and well. In addition to this, they relayed that they now had the orb but neglected to go into the details of how they obtained it. Mahdon took this as nothing but good news and expected a similar reaction from Maiya. That was not the case. She grew visibly angry and demanded to know where they were keeping it. When Aveen indicted that she didn't have that information readily available, Maiya expressed in no uncertain terms that it would be in her best interest to find out. If Aveen was unnerved by this reaction, she in no way made it known.

Mahdon watched her leave and then stopped Maiya before she could do the same. "What was that about? That was way over the top."

"I have a right to know."

"Yes, but berating her like that was uncalled for. Why the sudden rush to have it right now? We've been looking a long time; what's a few more days? We should be happy that they found it."

"Yes. I suppose you're right. I've been looking a very long time." She gave him a half smile and began to walk away. "What's one more day? You'll have to excuse me; I have some preparations to make."

"Preparations?"

"Yes, for when we see our friends again."

Mahdon allowed her to go without inquiring further and then preoccupied himself with a book until late evening. Once he was confident that he wasn't being watched, he removed several strands of hair from Maiya's brush, wrapped them in a bit of cloth, and pocketed them. He cracked the door of the study to check that Maiya wouldn't see his departure and found her preoccupied with the practicing of a spell. She took no notice of his gaze and continued to work diligently over the far desk. He let the door slip shut and headed down the stairs to the back doorway of the mansion. Doublechecking that no one was following him, he hurried off into the forest.

As the manor faded into the night and the only light he could see was from the starry sky overhead, he knew he was getting close. The sound of flowing water soon met his ears as he arrived at the pool where his union with Maiya had taken place. His eyes had adjusted nicely to the dark, and the reflection of light off the water illuminated the young tree the couple had planted a few months earlier.

"I'm sorry for doing this, Mai," Mahdon said to himself.

Mahdon took a quick look around to make sure he was still alone, and once satisfied that he was, removed his outer layer of clothing and stepped into the pool with the strands of hair in hand. He swam to the small cavern that housed the spring and exhaled slowly as he prepared himself for what he was about to do.

He held the hair between two fingers and placed it over the spring, then stepped into the water, and leaned back as the strands fizzled into nothingness. He closed his eyes as he slipped under the water and posed the question in his mind.

What happened between Brandon and Maiya while she was away?

Images began to course through his mind and brief glimpses of the past surrounded him. He saw Maiya in a place that appeared to be underground and faces that streaked around him in disarray. Her hair appeared disheveled and her wrists looked raw, as though they had been bound tightly for some time. The vision quickly faded to another and yet another after that.

One after another flew past until finally the question settled upon an answer. Mahdon watched as the vision came into focus and formed around him, appearing as solid as any other moment in reality. Bookshelves lined most of the walls around him, but the air chilled as he realized he was in a well carved and cared for cavern. The ceiling overhead was elaborate in its design, clearly unnatural in origin.

The room was dimly lit, but Mahdon could make out a man sitting behind a large desk on the far side of the room from where he stood. Moving closer to the desk, Mahdon squinted and could finally make out the face of the man who sat behind it. His features were partially obscured in the low light, but his clothing and mannerisms were unmistakable. Dressed in dark garments with a heavy fur and feather cloak draped over his shoulders, the man had a pen in hand as he flipped through the papers scattered on his desk.

Mahdon turned as a large set of doors opened behind him and the figure of a woman moved into the entryway. Brandon looked up as Maiya entered the room and closed the doors securely behind her. She stood tall and appeared menacing as her eyes flared with anger. She was covered in dried blood and her hair and wrists looked as they had in the image before, as though some abuse had come to her. Mahdon wondered what they had done to her and why the question had chosen to focus on this moment, rather than the events that produced the wounds she wore.

Brandon shot up from his chair, apparently stunned by her arrival. "What are you doing here?"

"I was wondering the same thing," Maiya said, then swept out a hand and sent Brandon flying across the room until he collided hard against the wall. The knockback made Mahdon wince reflexively, the force of the blow stronger than he thought Maiya capable of. Brandon slumped to the floor, leaning forward on his knees as he gasped for air. The long-time council leader looked to be in pain with every breath he took.

Maiya moved to where he fell and glared down at him, "Don't even think about shifting. No, wait. Go ahead and try. I think it will be amusing for the both of us."

Maiya spoke a few words in Fudarin, and Mahdon realized that he recognized it as a spell from the book they'd found several months earlier. As she did this, Brandon grew noticeably weaker and stared down at his hands in fear.

"What have you done to me?"

"I've simply... revoked... some privileges. You like that mask so much that I thought you might like to keep it."

"Please," Brandon said, holding his hands in front of him pleadingly, "You don't need to do this."

"Don't I?" Maiya circled the old council leader like a cat eyeing up its prey. "Isn't this what you wanted? To see what I'm capable of? Remember what I told you..."

A predatory look glistened in her eyes as dark sparks of energy danced across her fingertips. Something about the way the energy moved seemed unsettlingly familiar. Mahdon stepped closer, wishing he could analyze the magic that encircled Maiya now.

"I'm sure we can work this out," Brandon said, making no attempt to stand but putting on a diplomatic voice. "You are a reasonable being, are you not? I see no reason to spread further violence."

"Of course you don't. Not when the shoe is on the other foot."

"You're right. What I did was wrong."

"That's quite the understatement. It must be so much easier for you to say that now that you're mortal. Now that you know I can kill you."

"Why don't you go back to your mate and we can put this all behind us? You'll never be bothered again; I swear it."

"Spare me your lies. What good is your word? You're nothing more than a politician, playing the puppet master from the shadows, more power hungry than anyone else. Centuries of life have taught you nothing. You're not evolved; you're just fortunate enough to have extended life to the point that you have. We helped you. And for what? Only to find out that you're selfish and more of a threat to yourself than any natural cause ever could be."

She let out a long sigh and took a seat behind Brandon's desk. It seemed the fury had bled out of her. Her face looked gentle once more, but weary and pale. She smiled calmly at Brandon, who remained motionless on his knees.

"You wish to talk? Sit with me and we'll talk." Maiya motioned for him to join her. Brandon stood slowly and moved to sit awkwardly on the guest's side of his desk. Mahdon thought he looked like a student who had just been reprimanded. Brandon's shoulders relaxed slightly as he wondered if he should speak first or wait for permission.

"Why are you so invested in this little game of yours?" Maiya said at last, looking him squarely in the eyes.

"I don't believe I know what you mean," Brandon said.

"Why else would I be here? I hardly believe you'd have released me after draining my power. You haven't exactly been hospitable. After all, that is why you brought me here, isn't it? Once just wasn't enough. You tasted but a drop and you crave more." She leaned forward on the desk with a smile so unsettling that even Mahdon could see Brandon was visibly shaken. "I'd almost admire your handiwork if it weren't so sloppy. With all the time you've had, you should be far more destructive than you are now. It's embarrassing, really."

"What is it you want me to say? You should never have come here. I spent my entire life working to obtain what I had and then you showed up and destroyed it all in a matter of days." Brandon paused to look away, his voice filled with bitterness. "All I want is what should be rightfully mine."

"Well, well, aren't we an entitled one?" She nodded, twirling Brandon's pen about in her hand. "But that's not all there is to it, is there? There were fifteen others. You knew almost immediately that they didn't have what you sought, yet you kept them caged like animals anyway. You beat them and tested out your latest painful experiments on them, and when you got bored with them, you left them to die. It was more than possible for you to leave them be, but you chose not to. What you did, you did because you enjoyed it."

Mahdon could tell Maiya spoke the truth. He did not know what Brandon had done to them, but he could tell that the only way Brandon would ever offer freedom was if he felt he had no other choice. He could not deny it. Maiya stood, still twirling the pen between her fingers.

"And now that we have all those nasty details out in the open, how would you like to deal with me? Still wish to let me live my life in peace?"

"I have no quarrel with you any longer. Take a ship if you like; explore the universe. I don't care what you do, but please don't leave me like this. Return to me what is mine."

Maiya's eyes seemed to mist over for a moment as though she was deep in thought, then all at once they came alive, burning with a rage that sent shivers up Mahdon's spine. Brandon did not notice the dramatic shift, perhaps due to the way she so calmly walked around the desk while he awaited her response. Maiya pocketed the pen and stepped around behind Brandon, slipping her arms around him. For a moment, Mahdon thought she was giving him a hug. He watched as she brought her head close to one of Brandon's ears.

"You seem so very sincere," she said, "but I don't make the same mistakes twice. You made those same promises many, many years ago. After all you've put me through, I'm really going to enjoy this. I will never return to you what is rightfully *mine*."

Brandon's expression twisted into what Mahdon realized was a look of terrified recognition. "No... that isn't possible."

"How do you think I was able to break free and get in here so easily? Your basic stone barriers were no challenge for me."

Brandon now spoke in a suffocated whisper. "What is it you want?"

"You know what I want. Where is it?"

"I don't have it anymore. I sent it off with someone."

Maiya moved around in front of him and shook her head slowly. "That was rather foolish of you. You have no idea how long I've wanted to do this."

A vindictive smile crossed her face as she placed her hands on Brandon's chest. His body arched as though he had been shot with electricity and a scream escaped his throat. The scene had become so real that for a moment Mahdon shared in Brandon's pain and cried out for it to stop. He felt as though every nerve ending in his body was on fire, burning from flames that could not be extinguished. Mahdon saw a look of helplessness and fear in Brandon's eyes that he never imagined possible. Maiya removed her hands and Brandon fell to one side in the chair, whimpering. Unsettled by what he saw, Mahdon took a step back.

Maiya took Brandon's chin in one hand and lifted it to look in his eyes. "Now that wasn't so bad, was it? Before I go, I need one more thing from you. I need you to say it."

"Say what?"

"Oh, come now, surely you remember."

Tears streaked down his face. "Will you allow me to live?"

"Say it."

He dropped his head for a moment as he fought to steady his voice. "You are the one and only rightful ruler. I deserve everything that happens to me."

Maiya smiled, using one finger to lift his chin once again. "Yes, you do."

A guttural scream erupted from Brandon's throat as an incredible glow encased him. Mahdon had never heard a sound as terrible as he did at that moment when Brandon's body evaporated into ash, and Mahdon found he had to turn away. When he looked back, no trace of Brandon remained. He felt suddenly lost and shook his head in disbelief.

No, Mahdon thought, *this can't be right.*

The vision ended abruptly as his head broke the surface of the water. He stumbled from the pool, his mind reeling at the very notion that Maiya could do such a thing. Maiya wasn't a killer; she'd saved so many lives. This had to be a mistake. Even if Brandon had held her captive, tortured her – or worse – the woman he knew would never get such pleasure from taking a life. Would she?

Mahdon dropped to his back beside the wedding tree, unable to keep himself from shaking, and feeling alone for the first time in his long, long life. A man he'd known his entire life was dead by the hand of the woman he loved. A woman who had become a victim of whatever sick pleasures that very man desired. Mahdon had never felt so conflicted or unsure of his judgment. He laid on the ground for a great many hours, his mind in a haze while the constellations overhead moved toward the horizon.

When the morning light began to creep over the edge of Amertine, Mahdon climbed to his feet and dusted himself off.

I'm sure there is an explanation for this, he thought.

Later, as he returned to the manor, Mahdon looked once more into the study and saw Maiya as he expected, head down at the table where he left her, having fallen asleep in the middle of her work. He stood for a moment in the doorway, thinking she appeared as peaceful as he ever knew her, a woman incapable of bringing harm to even those who brought it to her. As the light of day filtered through the windows, Mahdon retired to the bedroom and curled up beneath the blankets alone.

CHAPTER 23

When Mahdon awakened, it was late that afternoon and the sweet scent of the evening meal already lingered in the air around him. Caught between sleep and full wakefulness, Mahdon rolled over and grasped for Maiya, sitting up when he realized she wasn't there. A moment of sleepy confusion washed over him before his mind reminded him of the vision and agreed to function once more. He frowned at the memory and made his way to the dining hall downstairs.

It wasn't common for them to have a formal dinner together, but when he entered, Maiya was in the process of setting out dinnerware for the two of them. He didn't think she noticed his absence during the night, but he couldn't say positively one way or the other.

Maiya greeted him with a smile. "I didn't want to wake you; you were sleeping so soundly. I thought I'd surprise you with dinner."

She placed a final fork and walked over to him. "Is something the matter?"

Mahdon caught himself staring at her and shook his head, "I'm fine. You were busy last night? You never came to bed."

"I'm sorry about that. I've just been so absorbed in my research lately that I've lost track of time."

She left the room and returned with a platter of meat and roasted vegetables. They sat to eat, and Maiya turned her attention to her plate. Mahdon watched her out of the corner of his eye, searching for some tell that she was not herself. Noticing nothing out of the ordinary, he felt both relieved and uneasy. If Maiya was no different than she ever had been, then the vision had to be wrong. Unless, of course, she was not the person he thought she was, which could prove to be more dangerous than a single crime of passion. She had acted unpredictably at times; was it possible this had happened during one of her blackouts?

Not having much of an appetite, he pushed the food around on his plate for a while before standing to put it away. Taking notice of this, Maiya set down her own utensils and put a hand gently on his arm as he passed. He reflexively jerked his arm away and then froze when he realized how badly he was shaking. Any hope he had of pretending everything was normal was gone in an instant. Maiya looked as though she'd been slapped.

"Did I do something wrong?"

"No, I just," he struggled to look at her while concealing the truth. "I'm not feeling very well. You startled me."

"You're sure that's all?"

Knowing that his hesitation and lack of eye contact had already given him away, he slowly sat back down.

"So, something is wrong, then?"

Mahdon nodded slowly. "I'm not sure. I need to ask you something."

Maiya looked uncomfortable now but not hostile. She sat silently and looked at him as she waited for him to continue.

"All this time spent practicing magic lately… what are you preparing for?"

Maiya wasn't expecting the question. She thought they were on the same page. "I don't want to be caught defenseless if Brandon or someone else decides one of us is next."

"Do you honestly think that's a real possibility?"

"Where is this coming from?"

He thought her confusion seemed genuine, but he needed more reassurance. He suspected she hadn't been forthcoming about further memory loss. "If we have the orb, do you think you can use it?"

"I don't think we even need it. It's probably best if no one has access to it. I don't want anyone else being tempted to try the same tactics as Brandon. But as long as he has it, I'm not going to feel safe."

"As long as he has it?"

Maiya gave him a look that needed no explanation. She knew he was trying to make a point, but he was being intentionally slow to get to it, and she hated when people beat around the bush. She sighed.

"Okay, out with it."

"You didn't ask the date today and I haven't told you. When was the last time we got a report from the security team?"

Maiya frowned and her heart sank. "I'm guessing yesterday based on that comment."

Mahdon relaxed somewhat and reached his hands across the table to take hers. "Something is very wrong. I know you don't remember it, but you aren't you all the time."

"How so?"

"You don't seem to care as much. Except when you're angry. You…" He stopped himself from sharing the vision he witnessed and chose to only provide the most basic of facts. He knew he couldn't shield her from the truth forever, but he was still coming to terms with it himself. "You're more hostile."

"The day that Tanin was murdered… do you think, maybe…" Her breath caught in her throat. She didn't need to say anything more for him to know what she was asking.

"We cannot disregard the possibility that you were involved."

Maiya's eyes misted over as she sat silently in thought. Mahdon knew her well enough to know she was trying to silence her anxiety before it presented itself as tears. She had no idea what to suggest but feared what would happen if this unexplained dark side of her showed its face again. At the same time, she was afraid that if she was voluntarily locked away, she'd be trapped should something else happen. Ultimately, she felt it was the only option to guarantee she wouldn't be the cause of anyone's death.

"If I've been compromised, you need to lock me away until we can stop this from happening again. There's protocol to follow for this, isn't there?"

"Yes. Typically, a temporary change in authority would involve a vote from all council members and supporting evidence, but if you do so willingly, that won't be necessary. The procedure we follow will be slightly different."

"What do you need me to do?"

"Where we are now is the most closely watched location since your return. I suggest we use that to our advantage. We'll have to update your

277

security on how to handle your movements and requests. Until that's done, they'll continue to follow every order you give. You'll need to tell them who will be your stand-in, and then my understanding is that they'll perform a security test to ensure the decision truly was made by you and not for you."

Maiya nodded. "Okay."

"Do you know who you will have be your substitute? I assume Naliz as you've given him the job in the past."

"If I have one of those 'episodes,' what's to stop me from taking the position back like I have before?"

"If you do this, your security clearance can only be re-established on the authority of the active council members. Are you certain this is what you want?"

"I don't think I have any other choice. I would rather you fill the role, though. It should be someone who spends a lot of time around me, and he's been absent lately."

Mahdon sat back, surprised. "I don't know how qualified I am for that role."

"I remember when I told you the same thing. You're a hell of a lot more qualified than I ever was. Besides, it won't be permanent, right?"

"I'll do my best."

They didn't waste any time contacting Aveen and proceeding with the power transfer arrangements. Neither of them went into detail on the reasons for the decision, but they were both taken to the headquarters separately for individual security screenings. Maiya's was much less invasive than the one she'd undergone to be granted the top security access. Though not as intense as Maiya's original screening, Mahdon's was more thorough than her latest one. When they were both back at the manor, they sat in the lounge in an awkward silence while Mahdon tried to determine the best way to break the news about the vision. Maiya was wrestling with her own thoughts about what would happen next. She wondered if they had already informed Naliz of the change, and if no one had, she wondered what the best thing was to say. She wondered what they would think of her. If she had gone crazy, was it even possible to help her?

"Did you tell them what we did?"

Mahdon sat forward in his chair. "I sent someone to relay the information. I did not get into the specifics as to why. That can wait until we once again gather in person."

"I can't imagine what they must think."

She wanted him to hold her and tell her it was going to turn out all right, but she could sense that even he was filled with uncertainty. A deep sadness rested in his eyes as he looked at her in the lingering silence. He moved to sit beside her and put his arm around her. Nothing more was said that night. Maiya fell asleep leaning against him, and he sat up through the night praying that she would still be herself in the morning.

The following day, confirmation came that their message was received and a meeting with Mahdon was requested. The wording in the response was clear that this would be a closed meeting at an undisclosed location. He would receive further instructions in a few days unless he indicated that more immediate action was needed. Maiya was uncomfortable being excluded but was understanding of the situation. Mahdon promised to let her know what was discussed about her, and they agreed that as long as she was acting normal, they wouldn't bring up the topic again until the meeting had taken place.

The next few days passed by quickly and somehow they both managed to pretend that things were normal. It even began to feel that way. Neither of them returned to their previous studies, choosing instead to spend their time together. It was becoming easier for Mahdon to live in denial about the vision until the night before he planned to meet with the council.

He found Maiya in their bedroom, running a brush through her hair and staring out at the night sky. His heart told him that something was not right, and he felt his worry would again betray him. Not wanting to disturb her, he took a seat on the side of the bed closest to her and sat silently, waiting for her to speak.

"We continue to waste too much time," she said at last. She didn't turn to face him but set the brush aside. "We should meet with the council tonight."

"I'm meeting with them tomorrow, and then we'll get this figured out."

"That's unacceptable. We must leave at once." Maiya shifted on her heels and Mahdon could once again see the fire in her eyes that had frightened him before. He knew immediately that she was not herself, that whatever had taken ahold of her was alive and well, and she would not be easily

279

swayed. Still he pressed, hoping he was mistaken and could bring about a fairer mood.

"We talked about this. I know you're anxious to get this resolved, but I promise we'll find a solution." He moved to her side and took her hands in his own. He felt her tension loosen slightly as he gave her hands a gentle squeeze. "You won't have to wait much longer."

Maiya's demeanor softened and a small smile crossed her lips.

"Perhaps you're right." She led him back to the bed, pulling him down beside her as they embraced. As they parted lips, their eyes met and for a moment Mahdon thought he caught a glimpse of pain in her eyes.

"I'm sorry that I have to do this," Maiya said.

"Have to do wha–?" Mahdon was cut short as Maiya sent him prone on the bed with a flick of her wrist. He attempted to move but found himself paralyzed. She moved to stand over him, her hand outstretched to maintain the spell that held him in place.

"I hoped it wouldn't come to this." Her tone was harsh and, to Mahdon, alarmingly steady. "This isn't easy for me. After all, this wouldn't have been possible without your help. It's unfortunate that you've chosen to stand in my way."

Mahdon's eyes grew wide with fear. What was she saying? How had her actions become so cold? So calculated? He scanned the room for any means of escape, seeing none that would break her spell over him. His only hope was to convince her to let him free or distract her long enough that her hold would weaken.

"What? Are you surprised? You look surprised." She laughed to herself and raised her other hand toward Mahdon as the air surrounding it began to crackle with energy. "I'm sure you know what became of Brandon after all his meddling and that pathetic attempt on my life. You were pressing the issue so much that you must have looked into that. Don't act like you wouldn't have tried something next. I've seen the way you look at me when you don't think I'm watching."

He searched her eyes for some sign that the woman he loved was still in there somewhere. "Mai, I don't know what Brandon did to you. I'm sorry for whatever happened to you, I truly am, but this isn't who you are. What's happened to you?"

"Me? I'm finally beginning to feel more like myself."

"Whatever's happened to you... maybe it can be undone. I want to help you."

"Enough of this prattle. I'm not the problem. You would have betrayed me as did the others. It's all a matter of time; that's all."

"I would never betray you."

"You didn't hesitate to take away my only access to them."

"Only at your behest. I gave up everything for you, and I would do it again. I love you."

Maiya flinched at his comment. Mahdon felt the resistance weaken and found he could free himself from her grip. She stepped back and sent him tumbling to the floor where she'd stood.

Mahdon peered up at her as a fiery light began to flicker in her right hand. "You have ten seconds before I change my mind. I won't tell you again."

"Maiya..."

"Nine."

Mahdon scrambled to his feet as the light grew brighter. Meeting her eyes one last time with a look of pity and pain washing over his face, he dashed for the exit and disappeared into the night. He waited within eyesight of the manor for the better part of the night, but if Maiya made any attempts at pursuit, they were not visible. After what seemed forever to him, Mahdon took to his feet and began heading north, toward what he believed to be the current location of the other council members. The brief struggle against Maiya's spell had left him exhausted and he soon sat to rest, taking shelter under a large tree he hoped would provide adequate cover come daylight. For hours, his mind raced with panicked thoughts until the exhaustion overtook him and he let sleep take hold at last.

He awoke in the midst of an argument between the remaining council members, and, more shockingly, within the confines of a moderately sized cavern. Mahdon looked around with a feeling of unease, unsure how they had managed to bring him here without waking him. Had Maiya's power drained him that much? He sat up on the bed they had been so courteous to provide, but they didn't seem to notice him as he peered over at what was obviously an important discussion.

"We need to address this immediately," Jo'dai said above the rest.

Saren nodded, but gave an exasperated sigh. "Yes, but we cannot go unprepared. It will do more harm than good to face this threat without knowing what we're up against."

"Arguing amongst ourselves does little good in the wake of – ah, I see he's awake," Naliz indicated to the others as he looked over in Mahdon's direction. "I trust you slept well. You didn't even stir when we brought you here. Why were you outside alone?"

Mahdon took a step closer as the events of the previous night swirled through his mind. Had that really happened? He took a few moments to compose himself as the council members waited in silence. "It's Maiya. She's... not well," he said at last.

Naliz's next question came cautiously. "Why didn't you send someone else to report this? We would have come there had we known."

"You don't understand," Mahdon said, "Maiya's lost her mind. She let me go, but I think she intended to kill me. I tried to talk to her, but she wouldn't listen. The way she spoke was unsettling, as though she doesn't know who she is. There's something wrong."

Naliz's face darkened, and he turned back to face the other two members. "Leave us."

They hesitated for a moment, then somewhat reluctantly, shifted from their forms and were gone from the cavern. Naliz waited a moment longer and directed Mahdon to sit with him. "I figured as much. At least that you would sense something. Her actions have been growing more erratic, but to attack you – that was unexpected."

"What will we do? We can't... kill her," Mahdon said, his voice wavering over the last two words.

Naliz leaned back in his chair. "If Maiya will attack you, what prevents her from killing any of us? How do we know she wasn't responsible for the disappearance of Brandon or the murder of Tanin?"

Mahdon said nothing in reply, wondering if Naliz suspected that he knew. It was at that moment that Naliz stood abruptly, stepped back from the table, and his face paled. He walked the length of the table and back again, looking ever more anxious. He stopped before Mahdon who was now staring up at him with wide-eyed confusion.

"How long?" Naliz asked.

"What?"

"How long have you known? Brandon is dead, isn't he? She killed him, didn't she?"

"I…I don't know what you mean."

Naliz slammed his fists down on the table before Mahdon, causing him to jump in his seat. He grabbed the arms of the chair and sat up rigidly. Naliz's eyes flared with a mix of fear and anger, and Mahdon worried what his friend might do next.

Naliz's voice was slower and quieter this time. "How long?"

"Nearly a week."

Naliz threw his hands up in the air and spun back around to face away. When he turned back, his expression gradually went from concerned to angry as he spoke. "Why would you keep such a thing to yourself? Damn it, Mahdon. He may not have been the only one. How many others has she killed? Did she tell you? Did you witness this? I certainly hope you were not involved! How did you come about this knowledge? Speak!"

Mahdon cowered under Naliz's penetrating gaze. "As you know, Maiya went missing. When she got back, she couldn't remember what happened. She began having more memory lapses from our time spent together after her return and she would act strangely during those times."

"So, you decided to do a little research of your own," Naliz said.

Mahdon nodded. "Yes. I took precautions to keep it secret from her, but I didn't want to believe it had happened. I still don't want to. I love her."

"Love," Naliz shook his head. "She would love nothing more than to use that against you, I'm sure."

"You don't know that. We don't know why this is happening to her."

"You cannot possibly understand what this means."

"Then explain it to me."

Naliz once again turned away. He sighed and dropped his head. "I can't."

"Then what am I doing here?" Mahdon pushed past Naliz and walked toward a slender hallway carved in the stone that he presumed to be the exit.

"Just where do you think you're going? We're all you have now. Even if you believe she can be saved, surely you must know that you can't do this alone."

Mahdon halted at the wall and stood in silence for a moment. He slumped to the floor at the edge of the cavern, holding his head in his hands. Though he tried to keep it hidden, Naliz could see that he was fighting back tears. Naliz immediately felt pity for him, fearing that the human form might drive him to take his own life. Naliz offered Mahdon his hand and, after a moment, Mahdon accepted and was pulled to his feet.

"Come," Naliz said, "Let us fetch you something to eat. Discussions can be had tomorrow. In the meantime, I will have a security team make contact to receive an update. For now, I don't find it necessary that they know what became of Brandon. Too much already weighs on their minds. And on yours."

CHAPTER 24

Several days had passed while the council made preparations in the confines of the cavern. Though it was difficult, Mahdon set aside his emotions to fulfill the role he'd accepted only days earlier. He shared the details of what he knew regarding Brandon and his unconfirmed suspicions that she was responsible for Tanin as well. The news was not entirely unexpected, but left a heavy atmosphere in its wake. The discussions that had been meant to last a few hours extended over two days, and a decision was finally reached that required some compromise on all parts. The council would be gathering their allies and inviting Maiya to join in negotiations that would, ideally, have better results than her last interactions with council members.

This was contrary to what Jo'dai wanted, stating that assassinating Maiya outright would be the safest outcome for everyone. While he personally harbored no ill will toward her, he believed it to be the most logical decision given what became of those who previously got in her way. In time, he argued, Mahdon would come to realize how irrational it was to believe she could be swayed. Saren pointed out that this approach, though sure to eliminate the problem they currently faced, would likely create further animosity toward the council from their own citizens. As Maiya became more dangerous, the common folk remained unaware of her actions, knowing only of those which were done to aid them. Any attempt on her life would be viewed as an attack on their own safety. She also expressed disinterest in killing someone she had come to consider a friend.

Mahdon did his best to remain impartial while each expressed their concerns, but was understandably relieved when Naliz presented the possibility of negotiations after the others had finished. The biggest problem Mahdon saw was that he had no idea what it was she actually wanted. She had expressed a great deal of interest in the orb, but at the time he had assumed that was because she wanted to prevent Brandon from using it against her. Now he knew otherwise. Why she wanted it remained a mystery to him, and the others were noticeably reluctant to part with it.

Naliz made arrangements to invite Maiya to talk, but when the night came and went without an update on the status of this, Mahdon became concerned and called Naliz to meet with him privately. When Naliz arrived, he was pacing up and down his makeshift quarters. He hadn't slept since he'd arrived and was still brimming with anxious energy. Naliz stood in the doorway with a look of concern mixed with mild annoyance.

"I need to see her."

Naliz sighed as he stepped into the room and took a seat on the bed. "You know that isn't wise."

"Maybe I could talk to her, bring some sense back to her. She's not like this; this isn't Maiya." Mahdon continued to pace, dropping his head into his hands and rubbing his temples in frustration. In all the time they'd known each other, Naliz had never seen him so emotional and lost in thought.

Naliz snorted. "That human body of yours is clouding your mind. You aren't thinking clearly, and neither is she. Going back there will be the end of you, especially as you are now - in that frail body you foolishly decided to keep."

Mahdon stopped pacing and eyed Naliz suspiciously. "It was clear you didn't know what happened to Brandon until I told you. And yet, you suspected and had already decided to keep your distance from us. What aren't you telling me?"

"What I do or do not know is irrelevant."

"You're dodging my question. Given my current position, there is nothing that should be hidden from me."

"I believe she's much more dangerous than you realize. That is all. If you truly wish to salvage what remains, you need to be prepared for what may be lost."

"Then I won't go alone. If we don't hear soon, I'll take a second team to confront her at the manor."

"You cannot do that."

Mahdon sighed. "Unless you have a better suggestion, I'm going to disregard that statement."

"Sit down. That is what I came here to tell you."

Mahdon sat down slowly on the bed, still regarding Naliz with suspicion. "You do have a plan then?"

"Yes," Naliz nodded. "But I'm afraid it won't be what you want to hear. The manor is gone, Mahdon. What remains now is no more than a pile of rubble. She burned it in the night."

Mahdon went pale. He suddenly felt exhausted. "Where is she now?"

"We don't know. But if we're going to find out, we need you to be in working order. You need to get some rest and then you'll need to be willing to be a bit more flexible."

"Meaning...?"

"The ruby. In your current form, you're no more than bait."

Mahdon shook his head, the disappointment he felt plainly reflected in his eyes. "How can you ask this of me?"

"Do you truly believe she sees any place for you in her life anymore?"

"I'm not confident that I know anything anymore."

"If she's still in there somewhere, I imagine she would understand. If she's not, well..." Naliz shrugged as he let the last word linger in the air.

"If she's not, then will it even matter if I have it back? She had no difficulty restoring Brandon's mortality."

"I do not believe she would dare try while we have the orb."

Mahdon sat up straighter. "Please tell me you aren't suggesting that we do what Brandon was trying to do."

"Of course not. Not forcibly, anyway. Think of it more as a defense tactic. She won't attack us if she knows it will leave her powerless."

Mahdon sighed. He stared at the floor for a long time before reluctantly nodding. "I pray she will forgive me."

After he agreed to Naliz's terms, Mahdon attempted to get some sleep but found it mostly restless. When nightfall came, he gave up any hope of feeling refreshed and headed out under the cover of dark. Naliz offered to accompany him, but feeling that what he was doing was a betrayal, he didn't wish to share the moment with anyone else. When Mahdon made it back to the union tree, he looked down at it in silence for a while, thinking back on how dramatically things had changed. He wondered if the same sad thoughts ever crossed Maiya's mind.

He knelt beside the tree and dug his fingers into the ground, pulling up clumps of dirt with the sparse grass that had only recently begun to grow. He did so slowly as to avoid injuring the roots and set the chunks of grass gently to the side. He removed one final handful of dirt and found the ruby nestled within a twist of roots. The gem glowed brightly as he wiped it clean and then dipped it in the pool to wash off the remaining soil. He moved back to the tree and was replacing the soil when he felt eyes on him.

"I suspected you'd come back here, but I wasn't expecting to find you digging that back up. I'd be lying if I said it didn't hurt a little."

"Maiya!" Mahdon jumped back from the hole, clutching the gem in one hand for dear life. Seeing her standing there so composed broke his heart. His heart raced as he watched her cautiously, considering Naliz's words and wondering if he had time to make an escape.

Maiya looked at his hand and then back up at his face and smiled. "Relax. I didn't come here to kill you. I've thought about what you said and have come to the conclusion that you would never harm this vessel. Let us drop this charade."

Mahdon narrowed his eyes at her but did not loosen his grip on the ruby. "Why are you talking like that?"

"Huh...he must not have told you. I really thought Naliz valued his friendships more than that." Maiya smiled to herself and then held out a hand to Mahdon. "If you help me, then I'll give you what you want."

"Help you what? Maiya, I don't know what's happened to you, but you're scaring me."

"It seems your friend hasn't been completely honest with you. You want to know what happened to me? Let me show you. Don't worry, I won't bite."

Mahdon stared at her outstretched hand for a moment in hesitation before pocketing the gem and extending his own. As their hands touched, he was immediately flooded with emotion as the world swirled around him and a vision formed before their eyes. A human woman with stunningly red hair and emerald eyes stood above a pit in the same dimly lit atmosphere of the council's chambers. Her hands were secured tightly behind her back and anger was apparent on her face. Mahdon recognized the location at once as being the cave in Ularia where the disease had originated.

On either side of her, Mahdon saw the familiar faces of four of the council members in a form that had long since become alien to him, though he had once been confined to it as they appeared to be now. A moment later Brandon approached her from behind, wearing the same human face he had been when he died. Mahdon looked around them in confusion.

"This is the old council chambers. They haven't been there in many years. Why does Brandon look like that already? Who is that woman?"

"His love for that form always astounded me given his loathing of humanity and anything he didn't understand. Just watch."

Mahon returned his attention to the vision, wondering who this woman could possibly be and why, given the bonds, the council would be interested in holding her prisoner. The Brandon of the distant past unsheathed a blade and cut the rope that restrained her, and for a brief moment Mahdon thought they were releasing her. Brandon grabbed her wrist and turned her roughly to face himself, meeting her eyes as he so-loved to do when delivering bad news.

"We would like to thank you for your assistance to our people, but I'm afraid your time with us has run out. Is there anything you wish to say?"

"You will live to regret this."

"I very much doubt that. I will give you one final chance to repent and proclaim your loyalty. Acknowledge that I am the one and only rightful ruler, and I will pardon you."

"You, pardon me?" She laughed. "Oh, Tribian, do you honestly believe this theft will break me? You dare to threaten me in the guise of an alien race? I promise you that it will be the last face you ever wear."

Mahdon gasped. As the woman spoke, recognition hit him and understanding unraveled in his mind. Recognition not of the woman as she appeared, but of the way she carried herself and her complete lack of fear. This woman, though she appeared human, was none other than the goddess Alurine, the one responsible for the immortality the Amerti had enjoyed for centuries.

"Alurine… it's her, isn't it?"

"Yes." Maiya's voice was calm and unwavering. "Tribian never was a merciful one. Not even back then."

"You deserve everything that happens to you," Brandon said, completely unaware of the onlookers' remarks. "We're finished here. Dispose of her."

Without a moment's pause, the four obeyed. Jo'dai grabbed her while the others blocked her escape. Alurine was forcefully thrown backwards into the pit and screamed from the pain as she landed hard on her back far below. The echo of her voice sent shivers down Mahdon's spine as the cold realization that no one would save her dripped sorrow into his heart.

The council members left the chamber, closing heavy doors behind them as Alurine yelled after them in angry desperation. Maiya turned away and the vision quickly faded.

"I was unfortunate enough to survive the fall, though I lacked the capacity to move. For nearly three days, I laid down there, trapped in a broken human body. Killing me directly would have been more merciful, but Brandon wanted me to suffer, so they left me to die. It was unforgivable. I chose to pay your planet a visit after so much time spent away, and those of your highest order repaid me with death."

Mahdon's eyes went wide. "The shadow in the council chambers... the one who began visiting Maiya... that was you? But how can you be Alurine? You had no limitations. How could you possibly be trapped like that?"

Maiya walked slowly alongside the pool. "Tribian," she nearly spat his name, "after hearing my foretelling of Jovienna's return, he requested a special honor – to see in what form the goddess would be reborn. Arrogant and trusting as I was, I agreed and took on the likeness of the woman you saw thrown to her eventual death. I did not realize at the time that they had found the Hokaruin orb – or that they understood its capabilities. Using my own naivety against me, they drained me of my power, forcing me to die in a weak and unfamiliar body.

"As I lay dying, I swore to put an end to them. Yet as a wandering soul, I couldn't touch them. All I needed to do was get close to them, but they had the means to prevent me from doing so. I needed a way to enter the physical realm before it was too late. Unfortunately, not just any creature would do; I needed a body with the potential for power like my own. Jovienna – Maiya – was my answer. Much like myself, she entered this plane of existence with magic in her veins. When I realized where my sister intended to go next, it complicated things. The council was very convincing that her presence was unnecessary, so I did what I had to do. I needed you to have a reason to bring her here, and you did."

Mahdon appeared crestfallen. "You're the one responsible for all those deaths. Why would you bring us the gift of life just to take it away?"

"How well do you remember that day – the day that you accepted immortality?"

He thought back, unsure why the question was relevant to his own. "I remember the council making the announcement at your temple in Fimbira. They told us of a fountain you had blessed before your departure. The water that flowed from it had an unusual shimmer about it, but I made the pilgrimage and drank of it. That's all there was to it."

"It sounds so innocent in your rendition of history. I didn't come here to give your people anything beyond someone to worship. I was bored and looking for a little bit of fun. That is all. That 'gift', as you like to call it, was stolen from me. That stone that you hold in your hand is but a fraction of my power. You can do so much more with it than you realize."

Mahdon immediately felt sick. The shame he felt for using something that wasn't given freely shook him to his core. He now understood her anger, but the fate of Maiya remained unclear.

"I had no idea. I never would have accepted it had I known. If you're Alurine, then what about Maiya? Is she still in there somewhere?"

"She's alive and well, I assure you. If not for her, I would not have stayed my hand. But now I must ask a favor of you."

"What is she then? Your prisoner? You speak of being trapped in a human body and aren't you trapping her in her own? How could you possibly expect me to do a favor for you?"

"You'll have her back. That is what you want, isn't it? Help me and I'll leave this body and give back the woman you love as you knew her."

"Why should I trust you? How can I trust the one who took her from me in the first place?"

Alurine smiled. "There's the beauty in it. You just have to. If you don't help me, the destruction of this vessel is guaranteed. If you do, she has a chance."

Mahdon's heart sank. He wanted to believe that she was bluffing, that only a fool would destroy what they had waited so long to acquire, but putting Maiya's life at stake was too high a risk. If he condemned Maiya to death by not accepting the offer, he would never forgive himself. Mahdon looked reluctantly to Alurine, feeling utterly powerless.

"I don't understand. Why do you need me to help? Why didn't you just take them all out when you had the chance?"

"After my..." Alurine paused for a moment to consider her word choice, "...discussion... with Tribian, I blacked out. The magic he so envied is incredibly draining. Once I recovered, I found the council had made some adjustments to prevent me from such an easy victory. I know very well where they are, but I can't touch them without your help."

"What do you want me to do?"

"You saw what they did to me, and now they have something that belongs to me. It's time to put an end to the council. All you need to do is help me get close. And once it's all said and done, you'll have her back."

"And you intend to murder them as you did the other two?"

Alurine laughed. "You make me sound so vicious. You must think I'm a monster. If anything, they were the monsters. Though if you must know, I didn't plan to kill them. I have something far more interesting in mind."

Mahdon looked relieved, but still frowned. "And that is?"

"In good time, you'll see."

"How can I help you get close? If you can't touch them with all your magic, how can I possibly make it possible for you to do so?"

"Let us make one thing very clear – this magic is not my own. It belongs to my sister. I want what is mine. I cannot recover it without the orb. They must have it in their current council chambers. If anyone has it on them now, it would be your friend. I just need you to recover it for me."

CHAPTER 25

When Mahdon returned, the council was already waiting for him around the table. They were noticeably silent, and the room was filled with a certain level of gloom. It was as though they were expecting to receive bad news.

Naliz stood the moment he saw Mahdon. "Did you retrieve the ruby?"

"Yes." He stopped just short of the table and looked at each of them in turn before looking back to Naliz. "But she was there waiting for me."

"And she let you live…" Naliz's voice dropped off. He sounded more frightened than surprised.

"Yes." Mahdon eyed Naliz with suspicion. "She showed me things; things that I wish not to believe, but I must ask you… Is it true?"

"You must know that anything that woman says is a lie. She's a killer, Mahdon."

"She would have me believe the same about you."

Naliz looked away, having no defense to offer.

"Were you privy to the murder of Alurine?"

The silence stretched out as they all refused to make eye contact with him. It was clear that the subject made them uncomfortable and, even after all this time, wasn't one they were prepared to discuss.

Jo'dai finally broke the silence. "You can't kill a god."

"Perhaps not. But what about the powerless physical embodiment of one? All these years we've survived on what was never meant to be ours."

"She would have used that magic against us to enslave us all. We did what had to be done." His response lacked emotion and was stated plainly as fact.

"And that included murder? If you truly believed that it was for the greater good, then why was it done in secret? Why have you kept this a secret all these years?" Mahdon soon turned his full attention to Naliz. "How could you do such a thing? How have you lived with this deed on your conscience?"

Naliz slammed his clenched fists on the table and his face grew bright red. "Do you think I am proud of my sins? You're an idealist, Mahdon. Good and evil aren't always black and white. Be grateful you were spared the details until now."

Saren stood slowly and shook her head sadly. "No, it isn't, but what we did wasn't done for anyone but ourselves. We deserve every bit of hell that awaits us."

"Now that you have this information, what do you intend to do with it?" Naliz asked.

"What would you have me do? I haven't been left with much of a choice. You've all confessed to a serious crime." Mahdon stepped forward and placed the ruby on the table. "I will not be the one to condemn you, but I can no longer assist you either. She's requested your presence at the falls."

"And if we refuse?" Naliz asked.

"The energy shield will be removed when I leave here. She knows you're here. One way or another, you will face your accuser." He turned and began walking away. "It's up to you if you want to be underground when that happens."

Naliz hurried after him, surprised by the response. "Why are you doing this? You'll be putting us at risk of death. Is that really what you want?"

Mahdon halted and turned to face him. "I never wanted any of this. If I'm understanding the situation correctly, and I believe I am, then everything bad that has happened is because our leaders — the ones meant to protect us — felt that they didn't have enough power. You've brought this upon yourselves."

"We merely did as we were told. It was Brandon's decision."

"Stop hiding behind your loyalty excuses. He was never as powerful as you allowed him to be. It's time for you to take some responsibility for your actions."

They watched Mahdon leave and then Naliz nodded back at Jo'dai. "Fetch the orb. We won't stand a chance if we leave here without it."

Jo'dai exited and returned quickly with a small wooden box, and then the three left in silence to meet Mahdon outside. He was waiting with a shuttlecraft and said nothing as they boarded. The flight, while short, was uncomfortably long due to the increased tensions between all involved. Mahdon felt angry and betrayed. He could sense a genuine aura of shame and sorrow from Saren, but the other two remained largely focused on self-preservation. He thought back on the many interactions he'd had with the council and felt embarrassed by all the signs he'd missed. They played him for a fool and continued to use him as a pawn in their games. All Naliz's actions cast doubt on whether or not they had ever been friends in the first place. How could they ever recover from this?

Alurine was standing along the edge of the canyon when they arrived. The remnants of the manor still smoldered in the background, not far from where she stood. She stepped away from the cliff as they landed and moved closer to the shuttle. They disembarked but kept their distance. Alurine looked them over, but Naliz was the first to speak.

"Alurine. It's been a while."

"Yes, it has."

Mahdon looked sharply over at Naliz. "Did you know who she was when you went into hiding? Or when you sent me to get the ruby?"

"I suspected."

Mahdon shook his head at him in disbelief. "Unbelievable."

"I don't think you would have listened had I told you."

Alurine gazed down at the box in Jo'dai's hands. "Have you brought me what I've asked of you?"

He tightened his grip. "We will not give you anything without first having negotiations."

She shifted her focus onto Mahdon with a small smile. "Oh, but I've already done that."

Everyone present now looked over to him as he reached into a bag he'd been carrying and pulled out the slightly humming artifact. Jo'dai opened the box he carried to reveal the replica that he'd had swapped out previously. All the color drained from his face as he gave Mahdon the same incredulous look that Mahdon had just given Naliz. Both men took a step back as Mahdon moved closer to Alurine.

"Please, Mahdon. You can't do this," Naliz begged. "If you allow her to deactivate that, you'll be condemning us all to death. It's the only protection we have. Nothing will be able to stop her."

"I'm sorry, Naliz. It's nothing personal."

"Isn't it? I understand why you're angry. You have every reason to be."

Mahdon sighed. All of the negative emotions had taken their toll, and all he wanted was to be rid of his role as middleman. "It's my duty to uphold the law. This is stolen property. Additionally, per the law, when there is adequate proof or an admission of guilt, the surviving family of a murder victim has the right to pass judgment and administer punishment should they so choose. The victim of an assault has the same right. This is an unusual case, but the facts remain the same."

Alurine stepped forward and lifted the orb slowly from his hand. She closed her eyes and held it to her chest for a moment before returning to the edge of the cliff. She extended both hands outward and released the orb. As she did so, it slowly rose and hovered in the air as it opened and let forth a much louder hum. She said nothing as she swept her hands past the orb as if to direct its power outward. A blinding light exploded across the land and then returned just as suddenly. The three long term council members fell to their knees as this happened, appearing weaker and afraid. The orb closed and fell dormant once again. Alurine reached out a hand to grab it as it fell from its position. She turned back to the group with a smile.

"Oh, how I've missed this! That immortality you took for granted will trouble you no more."

None of them dared to stand while she addressed them. Jo'dai stared straight ahead, almost as though he'd fallen into a trance. Naliz, on the other hand, kept his widened eyes on Alurine with every step that she took. Saren remained the furthest away, holding herself up with shaky hands. Mahdon had never seen her appear so fragile before and wondered what she must be thinking. Unaffected by the power transfer, Mahdon stood to the side and watched Alurine approach them.

She stopped before Jo'dai and regarded him with amusement. "I've waited thousands of years for this day. You used to stand so proudly. What happened?" She squatted down in front of him to be sure she was in his line of sight. "Have I broken you? I was hoping you'd be a bit more entertaining."

She stood back up and motioned for them to follow suit. "Rise. Follow me and you will be pardoned."

The response wasn't immediate, but Saren and Naliz slowly stood on unsteady legs. Jo'dai remained motionless, maintaining an unblinking stare.

Alurine stood over him, admiring his defiance. "Don't you wish to be absolved?"

"I will not willingly place the lives of our people in a sorceress' hands."

Though his voice was relatively steady, she could tell that he was afraid. His last defense mechanism was to dissociate from the situation. She had every intention to anchor him in the present.

Alurine placed a hand on his head. "Very well."

At first he appeared to be choking. His eyes grew wide and his mouth opened and closed like that of a fish, but no sound came out. When he threw his hands up to his throat, Mahdon rushed forward to intervene.

"Stop! He's harmless now. Show him mercy!"

Alurine raised her other hand and sent Mahdon careening toward the cliff. "Do not interfere. I did not come here to forgive, and I will not hesitate to kill you."

Mahdon rolled away from the canyon, having been so close to toppling over the edge that one leg was over nothing but air. A cold wind swept over him, bringing with it the scent of freshly spilled blood. Before Jo'dai collapsed to one side, Mahdon caught a fleeting glimpse of red as it seeped between the man's now motionless fingers. Alurine walked away from the body without another word. Mahdon watched from his position at ground level as she approached Saren and directed her to the cliff's edge. She smiled at Saren and stroked her hair as a mother might do to soothe a frightened child.

"You've taken on an appearance much like the one I did." She placed a hand gently on Saren's back and waved the other one slowly over the canyon. "All you must do is jump, and all is forgiven."

Mahdon could hardly hear what was being said, but he had no difficulty seeing the way the blood drained from Saren's face or how much her body trembled. "I'll die."

Alurine shrugged. "Perhaps. Perhaps not. It would be much in the way you killed me, but without the lingering."

"What good is forgiveness if I'm dead?"

"Despite what you may think, death is never permanent."

The sensation of vertigo was so strong that Saren nearly fell from the dizziness. What had once been beautiful filled her with fear. "What if I don't do it?"

Alurine peered over her shoulder at the blood-stained ground and the crumpled body it surrounded. "Would you rather suffer the same fate as him?"

Any flicker of hope Saren had been harboring was gone in an instant. She exchanged a despairing look with Mahdon. "I'm sorry, Mahdon, for everything that has happened."

He shook his head at her but was unable to get a word out before she closed her eyes, took a step, and disappeared from view. Alurine watched as she fell and then moved away from the cliff.

She gazed down at Mahdon with a slight smile. "A pity. I was beginning to like that one."

Mahdon pushed himself up to stand as she shifted her attention to Naliz and beckoned with a finger. Naliz trudged toward her as he cast his eyes first over the corpse, and then over Mahdon. Mahdon expected to see anger in his eyes, but all he saw was defeat. He wondered what dark game she intended to play next.

"Please don't do this," Mahdon begged. "No one else needs to die. It doesn't need to end like this."

Her smile broadened and a glint of satisfaction showed in her eyes. "No, but I'm quite enjoying myself. Would you have helped me had you known their fate? They're no less guilty than Brandon was; I'm simply dispensing justice."

Naliz had heard enough and broke down. "I'm not prepared to die. I will do anything you ask of me."

"I'm well aware. You'll follow anyone you fear, won't you?"

"I simply wish to make amends."

She raised an eyebrow. "Truly?"

"Yes."

She walked away for a moment, looking across the canyon as she pondered this. After several seconds, she turned back to address him. "I will restore your immortality. You shall never die." She returned to where he stood and continued. "In return, you will do my bidding. You will not question me. Do we have a deal?"

Mahdon wanted to tell him to say 'no', that it would be foolish to agree to such extreme terms, but he knew Naliz well enough to know that he would do anything for survival. He was understandably reluctant, but ultimately, he agreed. The arrangement was sealed with a handshake and, almost immediately, the man Mahdon knew disappeared before his eyes and was replaced by a very alarmed red fox. Mahdon dropped down beside him and sat frozen for a moment, supporting himself on one hand as he stared in shock at the cowering creature, wondering if Naliz really existed somewhere in that body.

Alurine bent low and admired her handiwork. "I always wanted a pet, but I could never find one intelligent enough for my tastes. He'll have to do."

Naliz whined at Mahdon, placing a paw on his leg. Mahdon continued to stare, unsure what to say and wishing to be done with all of the day's happenings. What he had seen and done was nothing he could ever condone or even forgive. He wondered if Maiya could possibly understand why he made the choices he had. He hoped she would be more forgiving of him than he felt he deserved. After giving himself a moment to compose himself, he nodded up at Alurine.

"You have your victory. Release her."

She gave him a look of disapproval. "You continue to speak to me as though we're equals. Have you no respect for your gods?"

Mahdon stood suddenly, the calm exiting his voice just as quickly. "I've done everything that you've asked of me. I dedicated my entire life to studying and understanding you. What more could you possibly expect from me?"

"You have, haven't you?" She said this slowly, as though she was mulling over a thought. "To show my gratitude, allow me to offer you a gift."

Mahdon was afraid to ask what she considered a gift. He suspected that, whatever it was, he had no say in whether or not he received it. "What gift?"

"The truth."

She leaned down and picked up the very squirmy Naliz. He whined and nipped at her until she scolded him. "Stop that or I'll have you muzzled and put on a leash."

He settled down but kept sad eyes locked on Mahdon. Alurine pet him as she continued. "We were never the creators you made us out to be. Your species was young when we first encountered you. We wanted to see you thrive... so we allowed you to believe what we had to. We never wanted you to fear us, and had you known what we were – that we were completely unlike you – our history could have turned out so differently."

Mahdon suddenly felt dizzy and nauseated. He didn't want to believe it. He threw a hand to his head and paced anxiously. "Everything... you're telling me that my entire life and everything I've ever believed is a lie." He stopped and looked back at her. "Why would you tell me this? Why must you destroy the only thing I have left?"

"I thought you would appreciate knowing. It seems I was mistaken."

Mahdon paled further as he was struck by the full force of what he'd done. Every decision he'd made was rooted in the belief that he was doing what was right and expected of him for eternal salvation. He'd abided by the law and she had a right to justice. What she got went beyond that, and now he questioned if his own participation would be what damned him. "What are you?"

"We call ourselves Mesorahk."

"And Maiya is one of you as well?"

"Yes, though she wouldn't know it. My sister grew bored some time ago and chose to experience life as various primitive species. She's been doing this ever since and only becomes aware of her true self with the proper triggers or upon the destruction of the vessel." She watched him for a moment before a smile crossed her face. "Oh, I do like the way you think. I can see it in your eyes. You're wondering what would happen if you killed me. It won't be that easy."

"You aren't going to let her go, are you?"

"You'll need to wait a bit longer. I still have need of her."

Mahdon could feel the anger building inside of him. Not only had she used him, now she was refusing to free the one person he had done it all for. "Now that you have your magic back, why do you need a host?"

She looked down at Naliz and stroked his fur. "I don't. This has nothing to do with the vessel itself." She glanced back up at Mahdon. "However, I don't expect she would come willingly should I leave it."

"Why are you doing this?"

"My business is my own. Once I'm finished with her, I'll release her. That's all you need to know. I can't promise that you'll see her again, but that's hardly my problem."

Mahdon's anger bubbled over and came out in a few gravelly words. "I'll kill you."

Alurine laughed. "You know as well as I that you aren't like them. Even if you were, you aren't stupid enough to try."

Mahdon wanted nothing more than to prove her wrong and free Maiya, but he knew she was right. The only thing he'd achieve by attempting such a feat was his own demise. He felt useless and defeated. In every way conceivable, she had won. This was the end of the road. What more could he possibly do? He was teetering on the edge of doing something foolish when she began walking away.

"Where are you going?"

"I already told you; my business is my own. Fulfill the prophecy and come find me. If you still wish to fight me then, I will welcome the challenge."

"Prophecy?" He laughed bitterly at the thought. "It was all based on lies."

"That doesn't make it any less true."

"Doesn't it? She can hardly lead with you holding her hostage."

Alurine shook her head. "Your naivety would be adorable if it wasn't so sad. You are the rightful leader now, are you not?"

The whole arrangement was supposed to be temporary. It hadn't occurred to him that he would be left in this position, but once again, she was right. He understood the implication and wasn't sure how to take it. Was she serious or mocking him?

He sighed heavily. "What can I possibly tell them? I've failed them. Their lives will be chaos."

"Then it's fortunate for them that there's a whole subsect of the population that never stole from me. I think you'll find that they can offer the necessary support system. Goodbye, Mahdon."

"Wait—"

He reached an arm out in her direction, but she was already gone. A light breeze tousled his hair as he looked around and saw no evidence that she had ever been there. Even where Jo'dai had fallen, the ground was now bare and unstained. Excluding the roar of the water below, the landscape around him was silent and he found that she'd left him entirely alone. Still crippled by the shock and unsure what to do with himself, he wandered into the remains of the house and began picking through the remnants of his life.

He wasn't sure what he was looking for, but each step through the ashes was heartbreaking. Much of what he found was charred beyond recognition or crumbled in his hands when he picked it up. As he neared what had been the rear of the house, he was certain that he heard a rustling in some of the unburned bushes ahead. He was just outside of the wreckage when Alurine showed her face again. She was eying up the bushes as he approached.

"One last thing," She turned back to face him. "I believe this belongs to you."

She held up three fingers and the ruby of Ar'ta appeared between them. When she moved her hand away, the ruby floated slowly to stop before Mahdon. He said nothing as he plucked it from the air.

"You never need to feel again if that's what you wish. Do with it what you will." She smiled at him one last time before once again vanishing into thin air.

Mahdon stood alone at the edge of the ruins, staring at the ruby in silence. As he pondered his situation, he heard a frightened meow coming from the closest bush. He crept slowly over and parted the branches to find both cats huddled together. He sat and gave them some time to become comfortable and crawl back out on their own. It didn't take them long to move over and allow him to carry them away from the ruins. The house now behind him, he gazed across the precipice at the golden city. As he closed his hand around the gem, he pledged silently to himself that this would not be the end.

"Let the new era begin."